Praise for Martin Edwards

GALLOWS COURT
The First Rachel Savernake Golden Age Mystery

2018 Dagger in the Library Winner
2019 eDunnit Award shortlist, Best Novel
2019 CWA Historical Dagger Award nominee

"Martin Edwards's *Gallows Court* seems awfully bloodthirsty for a traditionally designed mystery set in foggy old London in 1930… Fans of clean-cut heroes will be rooting for Jacob, although some of us would rather see devilish Rachel clean his clock. Either that or commit a clever, more refined murder of her own."

—*New York Times Book Review*

"Highly atmospheric, spine-tingling fun…the way that Edwards keeps deepening the creepiness of this mystery until the very end is utterly stunning."

—*Booklist*, Starred Review

"Exceptional series launch from Edgar-winner Edwards… The labyrinthine plot is one of Edwards's best, and he does a masterly job of maintaining suspense, besides getting the reader to invest in the fate of the two main characters. Fans of Edgar Wallace's classic *Four Just Men* won't want to miss this ⌐⌐ "

—*Publishers Weel¹* ⌐iew

THE FROZEN SHROUD
The Sixth Lake District Mystery

"Martin Edwards uses the lovely landscape of the Lake District to fine effect...clean prose and an engaging love for the territory."
—*Chicago Tribune*

THE HANGING WOOD
The Fifth Lake District Mystery

"With an unforgettable ending, this outstanding cold case will attract Lynda La Plante and Mo Hayder fans."
—*Library Journal*, Starred Review

THE SERPENT POOL
The Fourth Lake District Mystery

"An excellent choice for discerning readers who want an unusual and challenging puzzle mystery that will keep them guessing until the final pages. Wow!"
—*Library Journal*, Starred Review

THE ARSENIC LABYRINTH
The Third Lake District Mystery

"A beautifully crafted book."
—Ann Cleeves, CWA Gold Dagger winner

THE CIPHER GARDEN
The Second Lake District Mystery

"Fans of the British village mystery who are very particular about setting should trek to *The Cipher Garden*."
—*New York Times*

THE COFFIN TRAIL
The First Lake District Mystery

"A wonderful, absorbing read: a crime deeply rooted in the past, a beautifully evoked sense of the Lake District…"
—Peter Robinson, *New York Times* bestselling author

Other Awards

2019 CWA Short Story Dagger shortlist for
"Strangers in a Pub" (*Ten Year Stretch*)
Poirot Award 2017
Edgar Award for Best Biographical/Critical for
The Golden Age of Murder
The Red Herring Award 2011

Also by Martin Edwards

The Rachel Savernake Golden Age Mysteries
Gallows Court

The Lake District Mysteries

The Coffin Trail	*The Hanging Wood*
The Cipher Garden	*The Frozen Shroud*
The Arsenic Labyrinth	*The Dungeon House*
The Serpent Pool	

The Harry Devlin Series

All the Lonely People	*Eve of Destruction*
Suspicious Minds	*The Devil in Disguise*
I Remember You	*First Cut is the Deepest*
Yesterday's Papers	*Waterloo Sunset*

Fiction

Take My Breath Away	*Dancing for the Hangman*

Nonfiction

Catching Killers	*The Story of Classic Crime in*
Truly Criminal	*100 Books*
The Golden Age of Murder	

Mortmain Hall

MORTMAIN HALL

MARTIN EDWARDS

Poisoned Pen
PRESS

Published by Poisoned Pen Press, an imprint of Sourcebooks
P.O. Box 4410, Naperville, Illinois 60567-4410
(630) 961-3900
sourcebooks.com

Library of Congress Cataloging-in-Publication Data

Names: Edwards, Martin
Title: Mortmain Hall / Martin Edwards.
Description: Naperville, IL : Poisoned Pen Press, [2020] | Series: A Rachel
    Savernake Golden Age mystery | Summary: "Journalist Jacob Flint finds
    himself framed for murder after a surprise witness helps a man accused
    of a "blazing car" killing escape the gallows. To save himself, Jacob
    needs to discover what links these strange events to a remote estate on
    a northern coast, Mortmain Hall. But the house party culminates in
    tragedy when a body is found beneath the crumbling cliffs. Rachel
    Savernake, who's been invited to the party, proposes an intricate and
    dangerous solution to the assembled guests. Will her relentless quest
    for the truth bring down the British establishment?"-- Provided by
    publisher.
Identifiers: LCCN 2020001516 | (trade paperback)
Subjects: GSAFD: Mystery fiction.
Classification: LCC PR6055.D894 M67 2020 | DDC 823/.914--dc23
LC record available at https://lccn.loc.gov/2020001516

Printed and bound in the United States of America.
SB 10 9 8 7 6 5 4 3 2

Dedicated to Ann Cleeves,
with thanks for thirty years of friendship

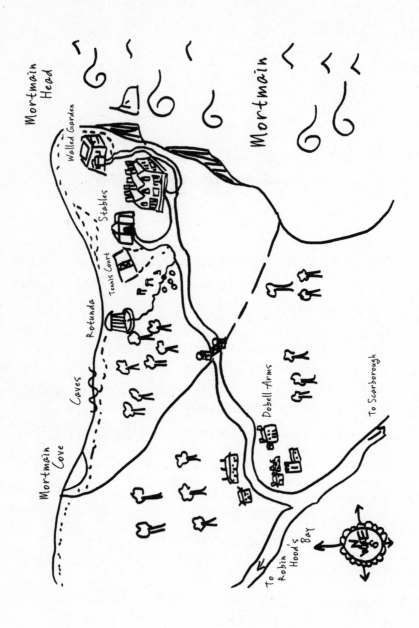

Epilogue

The man was dying. He knew it, and so did Rachel Savernake.

"You've discovered the truth, haven't you?" His voice was scratchy.

"Yes."

His hands trembled. "It was the perfect crime."

"Is there such a thing?" she asked.

He sighed, a long, low wheeze of surrender. "We thought so."

"Time is short." Leaning closer, she felt his sour breath on her cheeks. "Tell me what happened at Mortmain Hall."

Chapter 1

The ghost climbed out of a hackney carriage.

His head twitched from side to side as he checked to see if anyone was following him. Rachel Savernake was sure he'd failed to spot her. She stood deep in the shadows, on the opposite side of Westminster Bridge Road. A veil masked her face. Like the phantom, she was dressed in black from head to toe. During the half hour she'd waited for him to arrive, not one passer-by had given her a second glance. Women in mourning were a familiar sight outside the private station of the London Necropolis Company. This was the terminus for the funeral train.

With exaggerated care, the ghost pulled down the brim of his felt hat. During his years away, he'd grown a bushy moustache and beard. His left hand clutched a battered suitcase. As he limped towards the tall station building, Rachel stifled a groan.

The ghost's lameness gave him away. Gilbert Payne was still an amateur in deception.

Dodging between a double-decker bus and an ancient hearse, Rachel crossed to the station entrance. A curving road ran beneath a granite archway, affording access to the mortuary chambers. The building was fronted with red brick and warm terracotta; the white-glazed walls of the underpass were decorated with bay trees and palms. Behind the facade lurked a spindly pseudo-chimney which vented air to the morgues. Here coffined corpses became railway freight.

Ignoring the electric lift, she took long, athletic strides up the wrought-iron staircase. At the top she found herself beneath the glass roof of the first-class platform. The open doorway to the *chapelle ardente* revealed an oak catafalque, beige Wilton carpet, and walls treated in green and bronze. She considered the private waiting rooms. The first door bore a card with a name in neat script: *Mrs Cecilia Payne deceased*. It stood ajar, and Rachel glimpsed chairs upholstered in morocco, light oak panelling, and a shining parquet floor. Watercolour landscapes adorned the wall, as if this was a merchant's villa in Richmond. A tang of polish sharpened the air.

The ghost was nowhere to be seen.

A screen divided the platform. Behind it was the circulating area for third-class passengers. They had their own station entrance, so that those who paid for the privilege of a first-class funeral need not travel cheek-by-jowl with the grieving poor. The Necropolis Company prided itself on sensitivity to the feelings of the bereaved.

The ticket collector gave a discreet cough. He'd sprung out of his office like a bewhiskered jack-in-the-box. She thrust a small oblong of white card into his nicotine-stained hand.

"The express is waiting, ma'am." So it was, resplendent in olive-green livery, and belching steam, impatient as a starving dragon. "I'm afraid the hearse vans are already loaded."

While preparing for her journey, Rachel had learned that parties of first-class passengers were permitted to watch the coffin containing their loved one being loaded onto the funeral train. She marvelled at the entrepreneurs' ingenuity. They had transformed a moment of misery into a bonus for the privileged few.

"My fault for being late." She gave a nod of dismissal. "Thank you."

On the door of the nearest first-class compartment, a handwritten card matched the one outside the waiting room. A shadow was visible through the window. The ghost had taken his seat. Now he was trapped, as surely as if he'd locked himself in purgatory.

The air thickened with smoke and the smell of burning coal. The only person on the platform was a stout porter, shepherding an old lady into a third-class compartment at the end of the train. He spotted Rachel and broke into an unwise trot, puffing and grunting like an ancient locomotive destined for the breaker's yard.

"Just made it in time, ma'am," he wheezed. "We depart at eleven forty, sharp. Which party would you belong to?"

"The late Mrs Payne's." She thrust into his grimy paw a tip so extravagant that it risked making his heart stop. Her raised hand stifled his gasp of gratitude. "May I ask how many of our group are making the journey?"

He was sweating like a stoker. Rachel doubted his discomfiture was solely due to unaccustomed exercise. "I...well, ma'am, there seems to have been some confusion."

"Really?" She waited, confident that two gold sovereigns trumped any bribe paid to secure his silence.

"We expected six, ma'am, but only three gentlemen turned up. The pair who came early insisted they wouldn't travel in the compartment reserved for the...um, nearest and dearest. Most irregular. That's why the Company asks for bookings in advance. We don't want any mix-ups to spoil such a solemn occasion. Luckily, we only have one first-class funeral today."

A loyal servant, he didn't mention that the slump in trade

and rising unemployment had meant business was much less brisk in the aftermath of the Wall Street Crash.

"You managed to accommodate those two gentlemen elsewhere?"

A knobbly thumb jerked towards the compartment beyond the one allocated for mourners of the late Mrs Payne. "Right next door."

"Can you tell me anything about them?"

The porter mopped his brow. "I'm sorry, ma'am. We really need to…"

"Please forgive me. I can't explain why this is so important to me," she said, leaning closer so that he could inhale her perfume. "Personal reasons. You do understand?"

He peered through her veil. Something in her expression made him quail.

"Well, I'm…I'm sure you have good cause to ask. Quarrels happen in the best families, don't they? One chap's a cockney, dressed as a vicar. Surprised me, that did. I thought…"

"He didn't seem quite like an ordinary vicar?" Rachel suggested.

"Funny thing," the porter said. "I never saw a reverend gentleman with a tattoo on his hand in all my days. Takes all sorts, I suppose, but…"

"And his companion?"

The porter frowned. "Big fellow. Beefy. Mitts like coal shovels."

"Intimidating?"

"I really can't say any more, ma'am." He took another look at Rachel, and breathed out noisily. "Let's just say they tried to look posh, but forgot to shine their shoes. Funerals are funny; people aren't their normal selves. Why say they didn't want to disturb the rest of the party, when it turns out there's only one…?"

"Perhaps they just wanted to be considerate."

He flinched at her sarcasm. "Now, really, ma'am, please, I must ask you to board. We can't delay..."

"Of course not." Her smile lacked humour. "Thank you so much for your assistance."

He lumbered towards the compartment bearing the name of the late Mrs Payne, and opened the door. Ignoring his helping hand, Rachel jumped inside.

The compartment smelled of leather and tobacco. Seated at the far end, suitcase by his side, the ghost was gazing out of the window, lost in thought. One month short of his fortieth birthday, he seemed ten years older. Exile in northwest Africa's international zone had browned his cheeks and fattened his frame, but she doubted it was the sybaritic life that had aged him. The real cause was the never-ending dread of a knife thrust between his shoulder blades.

The porter slammed the door shut, knocking the ghost out of his reverie. Perched on the edge of the seat, Rachel gave a nod of greeting.

"Good morning," she said.

The ghost gave an anxious grunt. Her casual friendliness was all the more disturbing because her presence in the compartment was inexplicable. When he spoke, his voice trembled.

"Good...good morning."

"How pleasant to meet you," she said, "albeit in such sad circumstances."

A whistle sounded, and with a disconcerting jolt, the train began its journey to the cemetery. The ghost shuddered. Rachel pictured the cogwheels of his brain spinning. *Who was she? What, if anything, should he say?*

"My name," he said, "is—"

"You don't need to introduce yourself," Rachel said. "You're not really a ghost. You're Gilbert Payne, the missing publisher. Welcome back from the dead."

———

As the train rumbled down the track, the man rocked back and forth on his seat. The beard and moustache were fig leaves for naked vulnerability. His eyelids flickered under her scrutiny. She guessed his despair, but she hadn't followed him in order to sympathise. Long before his disappearance, he'd been notorious for recklessness. People found it easy to believe that it had cost him his life. He gulped, and she wondered if he was about to be sick.

"You…you are mistaken, madam," he muttered. "My name is Bertram Jones."

Rachel lifted her veil. His bloodshot eyes widened as he took in her youth, her beauty, and the chill of her smile.

"Not Bertram Jones, the old drinking chum of Gilbert Payne, who has lived in Tangier these past four years?"

"That's right!" He was as hapless as a man tumbling into a ravine, clutching at stubs of vegetation in the hope of salvation. "It's true…there is a…vague likeness between the two of us. A similarity in the cheekbones, perhaps. Poor Gilbert joked about it more than once before…"

"Before he feigned death by drowning, fled from London, and sailed under cover of darkness for the Continent?" Rachel asked. "Before he made his way in search of the esoteric delights of Tangier?"

The ghost slumped back in his seat, as if she'd thrust a hatpin into his heart.

"Long before he heard the tragic news of the death of the mother he'd adored?" She was relentless. "The woman who worshipped him, whose heart finally gave way without her knowing that her only child was still alive?"

"It's a lie, a cruel lie!" He stared at her. "In God's name, who are you?"

The train was picking up speed. Rachel was in no hurry. They were not at risk of being disturbed. The funeral express made no stops along the way.

"My name doesn't matter."

"What..." His voice was hoarse and barely audible. "What do you want with me?"

She pursed her lips. "I'm offering to save you from being murdered."

Chapter 2

Gilbert Payne said nothing until the train had escaped both slums and suburbs. The June sun had slipped out of sight. Above the open countryside, sprawling clouds were the colour of soot. Daubs of rain streaked the carriage windows.

Rachel's eyes never left him. It crossed her mind that he might fling open the far door of the compartment, and jump out. If he did, he'd more than likely break his neck. Terror had made him desperate.

"What…do you mean?" he said at last.

"I want to hear the story behind your disappearance. The truth, the whole truth, and nothing but. Tell me who helped you to get away from England, and why."

The farmsteads and smallholdings of Surrey slid by. Rachel tapped her heel on the compartment floor.

"I can't imagine why you're poking your nose into—poor Gilbert Payne's affairs." He swallowed, as if even he was unconvinced by this show of defiance. "Who in God's name are you?"

"Who I am is irrelevant. What concerns you is that I know your true identity, and I am prepared to help rescue you from the consequences of your own folly."

"I told you." He sounded like a child protesting innocence despite the evidence of grubby fingerprints. "I am Bertram Jones, late of Tangier."

She shook her head. "Time is precious. Don't waste it. We are halfway to Brookwood Cemetery. If you persist in your charade, there will be no second chance."

"You've given me no reason to talk to you on confidential terms," he said. "Nothing but a baseless slur."

Rachel gave an exaggerated sigh. "As Gilbert Payne, you enjoyed success in publishing. The business struggled until you started pumping out thrillers. Tales of derring-do. Manly Englishmen confronting sinister Orientals and crafty Continentals. Lion Lonsdale, Captain Chalmers, Sidney Smart-Fox, the names changed, but not their courage or patriotism. No matter how low a foul opponent stooped, our clean-living heroes always triumphed."

"Sneer if you wish, and be damned to you." His eyes flashed with anger. "Gilbert spotted an opening for decent entertainment. Exciting stories devoured by men whose bravery beat the Kaiser. As well as by keen young lads who wished they'd been old enough to fight."

"Unlike Gilbert Payne, of course," Rachel said. "Lame since childhood, and thus spared the chaos of the Western Front."

"I trust you're not suggesting Gilbert was a coward?" he retorted. "Nonsense! He served his country to the utmost of his ability. In his own way."

"His ways were unorthodox, weren't they?" Rachel said. "Entertaining the keen young lads?"

He curled his lip. "Your inference is contemptible, madam. Gilbert was a fine man. You only need read the books he published to see that he detested unnatural behaviour. He had a wide circle of friends. All of them, like me, were left distraught by his untimely passing."

"The face of the body they pulled out of the Thames was damaged beyond recognition, wasn't it?"

"After twenty-four hours in the murky depths, what would you expect?" His voice rose, as if declaiming a long-rehearsed speech. "The corpse was wearing Gilbert's monogrammed wristwatch. The coroner suggested that before falling into the water, the poor fellow had been knocked about by a boathook. To say nothing of the mischief done by sea life. An utter tragedy. Poor Gilbert had been out celebrating his firm's latest book, and he'd drunk more than usual. He fell victim to a robbery that went wrong. The inquest verdict was clear. Murder by person or persons unknown."

"Robbers who omitted to steal a valuable watch?"

"They panicked when they saw he was dead. All they wanted was to hide the evidence of their crime." His cheeks reddened; temper was strengthening his confidence. "And now you accuse me of assuming my friend's personality. Poppycock! I can't imagine who you are, or what your motives are, but it's a shameful falsehood. Today of all days, when Gilbert's mother will be laid to rest."

"I hate to be insensitive," Rachel said, "but where are the other mourners?"

He stiffened. "What do you mean?"

"Yesterday, when I arranged to join your party, the Necropolis Company was expecting Letty Mountford, Mrs Payne's lady help, to travel to Brookwood, together with your elderly aunt. Your mother's death came out of the blue. A devastating blow for you. You always intended to see her again one day, but the time was never right. The danger was too great. The least you could do was make sure she had a good send-off. Using the name Bertram Jones, you wired money to Letty Mountford, so your mother could be buried at Brookwood, alongside your father."

"How do you know this?" he whispered. "Why are you tormenting me?"

"What do you think happened to Miss Mountford and your Aunt Clara?"

"The porter said they'd sent a message that they were indisposed. A virulent bug of some kind."

"That same porter omitted to mention the two men who took their place."

"What men?"

"Were you too preoccupied to spot them in the compartment next door? It was prudent to leave your arrival at the station to the last minute, but you can be sure they made certain you boarded this train."

His face was white. "I can't...I can't imagine who they might be."

Rachel leaned towards him. "Use your intelligence, Mr Payne. If I've learned that you are back in Britain, so have others. Someone wanted you gone forever. Tell me why."

He glared. "Why on earth should I trust you? A woman who appears out of nowhere, who slanders my dead friend, and calls me a liar?"

"Because I am your only hope."

"Nonsense!"

In a sudden movement, she seized his wrists. He flinched at her iron grip. "Your enemies are on this train, but I have a fast car waiting at the South Station of the Necropolis. Attend your mother's service, then join me. That way, you will survive long enough to see another dawn."

She let his wrists go, and he sank forward on the seat, pushing his head into his hands.

"Has it occurred to you," he said in a muffled tone, "that regardless of your farrago, I might no longer care whether I live or die?"

"Unhappiness is suffocating you," she said. "Listen, I know what it means to lose a parent. Grief needn't destroy you. You sacrificed so much to stay alive."

He made no reply, but pulled himself upright, and turned to contemplate the passing landscape. She allowed him a few minutes of silent reflection before consulting a wristwatch brilliant with diamonds.

"Time is ticking, Mr Payne. Soon we arrive at Necropolis Junction."

"Why won't you listen?" There was something pitiful about his bluster. "Let me repeat myself. I am not Gilbert Payne."

She folded her arms. "I shall not attend the service. Consider my proposal while your mother is buried, and ask yourself whether she'd want you to follow her to the grave with such haste. I'll wait with my chauffeur. My car is parked close to the Keith Mausoleum. Grasp this lifeline, Mr Payne. There are no other straws to clutch."

He took a breath, and stared blankly past her, as if he'd put himself into a trance.

"I've given you my answer." His voice was hollow. "My name is Bertram Jones."

———

From the mainline junction, the funeral train reversed down the private cemetery line, through wooden boundary gates, and past laurel hedges, ornamental shrubs, late-flowering rhododendrons, and a redwood avenue formed by towering wellingtonia. They'd arrived in Brookwood Cemetery, the largest burial ground in England, some said in the world. Conceived by enlightened Victorians as a sanitary alternative to the capital's overcrowded graveyards, this estate was vast enough to accommodate London's corpses for centuries to come. A city of the dead.

First stop was the North Station, a low white-painted wooden building with green drainpipes and guttering and an overhanging roof. This was the halt for dissenters' funerals. Rachel's compartment stopped alongside a refreshment room for mourners. There was even a licensed bar. A stone's throw away stood the Nonconformist chapel.

A handful of mourners dismounted. They were greeted by functionaries of the Necropolis Company whose task was to escort the mourners to the service. They'd assembled in a line and taken off their hats as a mark of respect. Passengers fiddled with umbrellas in the drizzle. An attendant loaded a coffin onto a hand-bier.

Gilbert Payne's eyes were closed, but Rachel thought he was too frightened to doze. Perhaps he was hoping she belonged to a nightmare, and that when he looked again, she'd have vanished. Just as four years ago he'd gone in the blink of an eye.

The train set off again, and as they approached South Station, Rachel played her final card.

"Think about what I've said, Mr Payne." She lowered her veil. "The choice is yours. Life or death."

———

Jumping onto the platform, she glanced into the next compartment. The faces of the two men who had bribed the porter at Westminster Bridge Road were pressed to the window. They paid her no heed. Perhaps they assumed she'd made a mistake and travelled in the wrong compartment. Her impression was of men whose brutish muscularity didn't allow for a high opinion of female intelligence.

The weather was in keeping with the sombre atmosphere of the cemetery. As the mourning parties awaited direction from the cemetery staff, she hurried away past the Anglican chapels and towards her destination. The Keith Mausoleum was a Gothic edifice in marble, with stained-glass windows, and a cast-iron door bearing the family's name. Parked beyond the level crossing was her Rolls-Royce.

Trueman leaned against the bonnet of the Phantom, a mountainous figure, immaculate in his chauffeur's uniform and oblivious to the rain. A small pair of binoculars nestled in the palm of his huge right hand.

"What news?"

"I talked to Payne." She shook her head. "He clings to the pretence that his name is Bertram Jones."

"Anyone followed him?"

"Two hired thugs. They'll sit behind him in the chapel while the parson reads a eulogy to his dear departed mama. It's not a last act of kindness; it suits them better to bide their time. I expect the plan is to finish him off on the return journey."

Trueman nodded. "When his guard is down, and his thoughts are wandering. Easy prey."

"If he'd died before the funeral, there would be more awkward questions."

"Does he understand they mean to kill him?"

"I warned him in words of one syllable. The trouble is, he's lived a lie for too long."

"You'd better jump inside the car. No point in us both getting wet."

She took her place in the back of the Phantom, and waited.

The rain was easing off as Gilbert Payne emerged from the Anglican chapel. He'd trudged back there after following his mother's coffin to the graveside for the committal, while everyone else retreated to the refreshment room for a ham sandwich and a cup of tea. Had he been making his peace with God?

He limped towards the platform, still clutching his suitcase. It was nearly a quarter past two. The funeral train was ready to return to London. Studying him through the binoculars, like an ornithologist tracking the flight of an elusive bird, Trueman saw that he didn't even spare the Phantom a glance.

Rachel joined him and he passed her the glasses.

"Payne is supposed to be dead," he said. "There'll be no suppose about it, if he doesn't see sense."

"It's all too much for him," she murmured. "He's tired of running, of pretending to be someone he's not. He simply doesn't care anymore."

"Not care? After going to such lengths? Look at everything he threw away. Thriving business, swish home in Chelsea. His dear old mum."

"He was scared into believing he had no choice. Now he's had four years in the sun. Perhaps he's decided it was enough for a lifetime."

"Ready to die so young?"

Rachel shrugged. "I dare say he still hopes he can talk his way out of trouble. Negotiate. But he's not haggling with literary agents now. Come on, people are getting into the train."

They strolled forward, keeping sight of Gilbert Payne as he approached the throng of passengers on the platform. The two men following him were outside the refreshment room, waiting to see what he did next. He reached the compartment he'd shared with Rachel on the outward journey, and peeped inside. For a split second, he hesitated.

Had he expected to see her there again? Was he reconsidering her offer? As she and Trueman watched, he squared his shoulders. Decision made, he opened the door. The moment he was inside, he yanked it firmly shut.

Rachel let out a breath. Now he could not escape. Did he really believe he could survive?

The false vicar and his companion left their vantage point. The train was filling up, and a porter was urging everyone else to climb on board. Keeping to the timetable was a point of pride for the staff of the London Necropolis Company. When the two men were the only passengers left on the platform, their stride quickened. As the porter turned his back, they jumped into Gilbert Payne's compartment. A moment later, the flag was waved.

As the engine pulled away, Trueman shrugged.

"Jokers call it the dead meat train. They never spoke a truer word."

Chapter 3

As Rachel Savernake talked with a ghost, Jacob Flint sat cramped up with his fellow newspapermen on a hard, narrow bench in the Old Bailey. The final witness for the Crown in the case of *R v. Danskin* was giving evidence. This trial had knocked every other story off the front pages, but Minnie Brown wasn't basking in the limelight. She looked more frightened than the prisoner in the dock.

Minnie was only twenty-two, but already the cares of work and motherhood had taken their toll, stooping her shoulders and fading her pale prettiness. A waitress in the ABC teashop across the road from the Central Criminal Court, she had met the accused there two years ago when he had popped in for a cup of char and a crumpet.

Within days Clive Danskin had become her lover; inside twelve months he had fathered her child. Now Minnie could not bear to look him in the eye. Like everyone else in the court-room, she knew her tale of woe formed the last link in the chain of circumstantial evidence wrapped around the accused. A chain strong enough to drag him to the gallows.

Fiddling with his pince-nez, a habit born of nervous

energy rather than need, Sir Edgar Jackson KC consulted the Matterhorn of documents in front of him.

"And did the accused make payments to you in respect of your daughter?"

"Yes," Minnie whispered. "But the money didn't come in regular."

"Did you obtain at Guildhall Police Court, on 4 September last year, an order against the accused for maintenance of the child?"

She bowed her head. "I did."

"And did the prisoner make the payments ordered by the court?"

"Yes," she said, before looking up and noticing counsel's glare. "At least…he did until this March."

"March of this year?" the prosecutor demanded. "The month before the murder of which the prisoner stands accused?"

"Yes," she breathed.

The case against Clive Danskin was complete. Hooking his thumbs in his waistcoat pockets, Sir Edgar leaned back on his heels. He'd constructed an elaborate case like a legalistic Lutyens, and felt entitled to pause to admire the aesthetic excellence of his handiwork.

"Speak up, Miss Brown!" he bellowed.

"Yes."

Her voice echoed in the silence, loud and clear and mournful. Tears formed in her eyes. Tragic reluctance was precisely the picture Sir Edgar wanted to leave in the jury's mind. This wasn't a woman scorned, taking revenge on the cad who had betrayed her. Minnie Brown was a victim who still nursed a morsel of affection for a man she now knew to be not only a cruel deceiver but a callous murderer.

As Sir Edgar milked his triumph, the lawyers representing

Danskin shifted in their seats. The scarlet-robed judge yawned, his thoughts evidently drifting towards lunch. The jurors were sombre; they seemed to Jacob to have aged during the course of the trial, as if worn down by the knowledge of what a guilty verdict meant.

Jacob looked about him. His neighbour, chief crime correspondent of the *Witness*, was scrawling on his pad: *Final nail in coffin*. The stomach of the *Daily Mail* man rumbled; the fellow from the *Times* shot his cuffs. The other journalists, most of them twice Jacob's age, had sat through dozens of capital cases. A death sentence meant fifty thousand plus on their newspaper's circulation. Jacob hadn't yet reached the point where familiarity with the pomp and paraphernalia of the legal process bred contempt. Not that he'd admit it to a living soul, but he felt a chill every time he recalled that a man who lost in this game would pay with his neck.

Behind them, a bald, burly man was staring at Minnie Brown. His fierce concentration had nothing to do with curiosity, ill manners, or prurience. Roy Meadows was a courtroom artist who often contributed sketches from trials to Jacob's newspaper, the *Clarion*. The law forbade anyone to draw a picture or take a photograph in court, so the trick was to memorise the appearance of the principal characters in the drama: judge, jury, lawyers, witnesses, and above all the wretch in the dock. Meadows's technique was to identify a feature that brought a character to life. It might be something as simple as the way a barrister wore his wig. Poor Minnie must be a challenge. She was so nondescript.

Next to Meadows, the *Witness*'s courtroom artist, a pale, handsome fellow with straw-coloured hair and a beaky nose, alternated between nibbling his pencil and chewing at his fingernails. His gaze wandered from Minnie Brown and came to rest on a woman at the front of the public gallery. Jacob followed his eyes. It wasn't youth, beauty, or elegant grooming that had attracted the artist's attention. Her grey hair was an unruly mop, her chin sharp. She was craning her long neck forward, as if desperate not to miss a word that was said.

Jacob thought she looked like a witch. Add a broomstick and pointed hat, and you'd have a splendid caricature. Perhaps she intrigued the artist because she was a prominent public figure. Jacob couldn't place her, but the great and the good liked nothing better than to take in a few hours of the finest legal theatre. This trial had attracted an audience as eager as any found at an Aldwych farce. Without his press pass, Jacob would have been forced to join the long queue each morning to stand a chance of seeing Sir Edgar do his damnedest to hang Clive Danskin.

The witch was studying the prisoner. Searching for visible clues to the rottenness of his character, as a philatelist might inspect a rare stamp for flaws. Danskin struck Jacob as a remarkable specimen, as much a collector's item as a Penny Black. This wasn't because his appearance had special distinction. With his neatly combed brown hair, toothbrush moustache, and natty taste in suits, he was dapper enough to seduce impressionable tobacconists' assistants and teashop waitresses, but he'd never be mistaken for Ramon Novarro.

No, what made Clive Danskin extraordinary was his demeanour. Throughout the trial, he'd resembled a spectator at a game of croquet rather than a man on trial for his life. A few weeks hence, he would surely be executed. Yet as Sir Edgar built his case, he listened to each witness with a calm verging on indifference.

Motive, means, opportunity: the prosecutor had spelled out the whole sordid story. Danskin was a silk stocking salesman whose travels gave him endless opportunities to seduce lonely women. A married man, he was up to his ears in debt. After his car had been found on fire one night in a remote area of the north of England, a man's charred remains were discovered inside. A distinctive silver tip from the cane Danskin carried was found at the scene. At first, the police inferred that Danskin had been killed in a horrific accident, but when his photograph appeared in the papers, an irate creditor spotted him climbing into a taxi in Trafalgar Square. That same day, the police arrested him at Croydon Airport, minutes before he was due to board a flight for France.

To this day, the authorities had never identified the corpse. The dead man was presumed to be a passing tramp whom Danskin had picked up on the pretext of offering a lift, before bludgeoning him to death, and then dressing him in his second-best suit, his coat, and his trilby. According to the Crown's scientific expert, the fire was no act of God. Someone had deliberately set the car alight.

Danskin's private affairs were in disarray. The cost of maintaining an estranged wife and mistresses scattered around the country was crippling. He had a compelling motive to fake his own death by killing the tramp and pretending the corpse was his. The crime gave him the chance to break free of his responsibilities, and start a new life on the Continent, while his supposed widow benefited from the life insurance he'd taken out six months earlier.

He claimed that a tramp had stolen his car and possessions, but this seemed like an inept fabrication. The police had made strenuous efforts to trace the mysterious limousine, in which he claimed to have hitched a lift from northwest England to London, or its driver. The case had been widely publicised in the press and on the wireless, but no one had come forward. If the Good Samaritan existed, where was he?

"Thank you, Miss Brown," Sir Edgar said after testing the judge's patience as far as he dared. "Please remain where you are. My learned friend may wish to cross-examine you."

Minnie Brown trembled as Percival Lang KC rose slowly to his feet. Squat and sleepy-eyed, counsel for the defence never did anything in a hurry. His ponderous movements contrasted with his opponent's energy. Certainly there was no sign that he was capable of taking a sledgehammer to the case that Jackson had built.

"I have no questions for this witness, m'lud."

Next to Jacob, Haydn Williams scratched on his pad: *Hope abandoned: official.*

"Very well," Mr Justice Cairney said. "Sir Edgar?"

Learned counsel for the Crown jumped up, and treated the jury to a smirk of satisfaction. "That concludes the case for the prosecution, my lord."

The judge announced that it would be convenient to adjourn for luncheon, and the journalists scrambled to their feet. Two warders escorted the prisoner from the dock. Clive Danskin walked briskly, as if eager to tuck in to lunch. If he felt the noose tightening around his throat, he gave no sign of it. His *sangfroid* was remarkable. He looked as if for two pins, he'd whistle a happy tune.

———

"Nothing beats a good murder, my boy," Haydn Williams assured Jacob in the press room. They'd telephoned their offices with an update on the morning's developments, but there was no cause to hold the front page. The fireworks would come this afternoon, if Clive Danskin dared to take the stand.

Haydn was the doyen of Fleet Street's crime correspondents,

and his cynicism was as devout as the Presbyterian faith of his forebears in Merionethshire. He boasted that he'd seen all the great murderers in the dock, from that wretched pair Crippen and Le Neve to George Joseph Smith, the Brides in the Bath killer, and those poisonous lawyers Armstrong and Greenwood. If some wet-behind-the-ears newcomer to the press gallery fell into the trap, pointing out that Ethel Le Neve had been acquitted, and so had Harold Greenwood, Haydn would tap the side of his nose in a knowing manner before roaring with laughter at the tyro's naivete.

"You're sure that Sir Edgar has proved it was murder?" Jacob kept a straight face as he pointed to the black huddle of lawyers in the well of the court. "Danskin's counsel did his utmost to drill a hole in the engineer's expert evidence."

Haydn snorted. His trial reports were lurid confections of sex, scandal, and sensation. The wags among his rival journalists reckoned that if he turned his hand to fiction, he'd outsell Sapper and Sax Rohmer combined. For Haydn, what mattered was atmosphere. The smell of fear as a prisoner collapsed and sobbed for mercy, the deafening cheers as a jury set an accused woman free. Facts were an optional seasoning, a garnish reserved for cases where truth proved stranger than fiction, or as a last resort to deter a claim of libel.

"Desperation, my boy, pure desperation."

Haydn pushed a hand through his shock of white hair. Fifty-five years old, he could pass for seventy. The lines of his face were as deep as trenches, his eyes were bleary, and his paunch meant nobody could squeeze past him on the press bench. His clothing smelled of mothballs and stale beer. Jacob had seldom seen him drunk, and never completely sober.

"Faced with such an overwhelming case for the Crown, what jury could hesitate? They'll not need half an hour. Crippen was condemned within twenty minutes—did I ever tell you that tale? This business is done and dusted. A saint would be condemned to swing on what we've heard. Mark my words, Danskin will be six feet under in an unmarked grave before the summer's over."

Jacob felt nauseated. "The whole case is circumstantial."

"What more do you want?" Haydn's tufted eyebrows wiggled in mock astonishment. "A photograph of Danskin standing over the car with a lit match in his grubby paw? Really, boy, the only innocent round here is you."

Jacob had been promoted less than six months ago, following his predecessor's untimely death. Haydn maintained to all and sundry that he'd taken the lad under his wing and taught him everything he knew. Jacob enjoyed his tall tales and his company, but couldn't help wondering if the older man's jeering betrayed a pang of jealousy. Not of his job, but of his youth.

"Danskin is an unsavoury rascal," Jacob said. "He uses his charm to exploit the needy and naive. He's a liar and a cheat, but that doesn't make him a murderer."

"For a bright young spark, you can be as obstinate as a donkey. Old Edgar has shown he had means and opportunity. He's even gone to great pains to establish motive, though the jury could convict without it. What more can twelve good men and true dream of?"

Haydn's declamatory style was worthy of an old ham at the Hippodrome. Perhaps he was a barrister *manqué*. Stick a wig and gown on him, and the illusion would be complete.

"If the question is whether a man lives or dies," Jacob said, "shouldn't we give him the benefit of any doubt?"

"Never took you for a bleeding heart, boy. Next thing, you'll be telling me you don't believe in the noose."

"I'm no more a Bolshie than Baldwin," Jacob snapped. "All

I'm saying is that under cross-examination, the expert seemed vague. Can we be sure the tramp didn't die by accident? Even if he was murdered, how can we know Danskin set his own car on fire with this unknown man's body inside? What if he's telling the truth?"

"Pigs might fly, my boy."

"Suppose his car was stolen, and a stranger gave him a lift to London out of the goodness of his heart. Does it matter that no one has come forward to back up his alibi? That almost gives it the ring of truth. His story is so unlikely, why on earth would he make it up?"

"Load of cobblers, if you'll pardon the professional jargon. If you ask me, Danskin panicked, and came up with that tosh when the police first questioned him. Afterwards, he was stuck with it. Terrified that if he changed his statement, his credibility was shot."

Jacob gave a shrug of resignation. Haydn clapped him on the shoulder, and gestured to the door.

"Come on, boy, you're obviously under the weather if you think a fraud like Danskin deserves to walk out from here scot-free. Your imagination's got the better of you. Shove some proper sustenance into that skinny frame of yours. What do you say to washing a chop and chips down with a pint of Guinness at the Magpie?"

The Magpie and Stump, across the road from the Bailey, was Haydn's second home. When presiding at the bar, he loved to regale his listeners with his favourite story of Victorian enterprise. In the nineteenth century, the landlord rented out the room upstairs to wealthy peeping Toms who enjoyed a bird's-eye view of the public executions at Newgate Prison. If that wasn't enough to satisfy their appetite, they could devour a hanging breakfast of steak, devilled kidneys, and as much ale or porter as they could put away. Jacob had a queasy feeling that their descendants salivated over the trial reports in the *Clarion* and the *Witness*.

"No, thanks. I want to listen to the defence case with a clear head."

"It'll make more sense if you're three sheets to the wind. The minute Danskin starts answering questions about this mythical bloke who drove him to London, old Edgar will tie him up in knots."

"You think Danskin will give evidence?"

"Truth is, he's damned if he does, and damned if he doesn't. Some judge once talked about the cruel kindness of letting accused murderers testify on their own behalf. They usually end up hanging themselves. Danskin's got the gift of the gab when it comes to talking a shop girl into bed. Telling a cock-and-bull story to judge and jury in a murder trial is a different kettle of fish. But if Lang decides not to call him, the jury will presume that Danskin is afraid of getting caught out. Either way, his goose is cooked. Trust Uncle Haydn."

"I still need to work on my report," Jacob muttered.

"Mine's typed up already."

Haydn gave his belly a congratulatory pat. They joined the mass of people making their way outside. Jacob couldn't help scratching the itch of doubt.

"And if he's acquitted?"

"Same story, more or less. Only half as many column inches, tucked away on an inside page." Haydn's grin showed the gaps in his yellow front teeth. "But the question's academic; it doesn't arise. Trust me, boy. Clive Danskin is as guilty as sin. And may the Lord have mercy on his soul."

Chapter 4

As Haydn Williams stomped off in search of liquid refreshment, Jacob settled for a breath of damp air. The Old Bailey was no longer plagued by the stench of the old Newgate days, when judges carried posies of flowers to ward off gaol fever and the whiff of unwashed prisoners, but the ventilation was still hopelessly inadequate. He was glad to escape the suffocating atmosphere.

His thoughts far away, he lost his footing on a rain-slicked cobblestone, and collided with a solidly built woman who had halted right in front of him. She was gazing up at the bronze statue on the dome at the top of the building. Jacob recognised her as the witch who had caught the courtroom artist's eye.

"Pardon me," he said. "I wasn't looking where I was going."

"No harm done, young man."

There wasn't a hint of a witch's cackle; he even detected a comfortingly familiar Yorkshire accent. At a distance, he'd guessed she was a spinster of sixty. On closer inspection, she might be fifteen or twenty years younger. He'd also misjudged her marital status; the only jewellery she wore was a gold wedding ring. Swan-necked and formidably bosomed, she wore a garish mauve cape over an unflattering tweed suit that might have suited a portly gentleman farmer.

"Once again, my apologies."

"Nonsense, my fault for standing in your way." She waved her umbrella towards the figure on the dome. Justitia wielded a sword in her right hand and the scales of justice in her left. "According to the old legends, Lady Justice despaired of the evils of earth and retired to the heavens so as not to be sullied. Each time I come here, I pay my respects."

Jacob peered at the statue. "She isn't wearing her blindfold."

The woman snorted. "She never has. Not at the Old Bailey. In classical times, her dignity and maidenly form sufficed to inspire fear in the wicked and courage in the good. The notion of justice being blind came later, a wrong turning taken in mediaeval times. A judge needs clear sight, especially in a case as complicated as this Danskin business."

"You don't regard it as open and shut?"

"Far from it. The evidence against Danskin seems compelling. But who knows? Sir Edgar is always so cocksure. Perhaps he's swaggering too soon. I wouldn't be surprised if his carefully constructed case turns out to be founded on sand."

This was a woman who liked to swim against the tide, Jacob thought. Eccentric, possibly, but intelligent. He wondered if she was a campaigner against capital punishment, the sort who conducted a lonely vigil of protest outside the prison gates each time a convicted murderer took the eight o'clock walk.

"You're a sceptic, Mrs...?"

"Dobell is the name. And I prefer to describe myself as a realist, Mr Flint."

He was taken aback. "You know who I am?"

"I've a pair of eyes in my head, young man. You sit with the other journalists, and each morning you leaf through the *Clarion* before proceedings begin."

His interest quickened. "Do you have an interest in the case? Are you related to Danskin, by any chance?"

"Dear me, no." She paused. "Thank goodness."

"So you think he may be found guilty?"

"No, no, you must break with professional habit, and not put words in my mouth. I meant simply this. To be personally connected to a man on trial for his life is ghastly. It isn't only the prisoner who suffers, but those around him. Friends and family are tainted by association. Their lives are destroyed." Her voice trembled with emotion. "Danskin is an odious man, but does that make him a murderer?"

"Well, no, but…"

"Besides, we haven't heard the case for the defence. How can one possibly tell at this stage whether or not he committed the crime? Or does the *Clarion* prefer to prejudge?" Her gaze was piercing, accusatory.

"I'm sorry. You're right, of course. Innocent until proven guilty, and all that."

"A principle that newspapers seldom remember," she said. "I can only hope that as the years pass, you don't forget it."

"What do you make of the evidence we've heard so far?"

She shook her head. "The Crown has assembled a formidable case. But one should always expect the unexpected."

"You think Danskin's not as black as he's painted?"

"Who knows? Mud sticks, and there's plenty of mud to be thrown. And yet…" She waved her umbrella in the direction of the bronze lady on the dome. "Justice moves in mysterious ways, Mr Flint. Therein lies its eternal fascination."

And with a curt nod, she marched off down the road.

———

"Your name is Grenville Fitzroy Whitlow?"

"Correct."

Jacob's nickname for Percival Lang KC was the Tortoise. Counsel for the defence exuded caution, and his deliberate manner verged on lethargy. Sir Edgar, in contrast, was a born Hare. Even on the rare occasions when he raised an objection, the Tortoise's diffidence implied regret at interrupting his opponent's rhetoric. He wasn't noted as an advocate in capital cases; he usually specialised in advising government officers about the dusty by-ways of constitutional law. His opening remarks had struck Jacob as deplorably lacking in histrionics. More-in-sorrow-than-in-anger surely wasn't enough, when Danskin's life was at stake.

The Tortoise had chided Sir Edgar for his inability to establish that the man in the burned-out car had fallen victim to murder rather than a terrible accident, as well as for failing to show that his client's alibi was a dishonest charade. These shortcomings, he said, explained why he would not ask his client to testify. It was for the Crown to prove his guilt, not for him to disprove it. A bold strategy, but a sign of desperation.

The Tortoise took an age shuffling the papers in his brief. He never did anything in a hurry. Was his sluggishness calculated to provoke his opponent into an impatient outburst? As everyone waited, Sir Edgar muttered under his breath.

"I must apologise," the Tortoise said unexpectedly. "I should have said, you are Major Grenville Fitzroy Whitlow, DSO?"

The witness was lean and hawk-nosed, with short black hair. His movements were stiff and abrupt, and so was his manner. He kept his right hand inside a well-cut blazer.

"Yes."

"You were awarded the Distinguished Service Order for gallantry under fire in the autumn of 1917?"

"Yes."

"Forgive me, Major Whitlow, but am I right in understanding that you suffered grievous wounds in the action?"

The witness's grey eyes never flickered as he withdrew his right hand from his jacket. Except that it wasn't a hand, but a steel claw.

A low gasp from those sitting in the public gallery was quickly hushed into an embarrassed silence.

"I was blown up during an advance," he said. "We gained a good fifty yards that day."

"And your current occupation, Major Whitlow?"

"I work in Whitehall. My duties involve liaison between the Home Office and the FO." In the clipped tone of the Oxford common room, he said, "I gained a smattering of languages while operating behind enemy lines, so the authorities allowed me to make myself useful."

"I'm sure you do," the Tortoise said. "I have no wish to trespass on any area of national security, but would it be fair to say that you have recently been engaged on business of great urgency?"

"It would."

"Thank you." Having made clear why he'd called this witness first, the Tortoise indulged in a little page-shuffling. "Could you tell the court what you did on the evening of 3 February this year?"

Major Whitlow straightened his shoulders, and Jacob pictured him striding across a parade ground. No troops would wish to earn this man's displeasure.

"I was driving home from my mother's home. She lives in Kirkby Lonsdale in Westmorland."

"You're sure of the date? There is no possibility that you might be mistaken?"

"None whatsoever."

"Really? Why is that?"

Major Whitlow's frown suggested that he was unaccustomed to having his bare word questioned. "I have good reason to be certain. The following day, I was due to travel to Europe on urgent business for an indefinite period. My mother has a weak heart and had been suffering from poor health. I was concerned to see her before I flew out."

"You did not know," the Tortoise asked in a hushed and sympathetic tone, "whether you would have the chance to see her again once your...mission was complete?"

Major Whitlow bowed his head, but his voice remained steady. "Correct."

"Please describe what happened as you were driving back."

"I gave a man a lift."

"In what circumstances?"

"I spotted him standing by the roadside in north Lancashire. It was dark, and he was waving his hat to flag me down. He was respectably dressed, but wore no jacket. On a cold winter's night, with rain in the air, this struck me as extraordinary. Nor was he carrying any bags. He appeared to be agitated. I felt obliged to pull up and ask if I could be of assistance."

"What did he say?"

"He said he'd been driving along when he stopped for a man who was hitching a lift. A tramp."

"A tramp?"

"Yes, it was bitterly cold, and the tramp claimed that he'd been walking all day. The fellow took pity on him, and said he could hop in. He offered to take the tramp to Lancaster."

"Why Lancaster?"

"He was a salesman and he'd been on the road most of the day. Said he was tired. He planned to get up early and drive back to London the next morning."

"What did he say occurred after he picked up the tramp?"

"His car started giving trouble. He jumped out to look under the bonnet, and the next thing he knew, someone hit him on the head."

"Someone?"

"He presumed it was the tramp, but since he'd lost consciousness, he never saw what happened. When he came round, the car had disappeared, and so had his jacket. The tramp had gone, and so had his wallet and an overnight case stowed in the trunk of the car."

"What did you make of that account?"

"It sounded odd," Major Whitlow said. "For what it is worth, my impression was that he was telling me the truth, and that he'd suffered a dreadful experience as a result of an act of kindness."

Sir Edgar muttered grumpily to his junior, but kept his powder dry. Jacob glanced at the judge. The Tortoise was pushing his luck as regards the rules of evidence. If challenged, the Tortoise might argue that the vital question was not whether Danskin had actually been attacked, but what he'd told his rescuer. At all events, it was academic. Major Whitlow's air of authority was hypnotic.

"When did you form that opinion?"

"As soon as he told me what had happened."

"So quickly?"

"Making rapid judgements is a necessary part of my present duties." The witness looked up at the judge. Under his gaze, even the solemn, bewigged old man blinked. "It's a habit I developed during the war."

"One's very survival may depend on the accuracy of such judgements?"

The Tortoise glanced at his opponent, as if expecting an objection. The Hare remained in his seat. The witness was a war hero, a patriot whose personal sacrifice in the line of duty was plain to see.

"Indeed."

"Can you tell the court why you believed this man?"

"I have seen at firsthand the effects of concussion on the battlefield. His manner was consistent with his story. He seemed disorientated, although as far as I could tell, there were no signs of obvious physical damage."

"Any other reason?"

"Five minutes before I spotted the man by the roadside, I'd passed a bullnose Morris Oxford."

"A bullnose Morris Oxford," the Tortoise repeated, on the off-chance that there was a soul in the courtroom who failed to understand the significance of the make of car.

"Correct. The vehicle was travelling in the opposite direction, and I noticed it because of the erratic manner of driving. I needed to apply my brake to avoid a collision. The driver may have been under the influence of alcohol, but candidly, I took no notice of him. I was more concerned to preserve my safety, and that of my own car."

"I understand. What could you see of the driver?"

"Nothing. When the man I'd stopped for told me that his car was a bullnose Morris, I drew the obvious conclusion, that he was telling me the truth."

"So you agreed to take him—where?"

"He asked me about my own destination. I said I was returning directly to London. That suited him perfectly, he said. After the incident with the tramp, he didn't want to be stranded in Lancaster. If I didn't object, he would come back with me."

"What did you make of that?"

"I advised him to consult a doctor, as well as the police, at the earliest opportunity. Experience of combat has taught me that one can never be too careful with head injuries. He said he just wanted to get back home."

"And how did you respond?"

"I agreed to drive him to London."

"Did anything else happen on the journey?"

"No. He said he was exhausted, after such an upsetting incident. I suggested that he sit in the back of my car, and see if he could get forty winks."

"And did he?"

"He slept like a baby until we were almost there."

"Where did you drop him?"

"On the North Circular Road, sometime after midnight. He said that was close enough to his home. Of course, he had no possessions. They'd been stolen along with his car. I offered to take him to his front door, but he wouldn't hear of it. Said I'd done more than my bit. I tried to insist, but he saw I was weary, and he said that driving with a...handicap such as mine must be exhausting."

"Indeed." The Tortoise pursed his lips. "Did the man give you his name?"

"Yes."

"What was it?"

"Danskin."

"And do you recognise the person to whom you offered that lift in this courtroom today?"

For the first time, Major Whitlow turned towards the dock. Throughout the course of the trial, Clive Danskin had remained calm. Now, for the first time in the proceedings, a crack appeared in the smooth veneer. Eyes fixed on Major Whitlow, he gave a faint nod.

"That is the man." The claw pointed at the dock. "The prisoner."

———

"Well, blow me down with a feather," Haydn Williams said, diving into his bottomless well of clichés. "Game, set, and match. What a turn-up for the books!"

Clive Danskin's acquittal, and the judge's assurance, half drowned by cheers from the public gallery, that he left court without a blemish on his character, had become inevitable the moment Major Whitlow identified him in court. If Whitlow had passed the tramp driving the bullnose Morris minutes before picking up Danskin, the case for the Crown collapsed like a house of cards.

"The major was the perfect witness," Jacob said, as they headed towards the exit. "The fact he only arrived back in Britain last night explains why he didn't come forward earlier."

"Covert operations, I wouldn't be surprised." Haydn sighed. "I bet there's a story there, but we'll never prise it out of that oyster."

"No harm in trying. I thought I'd call his office, see if he'd like to say a few words."

"Good luck," Haydn said. "I'm telling you now, he won't play ball."

Jacob knew that such pessimism wouldn't deter the *Witness* from trying every trick in the book to steal a march on their rivals, but he simply said that he supposed Haydn was right.

"As always, my boy," the older man said complacently. "Trust Uncle Haydn. Tell you the truth, I wouldn't like to bump into the major in a dark alley. Slit your throat without a second thought, a fellow like that. No compunction, no moral qualms."

"Not like a journalist, eh?"

Haydn cringed at this low blow. "Where's your pride in your profession, you young whippersnapper? Anyhow, I don't have time to stand around gossiping with the likes of you. I need to fiddle about with my report. Don't want it to be an anticlimax. Nothing tops an eleventh-hour confession from a chap who has protested his innocence for months before being sentenced to hang. That's human interest for you. But there's some consolation. A mystery witness always sets the reader's pulse racing."

In the street outside, Jacob saw Clive Danskin pumping the Tortoise's hand. They were surrounded by gleeful female well-wishers heedless of the persistent drizzle. Several women looked quite adoring, as though they'd mistaken Danskin for a heartthrob of stage or screen.

"I should like to thank my legal representatives for their sterling efforts to secure my release," Danskin announced. "The last few months have been a ghastly ordeal. Forgive me if I don't make a speech. I certainly won't be selling my story to the press. Cruel things have been written about me, and the scars won't heal quickly. But I never lost my faith in British justice."

A handful of journalists lurking in the hope of an exclusive turned away in disgust. As the crowd thinned, Jacob spotted a familiar mauve cape, a flash of colour on a grey afternoon. Mrs Dobell was muttering in Clive Danskin's ear. Jacob moved closer, and watched Danskin consider for a moment before giving a quick nod. As a plump and adoring young woman seized Danskin's hand to give it a congratulatory shake, Mrs Dobell stepped away.

"You were right," Jacob said to her. "Justice does move in mysterious ways. I was wondering if you'd spare me a minute. I'm sure the *Clarion*'s readers would greatly value any insight…"

Her nose quivered, like a bloodhound picking up a suspicious scent. "I value my privacy, Mr Flint, and I never give interviews. All I will say is this. At the first trial I ever attended, long before your time, a judge's hostile summing-up caused a jury to find an innocent man guilty of murder. That same judge later cut his own wrists in the very same courtroom. His mind was warped. But the truth came out too late for the man he condemned."

"Judge Savernake." Jacob spoke before he could stop himself.

"I believe you are acquainted with the late Judge's daughter." The woman's sharp chin lifted. "Rachel Savernake."

He stared. How did Mrs Dobell know of his connection with Rachel?

He cleared his throat. "That's right."

She relaxed into a mischievous smile. "Next time you speak to Miss Savernake, please tell her to get in touch with me at the Circe Club. I should like to talk to her about murder."

Chapter 5

"Gilbert Payne is dead," Trueman announced as he marched into the elegant glass conservatory that served as the breakfast room of Gaunt House.

The air was spiced with kedgeree. Rachel buttered a thick slab of toast, smeared it with Hybla honey, and sliced it with a clean stroke of the knife. She was sitting at the table opposite her cook-housekeeper, Trueman's wife, looking out through the window on to a walled courtyard and garden. Putting down the knife, she arched her eyebrows. "Surely you mean Bertram Jones, late of Tangier?"

Trueman flourished a copy of the *Times*. Half a dozen other newspapers were tucked under his arm. "So the press call him, thanks to the false passport in his jacket pocket. Otherwise, the police would have struggled to identify him. His body was found on the railway line. The train that ran over him made a mess."

"Where was he found?"

"Three quarters of the way from Brookwood to London. According to the reports, he fell from the carriage just in time to be hit by the Waterloo express."

Hetty Trueman said, "If the body's unrecognisable, perhaps it isn't Payne."

Rachel drained her orange juice. "You think he faked his death again?"

"Why not? If he's done it before…"

Rachel shook her head. "An ingenious theory. If only it were true. But history hasn't repeated itself. Payne didn't have time to conjure up a substitute corpse."

"What do the reports say?" Hetty asked.

Her husband tossed the newspapers on to the table. "When they checked at the terminus, the door to Payne's compartment wasn't properly closed. His suitcase was still on the seat."

"There's no hint that it contained anything important?"

"None. Payne liked taking risks, but he wouldn't have been stupid enough to carry around anything revealing his true identity. Even if he had, the men who killed him would have removed it before they got off the train."

"The newspapers say the deceased was alone in the compartment, of course?" Rachel asked.

"Naturally. A witness did come forward, a vicar who said he occupied the adjoining compartment. He reported to a porter on arrival at Westminster Bridge Road that he'd seen something blow out from the train during the journey back to London. He said he was dozing, and the other person in his compartment was fast asleep, so couldn't be of any assistance. The reverend even wondered if he'd imagined it."

"Conveniently vague." Rachel chewed on her toast. "I don't suppose he left a name?"

"If he did, none of the accounts mention it. A clergyman from the colonies, according to the porter. Said he was on his way back to Canada."

"And therefore out of reach if the authorities wish to make further enquiries?"

"Exactly."

"So he won't attend the inquest. Which will duly return a verdict of misadventure. No nearest and dearest to bother about. Case closed."

Rachel gazed out through the window. The garden wall was topped with spikes. Gaunt House was situated on one of London's quietest and most select squares. The building had been refurbished at enormous expense by a millionaire swindler with his own reasons for craving privacy. After the police had finally caught up with him, Rachel had bought the house from his trustee in bankruptcy, renamed it after the island where she'd grown up, and installed herself and her tiny entourage. Despite the size of the property, the only servants were the three Truemans: Hetty, Clifford, and his sister Martha.

"A neat trick," Trueman said with grudging admiration. "That pair of villains made a song and dance about travelling in the next-door compartment on their way to the cemetery. If any member of the railway staff says he saw them getting into the dead man's compartment on the way back, the retort is obvious. They've got confused, simple as that. Impossible to prove otherwise."

"And how do the gentlemen of Fleet Street believe that Bertram Jones died?" Rachel asked. "Suicide or a freakish accident?"

"A bright spark from the London Necropolis Company has already come up with an explanation. He reckons Bertram Jones must have fallen asleep, then woken up in a dazed state. He opened the compartment door in the belief the carriage had a corridor, and fell out before he realised his mistake. A similar mishap befell some poor confused wretch a few years ago. An unspeakable tragedy, but hardly the fault of the company."

"Perish the thought." Rachel poured herself another cup of coffee. "The bright spark gets full marks for speed off the mark. It's worse for business if passengers on the railway kill themselves deliberately rather than succumbing to a misfortune in a million. The company doesn't want to be drumming up custom for the Suicide Train."

Trueman grunted. "Bad enough being known as the Stiffs' Express."

"He wasn't killed until late on in the journey," Rachel mused. "They must have questioned him to satisfy themselves that he gave nothing away to me."

"You didn't tell him your name?"

She gave him an old-fashioned look, but the housekeeper broke in. "Even if you wore a veil and widow's weeds, how long will it be before someone discovers you're poking your nose into affairs that don't concern you?"

Trueman said, "I hate to say it, but Hetty's right. You're playing a dangerous game. How many young women in London entertain themselves with strange cases of murder?"

"Gambling for high stakes is in my blood. You both know that."

"It's only a question of time before you're found out," Hetty said.

Rachel shrugged. "We've taken risks for as long as I can remember. All four of us. We're doing what we waited for all those years. It makes our lives worth living."

"Payne will have blabbed about his conversation with you," Trueman said.

"I didn't give anything away."

"I'm not saying you did, but what if…?"

"I don't care about *what ifs*." Rachel lowered her voice. "These men were crude thugs, hired to kill a man. They interrogated him at the point of a gun or knife and then stunned him before throwing him onto the track. They chose their moment carefully, timing things to perfection so that Payne's body would be torn to pieces by a fast train. They'd earned their pay. Why bother with an inconvenient complication like me? For all they know, I was a grieving relative of the late Mrs Payne."

"They'd already made sure the two women closest to Payne's mother didn't attend the funeral."

"I could have been a distant cousin or niece. That's what they will have told themselves. It's a simple explanation. Everybody loves an easy way out."

"Except you," Trueman said.

She gave a cool smile. "You know me too well."

Hetty Trueman could contain herself no longer. "Payne lived a lie, but he didn't deserve to be murdered. Was there nothing more you could do to make him see sense?"

Rachel rested her hand on the older woman's. "Other than kidnapping him in full view of the other mourners?"

"We'd have done that," Trueman said, "if we'd thought it would work."

"Payne abandoned hope," Rachel said. "Despair was written across his face. I wasn't surprised. In the fullness of time, even the charms of Tangier wear thin. Remember, he was living a lie long before he feigned death and fled this country. At least his love for his mother was genuine. Once he'd attended the funeral service, he didn't care what happened. He was living on borrowed time, and he was sick of hiding in fear. As soon as he realised his disguise had failed, he made up his mind. The end might as well come sooner rather than later."

"What about Reggie Vickers?" Hetty asked. "You were right. Everything he told you about Payne and the plot to kill him was true. I must admit, I had my doubts. It was such a wild story."

"He was too scared to be lying," Rachel said.

"And now he'll be in a blue funk," Trueman said. "I've said it before. You can't rely on Vickers."

"Without him," Rachel said mildly, "we'd never have known that Gilbert Payne was alive. Let alone that he was returning to Britain under a false name."

"Or that Clive Danskin would be acquitted of murder," Hetty said. "Or about those others. Henry Rolland and the woman. Or about Mortmain Hall."

Trueman said, "Vickers must realise he's already told you too much."

"He's not told me everything he knows," Rachel said. "He's held things back. Foolish of him. He may as well be hanged for a sheep as a lamb."

"Shall I have a word with him?"

"Please. He and I need to talk. Face to face."

"What if he begs you to forget everything he's ever said?"

"You won't forget," Hetty said. "Will you?"

"No," Rachel said. "I never forget."

———

Reggie Vickers stirred in his bed. His head was aching, his throat parched. Forcing open his eyes, he peered at the alarm clock on the small walnut table.

Five past eight. Surely he'd set it for seven. Why the devil hadn't the blasted contraption rung?

"Did you…?" he began, before realising he was alone.

He struggled out of bed, and pushed a hand through his tousled hair. One advantage of a set of bachelor rooms in the Albany was that it was only a short walk to his office in Whitehall. Parting the velvet curtain, he gazed down on to the courtyard.

Bright enough this morning, with no sign of rain, thank heaven. There was every chance of a full day's play at Lord's. He must nip over to St John's Wood, blow away the cobwebs. An afternoon at the cricket would do him a world of good.

Last night, he'd put away a hell of a lot of scotch, if the throbbing in his temples was anything to go by. Was Doodle right, was he drinking too much? Doodle seemed less understanding lately. They'd quarrelled last night, though now Reggie found it difficult to remember the precise cause of their spat. Oh, well. When a chap had so much on his mind, the bottle made for a decent refuge.

The bed was empty, and there was no sign of Doodle's neatly folded clothes. Was it possible that he'd slept through the alarm, while Doodle got ready for the day?

He kicked open the bedroom door with his bare foot, and called out. "Are you there?"

No answer.

Reggie groaned. He hoped Doodle wasn't sulking. That was the last thing a fellow needed, especially when he wasn't feeling too chipper.

He stumbled into the bathroom. A good wash always worked wonders, and by the time he'd dressed, his mood had lightened. Never mind if Doodle was hunched over the breakfast table, smouldering with resentment. The promise of a top-notch dinner this evening would work wonders. The Criterion was always reliable. Doodle had a taste for veeraswamy, but Reggie couldn't get on with Indian food. The place was nothing more than a curry club for ex-servicemen from the colonies.

Contemplating his reflection in the hall mirror, he took a deep breath, and plastered on a bright smile. That had been quite a bender last night, but he didn't look too rotten. The dark rings under his eyes would fade soon enough. The relentless expansion of his waistline was a worry, but damn it all, he was only thirty-two. Hardly one foot in the grave.

He strode into the kitchen, ready to utter a cheery greeting. The words died on his lips as he saw the envelope on the breakfast table, propped against the tin of coffee. His name was on the envelope, in Doodle's elegant script.

He yelped in dismay. Somehow he didn't need to rip open the envelope and read the letter inside to know what Doodle had written.

———

"And what about Jacob Flint?" Hetty demanded.

"What about him?" Rachel said.

"Have you lost interest in him?"

Rachel yawned. "It's barely five minutes since you accused me of being sweet on the poor devil."

"Sorry." The housekeeper bit her tongue. "I don't mean to cluck round you like a mother hen. But someone has to…"

"Our intrepid reporter amuses me. And he can make himself useful."

"Except that you sent him off with a flea in his ear."

"He'll be back."

"Don't be so sure."

"Jacob Flint has his hands full with the Danskin case," Rachel said. "I expect he recounted yesterday's sensation in court in breathless prose."

Trueman gestured to the pile of newspapers. "They're full of it."

"What does he say about Danskin's acquittal?"

Hetty pulled out the *Clarion* from the pile on the table. *Blazing Car Sensation!* screamed the front page. *Accused Man Cleared by War Hero Witness!*

Rachel glanced at the story. "He's made a decent fist of it, considering his editor must be furious. A death sentence means they can rush out a special edition. But if a man must evade the noose, it's some consolation if he's saved by a gallant veteran of the Western Front."

Trueman said, "A couple of newspapers haven't even mentioned Gilbert Payne's death."

"Only because," Rachel said, "they labour under the misapprehension that the corpse on the line belonged to an impoverished nobody called Bertram Jones. Even Danskin's escape from the gallows would take second billing if they knew that Jones was really Gilbert Payne."

———

The reproachful tone of Doodle's note hurt Reggie more than any torrent of recrimination or rage.

Last night you said I was a nobody. It's true. The first time we met, you said I'd always be your Valentine, but you didn't mean it. Now I'll go back to being a nobody.

Had he really been so stupid, even in his cups? Pity that his recollection of the previous evening was an incoherent blur. Yes, they'd exchanged harsh words, and this time it seemed he'd gone too far. The accusation of snobbishness was out of order. His lighthearted jokes were simply teasing, nothing more. If ever he talked out of turn, he was always quick to apologise.

Not that he'd been allowed a chance to say sorry. The last lines of the letter stabbed like a trench knife.

It's better to end it now. My mind's made up. There's no going back. Not to you or your posh friend Lulu. Please don't look for me. It won't do any good or make any difference. We won't meet again.

That was all. The letter wasn't even signed with a kiss, for old time's sake. At first, in frantic, unreasoning misery, Reggie contemplated setting off in hot pursuit. Not that he knew Doodle's address, just that it was somewhere in Hoxton. Probably he could find the place, given time. Cheap rooms in a dingy tenement, he supposed. Not a home to be proud of.

Within moments, he thought better of it. Doodle was stubborn, and the letter crystal clear. Mustn't make a fool of himself. Nothing worse than blubbing in front of a lover. He'd never been one to stand on his dignity, but to beg would be humiliating.

He was fumbling with the laces of his shoes when the shrill of the telephone broke the lonely silence. His heart lurched.

Doodle? Calling to explain, or apologise? Perhaps even to plead for forgiveness?

It was never too late. They could start again. He blundered across the room and snatched the receiver.

"This is Trueman."

A wave of nausea swept over him. For an instant, he thought he was about to be physically sick. Not Doodle, but that hulking brute who worked for the Savernake woman.

How he wished he'd never heard of her. Far less begged for her assistance.

"Did you hear me?" Trueman demanded.

Reggie summoned up what remained of his courage. "It's not convenient. Goodbye."

"Don't hang up," Trueman said. "Have you seen the newspapers?"

"Of course not!" The sheer absurdity of the question knocked him off balance. "I never bother with them until I arrive at the office."

"Gilbert Payne was killed yesterday."

The words smacked like a punch to the solar plexus. Reggie uttered a wail of pain.

"Run over by one train after being thrown out of another."
Trueman was remorseless. "The police call it an accident, but
you and I know better, don't we?"

Reggie's gorge rose. One body blow after another. How
much of a pummelling could he survive?

"Miss Savernake wants a word with you."

"No!"

"A few days ago, you pleaded with her for help."

Reggie gritted his teeth, forced himself to speak. "She
couldn't save Gilbert. He's dead. That…changes everything."

"It changes nothing. What happens at Mortmain Hall…"

"Look! I've done all I can. This must be the end of it. I never
want to hear from you again. Or from her."

"You've gone too far to back out now."

"I'm finished with the whole business. I can't possibly…"

"You're sure nobody knows you've talked to her?"

A pause. "Not a soul."

"I don't believe you."

"I've never breathed a word, I promise." He drew a breath.
"I'm begging you again. Just leave me alone."

"She'll expect you at Gaunt House this evening. Seven
o'clock."

"I can't."

"You must," Trueman said.

———

Putting down the phone, Trueman glared at his companions.
"Weakling."

"Nothing but a coward," Hetty said. "Showing himself in his
true colours."

"He's terrified," Rachel said.

"Last time," Trueman said, "Vickers insisted he'd told us all he knew."

"He was lying," Rachel said. "Unfortunately, Payne's death has knocked him sideways. All he cares about now is saving his own skin."

———

Each morning, senior reporters at the *Clarion* met in a poky, smoke-filled room to discuss the news agenda. Walter Gomersall, the editor, turned to Jacob Flint as soon as talk turned away from latest calamities to befall the hapless MacDonald's government.

"Good spread on the Danskin case, lad. Pity he dodged the scaffold, but you can't have everything."

"That fellow had the luck of the devil," moaned the City editor, a stern Calvinist by the name of Plenderleith. "Now he's free to carry on deceiving weak-willed and gullible women without let or hindrance. And that nincompoop of a judge said he left without a stain on his character! No wonder people think there's no justice on this earth."

Gomersall sucked on his pipe. "Pity the mysterious major is so taciturn, but at least those bastards at the *Witness* didn't have any joy in getting him to talk to them. Surely Danskin won't keep mum for long? Well, lad? Peculiar business. A victim with no name. A mysterious fire. Still plenty more to be said, if you ask me."

"His solicitors say they won't make a further public statement," Jacob said. "I spoke to them after the fuss had died down. Danskin has nothing to add to the story he gave the police. The tramp knocked him out and stole his car. When it broke down a few miles later, he must have investigated with a lighted match. The fireball killed him and destroyed the car, along with most of the evidence."

"Hence the experts arguing endlessly over how to interpret the bits and pieces fished from the cinders," Gomersall growled.

"Danskin won't talk. He wasn't even willing to give sworn evidence when his life was at stake."

"Because he was afraid of cross-examination. He's not on oath with us. Soft soap him, tell him he has a chance to set the record straight. Tell the world about the nightmare he's lived through."

"The solicitors say his health has broken down as a result of his ordeal."

Plenderleith snorted. "Spare us the violin strings."

"I'll tell you what's making Danskin poorly," Gomersall said. "Being forced to explain himself to his wife and his various mistresses. To say nothing of his creditors. Divorce isn't cheap. He must be desperate for hard cash. Those fancy lawyers cost a pretty penny. What better way to earn a few bob than an exclusive heart-to-heart with the *Clarion*?"

Jacob shook his head. "I tried every tack with the solicitors, I promise. No joy. The tramp is dead and buried, and nobody knows his name. Danskin doesn't seem worried about money. He reckons it would be wrong to profit from such a tragedy."

"Ye gods! Don't tell me he's acquired a conscience all of a sudden. There must be more to it than that. I bet he's keeping the juicy titbits back so he can write a book." Gomersall groaned. "All right, scout around for another story. Any bright ideas?"

"What about the body they found on the railway line yesterday?"

"The fellow who fell out of the funeral train and was cut to ribbons?" The editor grimaced. "What about him? The railway company is satisfied it was an accident."

"Predictably," Jacob said. "The Necropolis Company doesn't

want to scare off the bereaved. Kensal Green Cemetery is handier than Brookwood. Adverse publicity is bad for business."

"True, but the police aren't interested. The deceased spent years in Tangier, and we all know what that makes him, don't we? For my money, he topped himself. Either way, there's no mileage in it for us."

"It still might be worth digging around."

"You're a stubborn young devil." Gomersall blew a smoke ring. "What do you have in mind?"

"Let me try to find out something about him. What exactly did he get up to in Tangier? Did anyone have cause to wish him ill?"

Gomersall flicked the suggestion aside like ash from his pipe. "Hell of a long shot."

"You never know. This time yesterday, I'd have sworn that Danskin killed that tramp. Did Jones fall or was he pushed? I can see the headline now."

"We're all ears."

Jacob raised his voice to a roar worthy of Sir Edgar. "*Was Mystery Man from Morocco Murdered?*"

———

"Now Gilbert Payne is dead, that may be the end of it," Hetty Trueman said.

Rachel picked up a sheet of paper which was lying on the table. It bore four names in her neat handwriting.

Gilbert Payne
Sylvia Gorrie
Henry Rolland
Clive Danskin

"No," she said, crossing out the name of Gilbert Payne. "Remember what Vickers told us. This is only the beginning."

"You don't need to get involved."

"I watched a man walk to his death. Of course I'm involved."

"You couldn't do anything more."

"There's something I can do," Rachel said. "I can go to Mortmain Hall."

Chapter 6

Reggie Vickers blundered through the morning in a daze. Last night's binge was partly to blame, but hangovers were one thing, Doodle's departure and Gilbert Payne's death quite another. And then, to put the tin lid on it, Rachel Savernake's thug was bullying him. He wished he'd never heard of the woman, let alone told her about Gilbert and Mortmain Hall. How could he have been so stupid?

His head throbbed, his stomach ached, and his back was playing up. He felt feverish, and wondered if he was sickening for something. It was impossible to bury personal misery by throwing himself into his work. How could he begin to concentrate on the tedious memoranda heaped up in his pending tray? Frankly, it was as well that nobody cared what happened to the trivial nonsense he drudged over day after day.

The job was a sinecure. A blue-chip education—Christ's Hospital and Peterhouse—had ensured that he went out into the world with good connections and sophisticated table manners; he could also make up a four at bridge and keep a straight bat. At the tail end of the war, he'd joined the Royal Flying Corps. While training as a pilot, he crashed his Sopwith Pup in a farmer's field and fractured his spine. By the time he was walking again, the ink was dry on the Armistice. People said he was lucky to have survived in one piece, but in the darkest moments, his failure to make a worthwhile contribution to the war effort hurt more than his aching back. The story of his life was a tale of so near, yet so far.

After returning to Cambridge, he was approached about the possibility of joining the civil service. Apparently, his tutor had recommended him, which was quite a turn-up, given his academic indolence. He'd never made plans about a long-term career, but mouldering away behind a desk held no appeal. As a schoolboy he'd fantasised about playing cricket for Middlesex, but he'd never even broken into the university first eleven, and no enticing opportunities loomed on the horizon. When his pater, who was something in the City, died from a ruptured brain aneurysm and left behind a pile of unexpected debts, Reggie's hand was forced. His liking for the good life meant that he had little choice but to earn a crust in Whitehall.

Funny thing was, whenever he described himself to new acquaintances as a glorified pen-pusher, they thought he was joking, or excessively modest. Doodle had joked that he might be a secret agent, and seemed excited by the idea. The reality lacked glamour, even if he was playing his small part in keeping Britain on an even keel. At first he'd been glad of the chance to make himself useful by undertaking occasional extracurricular duties. Just bag-carrying, nothing risky or untoward.

His natural lack of curiosity was an asset in the job, since he never kicked up a rumpus by asking inconvenient questions. Everything chugged along merrily for years. Calling Britain a land fit for heroes might be stretching it somewhat, but at least they were keeping the Bolshies at bay. Things had quietened down since the collapse of the general strike fomented by agitators. But the powers-that-be would never rest easy. During the past twelve months, he'd been entrusted with more onerous tasks, and lately he'd begun to worry about where things might lead. When he'd cottoned on to the fact that Gilbert Payne was alive and well and in mortal danger, panic had set in.

He scribbled a few anodyne comments on a report about proposed amendments to the Defence of the Realm Act before deciding that he'd done enough for the time being. DORA always sapped his morale. He tidied up his desk, collected his hat, coat, briefcase, and umbrella, and hurried down the stairs.

Outside in Whitehall, the sky was blue, the sun high. A taxi approached. He was seized by a sudden urge to tell the driver to take him to Hoxton. If only he could make Doodle see sense! Of course it was hopeless. Even if he got down on bended knee, it would make no difference. Doodle was unfathomable, but also implacable. There was no hope of a change of heart. No hope at all…

"Afternoon, Vickers."

He started. A long-forgotten phrase from a poem he'd been taught at school sprang into his mind: *Like a guilty thing surprised*. The only line of Wordsworth he could remember. Ridiculous, what did he have to feel guilty about? If he was on edge, it was only natural after what he'd been through. He'd been so wrapped in his own thoughts that he hadn't noticed Major Whitlow coming out of the building.

"Oh, good afternoon, sir."

"Off somewhere?"

Reggie felt his cheeks burning. His thoughts jolted back to his schooldays. Pongo Yearsley, his house master, had caught him playing truant one afternoon, when the other lads were in the gymnasium. The occasion was etched on his memory. Pongo had exacted a high price for that misdemeanour.

He forced a little laugh. Even to his own ears, his attempt at hilarity sounded counterfeit. "Been working like billy-o this morning, sir. Rather fancied a break."

"Oh yes?"

The sight of the major's egg-and-bacon tie gave him a sudden inspiration. The tie betokened membership of the exclusive Marylebone Cricket Club. Reggie was also a member, and the second Test match had started today. England against Australia, battling for the Ashes.

"Actually, I was hoping to catch the afternoon session at Lord's."

Other than work, the major's abiding passion in life was cricket. He pursed thin lips. "Two minds with but a single thought, eh? My destination, too. Let's share a cab."

Reggie breathed out. At last on this dreadful day, he'd managed to get something right. It never did any harm to chew the fat with the department's big white chiefs. Especially with the major.

"Grand idea, sir."

"Taxi!"

The major lifted his arm, and within moments a taxi pulled up beside them. No cabbie could miss an upraised claw.

———

Munching a cheese-and-pickle sandwich over his desk, Jacob wondered what to do next. He'd devoted the morning to a series of futile attempts to learn more about Bertram Jones and his death. His contacts within the Metropolitan Police were no help. They were satisfied that Jones had suffered a regrettable accident. The London Necropolis Company was determined to say as little as possible, just in case a member of Jones's family appeared and made a song and dance about safety on the railway line. So far he'd learned nothing about Jones, other than the fact that he'd only been in the country for twenty-four hours prior to his death. He'd stayed at a guest house in Pimlico and kept himself to himself.

Why was he travelling on the funeral train? Had he come to England to say farewell to a loved one? The snag was that nobody called Jones had been buried at Brookwood yesterday. Had he mourned the death of a friend?

It was an odd business, but Jacob supposed Gomersall was right: he'd be better employed in finding a fresh angle to the Danskin case. Mrs Dobell was worth following up. Why did she haunt the Old Bailey, and how had she foreseen that Danskin might be acquitted?

And why did she want to talk to Rachel Savernake about murder?

Washing down his sandwich with a cup of milky tea, Jacob allowed his thoughts to stray to the young woman he'd met six months earlier. Rachel had arrived in the capital last year. She'd grown up on Gaunt, a tiny island off the coast of Cumberland, in the ancestral home of the Savernake family. After the death of Judge Savernake, she'd inherited a fortune. Notorious as a hanging judge, the old man had retired from the bench after his mind had begun to fail and he'd attempted suicide. His remaining years had been spent on the island as a recluse, descending deeper and deeper into a dark pit of madness.

Jacob's imagination was vivid, but even he found it impossible to comprehend how Rachel had endured life in that bleak and remote spot with a demented and dissolute old reprobate. The Trueman family supported her with extraordinary devotion; she said that without them, she'd never have survived. It must have been like serving a prison sentence. No wonder she never talked about it.

Even in London, she led a solitary life. She loved music, but her taste was for popular songs rather than the classics; she adored art, but spent eye-watering sums on surrealist pictures that struck Jacob as meaningless scrawls and splashes. When she'd involved herself in a sequence of bizarre killings, Jacob became convinced there was a story to be told about her, and that he was the man to tell it. The investigation had almost cost him his life. Her ruthlessness horrified him. He also found it strangely exciting.

To his dismay, he'd learned he was no match for Rachel Savernake. Never had he met a woman so formidable; never had he been so desperate to understand what was going on inside another person's head. Murder obsessed her, but her passion for justice had nothing to do with the niceties of the legal system. She danced to her own tune. He admired her, but he was afraid of her.

Jacob fancied himself as an amateur psychologist. He was convinced that her coldness was a form of disguise, a means of coping with the cruelty she'd suffered on the island of Gaunt. One day, he dreamed, she'd take him into her confidence. He'd sworn to her that he'd never publish a word about her unless she gave her consent.

Her mask never slipped. Like a fencing master, she parried every inquisitive thrust with ease. The last time he'd visited Gaunt House, frustration had overcome him. Emboldened by one glass too many of vintage claret, he complained that she treated him like a fool. With a shrug, she said that if he felt unwelcome, he was free to leave. Provoked, he grabbed his hat and coat. She watched him go without a word.

Since then, they'd had no contact, yet not a day passed without his thinking about her. Now the Dobell woman had given him a chance to speak to her again. He reached for the telephone.

———

"Everything all right, Vickers?"

"Absolutely, sir."

"Sure about that? You look…peaky."

What lay behind the question? The major wasn't given to displays of care for the welfare of his subordinates. Reggie eyed his companion warily, but as usual the major's face was emotionless as a statue on Easter Island.

Reggie had learned long ago that when you didn't want to give an honest answer, the safest course was to fall back on an edited version of the truth.

Venturing a confidential smile, he said, "After-effects of a vinous slumber, sir. I may have had one too many last night. It's made up my mind for me. I'm getting too long in the tooth to be letting my hair down and staying up till all hours."

The older man replied with a grunt. Did it imply displeasure? Reggie ground his teeth. His tongue was too loose. Better clarify, to avoid any misunderstanding.

"Not that I ever talk out of turn, even when I'm a bit the worse for wear."

"Glad to hear it." The major looked him straight in the eye, and Reggie shivered under the stony gaze. "Our work seems mundane, but society depends upon our rectitude. We are privy to many secrets."

"Absolutely, sir. I'd never…"

"Lives are at risk. Can't be too careful. Beware the enemy within."

"I couldn't agree more, sir," Reggie blurted out. "The drinking happens only once in a blue moon. Perhaps that's why the alcohol rather went to my head. I'm simply not used to it."

He stole a sideways glance, but the major had turned his

head to stare out of the cab window. Reggie wasn't even sure he was listening.

———

"You were right," Hetty Trueman said. "Jacob Flint is on the telephone for you."

"Tail between his legs," her husband said.

Rachel turned the page of her book. "I suppose it would be petty to say I'm busy."

They were in the roof garden on the top of Gaunt House, where they'd taken a leisurely lunch. Rachel had worked up an appetite by swimming thirty lengths in the pool. Now she was relaxing on a sun chair in her green silk swimsuit.

"It'd serve him right." Hetty eyed the telephone extension. "Shall I take a message? Or suggest that he calls later?"

"No." Rachel placed the book on the small wooden table by her side. "For once, his timing is impeccable."

———

In the heart of St John's Wood, thirty thousand people soaked up the sunshine as they absorbed the latest skirmish between sport's oldest rivals. Lord's cricket ground was packed to the rafters, but the privileges of MCC membership allowed Reggie and the major to make straight for the pavilion to find a vantage point in the Long Room.

Reggie loved this historic sanctum, an exclusive masculine preserve reeking of tobacco and history. In his dreams he often came here as a Test cricketer, padded up and bat under arm, on his way out to play the innings of his life for his country. He pictured himself jogging down the stairs, entering this packed room, striding past the paintings of famous players of yore, breathing in the thick fug of cigars, hearing the buzz of conversation, marching out into the fresh air, down the steps past the benches of spectators, and through the gate in the white picket fence, onto the hallowed turf.

A glance at the scoreboard revealed that on a benign pitch, England's batsmen had squandered their wickets. Only Duleepsinhji's flair had kept the Australian bowlers at bay, and now his innings almost died in inglorious fashion. He offered the Australian captain a simple catch, but the ball slipped through Woodfull's hands. The crowd gasped as it hit the ground.

"Butterfingers!" Reggie exclaimed, unable to contain his glee at the sight of the opposition skipper dropping a dolly. "That could be an expensive fluff. Young Duleep scored three hundred in a day down at Brighton the other week."

"It's a rule in life," the major murmured. "When you're given a chance, you need to take it. Opportunity never knocks twice."

Not like the major to wax philosophical, but Reggie thought he had a point. Cricket was a great leveller. One minute you were thrashing the bowlers to all corners of the ground, the next you were trudging back to the pavilion after throwing your wicket away with a wild slog. This contest was absorbing. Nothing like a cricket match for taking your mind off the cares of the world. Gilbert was dead and gone. At least he'd done his best for his old friend, although the Savernake woman had failed to save him. And even if he never saw Doodle again…no, he wouldn't think about that. Let the future take care of itself.

Within minutes, the enormity of Woodfull's howler became apparent, as the Indian kept driving ball after ball to the boundary. The applause became rapturous. Duleep was fast becoming not only an honorary Englishman but a national hero. Educated at Cheltenham and Cambridge,

Duleep possessed all the attributes of an English gentleman, not least being connected to all the right people. His uncle was the great Ranji, one of England's finest cricketers prior to becoming the Jam Sahib of Nawanagar. Nobody cared about the colour of his skin when his royal pedigree was unquestionable, and his batsmanship divine.

———

Like a penitent seeking absolution, Jacob tried to explain to Rachel why he'd called. Why on earth hadn't he rehearsed what he wanted to say? Her ironic amusement was painful on the ear.

"It was at the Old Bailey. Towards the end of the Danskin trial. I…met a woman."

"Congratulations."

"No, I mean…that is, she's certainly not our age. Much older. Looks like a witch. Just when Danskin looked to be in for the high jump, she said he might still get off. An oddball. But clever."

"For a woman?"

"Sorry. I'm not making myself clear. She knows you. Or rather, about you."

Silence.

"She wants to talk to you about murder."

"Does she, now?"

Her indifference made him feel like a conjuror who saws his assistant in half with a flourish, only to discover his audience is fast asleep.

"Yes." He added feebly, "She seemed…interesting."

"What's she called?"

Why did he sense that she'd already guessed the answer?

"Dobell. Mrs Dobell," he gabbled. "Sorry, I didn't get her first name."

"Don't worry, I know it," Rachel said. "Come to the house for a drink at nine this evening. You can tell me about her."

———

"Well played, sir!" Reggie cried, as Duleep crashed a poor delivery away for four more runs. At this rate, his hands would soon be sore from clapping. Beside him, the major was motionless. Hard to clap with a claw, of course. Funny cove, never seemed to get excited by anything. Perhaps after all he'd been through…

The Boche had tortured the major after capturing him behind enemy lines. It was said that even *in extremis,* he never let anything slip that might endanger the Tommies. Rumours abounded about the circumstances in which he'd lost his hand. Some of the stories were grisly; many were wild inventions. Nobody knew the details. The major never spoke about his wartime experiences. His personal life was as much a closed book as his precise role in the civil service.

Two spectators in the front row reminisced about the airship that had flown over the ground during the morning's play. Like watching a giant whale swim across the sky, they said. Reggie was sorry he'd missed such a marvel. The Imperial Airship Scheme was the pride and joy of British aviation, coupling technological wonders with the last word in luxurious travel. A pal in the Air Ministry often boasted of his chief's ambition. An airship with no need to refuel could knit together the scattered dominions of the British Empire.

Leaning towards the major, he said in a confidential tone, "Powerful beast, the R101. I hear the Air Minister reckons that Duleep could get to India in a fraction of the time it would take by sea or plane."

"The miracle of the socialist airship." The major's lip curled. "Time will tell if it flies or falls."

Deflated, Reggie kept his counsel until the tea interval. They made their way in silence across the Long Room's uncarpeted floor to the adjacent bar. When the major bought him a Scotch, Reggie stammered with gratitude. Thank the Lord he'd been forgiven for overindulging the previous night.

"To cricket," the major said, raising his glass. "The Masqueraders have a match coming up, with a return game thrown in. It will mean a few days in the wilds of Yorkshire. I trust you'll be available?"

"Rather!"

Reggie could barely restrain his jubilation. His tiny nook in Whitehall offered little in the way of social activity other than occasional invitations to play cricket. The Masqueraders were a wandering team, like I Zingari or the Free Foresters. They had no ground of their own, and an irregular fixture list. They usually played in out-of-the-way parts of the country, sometimes in inhospitable conditions and outside the usual cricket season. The side was organised by senior members of the department. The major himself captained the eleven, when his commitments allowed. With his left arm, he could bowl a useful wrong 'un.

"I'll ask Pennington to pass you the details." The major swallowed his whisky and checked his watch. "He'll give you a lift up there if you can cope with his driving. Now I have a meeting to attend. I'll leave you to it."

With that, he was gone. Reggie finished his drink, and ordered another. For a few moments during the taxi ride, he'd felt frightened. Had he been rumbled, despite all the care he'd taken? The major's inscrutability made him all the more menacing.

The invitation—command, almost—to turn out again for the Masqueraders was doubly precious. Taking part in a cricket tour, however brief, was far more enjoyable than slaving over a hot desk. Thank goodness, they still trusted him. Reggie felt comforted. His mistakes hadn't proved fatal. He squared his shoulders. The major had offered him a chance, and he meant to grab it.

Calmer now, he followed the ebb and flow of the teams' fortunes during the final session of play. Duleep was in sight of a brilliant double century when he suffered a rush of blood to the head. Having caressed a couple of boundaries off the bowling of the tireless Grimmett, he essayed a needless swipe, and found himself caught by Bradman.

Joining the crowd spilling out of the ground, Reggie told himself that anyone might get carried away. To err was human. If a sublimely talented prince could make a crass blunder, so could any ordinary mortal. The major had made himself clear. He'd take heed and become more circumspect. Why stick his neck out? Forget the doubts and questions, forget Doodle's desertion and the dreadful death of Gilbert Payne. It was time to look after number one.

He knew where his loyalties lay.

Damned shame about Doodle, but such was life. It had been fun while it lasted. As for Gilbert Payne, he'd done his utmost; his conscience was clear. Rachel Savernake could go to hell.

Glancing up, he saw a dark figure outlined against the brightness of the sky. The weather vane on top of the Grand Stand, tall as a man, was Father Time, complete with sickle. Despite the warm glow of early-evening sunshine, Reggie's spine felt a chill.

The Grim Reaper stared down at him.

Chapter 7

Reggie's resolve not to answer the telephone was tested within minutes of his return to the Albany. Twice the bell rang, and twice he ignored the imperious summons. He guessed who was calling. Rachel Savernake's brute, wanting to know why he'd failed to turn up at Gaunt House. Well, let him ring, let him ring, let him ring.

Or might it be Doodle, desperate to make amends? Was his heart so hardened that he could ignore a plea for mercy?

The telephone screamed for a third time. Reggie hesitated before stretching out a hand.

"Yes?"

"You missed your appointment," Trueman said.

Reggie cursed his feebleness. He'd only capitulated because he didn't want to hurt Doodle's feelings. Compassion was his fatal flaw. If he hadn't felt such pity for Gilbert Payne, he'd never have confided in Rachel Savernake. He had a sour taste in his mouth. Sheer frustration emboldened him.

"I want nothing more to do with you," he snapped. "Or your mistress."

"You're taking a risk. Playing with fire. What happened to Gilbert Payne…"

"Don't you dare threaten me!" Reggie shouted. "I'll report you to the police!"

He slammed down the receiver. It was a moment of bravado, the sort he'd hoped to show in the RFC before office life softened him. He gave a nod of satisfaction, although nobody else was there to see it, nobody to give him a round of applause or help him celebrate. Above all, Doodle wasn't there.

Ah, well, plenty more fish in the sea. He glanced at the ormolu clock on the mantelpiece. Half past seven, far too early to consider dropping in at the Clan. He'd dine at Kettner's before drifting over to Soho.

The morning's feverish unhappiness was already fading. Why shouldn't he go back to the Clan? Just for old time's sake. A quick drink, and then he'd head back home. He wouldn't stay out too late.

A tremor of anticipation rippled through his body.

———

"Vickers is stubborn," Trueman said.

"Scared," Rachel said.

A heavy sigh. "What do you want to do about it?"

"Nothing. Jacob Flint will cooperate."

"You're not giving up?"

"Have you ever known me to give up? I can't let sleeping murders lie. Especially after what happened to Gilbert Payne." She clapped the big man on the back. "Come on, I'm hungry. Time to eat."

———

Jacob adjusted his tie and cleared his throat as he rang the doorbell of Gaunt House. The last time he'd felt so nervous, he'd been waiting in an anteroom before his interview with the *Clarion*. He'd travelled down from Yorkshire, dreaming that he might make his name in the big city, yet quaking at the prospect of an inquisition by Walter Gomersall, Fleet Street's very own Torquemada. Calling on Rachel Savernake inspired a different kind of dread.

Martha Trueman opened the door. Like Rachel and Jacob, she was in her twenties. Tall and slim, with rich chestnut hair. The first time they'd met, her appearance had shocked him. Eleven years ago, a man had thrown acid at her. He'd meant to destroy her face, and succeeded in disfiguring her left cheek. Now Jacob felt ashamed that it had taken him so long to realise that Rachel was right. Despite the damage to her face, Martha was beautiful. He'd learned to look beyond the scars.

"Long time no see!" In the quiet of the square, his greeting sounded unnaturally loud. He tried again. "How are things, Martha? You're looking well."

The maid gave a wry smile. She treated him with less suspicion than her brother and sister-in-law, but like her employer, she never wasted words.

"You're to take a seat in the library. Rachel will see you presently."

An oddity of the little ménage at Gaunt House was that Rachel and the Truemans treated each other as equals. Within these walls, the servants never called her "madam" and never made a show of deference. Rachel encouraged their familiarity, and they only wore uniforms when the mood took them. Such flouting of convention wasn't the done thing. But then, Rachel scorned the done thing. During those years of living cheek-by-jowl on the island, these four people had forged a bond as strong as any blood tie. Their closeness was extraordinary. Almost as if they shared a dark secret.

He followed the maid down the long, spacious hall. On the thick carpet, their footsteps made no sound. A walnut long-case clock chimed nine. Rachel wasn't hurrying to greet him in person. A mirror reflected his forehead wrinkling in disappointment. Questions jostled in his brain, but Rachel would tell him nothing unless and until it suited her. By forcing him to wait, she was teaching him a lesson.

"The Chivas Regal is on the table," Martha said as she ushered him into the library. "Help yourself. Rachel says you can catch up with your reading while you have a drink."

The door closed behind her. At least he'd been forgiven for drinking heavily on his last visit here. After a long and unrewarding day, a tumbler of fine whisky represented welcome consolation. He poured himself an extravagant measure, and savoured the smoothness of the spirit as he made himself comfortable in a deep wing chair.

He'd never before set foot inside the library. Twenty feet long and fifteen wide, with floor-to-ceiling shelves on every wall, and not a single window, it was home to thousands of books, from calf-bound antiquarian tomes that Jacob couldn't imagine anyone reading to recent titles resplendent in colourful pictorial wrappers. The Savernakes were noted bibliophiles, and the late Judge's collection was said to be one of the finest in private hands. Since arriving in London, Rachel had added scores of recent titles.

In a rare confidence, she'd told Jacob that she'd educated herself from the books in Savernake Hall, just as she'd hardened her wiry frame by climbing rocks and swimming in the Irish Sea. It was a way of passing the time when, for all the Savernakes' wealth, she was scarcely more than a prisoner on the island of

Gaunt. Those long, lonely years had made her the woman she was. But who exactly was she? Jacob yearned to find out.

A chunky volume in a gaudy red-and-yellow dust jacket lay facedown on the low table that separated his chair from another. Someone—Rachel, he presumed—had placed inside it a white tasselled bookmark. What was she reading? Inquisitive as ever, he picked up the book, and turned it over.

The title was *Respectable Murders* and the publishers trumpeted the author, Leo Slaterbeck, as a distinguished criminologist. According to the description on the inside of the jacket, Slaterbeck's book comprised studies of cases in which life among the respectable British classes had been ripped apart by murder.

Rachel's bookmark was placed at the start of an account of a case that was only three years old, the trial for murder of Sylvia Gorrie. Her name sounded familiar, but Jacob couldn't place it. Three years ago, he'd barely put his first foot on the ladder as a cub reporter. He'd been more concerned with covering football matches in Leeds than following court cases in distant London.

Rachel had underlined the second paragraph in blue ink: "The Gorrie trial reminded observers of the tragedy of Edith Thompson. With one signal difference. Mrs Thompson was executed, although many of us consider that her crime was adultery, not murder. Unlike her predecessor, Sylvia Gorrie walked out of the court a free woman."

Why did that interest Rachel? He poured himself another whisky. Until she condescended to show herself, he'd while away the time by reading Slaterbeck's account of Sylvia Gorrie's story.

———

Sylvia Hardman's father was a Norfolk builder who was bankrupted after a strike by construction workers wrecked his business. Sylvia was undeterred by this calamity. Striking to look at, with lustrous blonde hair, she was determined to get on in life. She trained as a typist and moved to London a few months before war broke out; she was eighteen years old.

On arriving in the capital, she found secure employment in a government department, but in 1921 she moved to the offices of the London School of Economics. While working in that office, she met the economist and lecturer Walter Gorrie, an intellectual in his late forties and one of the most influential thinkers of the day. Having inherited a quarter of a million pounds from his father, an armaments manufacturer, Gorrie had devoted himself to campaigning for world peace coupled with radical change for the good of the ordinary working man.

Within six weeks of their first meeting, he and Sylvia became man and wife. The marriage astonished everyone in Gorrie's circle, since the couple appeared to have little in common, and Walter was universally pigeonholed as "a confirmed bachelor." As Slaterbeck remarked, nobody expected him to embrace such radical change for the good of an ordinary working woman.

Sylvia moved into her husband's home, a Georgian mansion complete with tennis court and an ornamental lake on the outskirts of Salisbury. No longer needing to work, she adored the trappings of wealth. When she wasn't swimming in the lake or practising her forehand with a succession of handsome young coaches, she'd go out shopping in her newest mink coat, or set off for a spin in her Sunbeam Tourer.

The Gorries' social life together was sterile. His circle, exclusively masculine, comprised economics students, Members of Parliament, and trade union leaders. He couldn't drive or swim, and hated tennis. Political arguments, meat and drink to her husband, sent Sylvia to sleep. Time passed, boredom set in.

Gorrie was often in London, leaving his wife to her own devices. With no children to keep her occupied, she joined an amateur dramatic society. Slaterbeck mentioned a series of flirtations, some of which developed into full-blown but short-lived romances. Then she became infatuated with Ralph Cullerton.

Cullerton was nine years younger than Sylvia. A clerk in an insurance brokerage, he hated office work and was hopelessly incompetent. If his uncle hadn't been senior partner in the firm, he'd have been out on his ear. Handsome if chinless, he dreamed of becoming a famous actor, but was as likely to set foot on the moon as to tread the boards of the Old Vic. His delivery was lifeless, and his butterfly brain was incapable of remembering lines. For most of his colleagues in the dramatic society, his long hair, winsome expression, and habitual sulkiness made him a laughing-stock.

Sylvia fell for him, head over heels. Making the most of Gorrie's frequent absences from home, they became intimate, and insatiable. They fantasised about running away together, and making a new life in a distant land, where jealous folk wouldn't mock her lowly origins or his yearning to make a name in the theatre.

The couple claimed that, in return for her helping him to learn his lines, Ralph was teaching Sylvia how to improve her backhand. But the snatched hours together were not enough. Neither could bear to be out of touch for long, so they wrote to each other, sometimes more than once a day.

"Ralph and Sylvia exchanged correspondence brimming with naive expressions of mutual ardour," Slaterbeck wrote, "and unconstrained by commonly accepted standards of decency.

Their language might embarrass a dock worker. Ralph's spelling and grammar would certainly shame an eleven-year-old."

Sylvia's marriage had never been consummated. She could have sought an annulment rather than a divorce, but although she wanted to be rid of Gorrie, she was less keen on losing her life of luxury. Panic sounded in her letters to Ralph as she begged him to do something. Each reply from Ralph was wilder than the last. His first instinct, to shoot himself with his father's old army revolver, met a wail of protest.

Sweety pie, but what about me?

As a romantic alternative, he proposed a suicide pact. Sylvia's appalled refusal made clear that she'd much prefer him to do something about Walter. Anything, she said, anything at all.

Ill have it out with him, promised Ralph. He had no time for apostrophes.

She begged her lover to be decisive. Come what may, she'd stand by him.

Ill do it. Cross my hart and hope to die.

Walter Gorrie returned to Salisbury from a meeting in London at two o'clock the next afternoon. A creature of habit, he took a constitutional around the ornamental lake at teatime, rain or shine. An April shower had left the grass damp and the stone paths slippery, but the sun broke through as he strolled by the water's edge. Lost in thought, he didn't see Ralph Cullerton step out from an oak tree's shade, waving a gun.

"Ralph! Please!"

Standing on the terrace at the back of the house, Sylvia watched as her lover confronted her husband. She shrieked wildly, and started to run towards them. One of the maids heard the commotion and pressed her nose to the kitchen window. As she later testified, Ralph Cullerton struck out at his rival, and after a brief, hectic struggle, Gorrie lost his footing on the treacherous York stone. Screaming with pain, he tumbled head-first into the water.

Gorrie's desperate cry paralysed Cullerton. Only as Sylvia, panting and sobbing, reached the lake did he pull himself together. It looked as though he might dive in to the water himself, but Sylvia banged her fists on his chest in a frenzy of distress. The maid watched the couple tussling with each other, and her own squeals of anguish acted as a summons to Wann, the elderly butler. Ordering her to telephone the police, Wann hurried outside himself. Sylvia kicked off her shoes and jumped into the lake. Cullerton jumped in after her, and they struggled with each other, as well as with the motionless body.

Walter Gorrie was dead before they hauled him out of the water.

———

Sylvia Gorrie and Ralph Cullerton were both charged with murdering her husband. Ralph insisted that he'd only meant to frighten Walter Gorrie into agreeing to divorce his wife and provide for her financially. The gun was a toy, a theatrical prop. The correspondence with Sylvia was simply an outpouring of romantic twaddle. Neither of them, he insisted, took a word of it seriously.

"Not even your expressions of mutual devotion?" enquired the attorney general, leading for the Crown.

"That was different!"

It was one of half a dozen foolish answers which knotted the noose around Ralph Cullerton's neck.

According to Leo Slaterbeck, Sylvia learned from the shocking precedent of Edith Thompson, whose inept testimony in her own defence had sealed her fate. Sylvia declined to go into the witness box. The case against her was, her counsel said, so piti-fully inadequate that she refused to dignify it with a response.

That decision was a risk, and Slaterbeck evidently thought the prosecution had a strong case. It wasn't simply that Sylvia had egged Ralph on, arguably inciting him to kill her husband. Her wild reaction to Ralph's attack had prevented him from rescuing Walter, while her own belated attempt to save her husband had done more harm than good.

The cards fell in her favour. The judge was an elderly puritan with a rabid attachment to the black cap who was showing alarming signs of senility. He'd not presided over a capital case for years, and many senior figures in the legal profession were appalled that he had been allowed a last hurrah. His summing-up savaged Sylvia, and his ranting about her moral turpitude made even journalists blanch. Her silent dignity in the dock impressed the jury. They took less than half an hour to acquit her, and tears of relief were still trickling down her cheeks, as in thunderous tones the judge sentenced Ralph Cullerton to death.

Ralph Cullerton was hanged a month later. Slaterbeck noted that he'd outlived the judge, who died of a stroke the day before the execution.

———

Replete after a dinner of succulent braised venison washed down with a bottle of full-bodied Grenache, Reggie Vickers emerged from the restaurant into the balmy Soho evening. Half past nine, and the street was quiet. It was still light—the longest day of the year was only a few days past—and the district never came fully to life until darkness fell.

Reggie loved Soho: the bright lights and raucous laughter, the smells from the restaurants and pubs, the flavour of danger

in the air when night-time came. There were innocent pleasures to be had, as well as forbidden delights. On a Saturday,
with nothing better to do, he'd wander around Berwick Street
Market, smell the spice and coffee, and indulge his craving for
salt beef sandwiches. A fruit seller who was rumoured to inject
his wares with water so as to make them juicier would cry, "A
glass of wine in every orange!"

Tonight Reggie felt a touch light-headed. Not unpleasantly
so: he wasn't drunk, or even woozy, just unfocused after a
strange day. Once again he was footloose and fancy-free. This
was quite like old times. There was no reason to steer clear of
the Clan, no reason at all.

Shame about Doodle, but his mood was philosophical. The
Grenache helped. Soon he'd be able to look back on their affair
with a tinge of nostalgia. The truth was, it could never have
worked. Their backgrounds were too different, and these things
mattered. He regretted calling Doodle a nobody, but who could
deny that he was right? They'd only been together for the blink
of an eye. As the initial pain of rejection eased, it felt easier to
bear than the responsibility of bringing the curtain down on a
relationship that had run its course. Sad, but there it was.

Yes, it would be fun to return to the Clan. He wouldn't linger.
Just one drink, and no playing cards. Call it a trip down memory
lane.

What harm could it do?

Chapter 8

"Ah, one of my favourite murders," Rachel Savernake said, glancing over Jacob's shoulder.

Immersed in Slaterbeck's narrative, Jacob hadn't heard the library door open. As Rachel spoke, he breathed in her perfume, a subtle fragrance of violet. He looked up. Her dark hair was soft and fine, like chiffon. Dropping the book on the table, he realised he was blushing. Anyone would think she'd caught him salivating over a smuggled copy of *Lady Chatterley's Lover*.

"Good evening." He couldn't help glancing at his watch. "Thanks for the invitation."

She took a seat in the wing chair facing him, but said nothing. Small talk held no interest for her. Nor did he expect an apology for the discourtesy of keeping him waiting for fully thirty minutes. Rachel Savernake always did as she pleased.

Nettled, he said, "You're interested in Sylvia Gorrie? I saw you'd marked up that chapter. I suppose the scandal ruined her?"

Rachel made a dismissive movement with her shoulders. The black crêpe frock, unfussy and elegant, suited her. The latest creation of one of her favourite Continental designers, he presumed, costing more than he earned in a year.

"Far from it. For a woman from a modest background, she has done remarkably well for herself. She no longer needs the diversion of a dramatic society; she has a new part to play. The respectable widow, plucky survivor of a human tragedy. With enough money to keep herself in furs and finery until kingdom come."

"Paid a high price, didn't she?"

"If she found the trial gruelling and the publicity unpleasant, she's not lacked compensations. To this day, she lives in that fine house outside Salisbury. I wonder what passes through her mind when she strolls past the ornamental lake."

"She lost the man she loved..."

"I wonder how much she really cared about Cullerton."

"She only escaped the scaffold by the skin of her teeth."

"You think she was lucky?"

"Slaterbeck obviously thinks so, even if our rotten laws of libel mean he has to watch his words. If the judge hadn't been so biased, the jury might have found her guilty. The man in the street..."

"Ah, the court of public opinion." Rachel pretended to stifle a yawn. "The prosecution case was founded on circumstantial evidence. Her letters to Cullerton never mentioned murder."

"She encouraged him. He was stupid; she was greedy. An innocent man died." Impatience was getting the better of him. He changed tack. "You didn't invite me here to chat about the Gorrie case. Whatever the rights and wrongs, it's old news."

"Not like the Danskin trial?" she suggested. "You met Mrs Dobell at the Old Bailey, and she wants to talk to me?"

"About murder, yes." He shook his head. "She watched your father presiding over a trial before the war. It made a great impression on her."

"Nobody who encountered the Judge is ever likely to forget him," Rachel said.

The shadow of a smile crossed her face. What game was she playing? He gritted his teeth. It was getting late. He'd wanted to see her again, far more than he liked to admit, but she seemed intent on teaching him a lesson. After a day of journalistic drudgery, he wasn't in the mood to humour her.

"I must apologise," she said abruptly, causing him to gape. An apology from Rachel Savernake was a collector's item. "I'm a rotten hostess. Your tumbler's empty. Let me pour you another measure. I'll keep you company."

"Thanks, but no. Some of us have to get up early for work tomorrow." A cheap retort, but he was sick of being patronised. "I've delivered my message. You can contact the woman at the Circe Club. I'd better go."

Without a word, she picked up the decanter, and filled both tumblers. Their eyes met for a moment, then he looked away. There was the rub. It wasn't just that she was beautiful. He found her mesmerising.

"Spare me another half hour, Jacob. Please."

He couldn't help feeling flattered. The woman had a knack of exploiting weakness. He was shrewd enough to realise that she was an expert in manipulation, but he hadn't learned how to resist.

She raised her glass. "To crime."

"To crime."

Again she smiled, this time without a trace of mockery. "Let me tell you about Mrs Dobell."

He considered. "Is this a story for the *Clarion*?"

"No."

What could he say? He drank some of the whisky. "Fire away."

"Very well." Rachel leaned back in her wing chair. "Leonora Dobell isn't a witch. She is one of England's foremost criminologists."

His eyes widened. "What?"

"Both her books on the subject earned critical acclaim. As I'm sure you will understand, after reading her latest." She gestured towards *Respectable Murders*. "Of course, she writes under her maiden name."

"Slaterbeck?" He groaned. "Leo is really Leonora?"

Rachel savoured her drink before speaking again.

"At the tail end of the war, she married a man called Felix Dobell who had been severely injured in the fighting. He comes from an old Yorkshire family, and was born and bred on the family estate. Their home is on the northeast coast. It's called Mortmain Hall."

———

"Fancy a nice time, dearie?"

Darkness had fallen in Soho. The woman had russet hair and wore a fake fox fur. Her mouth was a lurid crimson gash. The brightness of her voice sounded false, and her shoulders were sagging with fatigue. Cheap scent teased Reggie's sinuses. This backstreet was her patch, and he'd seen her many a time on his way to the Clan.

"Sorry. Not today, thank you."

With a courteous smile, he shook his head. Such invitations regularly came his way as he walked these streets, and he always declined. Unlike many men, he took pains to be polite, however crude the overture. It would be absurd to take offence, and stupid to risk retaliation. Live and let live. The last thing he wanted was trouble.

Pungent beer fumes seeped into the night as he passed a pub. Inside, someone was singing out of tune. He was conscious of a bulky male figure emerging from the shadowy doorway. The man's footsteps smacked the pavement. Reggie didn't glance over his shoulder, but slowed down so that the man could get by. Instead, he remained close behind. Was this a thug who protected the prostitute? Thank goodness for the unwritten law. Only customers who cut up rough or refused to pay got themselves hurt.

Fifty yards ahead was an alleyway leading to his destination. The Clan was a safe haven, even if the man had robbery on his mind. No need to worry unduly about being followed. When coming to Soho at night, he left his gold watch at home, and never carried a large amount of cash. If the need ever arose, he wrote an IOU.

He hurried towards the alley. Once there, he'd break into a run. He was still quick on his feet over a short distance. The fellow behind him mightn't even give chase.

Almost there now. He gulped night air into his lungs. Turning the corner, he set off from a standing start, only to cannon into someone else. Another big, hulking fellow.

As he lost his footing, he realised that like Duleepsinhji at Lord's, he'd been lured into an appalling misjudgement. He'd been caught in a trap.

———

"Now I see why Mrs Dobell haunts the Old Bailey." Jacob drained his tumbler. "The pseudonym deceived me. It never occurred to me that Slaterbeck was female."

"It's a common ploy," Rachel said. "Her principal competitor is another female criminologist who writes as F. Tennyson Jesse. Publishers are alert to public taste. Readers won't take a book about murder cases seriously if they think it's not written by a man."

"Yes, I suppose I can…" Jacob's voice faded away as Rachel's features hardened. "What I don't understand is how Mrs Dobell knew that we're acquainted."

"You kept your promise?" Rachel asked.

Her determination to preserve her privacy bordered on the fanatical. Never had he known a woman so secretive. Earlier this year, she'd saved his life. Gratitude didn't interest her, but she'd extracted his solemn assurance that he'd never talk about her with other people.

"You know you can trust me."

She considered him with the calm detachment of a pathologist examining human tissue. "I trust no one except the Truemans."

"I'm a man of my word." Even to his own ears, the phrase sounded pathetically old-fashioned and defensive.

"No need to bluster, Jacob." She savoured the Chivas Regal. "As it happens, I've become interested in Leonora Dobell. She doesn't skimp on research, as her books demonstrate. I gather she's been assiduous in making friends in high places. Especially within Scotland Yard. She's acquainted with Inspector Oakes and on dining terms with Sir Godfrey Mulhearn. Our mutual friend, the good inspector, keeps his lips buttoned. If someone has talked out of turn, it's Mulhearn."

Jacob nodded, pleased to be let off the hook. The commissioner of the Metropolitan Police was vain and talkative. It was easy to picture the old buffer boasting about his acquaintance with the lovely daughter of the late Judge Savernake.

"I can almost hear Sir Godfrey bragging after a few drinks." Jacob drew back his shoulders and puffed out his chest, raising his voice to a fruity roar. "Damned attractive filly, I must say. If I were twenty years younger, ha! Mark my words, though. Her father was a rum 'un, and she's a chip off the old block. Poked her nose into some funny business a while back. The Chorus Girl case...you may remember all the fuss. Murky affair, can't talk about it. Top secret, frankly. Our fellows sorted it out, thank heaven. Good man, Oakes. Youngest inspector at the Yard and one of the smartest. Saved the life of a journalist. Flint, they call him. Impetuous boy, certainly not top-drawer. But that's reporters for you. They don't make our life any easier. Sometimes I wonder whose side the blighters are on."

Rachel rewarded his mimicry with a round of applause. Her eyes sparkled with pleasure; her laughter was musical, a rare and joyful sound.

"Bravo! If the *Clarion* gives you the sack, you have a future in vaudeville. And yes, Mulhearn will have let it slip rather like that. His tongue is too loose."

"Doesn't matter, does it?" Jacob was relaxing. The whisky made him sleepy.

"I prefer to keep myself to myself."

He beat a hasty retreat. "Yes, yes, absolutely. But will you talk to Mrs Dobell?"

"Yes, she intrigues me."

"You think she'll explore the Danskin case in her next book?"

"Why not? A mystery with so many facets offers something to suit every taste. An unidentified corpse, a dubious alibi, a surprise witness. And at the eleventh hour, a prisoner dodging the noose." Rachel paused before adding, "Just like Sylvia Gorrie."

"The two cases are very different."

"So it seems."

"You sound sceptical."

She shrugged, but didn't respond.

"The blazing car case isn't a bad story." He contemplated the bottom of his tumbler. "Despite the anticlimax. So much hoo-ha, and then it turns out the tramp wasn't murdered after all."

Looking up, he saw her gaze fixed on him. Almost as if she setting him a test.

"The fire was simply a tragic accident?" she asked.

"What else?" He sighed. "It's like that death on the railway line yesterday afternoon. The chap who was run over by the Waterloo express."

"I read about it." Rachel's face was a blank.

"I wondered if it might be the exact opposite of the Danskin business. A case where murder is done, but never suspected."

———

The man in the alleyway held a blade to Reggie's throat while his colleague kept watch.

"Please," Reggie whimpered. "I'll give you money. All the cash I have…"

"I don't want your money," the man hissed. "Who have you been talking to?"

Reggie blinked. "No one. I swear it."

"The Dobell woman?"

Reggie's heart skipped a beat. "Who?"

The blade scratched his skin. He closed his eyes. Was this how it would end, in a dark and litter-strewn alley?

"Talk, and you're done for."

"I swear," Reggie said. "I haven't said a word."

"Keep it like that if you don't want to taste a knife."

Reggie felt a flicker of hope. Might he yet survive? His assailant must be open to reason. Despite his size and strength, he wasn't a roughneck at all. Incredibly, he spoke in the well-modulated tones of a man educated at one of the better public schools.

He was a gentleman.

———

Rachel's face gave away nothing. Jacob felt compelled to defend his theory. "It's not so absurd to suggest that Bertram Jones was murdered," he said. "For a middle-aged man simply to fall out of a railway carriage and onto the track, at exactly the time a fast train is heading in the opposite direction, seems rather a coincidence."

"It's happened before. On that very line. There was no question of foul play on that occasion."

"A helpful precedent, if you want to commit a murder and pass it off as an accident. Today I made a few enquiries, but they got me nowhere."

"A pity."

"Yes, the police have written the death off as a piece of bad luck. The Necropolis Company doesn't want anyone stirring things up." He stifled a yawn. "The deceased has no nearest and dearest to kick up a stink on his behalf. I don't even know if he actually attended a funeral at Brookwood. I might go there, to check if anyone saw him at a service or by a graveside."

"If I were you," Rachel said, "I wouldn't waste my time prowling around a cemetery."

At once he became alert. "You wouldn't?"

A decisive shake of the head.

"All right." He chose his words with care. "What would you do, if you were me?"

Rachel stretched in her chair. Lithe, graceful, feline. "I'll take you into my confidence. Provided you swear that nothing I say will find its way into the *Clarion*."

"Why be so mysterious?"

"Put it down to a flaw in my character." A thin smile. "It's not my only failing. Well?"

"I'm a professional newspaperman. You can't…"

"If you prefer, we can forget this conversation ever took place."

He bowed to the inevitable. "You have my promise."

"Thank you. On the shelf to your left is a run of first editions. Can you see a book in a rather horrid orange wrapper called *Murder and Mysteries*?"

He jumped to his feet and plucked the book from its place. "Written by Leo Slaterbeck, who else?"

"Take both her books home. You'll find that she has a thought-provoking knack of describing a case factually while implying that all is not as it seems. *Murder and Mysteries* includes a chapter called 'The Demise of Gilbert Payne.'"

"What does this have to do with Jones's death on a railway track?"

"The name of the man who was killed," Rachel said, "was not Jones, but Gilbert Payne."

———

Reggie Vickers fainted as his two assailants let him go. They'd kicked him in the kidneys before dumping him in the alley like a sack of rubbish, with the rest of the rotting debris.

When he came round, he wasn't sure if he was still alive. The buzzing in his head made him feel giddy. Everything seemed unreal. His kidneys hurt, and his neck stung where the blade had touched it. Groggy and frightened, he touched his throat. He felt a sticky smear. Blood stained his finger.

They'd cut him, and in his terror he'd not realised.

Gentle probing established that the slit was not a gaping wound. He pulled out a handkerchief and held it against his throat. Unsteadily, he levered himself upright. His flat was five minutes away. Despite the pain in his kidneys, he could just about hobble there.

All that mattered was that he was alive.

———

Jacob stared at Rachel. "Jones was an imposter?"

"Everyone believes Payne was murdered, and his body thrown in the Thames. Leonora Dobell's investigations led her to question the official version of events, but she didn't know the whole truth. In fact, he's hidden in Tangier ever since staging his disappearance. He only came back to Britain because his beloved mother had died. Hence the visit to Brookwood."

"How do you know all this?"

"I was told by a friend of his called Vickers. He was fearful about Payne's safety."

"Rightly so."

"Yes, but Payne's death has frightened him into silence."

"So my instinct was right," Jacob said. "He was murdered. And you'd like me to poke around, see what I can find?"

Rachel shrugged. "Trueman has made some enquiries on my behalf. What you do is entirely your decision."

Jacob's mind was racing. "Who wanted Payne dead?"

"Good question. Payne's personal life was…tangled. Before he vanished, he was an *habitué* of the Soho *demi-monde*. There's a club known as the Clandestine, or simply as the Clan. Very different from the Garrick and the Reform, but he was a regular."

"You think he made enemies?"

"I think you should take good care of yourself. So should Leonora Dobell."

"Is she in jeopardy too?"

"Vickers thinks so," Rachel said. "And remember this. Investigate Gilbert Payne and Leonora Dobell, and your life will be in danger too."

Chapter 9

Jacob slept fitfully. He wasn't accustomed to drinking whisky, and shouldn't have allowed Rachel to keep refilling his glass. He was easily persuaded, that was the trouble, and she traded on it. She was using him, but he was sufficiently under her spell not to find that an intolerable insult. What gnawed at him was his bafflement about what precisely was in her mind.

Spending time with her always left him with muddled emotions. He'd never admit it to another soul, but he was physically attracted to her; it wasn't merely her looks, but the strength of her character. Yet her remoteness made her untouchable. He suspected that she found him amusing, and also that if the need arose, she'd sacrifice him without a second thought.

He was restless under the blanket, thoughts roaming far and wide. This business about Gilbert Payne and Leonora Dobell. How seriously should he take her warning? Rachel loved a touch of melodrama; she might be exaggerating the threat to keep him on his mettle. Then again…

At six o'clock he dragged himself out of bed. Parting the bedroom curtains, he peered down at the street. A handful of people were already about. In spring, he'd moved into rooms in

Exmouth Market, above a cheesemonger's. He loved this part of London; the shops, stalls, and pubs within a stone's throw supplied him with everything he needed, as well as delicacies such as stewed eels that he wouldn't touch for a gold clock. The street teemed with life from dawn till dusk and the air was thick with the smell of cabbages and coffee. He loved the market traders' cheerful rowdiness, and it took him only twenty minutes to walk to Clarion House. Less if he cycled.

He made himself a pot of tea and two rounds of buttered toast. He worked on Saturday mornings but wasn't due at the office until half eight. As well as *Murder and Mysteries*, Rachel had wanted him to read *Respectable Murders*. There were one or two stories he might find especially interesting, she said; the Wirral Bungalow murder, for instance.

Why did he sense that she was setting him a challenge? Her hint—if it was a hint—that the Sylvia Gorrie case had some connection with the Danskin trial was equally frustrating. She'd given him pieces in a puzzle, but the picture he could make with them was incomplete. Even if her aim was to protect him from harm, she was maddening. He wasn't a child. He could look after himself.

In a grumpy mood, he settled down on the sofa in his tiny sitting room, and began to read "The Demise of Gilbert Payne."

———

Reggie Vickers didn't sleep at all. Lying on his back, staring at his bedroom ceiling, he told himself that insomnia was a fate better than death.

His neck stung, and his kidneys ached, but he'd been lucky. The blade could have slit his throat from ear to ear. He'd bled profusely, but the damage was superficial. The mark would take some explaining. He'd tell anyone who asked that he'd had a messy accident after his hand slipped while wielding a cut-throat razor. It was plausible. Just about.

"Thank your lucky stars you didn't call on the Savernake woman," he murmured to himself. If anyone got wind that he'd spoken to her...

How right he'd been to refuse to bow to pressure from her hireling. And to be so wary when approaching her in the first place. As the pea-souper in his mind began to clear, he realised why he'd been threatened.

News of Gilbert Payne's death was bound to shake him, make him vulnerable. Probably he was regarded as unreliable. The warning he'd received was a preemptive blow, a calculated reminder of the risk he'd run if he let anything slip.

Not that he knew much, in all honesty. Only what he needed to be told.

If only he'd never uttered a word. To Doodle, to Rachel Savernake. With Doodle, he'd been trying to impress, and failing. As it was, the shock of Doodle's defection had helped to anaesthetise him to the loss of Payne. And he'd never believed there was much hope for poor Gilbert. To be run over by a fast train was a rotten way to go, but at least it was quick.

No, it was Rachel Savernake he needed to worry about. He tumbled out of bed and, for the first time since he'd been assaulted by two older boys at school, he said a prayer.

"Oh Lord, don't let her keep pursuing me."

———

"Sleep well?" Martha asked as Rachel strolled into the kitchen.

"The sleep of the just."

The two women exchanged smiles as Martha put the teapot

on the stove. This little joke had become a ritual between them. The maid found comfort in familiar routines. But Rachel never asked her how she'd slept. Ever since the acid attack, Martha had suffered from foul and recurrent nightmares. Only since the death of Judge Savernake, and the household's departure from the little island, had the terrors of her adolescence abated. Even her physical scars were beginning to fade.

"You told Jacob Flint that Jones was Gilbert Payne?"

"Also that Leonora Dobell is playing with fire. That's enough for him to get his teeth into. I warned him about the risk, but he's intrepid. Or naive."

"Or both," Martha said. "You're sure this is better than asking an enquiry agent to help? Jacob's just an ordinary young man, when all's said and done."

"He's as dogged as any private investigator. And we can rely on him."

"I suppose you're right."

Rachel shot her a sidelong glance. "You like him, don't you?"

When Martha blushed, it made her look sixteen again. "Oh, he'd never look at me. Not if he had the chance to turn in the other direction."

"Don't be so sure." Rachel reached out and stroked the maid's hair. "And don't forget this, either. Jacob's ordinariness is an asset. He makes it so easy for people to underestimate him."

———

Gilbert Payne was born with a silver spoon in his mouth. The only child of elderly parents, he grew up in a country house in the wilds of Shropshire. His father was a furrier from Manchester and his mother a member of an old Oswestry family. Cissie Payne became pregnant at a stage in her life when, after innumerable miscarriages, she despaired of ever carrying a child to term. This time, she gave birth to a son. Gilbert was the apple of her eye. When an attack of infantile paralysis nearly did for him at the age of five, Cissie became even more protective and doting. Polio lamed him, but he survived and his mother spoiled him endlessly.

In her book, Leonora Dobell, alias Leo Slaterbeck, made no secret of her disapproval. Gilbert Payne was sensitive and intelligent, but softened by parental indulgence. At school, he was bullied, and took refuge in books. After earning a scholarship to Cambridge, he wrote enough poetry to fill a slim volume. When nobody wanted to publish it, he produced five hundred copies, and called it a limited edition.

Critical indifference and public apathy greeted the book's appearance. Yet Payne's efforts weren't a total failure. They introduced him to publishing's pleasures as well as its pitfalls, and inspired him to take it up as a career. On graduating, he took a position in Bonnell's before deciding to set up on his own. Following the death of his father, he sold the estate in Shropshire, bought a house in Hampstead for his mother, a flat in Chelsea for himself, and sank a large amount of money into his new venture.

At first he specialised in poetry, with a sideline in political and philosophical monographs. His aim was to build an imprint with literary respectability, but the business drained his capital at an alarming rate. The turning point came in a casual conversation in Payne's club.

"Publishers don't give a fig for young British patriots," a friend complained to him. "We couldn't care less about the blasted Bloomsbury set. The war's over, thank God, but we still yearn for excitement. Stories of adventure. Yarns about chaps showing the spirit that vanquished the Hun. Tales where the best man wins."

Lo and behold! Leonora proclaimed. Within weeks, Payne had his breakthrough. A major who had been invalided out of the Grenadiers had written a tale of blood and thunder starring Lion Lonsdale, a much-decorated war hero who didn't allow the Armistice to get in the way of a good punch-up. The dog-eared manuscript of *Action in the Ardennes* had received two dozen rejections by the time it reached Payne's desk. Refreshed with a new title, the story sold fifty thousand copies. *The Best Man Wins* launched a long line of Lion Lonsdale stories. Gilbert Payne's fortune was made.

Payne wasn't the marrying kind; he haunted the darker corners of Soho, hobnobbing with folk on the outer fringes of respectable society. One evening, he hosted a party in the West End to celebrate the publication of Lion Lonsdale's latest escapade. When the gathering broke up, he announced to anyone who cared to listen that he was off for a nightcap at his club. That was the last anyone saw of him.

His secretary reported him missing when he failed to turn up the next morning. For him to absent himself without warning was out of character. Once a body was fished out of the Thames mud near Limehouse, a murder enquiry began. The remains were presumed to belong to Payne; even though a boathook had destroyed his features, the body hadn't quite been stripped bare in the water. At the mortuary, Payne's distraught mother identified his watch, and confirmed that the corpse was the right height, weight, and age.

So who had killed him? Leonora Dobell explored theories ranging from a commonplace robbery to a revenge attack on the part of a disgruntled lover, although she took care to avoid naming any likely suspect. The conclusion of her account struck Jacob as oddly inconclusive:

"And there remains one other possibility, remote yet

tantalising. What if the body in the Thames was not Gilbert Payne's? What if he vanished for reasons of his own? If so, he may be among us right now, strolling the streets of London in disguise. Even that doesn't solve the mystery of the disappearance of Gilbert Payne. The fundamental question remains:

"Why did he vanish?"

———

"This is an unexpected pleasure," Leonora Dobell said into the telephone when Rachel called the Circe Club.

"Didn't you trust Jacob Flint to pass on your message?"

"Oh, he seems well-meaning enough. For a journalist. I wasn't sure you'd be willing to speak to me. Or know who I am."

"You're too modest," Rachel said. "As you've gathered, I am another student of crime. I've read your books, and your insights into the murderous mind intrigue me. I couldn't resist making enquiries about you."

"Oh, yes?" A cautious note entered the other woman's voice.

"I learned about your past. And the connection between us. Or rather, between our fathers."

After a pause, Leonora Dobell said, "Then you'll know that we share a taste for detection. Perhaps we can meet?"

"I'd like that," Rachel said.

"I stay here at the Circe when I'm carrying out my researches, but I'm about to catch a train home. My husband is an invalid, and I don't trust his nurse."

"I'm sorry to hear that," Rachel said. "Will you be back in London soon?"

"Oh, yes, it's only a flying visit. As much to keep Bernice, the wretched nurse, on her toes as anything else. I'll be back by Monday afternoon. What time would suit you?"

"Shall we say three o'clock, outside Burlington House?" Rachel took a breath. "Perhaps you will allow me to introduce you to a murderer."

She rang off without waiting for a reply.

———

As the *Clarion*'s morning news conference broke up, Jacob turned his mind back to the puzzle of Gilbert Payne. He shut his office door, and lounged in his chair, feet up on the desk. What had he learned from Leonora Dobell's book? She suspected there was more to Payne's disappearance than met the eye, but had found no evidence to substantiate her theory. Unless, Jacob thought, she hadn't dared to publish everything she'd discovered, for fear of a defamation claim. For anyone writing about a controversial subject, it was a familiar dilemma. You couldn't tell the whole truth, because you couldn't always prove it.

If she was in danger, she must have angered someone. *Murder and Mysteries* had been published last autumn. Nine months later, she'd not come to any harm. What had changed?

Payne's mother had died, Jacob told himself, causing him to break cover. Yes, that must be the answer. While Payne was tucked safely away in exotic Tangier, any suggestion that he was still alive could be brushed away as mischievous speculation. His return to Britain made all the difference.

Leonora wasn't as well informed as Rachel. If she'd known that Payne was back in the country for the funeral, surely she wouldn't have been content to linger at the Old Bailey?

Rachel wanted him to undertake some detective work but was unwilling to tell him everything or even let him write up the story. A one-sided bargain and ridiculously unfair, but those were her terms, take them or leave them. He dared not cross her. She'd always played by her own rules.

———

"The Aussies are batting at Lord's." A fellow cricket fanatic, Basil Pennington, accosted Reggie Vickers as they left the office at lunchtime. "Our tail didn't wag, and they've made a good start... Heavens, what have you done to your neck?"

"Ah." Reggie had prepared his answer. "Cut myself shaving with the old cut-throat. A real butterfingers. Bad as those dollies the Aussies dropped yesterday, eh?"

"You need to take care," Pennington advised.

"I will," Reggie said to himself. "Depend on it."

During the morning, his mood had lightened. The pain in his kidneys had subsided to a dull ache, and the Savernake woman hadn't been in touch again. Thank God he'd held his nerve. She must have got the message.

Everything was going to be all right.

Chapter 10

"Payne?" Throaty laughter came down the telephone line. "Aye, a good name for a publisher. Dealing with 'em is always painful for a writer."

Jacob forced an appreciative chuckle. He was at Clarion House, making his latest call to an author from Payne's list. So far, he'd learned nothing new. Now he was talking to Alexander Mudie, who was in his seventies and hadn't published a word for years. As an officer of the Black Watch, Mudie had fought in the Boer War and served in the Punjab. Following the Armistice, he'd enjoyed a brief vogue with half a dozen thrillers recounting the daredevil exploits of Mackintosh Trueblood. In his youth, Jacob had devoured them all.

"I'm researching an article about his murder. An unsolved mystery, you may recall?"

"Can't help, I'm afraid. I'd not heard from him for some time before he died. He used to pester me for another manuscript, but the well had run dry. I couldn't come up with a new idea."

Jacob's memories of the Trueblood saga suggested that he'd run out of inspiration long before that. Each story followed precisely the same template.

"You knew him well?"

"Only met him the once, when he held a party for his authors." Mudie clicked his tongue. "And once was enough. London makes my head spin; give me the Lowlands any day."

"What do you remember of him?"

"Well, *de mortuis*, you know, but Payne wasn't my cup of tea. He was more at home with poets and political types. Oddballs, agitators."

Jacob found himself offering sympathy. "Oh dear."

"Aye, and as if that wasn't bad enough, he invited along his friends as well as his scribblers. Very rum crowd. There was a young fellow who fawned on him, rather embarrassing. Wouldn't have gone down well in the Black Watch."

"Perhaps he could help. Can you remember his name?"

"Sorry, mind's a blank. There was plenty to drink that night, thank the Lord. That made it just about bearable. Not much else I can tell you."

"If the chap's name comes to mind, perhaps you'd give me a ring."

"Don't hold your breath, Mr…um, Flint." Another throaty laugh. "You've read my yarns, you say? As it happens, I'm thinking of picking up the old quill again. If you care for an interview…"

"Most generous of you," Jacob interrupted. "We must talk about Trueblood some other time. Perhaps when you call back with that name."

———

He took a break from the telephone to wander to the *Clarion's* reference room, where an eclectic stock of books and periodicals supplemented back issues of the newspaper and even a couple of its competitors'.

Perhaps he could discover something about Leonora Dobell. The jackets of her books included no biographical notes about the author. Back copies of the newspaper included a couple of reviews, but revealed nothing about her, under her married name or pseudonym.

A woman of mystery, yes, but no hermit. She'd been quite happy to talk to him at the Old Bailey, and according to Rachel, she mixed with people from Scotland Yard. He plucked the latest edition of *Who's Who* from the shelves, and found that she merited an entry.

Slaterbeck, Leonora (Mrs Leonora Dobell), writer on criminology, *b.* Osbaldwick, 1887, *d.* of the late N.O. Slaterbeck, *m.* Felix Dobell, 1918. *Educ.* Harrogate Ladies' College. *Publications:* Murder and Mysteries, Respectable Murders. *Recreations*: attending trials. *Address*: Mortmain Hall, Yorkshire.

Short and to the point. This was not a woman with the time or inclination for knitting, cookery, or flower arranging. Her single-mindedness reminded him of Rachel. But what had inspired such devotion to the study of crime and the machinery of law and justice?

A gazetteer told him that Mortmain Hall had been the seat of the Dobells for two hundred years. What must it be like to live in a mansion handed down through the family from generation to generation? He felt no nostalgia for the terraced house in Armley where he'd grown up, but he could imagine that those to the manor born saw things differently.

The Mortmain estate occupied a finger of land on the north Yorkshire coast, pointing out into the North Sea. Jacob was familiar with bustling Scarborough, the fishing village of Robin Hood's Bay, and Whitby, home to an ancient abbey; but he didn't know Mortmain.

The last people to pay much attention to the place seemed to have been the Romans, who had built a signalling station there. The winding coast road bypassed the tiny settlement. It was a lonely stretch of country, exposed and wild. Merely to imagine the northeast gales lashing grey waves into a snarling frenzy made Jacob shiver.

———

"Between you, me, and the gatepost, I never cared for the chap."

It was half past five. Charles Bonnell had invited Jacob to join him at his club for a preprandial snifter. This was Jacob's first visit to the Bookman's Club, but he surmised that his host spent more time here than at the office. At forty-five, Bonnell had the jowls and greying whiskers of a man twenty years his senior. His hair was thinning, his eyes watered, and gout kept making him wince. He represented the Bonnell publishing dynasty's third—and, Jacob guessed, final—generation. Already he'd explained that the key to managing a business involved letting the staff get on with it. While one got on with the task of consuming the profits, presumably.

"Unreliable?" Jacob suggested.

"Yes and no, as the legal johnnies would say," Bonnell replied unhelpfully. "I mean, he wasn't bad at his job, even if his literary pretensions were an embarrassment."

The nutty flavour of the Oloroso teased Jacob's taste buds as he inhaled the odour of leather upholstery and tobacco. He was as unaccustomed to opulence as to fine sherry. The pubs around Fleet Street and Exmouth Market where he guzzled pints of bitter were crowded and noisy. Here you could hear an aitch drop—if one ever did.

His luck had turned after largely fruitless efforts to track down people in Gilbert Payne's circle. Bonnell's willingness to talk had perplexed him until it became clear that the publisher's priority was to find a drinking companion before dinner rather than gaining coverage in the press. His wife had left him six months ago, Bonnell said, and he hadn't eaten at home since.

"My father took Payne on, you understand. I'd never give a chap like that house room. Fellow hankered after being a poet. Most of his stuff didn't even rhyme. Bad idea, to run with the horses and hunt with the hounds. One is either a publisher or a writer, need to nail one's colours to the mast. Took him a few years to see the light."

"And when he did see the light?" Jacob prompted.

"What did he do but hand in his notice?" Bonnell tutted at the memory of base ingratitude. "My father trained him up, taught him everything we knew, and then he deserted us. Thankfully, he didn't try to poach our popular authors. Romance and comedy, with a few 'tec yarns thrown in, that's our recipe. Only one of our writers followed him, and he never fitted our list. Papa only took him on because they'd gone to the same school. Damned Bolshevik, frankly. Not that Payne was much sounder."

"Did Payne's politics make him unreliable?"

The fleshy jowls wobbled as their owner weighed up his answer. "That wasn't what I had in mind. Payne got on well enough with the Reds, and called himself a socialist, but he was a man of good family. Can't believe his heart was in it. Look what a mess that numbskull MacDonald has got the country into. Just look!"

Jacob didn't want to look. Political arguments made his heart sink. "What did you have in mind?"

Bonnell made short work of his sherry, and snapped his fingers to summon a waiter. "Have another? To be candid, I never cared for the company he kept. Publishing's a funny game, mind; one meets all sorts. I'm as broad-minded as the next man, but one has to draw the line somewhere."

"Did Gilbert Payne…"Jacob groped for the right phrase. "… mix business with pleasure?"

"Not to my knowledge," Bonnell said hastily. "Not while he was with us, at any rate. And in fairness, when he set up on his own, he put out some decent books. Stories about Trueblood, Lonsdale, chaps who were the salt of the earth."

"Then…"

"One hears gossip," Bonnell said. "In publishing, it swirls like fog. Not that I took much notice. Our paths seldom crossed after he went his own way."

"He wasn't a member of the Bookman's?"

"Good grief, no. Too staid for him."

Behind them, someone was snoring. The atmosphere in the Smoking Room was soporific even without an unnecessary fire that blazed warmly enough to make anyone's eyelids droop. In one corner of the room, two whiskery old men were playing bezique for matchsticks. Wilkie Collins peered myopically down from a huge gilt-framed oil painting above their heads. Jacob also recognised other luminaries of Victorian literature on the wall: Thackeray, Dickens, Hardy, Trollope, and Bulwer Lytton. There was no room for Eliot, Gaskell, or the Brontës, far less Braddon or Oliphant. Like the Long Room, this place was a male refuge.

"But he was a club man, wasn't he? Someone mentioned to me…" Jacob went through a pantomime of trawling through his memory. "A club called The Clandestine?"

"Ah." A flush came to Bonnell's puffy cheeks. "That may be so. I've heard tell of the place. Can't tell you anything about it."

"When I looked it up in the directories," Jacob said, "I couldn't find any information. It's simply not mentioned."

Bonnell grimaced, perhaps at a twinge of pain from his gouty foot. "There's a very good reason for that, Mr Flint. That place has an extremely dubious reputation. Attracts the wrong sort… Mummy's boys, if you get my drift."

Jacob did get his drift. "Could something in his personal life have led to his murder?"

"Wouldn't surprise me, frankly." A worried look crept into Bonnell's tired eyes. "This is all off the record, of course."

"Word of honour." Jacob wore his best choirboy expression. "As you see, I left my notebook in the office."

"Capital. Wouldn't do to conduct business within these hallowed portals in any case, goodness me. What did you intend to write about Payne?"

"To be honest," Jacob said, "it's unlikely that I'll get the go-ahead to publish an article about him. The *Clarion* is a family newspaper, and from what you've told me… All the same, I'm grateful for your time. I must remind our literary editor to take a look at your latest catalogue."

"Good of you. Things are ticklish in publishing at the moment, with the economy in such a mess."

The waiter arrived with more sherry. As Bonnell rapidly emptied his glass, Jacob reflected that just as in Yorkshire, farmers always moaned about hard times, so in London people in publishing routinely expressed despair about the state of the market. In both worlds, pessimism sprang eternal.

"I suppose," Jacob said in an artless tone, "there's no doubt it was Payne's body they found?"

"None whatsoever. His poor mother was beside herself."

"Odd business," Jacob mused. "I wonder who would want to kill him."

Bonnell patted his corporation. "Damned odd. Scotland Yard never got to the bottom of it. Lovers' tiff, if you ask me. Things can get pretty nasty among that bunch." When Jacob gave him an enquiring look, he added quickly, "So I'm told, so I'm told."

"You think there was a personal motive? Spite, revenge, jealousy?"

"What else?" Bonnell chortled. "Don't tell me it was an author who felt cheated out of his royalties!"

"After he died," Jacob said, "you took over his firm."

"Correct." Bonnell frowned. "Cecilia Payne had no head for business. She was heartbroken over the death of her darling boy. The last thing she needed was the responsibility of running a publishing house. My father and I were happy to take it off her hands."

Jacob could imagine. Payne's firm was thriving, while the one he'd left stagnated, but his mother would have been no match for the Bonnells in a negotiation. Cissie had sold out for a song. The acquisition had given Bonnell's a much-needed shot in the arm, even if the jingoism and fisticuffs beloved of clubland heroes were falling out of fashion.

"So you now publish the Lion Lonsdale series, and all the rest?"

"Inevitably, one or two people fall by the wayside. That's the nature of publishing."

"The authors who write about politics and philosophy?"

"Politics and philosophy got this country into its present mess," Bonnell said. "What people want from us is decent entertainment. Nothing more, nothing less."

"And the one author Payne poached from you? Did you welcome him back, or has he gone too?"

Bonnell sighed. "Between you, me, and the gatepost, his stuff never was our cup of tea. We don't live in Utopia, Mr Flint, and never will. He didn't write anything for us in the last few years; he was too busy trying to change the world. Though technically he remained on our list until the tragedy."

"Tragedy?" Jacob was nonplussed.

"Yes, the poor wretch was killed by his wife's fancy man. Shocking affair, in more ways than one. His wife was charged, along with the boyfriend. He was hanged, she got away with it. Not that anyone should be surprised. Juries can never resist a pretty face. If I ever want to murder anyone, I'll pretend to be a flapper."

Jacob had to ask. "What was her name?"

"Sylvia Gorrie."

———

Was Bonnell feasting on beef Wellington, lobster thermidor, or a chateaubriand steak? Jacob played a guessing game as he left the fish-and-chip shop on Exmouth Street. His own dinner was wrapped up in a newspaper. Happily, it was the *Witness* rather than the *Clarion* that was sodden with grease and vinegar.

It was a fine evening, and he'd cycled home from the Bookman's Club. At one point, he'd gained the impression that a black car was following him. As he reached Gray's Inn Road, he risked a glance over his shoulder, but the car was nowhere to be seen.

He reached the door next to the cheesemonger's front window, and took the key to the mortice lock from his pocket. Looking round, he spotted a black Austin Twenty parked near the Exmouth Arms. Hardly unusual. He let himself in, and scolded himself for conjuring up worries out of thin air.

A couple of minutes later, he was at the kitchen table, putting the finishing touches to his meal. Let publishers gorge on the Bookman's legendary haute cuisine. For a journalist from Leeds, happiness meant coating his cod and chips with thick brown smears of HP sauce and an extra sprinkling of salt. And being young and fit enough for it not to add an ounce to his weight.

His thoughts wandered. Was it pure chance that Gilbert Payne had known Walter Gorrie? Jacob distrusted coincidences. But what else could this be? Payne and Gorrie were affluent, intelligent, attached to the written word; it would be peculiar if they didn't move in the same orbit. For all its vastness, London was a small world of cliques and close connections. Who you knew counted for as much as what you did.

After he'd washed up, he repaired to his tiny sitting room. Leonora Dobell's books were on the sideboard, but he'd had enough of Gilbert Payne for one day. He toyed with the idea of ambling over to the Exmouth Arms for a jar or two, but inertia prevailed. He'd had enough to drink as well. Sherry wasn't his tipple, and he hadn't expected it to make him feel so mellow.

Yawning, he peered out of the window and down on the street. No sign of the Austin Twenty. No dark silhouette skulking in a shop entrance. No need for his imagination to run riot. He was cross with himself for bothering to check. Blame Rachel Savernake. Her talk of danger was unsettling.

Five minutes later he was snoring loudly enough to be mistaken for a member of the Bookman's Club.

———

Charles Bonnell was usually the last to drag himself away from the Bookman's at the end of the day. Tonight was no exception. After his dining companions bade him goodnight, he contemplated having one for the road to dull the pain of his gout. Better not; he didn't want to finish up an old soak like Grandpa. Rising unsteadily to his feet, he tottered out of the Dining Room and made for an alcove next to the cloakroom. A telephone sat on a small Chippendale table, and he dialled with exaggerated care.

"Talked to the…um…reporter chap." Dammit, surely he wasn't slurring his words? "Nothing to worry about there."

"You think so?" said the calm voice at the other end of the line.

"Not too bright, if you ask me. Certainly not a pukka sahib, either. North-country accent, glorified bumpkin. Didn't invite him for dinner, he's probably gone back to some hovel to chew straw."

"What did he want to know about Payne?"

"Seemed to me that he was just fishing."

"Did he ask about Payne's death?"

"In passing. I told him my money was on a squabble with a boyfriend. 'These things can turn very nasty,' I said. That seemed to satisfy him."

"Anything else?"

"The Clandestine was mentioned. He knows Payne frequented the place, but that's as far as he's got."

"You're sure?"

"Shouldn't blow one's own trumpet, but actually it went rather well." He coughed. "Now, about that injection of capital…"

"I'm sure something can be arranged," the voice said smoothly.

"Sooner the better, frankly. Got a rather ticklish interview with the bank manager on the old horizon. I suppose you're waiting to see what happens next. Don't worry your head about that. You've nothing to fear from Jacob Flint."

Chapter 11

"All aboard the funeral express!"

In his dream, Jacob was running along an endless platform as the steam-belching train began to move. A conductor wearing a black cap thrust a ticket into his hand as he raced by.

In the nick of time, he grabbed the handle to the door of the last compartment. Yanking it open, he threw himself inside.

An elderly woman wearing a heavy coat and an old-fashioned bonnet was the only other occupant. Her face was turned away from Jacob.

"Where are we going?" he gasped.

She shuffled around in her seat, so that he could see her face. Except there was no face. Only a smiling skull, speaking in a whisper.

"To the end of the line."

He opened his palm and looked at the piece of card the conductor had pushed at him. It only bore two words.

No return.

———

He woke, sweating. Who would have thought the Bookman's Oloroso packed such a punch?

A mug of coffee revived him, and over breakfast he caught up with the morning's newspapers, including England's dire showing in the field on the second day of the Test, before picking up *Respectable Murders*.

If Rachel was right, Leonora's life was in danger. Had her writing and researches jeopardised someone's respectability? And if she found out, would she be amused by the irony?

On such a fine morning, it would be a criminal waste to linger indoors. He took himself off with his book to Wilmington Square, a green and pleasant oasis off Rosebery Avenue. The asphalt paths were busy with children racing around on tiny scooters, while old men slaked their thirst at the drinking fountain. Jacob found a bench, and settled down to read a story Rachel had marked. Leonora called it "The Wirral Bungalow Murder."

———

On a Friday evening in September 1928, a young couple took a romantic walk along a beach on the tip of the peninsula separating the Dee from the Mersey. The gaudy resort of New Brighton down the coast had never been quite as popular since the colossal tower was pulled down after the war, and with the holiday season over, few visitors strolled this far. There were no fairground rides to lure them, no candyfloss to devour. Eileen O'Connor and Jim Ashton often cycled here from Saughall Massie, intent on escaping their younger siblings, none of whom understood why the pair wanted to be alone.

This stretch of beach suited them to perfection, and low sand dunes offered additional privacy. Apart from lovers and a few people walking their dogs, at this time of day there was seldom anyone else about. Today they were in luck. The place was deserted. The sky was streaked orange and purple as the sun set above the water. Jim tightened his grip on Eileen's waist.

As he bent down to kiss her, the idyll was shattered by a shriek that became a gurgling scream.

"Did you hear that?" Eileen asked. "What was it?"

"A girl," Jim said. "She sounds panic-stricken."

"Is she in the dunes? Has someone attacked her?"

"Not sure. I'll go and see what's up. You wait here."

"Not on your life, I'm coming too!"

As the two of them hurried along a narrow path winding through the sand dunes, they heard the engine of a car roaring into life. Jim halted in mid-stride.

"Hear that? Someone's on the move!"

Nestling in a hollow beyond the dunes was a tiny wooden bungalow, painted lime-green and surrounded by a low white fence. Its garden was a tangle of ferns and shrubs. The curtains were drawn and there was no sign of life. A stony track led from the bungalow through a scattering of beech trees to the nearest road.

The car was out of sight.

"What should we do?" Eileen asked. "Ask if the people in the bungalow heard anything?"

"Doesn't look as if anyone's in."

"We ought to report it."

"None of our business."

"What if something awful has happened? I wouldn't want that on my conscience."

"Don't be silly. I bet it was just someone mucking about."

"Well, if you're sure..."

Jim later admitted to the police that he wasn't sure at all, but he didn't want to cause trouble. Or have his evening ruined. But the scream had broken the spell. They cycled home in silence.

Next day, Eileen's conscience got the better of her. She cycled over to Meols to pop in on her cousin, a young police constable. After listening to her story, he assured her there was probably nothing to worry about. There had been no reports of trouble anywhere close to the beach, but he was willing to take a nosey around the place.

Nobody answered his knock on the bungalow's front door. When he peered through a narrow gap in the curtains at the back window, one glimpse was enough to confirm cousin Eileen's premonition.

She was right. Something awful had happened.

————

The corpse belonged to a woman in her early twenties. Her hair was dyed blonde, her lipstick a dazzling scarlet. She wore a wedding ring, an apricot satin chemise, and nothing else. Someone had strangled her with his bare hands.

A double bed with silk sheets was crammed into the small, solitary bedroom. The few clothes in the wardrobe and chest of drawers were expensive and matched the dead woman's measurements. Beside the wardrobe, the police found a small, empty suitcase. The inference was that she didn't live in the bungalow, but had brought along enough things for a weekend visit.

Local enquiries established that the bungalow had been built eighteen months earlier for a wealthy Liverpool businessman called Green. Nobody saw much of him, and his determination to keep himself to himself provoked plenty of gossip. The gleeful consensus was that the bungalow was a "love nest." Green's nearest neighbour walked her collie over the dunes every day, and saw it as her duty to keep a sharp eye out for any evidence of untoward behaviour. Two or three times in the past couple of months, she'd seen a young woman, all dolled up and hanging about the premises. When the woman had spotted her, she'd hurried back inside. It all seemed most unsavoury. The description of the woman's hair and figure tallied with the deceased.

It didn't take the police long to identify the bungalow's owner. Green was an alias. His real name was Henry Rolland, and he was chairman and chief shareholder of a large engineering company in Garston. For the past ten years, he'd lived in a double-fronted house looking out over Sefton Park with his wife and sons. But when the detectives came to call, they found the Rollands' home deserted.

According to information received, the two boys were away at boarding school. Mrs Rolland had departed the previous weekend, to move back in with her mother. The old lady was a widow whose husband had taken on Rolland as an apprentice. He'd retired from the business when Rolland married his daughter, and transferred ownership to his son-in-law in return for a generous pension. Six months later he died of a heart attack; within a year, the company was renamed Rolland Castings Limited.

Over a decade, the small firm on the city's outskirts had grown to become one of the largest in its field. Rolland's hard work and determination had made him a Daimler-driving millionaire. He'd carved a reputation as a ruthless boss who believed that the end justified the means. As he ticked off his ambitions in the commercial world, he concentrated increasingly on the relentless pursuit of beautiful young women. The most recent target of his attention had been his secretary. The girl was also married, but such trifles didn't concern Rolland. His obsession with Phoebe Evison had driven his wife to the brink of a nervous breakdown.

The car Jim and Eileen had heard starting up was presumably Rolland's Daimler. That too was missing. Where he'd driven to after leaving his bungalow, nobody knew.

The urgency of the hunt for Rolland intensified with news from the forensic pathologist. The killer had strangled the deceased with bare hands. She'd been ten weeks pregnant.

———

The dead woman was identified as Phoebe Evison even before Mrs Rolland was interviewed. Phoebe's older sister, Maisie, came forward as soon as a description was circulated. Phoebe was twenty-two, a typist who had joined Rolland Castings six months before to become the chairman's confidential secretary. The pay was exceptional by Liverpool standards, but she'd fallen out with her husband as a result of taking the job.

"Why would that be?" asked a sympathetic police sergeant.

"A born troublemaker, is Dermot Evison. Jealous, too, and bitter. Hated seeing Phoebe get on. Out of work himself, with no prospect of a decent position. As far as he was concerned, Rolland was a filthy capitalist who exploited his workers. Phoebe was consorting with the enemy. But Phoebe said they couldn't rely on what Evison brought in from doing odd jobs for his mates. They had to eat. And she loved looking nice."

"How did she get on with Henry Rolland?"

"Phoebe was bonny, and she knew it. I warned her Evison was a good-for-nothing, but did she take any notice? Not likely. Headstrong, that was poor Phoebe. You couldn't tell her anything."

"Was something going on between her and Rolland?"

Maisie sniffed. "Rich men who employ a pretty girl are usually after only one thing. And I'll tell you this for nothing. It isn't help with the filing."

———

Henry Rolland's movements during Friday afternoon were quickly traced. Following lunch with a supplier, he'd spent half an hour closeted in his private office with Phoebe Evison, and then had a meeting with his chief engineer. Rolland had left the factory on the dot of five, before his secretary. After that, his trail went cold.

The investigators could picture what had happened. The couple made their way separately to the bungalow, and Phoebe put on her nightgown. Her aim was to create a mood of romance prior to breaking the news that she was expecting a baby.

When the bombshell dropped, Rolland's reaction was easy to predict. Was the child his or her husband's? Not that Rolland cared; he'd pay whatever was needed to make the problem go away.

But Phoebe was desperate for a child of her own. The pregnancy was the perfect reason to persuade her lover to divorce his wife while she ended her marriage to her feckless husband. She'd give up work, and the three of them could live happily ever after.

Easy to see how a quarrel might start. Cajolery fails, complaints and accusations fly around. Threats are made, voices are raised. Two angry people, neither willing to back down. The woman becomes frightened, and opens the door, about to run out into the open in her chemise. Making a spectacle of herself, humiliating her lover.

He needs to stop her. When he grabs hold of her, she screams. He must shut her up. Hands around her throat, squeezing...

Within moments, she is silent. Her limp body sags. He's gone too far.

He is beside himself with fear. All he knows is that he has to get away. Impossible to go home. He must hide, even though he knows in his heart that he can't run forever.

Yes, it would be something like that.

———

Phoebe had kept quiet about her plans for the weekend, which the other typists said was par for the course. They regarded her as a brazen schemer who had set out to seduce her boss, with disgusting success. For her part, she did her best to ignore her colleagues. None of them had noticed her suitcase; she'd made sure she was first to arrive in the office that day, and the last one to leave. She'd travelled to the Wirral on her own, by taxi.

Dermot Evison wasn't at home when the police hammered on the door of his scruffy terraced house in Vauxhall. When questioned about him, the people who lived on either side wrinkled their noses. They'd seen neither hide nor hair of him for the past few days. What's more, whenever they did see him again, it would be too soon.

Evison was a firebrand. All his life, he'd campaigned with a fierce passion for unfashionable causes, but at the age of forty, he was running to seed. He had a weakness for Guinness as well as a hair-trigger temper. These days he dissolved into tears of maudlin self-pity as often as he flared into rage.

The marriage to Phoebe was his second. His first wife put up with adultery and repeated beatings over the years, but obtained a divorce after he was sent to prison for affray.

Even before that, he was known to the police. The most remarkable discovery that detectives made about Dermot Evison was that he'd once been one of their own. For six months after the war, he held the office of constable in the Liverpool City force.

———

Henry Rolland was not a man to do things by halves. When handing himself in to the authorities, he wasn't content to appear at his local police station. Instead, he reported to Scotland Yard.

The suave, well-groomed businessman was now haggard and unshaven. He wanted to make a clean breast of things, he said, and he didn't mean to insult anyone's intelligence with a string of crude denials. Yes, he'd bought the bungalow under a false name and he made no bones about his motive. It was convenient for illicit assignations, only a few miles from home as the crow flew, but on the other side of the water from Liverpool. There was little risk of being recognised as long as he kept his head down. Since buying the property, he'd taken a succession of friends there. Those ladies meant nothing to him. With Phoebe Evison, it was very different.

Phoebe's vivacity appealed to him as much as her looks, but it had taken time to break down her defences. Her insistence that she was a married woman who believed in "until death do us part" simply fuelled his desire. When she finally agreed to spend a single night with him in the bungalow, it was the happiest moment of his life.

Phoebe made him feel young again. They began to make plans for divorcing their spouses and marrying after a decent interval. At a rendezvous at the bungalow the weekend before her death, Phoebe had broken the news that she was pregnant. The child was his, beyond question. She'd stopped having relations with her husband months ago; he'd no doubt she was telling him the truth. The news that they were to become parents made him ecstatic. He wasn't bothered about decent intervals. The divorces and their marriage must take place as soon as possible.

His response thrilled her, but she urged caution. Dermot Evison was violent as well as jealous. He'd need careful handling. They'd work out their plans in detail at the bungalow the following weekend. Meanwhile, Henry would provoke a row with his wife, so that she'd move out, the first step in the separation.

He spent the week in a daze of happiness, untouched even by a bitter quarrel with his wife. Once she'd packed her bags, he suggested to Phoebe that they spend the weekend together at his home in Sefton Park. She wouldn't hear of it. They'd meet at the bungalow, just as before, until she'd made the break from Evison. She was afraid he suspected their affair, and she couldn't take the risk that in his fury at the betrayal, he might hurt her lover. Or even kill him.

At this point, Rolland's stiff upper lip gave way and he dissolved into tears.

When he recovered, he explained that he'd turned up at the bungalow at the appointed time. Phoebe had promised she'd be ready and waiting in her new satin chemise.

But he was too late. Dermot Evison had reached the bungalow before him.

Phoebe was right to suspect that her husband was capable of murder. Her mistake was to believe that Evison would kill her lover. He'd taken his revenge by strangling her.

———

The police didn't take Rolland's statement at face value. Too much was open to question. Why hadn't he driven straight from the factory to the bungalow, ready to greet his mistress? His story was that he'd gone back home first, because he'd forgotten to pack his own suitcase, but nobody had seen him.

Rolland claimed that Phoebe had her own key to the

bungalow, but it hadn't been found. And what of the scream that Jim and Eileen had heard, shortly before the car engine started up? All Rolland could say was that, after finding Phoebe's corpse, he'd cried out in horror and disbelief. The young couple were wrong to jump to the conclusion that the shriek came from a woman; it was understandable, but they were mistaken.

He said he'd fled from the bungalow because he was terrified. The woman he loved had been brutally murdered. Her husband must be responsible, and he could only hang once. For all Rolland knew, Dermot Evison was lurking in the vicinity of the bungalow, ready to kill again.

Numb with shock, he'd driven aimlessly through the night. He couldn't go back to Sefton Park. He was too afraid of how things would look. His mistress had been strangled in his bungalow, and he was the obvious suspect, despite the strength of Evison's motive. The publicity surrounding the crime, he maintained, proved the point.

His vagueness about his movements was unsatisfactory. He claimed to have snatched an hour or two of sleep in his car during the early hours of Saturday, before making his way to London. There he booked in to a seedy boardinghouse in Hackney. Poring over the newspapers, in which he was practically accused of killing Phoebe, he realised that, whatever the cost, he had no choice but to come forward and try to clear his name.

———

In Liverpool, the police were piecing together the story of Dermot Evison's life. Time and again, he'd been sacked for insubordination. He spent much of the war in a military hospital after being badly wounded on the battlefield. When peace came, he joined the police, but his career ended in ignominy. A radical to his bones, he joined the local branch of the newly formed National Union of Police and Prison Officers and took a leading role in organising picket lines during the strike of 1919. The mutiny crumbled and he was dismissed from the force.

After that, Evison drifted from job to job; his drinking companions were political agitators, and he was forever arguing for higher wages and better working conditions. On one occasion, a row with a foreman led to a fist fight. The foreman was badly beaten, and Evison was sent to gaol.

His wife divorced him, but on the day of his release, he met Phoebe and swept her off her feet. Within six weeks they were man and wife, but following the General Strike, employers viewed Evison and his kind with suspicion. To keep afloat, he had to resort to odd-job work. That, and relying on his smart young wife's earnings.

Three days after his wife's murder, the police broke into a disused shed in Everton. It belonged to an old Communist pal of Evison, a toolmaker, who was at present serving a prison sentence for obstructing the King's highway.

Evison's body was hanging from a rafter. On the floor below his feet was a note. Only with difficulty could they decipher the wild scrawl.

She deserved what she got but I can't live without her.

———

The sun was scorching Jacob's forehead as he reached the final page. He'd forgotten to bring a hat. The park was packed with parents strolling around in conversation as their children filled the air with whoops of glee. A young couple had squeezed down onto the bench next to Jacob, and were kissing noisily.

Two hundred miles away, Henry Rolland was also probably relishing the sunshine. The police had never charged him. For all the oddities and gaps in his testimony, there was no proof that he'd lied. Without fuss or fanfare, the police investigation fizzled out. At the inquest into Phoebe's death, the coroner suggested that Evison's history, coupled with his suicide and the note he'd left, made the jury's task straightforward. They took the hint, and named Evison as Phoebe's murderer.

According to Leonora Dobell, Rolland didn't survive the scandal unscathed. His wife divorced him, and the company suffered. After selling his shares to a competitor for a quarter of their previous value, he buried himself in a quiet village in Cheshire. He was still a wealthy man, with decades of life ahead of him.

Leonora's concluding paragraphs were worded, Jacob thought, with a politician's flair for evasion. The dead were fair game, but she was too shrewd to shoot accusations at the living, especially if they had the money and ammunition to fire back in court.

Even so, he was sure Leonora suspected that Phoebe's murderer was not her husband, but Henry Rolland.

Chapter 12

"Are you certain?" Jacob leaned back in his office chair, trying to make sense of what he'd been told.

"Quite certain."

Ice entered the voice at the other end of the line. The secretary of Harrogate Ladies' College did not expect her word to be questioned by a London journalist, even if he did speak in a Yorkshire accent.

"Not for any period, however short?"

"Our record-keeping is second to none, Mr Flint. I can assure you that we have no record of a pupil called Slaterbeck. Now, if you'll forgive me, I have other matters to attend to. Good morning."

The secretary put down the phone, leaving Jacob to frown at the heap of directories on his desk. He'd spent half the morning trying to find out something about Leonora Dobell, and he'd set about the task methodically. Begin at the beginning, Gomersall advised reporters researching a story. Jacob hadn't expected Leonora's beginnings to be shrouded in mystery.

Slaterbeck was an uncommon surname, and he'd not been able to trace either Leonora or her father. It was as if she'd never existed prior to her marriage. He opened the office copy of *Who's Who*, where he'd bookmarked her entry. As he stared at it, the truth finally dawned.

Who's Who relied on the good faith of the great and the good; it wasn't seemly to double-check every piece of information it was given. The old witch had named her father as N.O. Slaterbeck as a joke.

There was literally no Slaterbeck.

———

"Delighted to meet you, Miss Savernake." Leonora Dobell extended her hand in greeting. They were outside the main entrance to the home of the Royal Academy in Burlington House. "Not that I think of you as a stranger. We have a great deal in common. I feel as I've known you for a long time."

"You're a student of the criminal mind." Rachel gripped the older woman's hand. "Perhaps I should be apprehensive."

"I hear you take after your father. He didn't have a nerve in his body."

"It's no secret," Rachel said. "There was no love lost between the Judge and me."

"Surely as he became older, increasingly frail…"

"All I will say is this. Nobody shed any tears when he died. Certainly not me."

Leonora studied her, as if trying to fathom a cipher. "Such a pity, family quarrels. I was devoted to my own father. As for Judge Savernake…well, you could say that everything I've done since has been inspired by the Judge."

Rachel looked into the dark, glittering eyes. Leonora gazed back at her. Like opponents in a fencing duel, each was trying to get the measure of the other.

"I prefer not to think about him, Mrs Dobell," Rachel said. "Or should I call you Miss Slaterbeck?"

"Leonora, please." The older woman beamed. "I hate people standing on ceremony. I suspect you feel the same. Ever since I learned of your arrival in London, I've longed to meet you."

"When you told Jacob Flint you wanted to talk to me about murder, you didn't explain what you had in mind."

"Mr Flint is young and charming, but he's a journalist to his inky fingertips. Ingenuous as he seems, I'm sure you watch your words with him. As I did."

"You bumped into him by accident?"

"He thought so." Leonora gave a sly smile. "Between you and me, I made sure we had the chance of a conversation. I'd heard you and he are acquainted."

"You're well informed."

"It's my business to be. My researches keep me in touch with Scotland Yard, and your name cropped up. Not that anyone seems to have deduced much about you, not even Jacob Flint. Murder obsesses you, that's perfectly clear. What isn't quite so obvious is…why?"

"People might say the same about you," Rachel said.

Leonora stared hard at her. "Touché."

Rachel waved towards the Palladian splendour of Burlington House. "You're an art lover, I believe. Isn't the Mortmain collection one of the finest in Yorkshire?"

Leonora sighed. "Unfortunately, maintaining the property and estate is wickedly expensive. My husband needs nursing care, and my royalties are swallowed up by everyday expenses. When the roof springs a leak or the carpets need replacing, I have to auction an oil painting to pay the bill."

"Eminently practical. And your husband approves?"

"Nowadays, Felix's life revolves around completing jigsaw

puzzles and flirting with his nurses. The latest woman is especially tiresome. She encourages him to snipe at me. But her wages don't come out of thin air. Hence the need to sell the pictures. He understands that there is no alternative."

"I see the dilemma."

"And so does old Mulkerrin, the other trustee. As I say to Felix, it's preferable to allowing a tycoon to bulldoze the Hall and build fifty bungalows. The Dobells have always been determined to make sure the estate remains in their hands." She smiled at Rachel. "The belief that it's important for families to endure is common enough. I suppose the Savernakes are the same?"

"I'm the last of the line," Rachel said. "I feel no sentimental attachment to Gaunt."

"You're young. One day you'll have children."

"I don't care to be beholden to others."

Leonora frowned. "You said you'd introduce me to a murderer."

Rachel gave a wry smile. "He's hanging around in the Royal Academy Schools."

"Aren't the Schools out-of-bounds to members of the public?"

"Indeed, but I became a patron of Academy following the Italian art exhibition."

"I saw it in January." Leonora closed her eyes, as if picturing *Birth of Venus* in her mind. "Botticelli, Raphael…"

"To say nothing of the Old Master of propaganda, Signor Mussolini." Rachel frowned. "The Academy isn't a stage for dictators to strut around."

"Il Duce is not to everyone's taste, but he gets things done." Leonora exhaled. "Strong leadership is sadly lacking in this country."

"In that case," Rachel said coolly, "let me lead the way."

———

Jacob's excitement at having discovered Leonora's deception evaporated in minutes. When all was said and done, the woman was a writer, and writers commonly hid behind pseudonyms. To falsify an entry in *Who's Who* was taking a joke to an extreme, but she was a woman with a peculiar sense of humour.

Flicking again through her books, he noticed that Rachel had underlined the printed words on each of the two dedication pages. Clues to solve a puzzle?

Murder and Mysteries was dedicated simply "In Memory of My Father". The dedication in *Respectable Murders* was longer: "To George R. Sims, William Roughead, and other campaigners against injustice."

Sims and Roughead? Their names rang bells. When he looked them up, he had his answer. Sims was a journalist, Roughead a Scottish criminologist. They had earned respect for their crusades on behalf of two men falsely accused of murder. One was called Adolf Beck, the other Oscar Slater.

Leonora had chosen Slaterbeck as a pen name in tribute to victims of miscarriages of justice.

———

The corpse of an old man, flayed to the muscle with arms outstretched, was nailed to a wooden cross. A creature in torment, laid bare in anatomical detail. A figure too grotesque for sensitive public stomachs.

Leonora gasped.

"A plaster cast, believe it or not," Rachel said. "I've met creatures of flesh and blood who seem less real than James Legg."

They were in a room reached by way of a corridor for

servants rather than students. It was kept locked, but Rachel had collected a key from the porter.

"Most of the *écorché* figures are kept in the Life Room." Rachel pointed to a door in the wall opposite the flayed corpse. "We're forbidden to go in, for reasons of moral propriety. The only women admitted are models willing to strip off their clothes. The artists need to study the finer points of the female form."

Leonora indicated the crucified man. "And this poor devil?"

"James Legg was in his seventies, a Chelsea pensioner. One day, out of the blue, he shot a fellow resident of the Royal Hospital. Demented as he was, a plea of insanity failed. The judge sentenced him to be hanged and anatomised."

"There's nothing new about injustice," Leonora said in a low voice.

"The execution helped a group of Academicians to settle an argument. They believed that depictions of Christ on the cross misunderstood human anatomy. So they persuaded the authorities to allow an experiment in the interests of authenticity in art. With Legg's body still warm from the gallows, they nailed it to this cross."

"Extraordinary," Leonora breathed.

"The cadaver was flayed by an eminent surgeon. All the skin and fat cut away to expose the inner man. A sculptor made this cast for the Academy, so young artists could see for themselves the precise effect of crucifixion on the human form. During the war, an inconsiderate Zeppelin dropped a bomb on this building, but Legg survived unscathed. He's led a charmed death."

Leonora seemed hypnotised by the corpse. "And now he's achieved a curious form of immortality."

"Like so many notorious murderers," Rachel said. "Guilt is so much more memorable than innocence. We all remember

George Joseph Smith. How many of us can name those pitiful brides he drowned in the bath?"

"Nobody," Leonora said. "Like you, I'm a cynic. But let me explain why I wanted us to meet. I am about to hold a little house party at Mortmain Hall. I'd love it if you could join us."

"I'm notoriously unsociable."

"This is a very special gathering," Leonora said.

"Who are the other guests?"

"You're familiar with their names." Leonora ticked them off on her bony fingers. "Sylvia Gorrie, Henry Rolland, and Clive Danskin."

———

"What brings you here, young fellah-me-lad?" Haydn Williams demanded during a rare pause for breath.

Haydn was holding court in the Magpie and Stump, telling anyone who cared to listen that murder wasn't what it used to be. Even cut-and-dried capital crimes crumbled into anticlimax. Not like the good old days.

Jacob put two foaming tankards on the bar counter, and insinuated himself next to the older man. Haydn's audience needed no further encouragement to melt away. With no murder trials on at the Old Bailey, Jacob hadn't needed to be much of a detective to deduce where to find his quarry. He wanted to confirm his theory about Leonora Dobell's past, and when it came to old murder cases, Haydn was a walking encyclopaedia.

"Cheers. Wanted to pick your brains, actually."

Haydn took a gulp of beer. "Eyeing up a career as a crime reporter? Think again, my boy. It's yesterday's profession. Today's criminals aren't a patch on their predecessors. If you fancy a long life in print, you'll be better off compiling bloody crosswords."

"It's crimes of the past I'm interested in. Thought I'd come to the oracle."

"Flattery will get you everywhere." Haydn belched. "Unless you're hoping to scoop the *Witness*."

"Wouldn't dream of it," Jacob lied. "This isn't hold-the-front-page stuff. I was thinking of a feature about miscarriages of justice."

Haydn considered his reply with the help of another swig of bitter. "Careful, boy. Gomersall hates pandering to cranks who want to get rid of the rope."

"Heaven forbid. I thought I'd research old cases, where the people in question are likely to be dead. The accused, the witnesses." Jacob paused. "The judges who got things wrong."

"Tell you what I like about judges, boy. They turn the other cheek. They never sue, whatever you write about them."

"Not even the fearsome Judge Savernake?"

"Specially not him." Haydn wrinkled his nose, as if smelling a story. "Didn't you come across his daughter?"

"She keeps out of the public eye," Jacob said evasively. "A recluse, almost."

Haydn jabbed him in the midriff. "Sniffing around, were you, boy? Word is, she's a stunner. Not exactly a chip off the old block."

"I don't think she and her father were close."

"In his pomp, he was a terror, the Judge."

Jacob pretended to rack his brains. "What was the name of that chap he condemned, the one who turned out to be innocent?"

Haydn wagged a stubby finger. "Don't forget, a judge never finds a man guilty. It's always a jury which returns the verdict."

"But that's not the whole truth, is it? Some jurors are like sheep, they take their lead from the summing-up. If the judge is hostile…"

Haydn knocked back the rest of his bitter. "A hard man, Judge Savernake. I felt as guilty as sin whenever he cast his beady eye over me, and I was just a runny-nosed kid in the press gallery. But until his brain turned to mush, he was as sharp as a knife."

"You don't recall the case?" Jacob's show of disappointment was intended to provoke. Haydn prided himself on his formidable memory.

"Wait, wait. Give me a chance." Haydn banged his tankard on the door, and Jacob signalled to the barman for a refill. "Old Savernake didn't get much wrong. Except for the Gee trial."

"That's the one!" Jacob exclaimed in admiration, as he crossed his fingers behind his back.

Haydn tapped the side of his head. "There's more stuff up here than in the London Library, boy. Yes, must be Gee you're thinking of. Sad story."

"A real tear-jerker," Jacob agreed. "Remind me, what was it all about?"

"The usual." Haydn sighed. "Wife murder, of course."

Haydn's wife had run off with a tallyman twenty years ago. Haydn often boasted that it was only her desertion that had saved him from the noose, although he'd have had a good case for justifiable homicide. Jacob's sympathies lay with the former Mrs Williams.

He hazarded a guess. "Suffocated, wasn't she?"

"Lord, no. Beaten to a pulp with a poker in her own back parlour. Messy, very." Haydn lifted his replenished tankard. "Here's to crime. Come on, boy, drink up."

Jacob took a sip, washing the sour taste from his mouth. "I suppose it looked like an open-and-shut case?"

"Plain as the nose on your face, boy. Gee was a teacher at a school near York. The henpecked type. He'd married an older woman, and she wore the trousers. The police presumed that one day, he finally snapped. His alibi was so feeble it was embarrassing. It was almost an insult to the intelligence to ask people to believe him."

"Did nobody back it up?"

"Not a soul. Claimed he'd been telephoned by a stranger, who said he was passing on a message. Gee was asked to meet the headmaster urgently at the school one evening. When he showed up, nobody was there. He hung around for a while, then went back home to find his wife murdered. Nobody believed his story. The headmaster denied having sent any message. That was enough for the chief constable. He ordered his men to go in with all guns blazing, and they browbeat Gee into enough contradictions to justify an arrest. Feelings ran high because the killing was so vicious. Gee came up in front of old Savernake. I was sent up to cover the case, and the summing-up froze me to the marrow. To this day, I've never heard sarcasm as cruel."

As Haydn paused for a sup of beer, Jacob said, "He was biased against Gee?"

"It wasn't personal. The old bastard hated everyone. He was sure Gee was guilty, that was all. The Crown case wasn't watertight, and he didn't want the jury to be swayed by sympathy. Gee cut a pathetic figure in the dock. Sounded as though he was making up answers as he went along."

"And so he was found guilty of killing his wife?"

"Oh, yes. He'd have swung if the real killer hadn't been caught."

"Who was the murderer?"

Haydn searched his memory, aided by another mouthful of beer. "The school caretaker. Chap called McLean. He'd heard Gee say he'd won a tidy sum of cash on the Grand National sweepstake. Fifty quid, if memory serves. Beginner's luck: he wasn't even a betting man. His daughter was away at boarding school, and Mrs Gee was supposed to be visiting an aunt. McLean made the phone call in a disguised voice to lure Gee out of the house. Common or garden burglary. Snag was that Mrs Gee had a migraine, and stayed at home in bed. When she heard McLean breaking in, she went downstairs, and he panicked. The poker was just too tempting."

"Gee was released from prison?"

"Once the Home Secretary got his skates on. There was a public outcry, questions asked in Parliament. The fuss probably tipped the Judge over the edge. Not that it did Gee any good."

"Why not?"

"The trial made mincemeat of him. He'd lost his wife, then been convicted of a crime he didn't commit. Unbearable for a fellow with a weak heart. He'd only been home a week when he dropped down dead in his own back parlour. The very spot where his wife was murdered." He took another swig from the tankard. "You know what I call that?"

"No."

Haydn stared moodily into the middle distance. "Poetic injustice, that's what."

———

"You've arranged a very exclusive gathering," Rachel said. "Three guests who were accused of murder. Each of them narrowly escaped being sentenced to death."

"Each noted as a victim of a miscarriage of justice," Leonora said.

There was a challenge in her dark eyes. Once again, the two women were like duellists *en garde* as they faced each other in the company of the flayed remains of a murderer.

"Surely they'd prefer to bury the past?" Rachel asked.

"I can be very persuasive," Leonora said softly. "It will be a unique occasion. I do hope you can be tempted."

"How kind of you to want to include me." Rachel relaxed into a smile. "You're right. I simply can't resist."

———

Five minutes after leaving the Magpie and Stump, Jacob was back at Clarion House. Haydn had given him plenty of leads to follow up in the archives. On his way into the entrance vestibule, he bumped into George Poyser.

"And where are you off to in such a tearing rush? You were very quiet at the conference this morning. Don't tell me you've come up with a scoop?"

"If only. I want to look up an old trial. You may remember it. A man named Gee was found guilty of battering his wife to death. He was saved from the gallows because the real killer was found."

"Gee, you say?" A faraway look came into the news editor's protuberant eyes. Poyser wasn't a crime specialist, but his powers of recall were phenomenal. "Hmmm, the name rings a bell. Can you give me more to go on?"

"The crime was committed in Yorkshire, about a quarter of a century ago. I'm not sure how the police managed to find the real culprit. Or why they didn't do so before Gee was tried and convicted."

"Sorry, I'm not sure I can…oh, wait! Was Gee the chap with the daughter, seventeen or eighteen years old?"

Jacob was taken aback. "Yes, as it happens."

"That's the one!" Poyser beamed in self-congratulation. "Yes, it was a nine days' wonder."

"Why do you ask about the daughter?"

"Because she played the detective. If not for her, the murder might never have been solved."

———

"So you got what you wanted," Clifford Trueman said.

Rachel had joined the three Truemans in the conservatory at Gaunt House. Outside, roses entwined around the redwood pergola had burst into crimson bloom. Through an open window, she caught a scent of damask.

"She always does," his wife said.

Trueman shrugged. "Better to be born lucky than rich."

"She's lucky and rich," Hetty said. "To prove it, I've made her favourite soup. Jerusalem artichoke."

Hetty was a devotee of Mrs Beeton. Rachel laughed. "I've earned it. We've been invited to Mortmain Hall."

"What did you learn from the Dobell woman?" Martha asked.

"First and foremost, Vickers told the truth, what little he knew of it. The house party is going ahead. Danskin has joined Sylvia Gorrie and Rolland on the guest list. As for selling off the Mortmain art treasures, she's quite brazen about it. Admits her husband is in no position to argue. She reckons she's got the green light from the solicitor to the family trust. It's a West End firm, Mulkerrin and Morgans. Said to be highly respectable."

Hetty sniffed. "A likely story."

"I believe her. In this day and age, running an estate in the country costs a fortune. And there must be some respectable lawyers."

"It's not like you to be so trusting. What's her game?"

"I'm sure she's hugging herself with delight at the prospect of playing lady of the manor with three people who were tried for murder, and the daughter of a sadistic judge."

"Just for her own private amusement?"

"I wouldn't put it past her. Besides, why am I poking my nose into her affairs? Just because I can, and I'm inquisitive, and there's a mystery to be solved. At least she can fall back on the author's excuse for indulging in frivolity. She might get a book out of it."

"Murder isn't a game."

"Games can be deadly serious."

"There's something else," Martha said.

During their years together on the island, she'd rarely spoken up. Even in London, Martha much preferred to listen, and keep her opinions to herself. The others looked at her.

Rachel said quietly, "What is it?"

"In Leonora Dobell's eyes, the Judge was your father."

"She thinks he was, yes. Everyone must think so, forever and a day."

"Then she believes your father condemned hers to death."

"Hubert Gee didn't hang," Trueman said.

"Martha is right, though," Rachel said. "The trial destroyed him."

"Have you considered what that means for you?" Martha folded her arms. "What if Leonora wants to avenge him?"

Chapter 13

During the afternoon, Jacob trawled through the archives of the *Clarion*, piecing together a picture of the Gee tragedy. Haydn's memory hadn't betrayed him. The murder of Priscilla Gee was bloody and brutal enough to make the story supremely newsworthy. For a schoolteacher to be prime suspect put the icing on the journalists' cake. The dead woman was a martinet who had led her diffident husband a dog's life. The police wasted no time in charging him, and very little in pursuing other lines of enquiry.

The couple had one daughter, but no mention was made of her in the press until after her father was sentenced to death. At that point came news of McLean's arrest. Leonora Gee, horrified by the trial but determined to prove her father's innocence, had played the amateur detective.

She'd befriended a burly young police officer who resented the way the chief constable had bullied his subordinates into making a quick arrest. In the hope of making a name for himself, he'd asked around, and discovered that ever since the murder, McLean had been splashing money as if there were no tomorrow. Leonora telephoned the caretaker, giving a false name and claiming to have seen him leaving the Gees' house after the crime. She demanded ten pounds in return for her silence.

Deceiving him by telephone, just as he'd deceived her father, appealed to her sense of justice. Once again, a simple ruse worked a treat. McLean turned up at the rendezvous point, an empty warehouse in York, but instead of an envelope stuffed with banknotes, he brought along a ball-peen hammer. She'd talked the young constable into joining her in the warehouse, and he gave McLean a taste of his truncheon before any more harm could be done.

Leonora Gee shrank from the public gaze. The story cried out for a heroine with fair curls, dimples, and rosy cheeks, not a plain young woman with an abrupt manner who hated the press for presuming her father's guilt. The newspapermen's dismay was compounded when their hopes of a burgeoning romance were stillborn. The young constable earned a commendation and lapped up the publicity, but he'd served his purpose. Leonora never saw him again.

When her father died, she suffered an emotional collapse. The last information Jacob could find was that after spending a fortnight in hospital, she'd gone to live with an elderly aunt. All requests for interviews were refused. The old lady regarded journalists as spawn of the devil. They'd hounded Gee, and they wouldn't be allowed to torment his ailing daughter.

The press was even deprived of an execution when McLean strangled himself with a bootlace in his prison cell. There was nothing left to say. Hardly anyone mourned Priscilla Gee, and her husband had few friends. Today's sensation became yesterday's news, and Leonora Gee disappeared from public view. Jacob could trace no further mention of the name.

Only in 1918 did she resurface, with the announcement of her engagement. Miss Leonora Slaterbeck was to marry Mr Felix Dobell of Mortmain Hall. There was no hint of a connection to a pre-war *cause célèbre*. Priscilla and Hubert Gee were dead, buried, and forgotten.

———

"Bryce, a word in your ear."

A firm hand grasped the bony shoulder of Wesley Bryce, Assistant Commissioner (Crime) in the Metropolitan Police. He'd just slipped into Lord's for half an hour's cricket in between business engagements at the Yard. A chap needed a break; he compared it to cleansing the palate. Just a pity that England's bowlers were being put to the sword by the Aussies.

Looking up into the cold blue eyes of Colonel Hemmings, he felt like a schoolboy caught playing truant. Was it absurd to suspect the colonel of turning up in the Long Room precisely because he expected to find him here?

"Afternoon, Colonel." He gestured towards the field of play. "Damn good game."

"We let them off the hook." The colonel was not to be sidetracked. "There's a newspaper reporter, name of Flint."

"Writes for the *Clarion*." Wesley Bryce liked to be regarded as well informed, up to date, on top of his job. He was hopeful about his prospects when the present commissioner retired. "We know of him at the Yard. Inspector Oakes..."

"Yes, there was that business earlier in the year."

Bryce frowned. "You're aware of that?"

"We like to keep tabs on things." The colonel's face never gave anything away. It was one of the reasons why Bryce disliked him. "Flint is making a nuisance of himself."

"Sorry to hear that," Bryce said, not sounding in the least apologetic. "Asking questions, is he? Writing articles? I suppose reporters have to do something to occupy their time."

Sarcasm bounced off the colonel like pellets off a tank. "He's raking over old coals. Unwise. People can still get burned."

"Any particular coals?"

The colonel's eyes narrowed. "No names, no pack drill."

"It's rather difficult, if you won't..."

"He's a crime correspondent. Plenty of crime for him to report in this city, as you're well aware. People are saying the streets of London aren't safe to walk down."

Bryce gritted his teeth. "Our manpower..."

"Put a stop to it, will you, before any harm is done? There's a good chap."

The colonel's tone was casual; he might have been commenting on the state of the wicket. For all the warmth of the Long Room on the last day of June, however, Bryce felt a sudden chill.

"It's a free country." It was time to make a stand. "We can't control the press."

"It's a free country because we take pains to guard the national interest," the colonel said softly. "Have Oakes speak to him."

"Flint's a journalist. He doesn't..."

"I'll leave it in your capable hands." Resigned applause rippled around them as a batsman in a baggy green cap crashed another boundary to the boards. "I'll be getting back to the office. You might do the same. Plenty in your in-tray, I'll be bound. And this match is a lost cause."

"It's too soon to write the game off," Bryce retorted. "We shouldn't give up."

"Sometimes," the colonel said, "one needs to realise when one is beaten."

———

"I made enquiries at the Law Society," Trueman said on rejoining the others in the conservatory.

"Any luck?" Rachel asked.

"More than I expected. I spoke to a very helpful young lady."

Hetty grunted. "You meet a lot of very helpful young ladies, Cliff Trueman."

"True enough," Rachel said. "That rugged exterior is deceptive. He can turn on the charm like a tap."

"Are you going to let me get a word in?" he demanded.

Rachel took a swig of lemonade. "I'm all ears."

"There are two partners in the firm. Mulkerrin runs the show. Famously discreet; you'll not get much change out of him. His partner Morgans died a year back, shortly after his son came into the firm. Morgans junior is a different kettle of fish. At first he refused to follow family tradition and go into legal practice. Effete type, by the sound of him. Fancies himself as a writer."

"How dreadful," Rachel said. "What does he write?"

"Poetry or some such." Cliff's taste in verse didn't extend beyond "Vitaï Lampada". "It was only when his father took ill that he was forced to buckle down and go into the business. Mulkerrin has no time for his dilettante ways. Or his tendency to gossip."

"It's a truth universally acknowledged," Rachel said, "that a single woman in possession of a good fortune must be in want of legal advice. I think I should call on young Morgans. We can have a good gossip."

The telephone rang and Hetty answered. After listening for a moment, she mouthed "Jacob Flint."

"Let me talk to him." Rachel took the receiver. "Hello, Jacob. Done your homework?"

"I've made enquiries about Gilbert Payne." He sounded breathless, excited.

"And the Clandestine Club?"

"I'll pay it a visit as soon as I can. As for Henry Rolland, reading between the lines, Leonora Dobell suspects that he murdered Phoebe Evison. Just as she hinted that Sylvia Gorrie wasn't innocent of her husband's death."

"Leonora likes playing with fire."

"What's more, I've discovered that her maiden name wasn't Slaterbeck but Gee."

"Good work," Rachel said. "Congratulations."

"You knew already, I suppose?" He couldn't quite squeeze the disappointment out of his voice. "And that her own father was convicted of murder?"

"Yes."

"I'm not sure I can tell you anything you don't know," he said sulkily.

"I had a head start," she said. "When I lived on the island, Foyle's delivered a fat parcel of books every month. The Judge kept abreast of everything that dealt with crime and the law. He also kept detailed papers of his own. When he was too gaga to care, I carried on reading. His library was his one gift to me. No university could have offered me a better education. Years ago, I learned about the Gee case. It's only lately that I've made the connection with Leonora Slaterbeck."

"Why did she change her name? It doesn't make sense. Thanks to her, Hubert Gee was vindicated. He was as much a victim as his wife."

"A victim of the Judge, you mean. But can't you see? Leonora was desperate to put the murder and the trial behind her. No wonder her health collapsed after her father's death. Who could bear to be haunted by those memories? In her shoes, I'd have changed my name as well."

Trueman flashed a warning look, and Hetty put her hand to her mouth. Rachel stuck out the tip of her tongue.

"And then," Jacob said, "she married into the Dobell family."

"In the war, Mortmain Hall was transformed into a military hospital. Leonora worked there as a VAD. Felix Dobell was badly injured in France and came home as a patient. After his wife's death, he turned to Leonora."

"Have you met her?"

"Yes, but she's going back up to Yorkshire for the weekend. She's invited me to a house party."

"At Mortmain Hall?"

"Yes. The guest list is small and select, if I say so myself. The other names you know. Sylvia Gorrie, Henry Rolland, Clive Danskin."

He exhaled. "What's she playing at?"

"All may be revealed over the weekend."

"Be careful. Judge Savernake's summing-up condemned her father."

"You believe I'm in danger?" Rachel laughed. "Great minds think alike. Martha has already warned me to watch my step."

"Have you accepted this invitation?"

"How could I refuse?"

"But…"

"I can take care of myself. My main concern is you."

"Me?"

"Especially if you go to the Clandestine Club."

"What do you know about it?"

"Not enough. But I know what happened to Gilbert Payne."

———

"Seen anything of Flint lately?" Wesley Bryce asked as Inspector Philip Oakes was about to leave his room.

Oakes stopped by the door. He'd been called in ostensibly

to give Bryce an update on an investigation into dope smuggling from France. Oakes was that rarity among police officers, a graduate of Caius rather than the university of life. His prosperous background, good looks, and intellectual agility hadn't made him popular among his fellow officers, but his thirst for hard work and an ability to get results had earned a grudging respect from all but the chronically prejudiced.

"Not for some time. He covered the Danskin trial. I read his reports. He was obviously as surprised at the outcome as we all were."

"You read the *Clarion*?" Bryce believed that a touch of levity with one's subordinates worked wonders when a difficult conversation loomed. As long as people didn't become too familiar. "I'd have put you down as a *Times* man."

"That too, sir. I like to keep in touch."

"Excellent." Bryce's smile of encouragement faded. "The devil of it is, Flint is putting one or two Very Important Noses out of joint. Raking over old coals, that's all I've been told. I wonder if you could give him a nudge?"

"A nudge, sir?" Oakes was impassive.

"All right, I won't make any bones about it," Bryce said. "I've been asked to make sure that he's warned off."

"Although we don't know what we're warning him about?"

It didn't take much to rub away Bryce's veneer of good humour. His thin lips almost disappeared as he pressed them together. "Damn it, I've told you all that I know. See to it, will you?"

"Very well, sir."

———

No sooner had Jacob finished speaking to Rachel, then a call came through from Scotland Yard. After the routine pleasantries,

Oakes said it would be grand to catch up; they could have a bite, his treat. Jacob wondered what he was after. High-flying detectives didn't stand crime reporters lunch for the fun of it.

Come to that, what was Leonora Dobell playing at? A house party for acquitted murder suspects at Mortmain Hall? He'd love to be a fly on the wall. There was much more to that woman than met the eye. And what about the Clandestine Club? Rachel's warning only spurred him on.

Returning to the reference room, he picked up *Who's Who* and looked up Leonora's husband. His entry was brief:

Dobell, Felix, landowner, *b*. Mortmain, 1879, *o.surv.s.* of the late Oswyn Dobell, 1 s. (*dec'd*), *m*. Elspeth Barnes, (*dec'd*), 1906, Leonora Slaterbeck, 1918, *Educ:* Giggleswick School. *Recreations*: jigsaw puzzles. *Address:* Mortmain Hall, Yorkshire.

Jigsaws! A means for an invalid to pass the time, Jacob supposed. It couldn't be much of a life, stuck in a draughty old mansion, especially if you were old and frail and your only child was dead. No wonder Leonora escaped to London. He wondered about their marriage. A decision to spend the rest of your life with another person struck him as an extraordinary gamble. His own parents had enjoyed a blissful union until his father's death during the war, but few couples lived in such harmony. Jacob loved the company of women, but he'd not come close to finding anyone he wanted to live with forever.

There was scant information about the Dobells in the books. Time to take another tack. He'd consult the *Clarion*'s expert on tittle-tattle about the gentry, Griselda Farquharson. A conversation with a woman so overpowering and loquacious was not for the faint-hearted, but a lifetime in the social whirl had given Griselda an unrivalled knowledge of the upper echelons of society. Most of the *Clarion*'s staff gave her a wide berth, but Jacob rather liked her. Her snobbishness and vanity had a satiric edge.

After signing his correspondence for the day, he wandered out to the lobby. The *Clarion* had a pretty new girl on the main desk, a Scot whose curly hair, cherubic features, and cheeky sense of humour reminded him of the actress Renee Houston. He enjoyed flirting with her, and it had crossed his mind to invite her out for a drink. She was already putting on her hat and coat, and he realised with a start that it was half past five.

"I don't want to keep you, Maggie, but one last thing before you go, if you don't mind."

"For you, Mr Flint, anything." She arched her eyebrows. "And I wouldn't say that to everyone. Specially not when I'm in a tearing hurry."

"You're very kind. And how many times do I need to tell you, my name's Jacob?" He grinned. "Do you have a number for Griselda Farquharson?"

She giggled. "Biting off more than you can chew there, aren't you? She may be a hundred years old, but they say she's still a man-eater."

"Don't worry, I can look after myself."

"Brave words, Jacob." She checked her notepad and scrawled down a number in a large, unformed hand. "There you are. Now, I'd love to stop and chat, but I mustn't be late."

"Thanks, Maggie. And where are you off to in such a rush?"

"My young man's taking me out for dinner, and then to the Lyceum." Another giggle. "Guess which show he's chosen?"

"I'm hopeless at guessing."

"A likely story! You're a reporter, aren't you? Anyway, it's *Here Comes the Bride*. Ever so popular. You must know the songs?" She warbled a few bars that Jacob found hopelessly unrecognisable. "Swear not to tell a soul, but I think he's going to pop the question."

He forced a smile. Anyway, she wasn't really his type. "Have a marvellous time."

"You bet I will!"

With that, Maggie was gone, leaving Jacob to spend another night on his own in Exmouth Market.

Chapter 14

Mulkerrin and Morgans had guarded the secrets of the wealthy for generations. Their inconspicuous offices were in keeping with the discretion for which the firm was noted. The entrance was tucked away in a passage off Albemarle Street, and the lettering of the ancient brass plate on the wall was faded almost to illegibility. The door was painted grey, the step that led up to it well worn. There was no bell-push, only a venerable cast-iron knocker decorated with the face of a disapproving owl.

It took fully one minute for the door to open in response to Rachel's knock. A wizened face peered out. It belonged to an aged, Tiresias-like figure whose inscrutability made the Sphinx seem rubber-faced.

"My name is Rachel Savernake. I have an appointment at noon."

Tiresias indicated with an age-spotted paw that she should go into a waiting room. The austere decor was confined to yellowing professional certificates of long-dead partners in the firm. The *Times* was on the table; a wall shelf was occupied by *Who's Who*, *Debrett's*, *Crockford's*, and the *Law List*.

The door opened, and a sonorous voice enquired, "Miss Savernake?"

A portly man in his fifties, with wispy sandy hair combed in a doomed attempt to conceal a bald patch, considered her through gold-rimmed pince-nez, like a country doctor examining a patient for symptoms. Rachel returned his gaze, unblinking. He gave a cough which sounded like an admission of defeat.

"Permit me to introduce myself." Beaming, he slipped into his best bedside manner. "Angus Mulkerrin, senior partner. Delighted to meet you."

Rachel stood up. As they shook hands, he winced at the firmness of her grip.

"I was expecting to see Mr Morgans."

"Ah yes." He coughed again. "Perhaps you'd be good enough to spare me a moment?"

Without waiting for a reply, he waddled down a short corridor into a large room, his personal fiefdom. A wall of shelves held a row of law reports arranged in date order. The furniture was in the style of Sheraton, the carpet was Persian.

Mulkerrin ushered her into a chair and took a seat at his desk. Behind him hung an oil painting of a bald man with an extravagant sandy moustache and gold pince-nez. A nineteenth-century ancestor; the pince-nez must be a Mulkerrin family heirloom.

"A privilege to meet you, Miss Savernake. Your father's long illness and subsequent death was a grievous loss to the English legal profession."

"So I've been told."

"Our paths never crossed, I'm sorry to say. He rose to eminence in the field of criminal law, whereas I'm merely a humble practitioner in the law of wills, trusts, and probate."

Mulkerrin struck Rachel as being precisely as humble as every other professional man she'd ever met. "I was given your firm's name by Leonora Dobell of Mortmain Hall. I believe you have acted for the Dobell family for many years."

He bestowed an ingratiating smile. "Of course, it would be unprofessional to comment on the existence or otherwise of a relationship with a client, but I can say that we value any recommendation most highly."

Trueman's information about Mulkerrin's devotion to confidentiality was spot on. Rachel gave him another chance to rise to the bait. "She spoke highly of you."

"Most kind, most kind. It will be my pleasure to assist you to the best of my ability. How may I...?"

"Forgive me, Mr Mulkerrin. I don't mean to seem rude or ungrateful, but I did make a specific arrangement to see your partner and I don't want to trouble you unnecessarily."

Mulkerrin's sandy eyebrows twitched. It was probably as close as he ever came to registering astonishment. "Of course, dear lady, of course. But let me first explain myself. If I may say so, I have toiled for thirty years in the vineyards of Chancery law. This firm has served some of the country's most distinguished families. Louis Morgans's father and I belonged to the third generation of partners. Louis joined the practice shortly before Humphrey Morgans's untimely demise, but he is young and..."

"Mr Morgans's lack of experience doesn't concern me. He can turn to you for wise counsel whenever the need arises."

"Naturally, my dear young lady. But—"

"Judge Savernake's estate is, to put it with a lawyer's delicacy, not inconsiderable. His affairs were looked after by Gabriel Hannaway, who died earlier this year."

"Ah yes, such a tragedy." Mulkerrin's regret was perfunctory.

"I need to consider which firm to retain for the long term. So it's only right that I should speak to the younger members of the practices in question before arriving at a decision. I'm sure you understand."

The eyebrows twitched again. "Do I understand that you are seeking to…draw a comparison between ourselves and professional colleagues in other firms?"

Rachel put a hand to her mouth. "Please forgive me if I seem impolite. It's simply that I lack the business experience of a man of the world. I do hope you will indulge me."

Angus Mulkerrin hadn't toiled in the vineyards for thirty years without knowing a fait accompli when he saw one. He coughed long enough to adjust to the inevitable.

"Your approach is certainly novel, Miss Savernake. If you are quite certain…"

"I am." She smiled sweetly and folded her arms.

"Very well." Another cough. "It may be that your…unorthodoxy will strike a chord with Louis."

Rachel was sure that Mulkerrin yearned to make the best of a bad job. The fees to be earned for looking after the Savernake fortune were not to be coughed at. He rang a bell, and Louis Morgans came in.

Mulkerrin made the introductions and said, "I'm sure the two of you will get on like a house on fire."

Rachel surrendered to an irresistible urge to simper. "Oh, I do so hope we will."

———

"Judge Savernake, eh?" Louis Morgans asked. "Lord, what a turn-up for the books. He sat on the bench long before my time, but I've heard a few stories. Quite a tartar, eh?"

They were ensconced in the junior partner's cubbyhole, a fraction of the size of Mulkerrin's domain. It was a warm day, and the atmosphere was stuffy; by opening the sash window, Morgans had allowed the smells of the rubbish bins in the passageway to drift inside. Every available surface was cluttered with papers tied with pink ribbon; Rachel inferred that whenever he was given a legal problem to chew over, Morgans bailed himself out of trouble by briefing learned counsel to do whatever was necessary.

Rachel leaned towards him in conspiratorial fashion. "Between you and me, he was an old terror."

He smirked at this confidence. "Parents, eh?"

Louis Morgans was pale and sleepy-eyed, with a weak chin and an even weaker handshake. Long brown hair and a dazzling yellow tie were token gestures towards bohemianism. His languid pose suggested that he'd rather be reclining on a sofa, cigar holder in one hand and gin rickey in the other. Rachel diagnosed a character fashioned by a mother's worship and a father's contempt.

She waved at a pile of deed boxes in a corner of the room. The second box from the top bore the name *Dobell*. "I was delighted when Leonora Dobell gave me your firm's name," she said. "I must admit I find myself bewildered by legal affairs."

"Frankly, Miss Savernake, I sympathise." He treated her to an impudent smirk. "Take it from me, they're much duller than most affairs."

"Please call me Rachel." Her tone was coquettish.

"Splendid! And I'm Louis." He smirked again. "So you want a guiding hand, eh?"

"If it's not too much trouble."

"Perish the thought! No need to fuss over the legal niceties. Your pater died last year, didn't he? Probate granted, and whatnot?"

"The formalities have been dealt with. I wish to look forward, not back."

"It will be an honour to serve you, Rachel. Let me assure you of my closest personal attention."

"That's very good of you, Louis. It would take such a weight off my mind."

"Think nothing of it. Absolute pleasure." He flapped a neatly manicured hand. "Tell you what, might you fancy dinner sometime? My treat, of course. No question of the old taxi meter running. Just a chance for us to get to know each other better."

"How kind! I'd love to."

Fishing a leather-bound diary out of a desk drawer, he said, "When would suit you?"

"It just so happens," she said, "that I'm free tomorrow evening."

His eyebrows shot up. "Splendid! Shall we say seven?"

"Your wish is my command."

For a fleeting moment, Rachel thought she'd overplayed her hand, but Louis Morgans's grin made clear that he took subservience as his due.

"Do you know Foibles in Soho, by any chance? I'll have my secretary reserve a private booth, so that we can...talk undisturbed. As it happens, I'm on rather good terms with both the head waiter and the sommelier." He leaned back in his chair. "That's the secret, Rachel. It's all about who you know."

"I'm sure," she said meekly, "you never spoke a truer word."

———

After Clifford Trueman had driven her back to Gaunt House, Rachel changed into a new Jantzen swimsuit, a fetching shade of carmine. She swam a dozen lengths in the rooftop pool before joining the Truemans. As she towelled her hair, she regaled Martha and Hetty with an account of her visit to Albemarle Street.

"Tomorrow night, I'll pump Morgans about Leonora and her

husband. Meanwhile, Cliff can do a little breaking and entering. I'd like to peek inside the Dobells' deed box."

"You know where it's kept?" Martha asked.

"In plain sight in Morgans's office. The sash window is easy to force, even if Morgans closes it before he leaves for the day."

"You expect Morgans to talk about Leonora?" Hetty asked.

"If my personal charms aren't enough to loosen his tongue, the prospect of fat fees should do the trick. And I'll ask about Gilbert Payne. Who knows, their mutual love of poetry may have brought them together."

"At the Clandestine Club?" Martha asked.

"Where else?"

———

"Let me get this clear." Jacob washed down the last slice of his veal-and-ham pie with a mouthful of pale ale. "I've blotted my copybook with someone in authority. You don't know who or how or why. But I've been found guilty of raking over old coals. Whatever the hell that means."

Oakes put down his soup spoon. They were lunching at Stone's Chop House on Panton Street. Jacob had chosen the venue partly because he'd heard that the helpings were lavish and the beer excellent and partly to see whether it was true that the waiters wore brown knickerbockers and red waistcoats; and indeed it was.

"That's about the size of it." Oakes considered his companion. "You'll know what they are talking about."

"Perhaps I do," Jacob said. "Perhaps I don't."

"I bet you do. Care to let me in on the secret?"

Jacob rubbed his chin. "I reported the Danskin trial. It prompted my interest in previous miscarriages of justice."

"I've heard it said," Oakes snapped, "that Danskin's acquittal was the miscarriage of justice."

"Careful what you say, Inspector." Jacob grinned. "He's an innocent man. Isn't he?"

"So the court ruled." Oakes shook his head. "It wasn't my case, but the experts were morally certain that he set the car on fire with malice aforethought. Which isn't the same as proving it. Beyond reasonable doubt is a high threshold."

"Better that a hundred guilty men go free than one innocent man be convicted."

"I'd take a lot of convincing if the guilty man had killed someone I cared for."

"But not if you were the innocent man?"

"Maybe not." Oakes tapped his spoon on the table. "Do you mind telling me which cases you're looking into?"

"Not at all," Jacob said disingenuously. He didn't intend to mention Gilbert Payne's resurrection in the form of Bertram Jones. "As long as you promise not to spill the beans to the *Witness* or the *Trumpet*."

"Cross my heart and hope to die."

"The Wirral bungalow murder is one case. The Gorrie trial is another."

Oakes's brow wrinkled. "Going back a while, aren't you? Refresh my memory."

"A Liverpool businessman was arrested on a count of strangling his mistress in their love nest. Just in time, the cuckolded husband was discovered to be the culprit. As for Mrs Gorrie, her boyfriend murdered her old man, but she was charged too. She'd egged her lover on, but she was acquitted."

Oakes gave him a sharp glance. "Is that all?"

"This complaint you've had, it's a mystery to me."

"Very well, I've passed the message on to you. What happens

now is no concern of mine." Oakes beckoned for the bill. "So how is Miss Rachel Savernake these days?"

"I've barely seen her."

"You surprise me. Such an extraordinary woman."

"She isn't easy to get to know."

"I can imagine." Oakes eyed him speculatively. "You'd like to get to know her better?"

"She's rich, clever, and beautiful." Jacob laughed. "Draw your own conclusions. If only I were rich, clever, and handsome, I might stand a chance."

"I wonder if she's lonely."

"In London, with its teeming millions?"

"Especially in London."

Jacob leaned forward. "Mind if I ask a question?"

"Fire away."

"What do you know about the Clandestine Club?"

Oakes frowned. "Why do you ask?"

"No particular reason."

"Reporters don't ask questions for no particular reason any more than policeman do." Jacob said nothing. "Is this anything to do with those old coals you've raked over?"

"Sylvia Gorrie and Henry Rolland?" Jacob still didn't want to let slip his interest in Gilbert Payne. "They're not connected with the Clandestine Cub, as far as I know."

"Then why ask?"

"I've heard of the place, but I don't know anything about it. Call it an innocent enquiry."

"There's nothing innocent about the Clandestine Club."

"You've piqued my curiosity. What do you know about the Clandestine?"

"Your maiden aunt would call it a sink of iniquity."

"Now I'm even more interested."

Oakes grunted. "You'll find the Clan in a smoky basement in Soho, not ten minutes' walk from here. There's no name on the door, and no official telephone number. It's for people in the know."

"Why don't the police shut it down?"

Oakes glowered at him. Both men knew that when it came to Soho clubs, officers of the Metropolitan Police had an embarrassing history of turning blind eyes and pocketing bribes.

"The Clan isn't a conventional vice den. People run nightclubs to make easy money by robbing their clients blind. They lack patience and discipline, so they take shortcuts, break rules. Sometimes I think these places are called disorderly houses because the managements are so inept. They flout the licensing laws, they harbour criminals and prostitutes, they allow every Tom, Dick, and Harry to become a member. And then they have the brass neck to squeal because Harry happens to be a plainclothes policeman."

"But the Clandestine Club is a legitimate set-up?"

"It's a haven for rich decadents, but thank the Lord I'm not responsible for policing nightlife in Soho. Between you and me, I'm glad the Clan isn't my pigeon."

"But?"

"I smell something rotten. Call it instinct." Oakes sighed. "Or just call me old-fashioned and strait-laced."

"If the club attracts undesirables, why don't your colleagues raid it one night? Make a few arrests, send out a message?"

"Easier said than done. As with Danskin, reasonable belief is one thing. Proving guilt to a criminal standard gives us a mountain to climb. Hearsay, gossip, rumour, that's our stock-in-trade, just like your game. But it's not enough to bring a case to court."

"I've never read about the place in the press."

"Other nightclubs thrive on publicity, good or bad. The

Clandestine lives up to its name." Oakes heaved a sigh. "Nobody blabs to the *News of the World*, no crimes on the premises are ever reported. The club started up ten years ago, and it's survived when most of the competition has closed because there are so few customers around. The idle rich are a dying breed."

Jacob grinned. "At least one good thing came out of the Wall Street Crash, then?"

Oakes wasn't in the mood for levity. "I hear the Krug costs less than you pay at the Criterion. The members aren't exploited financially. They aren't your common or garden undesirables."

"So who are they?"

"People with money, breeding, the right sort of background. And with tastes for the…exotic, of course."

"Or so you believe."

Oakes gave a weary shrug of the shoulders. They walked to the door. "You asked the question. I'm trying to give an honest answer."

"Thanks," Jacob said. "Who owns the Clan?"

"Wish I knew. There's a tangled web of holding companies, subsidiaries, and frontmen. Who holds the purse strings, I don't know. Whoever they may be, they are very well advised. Police powers of entry aren't as wide as everyone thinks."

"Or as Scotland Yard likes to make out?"

The inspector's rueful smile spoke for itself. They stepped into the street. The sun was high, with not a cloud to be seen. "In the absence of evidence of wrongdoing, what can we do?"

"So you've given up?"

Oakes glanced around. Nobody was in earshot. "We're still off the record?"

"You can trust me."

A bitten-off laugh. "As much as I trust any reporter."

"I'll take that as a compliment."

"Don't get carried away; there's no other journalist I'd trust an inch. Officers from C Division have tried to get in once or twice, but their efforts always backfire. The people who run the Clan keep one step ahead of us. The minute that m'learned friends send a stiff letter to the commissioner, threatening injunctions and Lord knows what else, he runs a mile."

"Due to retire next year, isn't he?"

A rare note of bitterness sharpened the inspector's voice. "All he wants is a quiet life."

"Don't we all?"

Oakes looked him in the eye. "Not you and me. Good luck with investigating the Clandestine. You'll need it."

Jacob shook his hand. "I didn't say I was conducting an investigation."

"Of course you didn't." Oakes gave him a bleak smile. "Nobody has asked me to warn you off the Clandestine, as it happens."

"If it's so well run, how can I get in, when I'm not a member?"

Oakes thought for a moment. "Are you free tomorrow? Very well, leave it with me."

"Thanks."

"If curiosity does get the better of you, remember that the people behind the Clan are ruthless. Take good care of yourself."

Chapter 15

"Jacob darling, how marvellous!"

Griselda Farquharson's kiss of greeting was as exuberant as her tumbling black curls, her kohl-smeared eyes, and her plump, powdered cheeks. Shocking-pink lipstick matched her chiffon dress, complete with train sweeping down from her shoulders. Her lavender perfume was so pungent that it brought tears to Jacob's eyes. He'd met her only half a dozen times in his life, but she hugged him to her voluminous curves as if he were a long-lost son.

Her embrace knocked the breath out of him. Effusiveness was hardly conduct becoming to the august environs of the Highgate Literary and Scientific Institute. The Reading Room was supposed to be an oasis of tranquillity. A bust occupied an alcove, paintings of former presidents adorned the wall by the door, and beneath them stood a large globe. At the rear of the room, steps led up to the librarian's rooms, with a bell next to the door.

The door had a peephole. Jacob wondered if the librarian used it to check if Griselda had gone before emerging. The members present had buried their heads in their books and newspapers. Nobody tutted in disapproval, or tried to shush Griselda into silence. Any attempt to cow her into conformity was doomed to failure. Griselda was a law unto herself. Genteel yet outrageous; vain yet amusing; snobbish yet brimming with *joie de vivre*. A force of nature.

Not that there was anything natural about her appearance. He couldn't make out whether she wore a wig or employed an eccentric hairdresser, and he'd no idea how old she might be. Sixty-five, seventy, seventy-five? Surely not eighty? With extraordinary cunning, she'd made it impossible for anyone to guess.

"Good of you to spare me half an hour," he mumbled once he'd got his breath back.

"My pleasure, dear Jacob. The very least I can do for a fellow scribe."

Griselda had written the *Clarion's* weekly society column for upward of twenty years. For a newspaper aimed at the working and lower-middle classes, gossip about the idle rich, or what remained of them following the collapse in the stock market, seemed as out of place as a hymn in a pantomime. Yet readers lapped up her accounts of the high life, and Walter Gomersall wouldn't hear of dropping them. When hard-bitten journalists moaned that Griselda was a joke, he pointed out that they didn't object to the *Clarion's* cartoons. If someone suggested that she made up anecdotes whenever she ran short of material, he said that truth was stranger than fiction, especially when it came to Britain's upper crust.

"Thanks. Sorry to interrupt your researches."

Griselda lived in Highgate. On the telephone, she'd announced she was spending every spare moment in the Institute, researching her family background. All he knew was that she'd buried three husbands. Unkind colleagues said they'd died of exhaustion.

"Think nothing of it! I've been ploughing through old direc-tories. I'm a Highgate girl, you know, born and bred. My mother was a maidservant, worked in the big villas. I'm trying to decide which of the local masters of the house was my father."

"Really?" Jacob didn't know what else to say.

"Goodness me, don't blush! Surely you knew I was born on the wrong side of the blanket? There's no shame in bastardy; only prudes think otherwise. A by-blow or two are *de rigueur* in the best families, don't you agree?"

Jacob's experience of the best families was minimal. He nod-ded helplessly.

"Mamma was a pretty young slip of a thing, I get my cheek-bones and the shape of my nose from her, you know. Six months after I was born, she married a potman from the Spaniards Inn, and I grew up as Edna Bratt. Not a name to conjure with, but I'm a romantic at heart. From childhood days, I've imagined myself as Griselda Farquharson, scion of one of England's old-est families."

"And now you're trying to discover your roots?"

"In days gone by, dear Jacob, I preferred my fantasies. So much more nourishing than real life, don't you think? But lately, I've begun to wonder. Not that I hope to make any claims on a rich estate, perish the thought. The legal prejudice against chil-dren born out of wedlock is a disgrace. I'll be proud to flaunt a bar sinister on my coat of arms."

How easy to drown in the flood of chatter. Jacob had never met anyone with such perfect recall of the inconsequential.

"As I said, I'd like to pick your brains about the Dobell family."

"My pleasure to assist, dear Jacob. Shall we adjourn for tea?"

Griselda and her pink train billowed out of the room, leaving him to trail in her wake. Five minutes later, they were consulting menus in the Misses Williamsons' tea room on the High Street.

She'd greeted the waitress like a daughter, though the woman was fifty if she was a day.

"I have a sweet tooth," she confided, after ordering a large pot of Darjeeling and a plate of fairy cakes. "There used to be a wonderful little café in Chelsea which served the most divine meringues and marshmallows..."

"About the Dobells," Jacob said firmly, trying to drive out of his mind an image of Griselda as a human meringue.

"Ah yes. Such an unlucky family."

"Unlucky?"

"One tragedy after another," Griselda said brightly. "So very sad."

"They come from Yorkshire, my home turf. I wasn't sure you'd know them."

"Ah, the county of broad acres! Land of the Brontës! Haworth Parsonage, *Wuthering Heights*! So romantic. Wild and mysterious." Under the table, Griselda's plump leg rubbed sociably against Jacob's. "Not that I've ever been that far north, of course."

"Of course not," Jacob said. "How did you come across the Dobells?"

A dreamy look came into Griselda's eyes. "I married very young, Jacob. My first husband, bless his heart, was old enough to be my grandfather. He couldn't keep up with a young bride. I loved parties, and I mixed with a fast crowd. That's how I met a charming bachelor called Oswyn Dobell."

"Oswyn?" Jacob cast his mind back to Felix's entry in *Who's Who*. She must be going back to the seventies.

"He'd come to London to further his ambitions as an artist. Alaric, his father, was an amateur watercolourist before he devoted himself to collecting art. Commissioning Millais and suchlike to paint Yorkshire landscapes. Oswyn shared his love of the pre-Raphaelites, but he loved the ladies even more."

"And did you love him?"

Griselda gave him a roguish smile, and tapped the side of her nose. "All of us girls did. Cupid's dart landed on a pretty debutante. When she found out she was expecting, Oswyn did the decent thing, and proposed, but she was a sickly creature. Had a miscarriage, and died in his arms a month before the wedding day. The poor lamb was heartbroken. On the rebound, he married a brigadier's daughter and took her back to Mortmain. My own husband died six months later. I often think that if things had been different—"

"And Oswyn's son?" Jacob said. "Did you know him?"

"There were two boys, not one. Maurice and Felix." The tea arrived, together with two plates piled high with cakes. "Their mother died when they were young. By then I'd remarried, and there was no question of Oswyn and me—"

"About his sons," Jacob said firmly.

"Ah, yes. They were looked after by governesses. Young, winsome girls who looked after Oswyn as well." She chortled. "The last of them became his secretary. Delightful euphemism, don't you think? Eventually she became his second wife. That would have been in, let me see, 1900, just before Alaric died."

"By that time, his sons were grown men. What happened to them?"

"Maurice had left Sandhurst and joined the Grenadier Guards. His mother's people were all military types. He loved soldiering."

"And Felix?"

"Artistic boy, softer than his brother. He followed in Oswyn's footsteps, and moved to London. I came across him once or twice. He got mixed up with an actress, and she gave birth to his baby. She was the neurasthenic type. Prone to hysterics."

"Ah."

Jacob didn't know what else to say. Griselda turned her attention to the fairy cakes. They were chocolate, with a topping of marzipan.

"Felix said he'd pay for Valentine's upbringing, but marriage was out of the question. Perfectly understandable. The girl was hardly top-drawer. No breeding."

"Pity."

"So important that people know their place in the world, don't you agree? How else can society function? The poor creature was hopelessly unstable. Booked into a hotel in Bloomsbury, and threw herself out of a fourth-floor window. On the very day of Queen Victoria's funeral!" Griselda polished off another fairy cake. "Hideously selfish, when people simply wanted to pay their respects to Her Majesty. Though in the long run, I suppose it was for the best."

Jacob couldn't help saying, "Except for the actress."

"Perhaps even for her, dear boy. She left a note saying everything had just become too much for her. Thankfully, she had the good grace to make clear that she didn't hold Felix responsible. Otherwise he might have blamed himself."

"Perish the thought." Jacob drew a breath. "About Felix's marriage…"

"I'm coming to that." Griselda wagged a marzipan-smeared finger at him. "Men are always in a such a hurry. Never rush a lady, Jacob. I remember one rather good-looking young rip—"

"I'm so sorry," Jacob said with a touch of desperation, "but you've got me fascinated by the Dobells. You were talking about their bad luck?"

"It's very sad." She wiped her mouth with a napkin. "Poor Oswyn's second wife died in childbirth, and the baby was stillborn. After that, he pined away. As for Felix, he ran out of money. Alaric disapproved of him, but once he died, the prodigal returned. Like father, like son. He and Oswyn did have a lot in common. The only difference was that Felix married the daughter of the chief constable rather than a brigadier. Haughty woman, Elspeth, but there was money in the family, which was what mattered."

"So the bohemian artist sacrificed ambition for financial security and rural respectability?"

Griselda sighed. "Dreadfully boring, don't you think? Felix was a charmer, but rather selfish. Not that he lacked courage. Once war was declared, he joined up straight away. Oswyn was very frail by this time, and Elspeth ruled the roost. With thousands of men being wounded in France, the ordinary hospitals and nursing homes were overwhelmed. Country houses like Mortmain were pressed into service. Elspeth turned the Hall into a military hospital."

Jacob breathed a sigh of relief. At last she was getting to it.

"The last year of the war was calamitous for the whole Dobell family. An endless sequence of disasters."

"What happened?"

"Maurice was killed by a sniper's bullet. That was bad enough, but it was only the start. During his first week in France, Felix's poor little bastard son suffered shell shock and amnesia. He deserted, and was lucky not to be shot. A coward, you see, just like his mother. Felix was told when he got home on leave, and cut him off without a penny. The boy might as well have died on the front."

Griselda let out a long, low sigh. "If only Felix had a yellow streak! He went straight back to the trenches, and was blown up for his pains. Next time he came back to Mortmain, he was a husk of a man with just one leg. And that wasn't all."

"Surely it was enough." Jacob was feeling rather shell-shocked himself.

Griselda shook her head. "Just after the news came through that he'd been hurt, Elspeth took ill and died."

"Spanish 'flu?"

"Gastritis, I believe. Then within a month, poor Oswyn's heart finally gave way. Can you believe it? As far as Felix was concerned, his whole family had been wiped out. As if there was a curse on Mortmain Hall and everyone associated with it."

In a hushed, melodramatic tone, Jacob said, "The curse of the Dobells?"

Griselda nodded solemnly. "Felix survived, but nothing was ever the same again."

"Yet he did find some comfort." At last he could turn the conversation towards Leonora. "He found a second wife."

Griselda sniffed. "His nurse."

"Leonora Slaterbeck."

"Was that her name?" Griselda wrinkled her nose. "I'm afraid I lost track of the Dobells. Not heard of them for years. All that promise, come to nothing. Tragic, I tell you."

"So you can't tell me anything about Leonora?"

"Nothing, my dear. She came from plebeian stock, I suppose. That's what the war did to this country. Turned everything upside down."

Actually, Griselda had told him something about Leonora. The change of name had worked. She'd kept her secret. If Griselda didn't know of her connection with the Gee case, nobody else would. Did even Felix know her true identity? And would he care if he did?

Griselda dug him in the ribs. "Here am I, nattering on, and you never told me why you are so interested in the Dobells."

"Felix's wife has invited someone I know to Mortmain for the weekend."

"Goodness, a house party? How wonderful." Griselda helped

herself to the last of the fairy cakes. "Do pass on any snippets I can use in my column. Things are so wretched these days. Nobody has any money, the world is so dreary. People love to be cheered up with a glimpse of the high life."

"I'm sure they do."

"And do ask your friend to give my regards to Felix. I don't suppose he remembers me."

Jacob mustered a gallant smile. "How could anyone possibly forget?"

———

"Almost there!" Pennington cried cheerily.

He was the adoring owner of a Bugatti 38 tourer, built to fly like the wind. As they drove up to Yorkshire, Reggie Vickers feared they'd be blown to oblivion, such was the speed with which they hurtled round every bend. Pennington boasted that they'd saved more than two hours, but the damage to Reggie's nerves had shortened his life by a much longer span. He'd found it impossible to doze, what with the bellow of the engine and Pennington harping on about the finer points of the Bugatti's manufacture. Reggie had no idea what a single overhead camshaft was, far less a triple ball bearing crankshaft.

"Good show," Reggie said through gritted teeth.

At least he had a game of cricket to look forward to. His superiors' enthusiasm for the game was the most attractive perk of his job; in fact it was the only one, if you didn't count the fact that nobody cared how little paperwork he ploughed through each day. He was glad to get out of London, and put Doodle, Lulu, and that wretched Savernake woman out of his mind. As Pennington pressed down on the accelerator, Reggie's only concern was whether he'd reach his destination in one piece.

"This must be Tunnicliffe!" Pennington braked fiercely, sending a shudder through Reggie. The car turned into an arched entrance beneath a gatehouse topped with a clock tower. "Phew, nearly missed it!"

"Thank goodness," Reggie said faintly. "I could do with a drink."

"You're in luck. I hear our host has a well-stocked cellar." Pennington chortled. "We've made such good time, we'll be well oiled long before the slowcoaches arrive."

The sun bathed the grounds of Tunnicliffe as they sped along. A long row of poplars stood on either side of the drive like sentries forming a guard of honour. There was an oval lake, and Reggie glimpsed white cricket sight screens and a cricket pavilion with a thatched roof. The house loomed ahead of them, a vast red-brick pile in the Jacobean style. The former owners had fallen on hard times after the war and sold Tunnicliffe to Sir Samuel Dackins.

The former Sammy Dackins had founded a business which became one of Europe's biggest soap-making companies. On turning fifty, he'd sold up and retired on the proceeds, exploring the world before buying Tunnicliffe and devoting himself to life as a lord of the manor. As a red-blooded Yorkshireman, one of his first acts was to establish his own team of cricketers, comprised of men who worked on his estate, and appoint himself captain.

He'd been thrilled to accept Major Whitlow's proposal of a match against the Masqueraders, Pennington said, before adding jocularly: "He'd have bitten off the major's right hand if he'd had one."

The Bugatti swerved past an ornate stone fountain and round the final bend in the drive before coming to a juddering halt beneath the porte cochère. Reggie stifled a gasp of relief.

"Made it!" Pennington exclaimed. "Thanks for your company, Vickers. So difficult to get to know a chap properly while we're beavering away in the wretched office. That's the beauty of cricket trips. Wonderful for esprit de corps. Good to have the chance of a decent chinwag. Never knew you were such a car fanatic."

Reggie clambered down and waited as Pennington lifted out their suitcases and cricket gear with nonchalant ease. He was a broad-shouldered six-footer, more at home in a tweed jacket and flannels than in Whitehall pinstripes.

A distant roar shattered the silence.

Reggie clutched Pennington's beefy arm. "What was that?"

"A lion, I suppose."

"Pennington, please. We've had a long drive, and I'm not in the mood for silly jokes."

"You should have more faith in me, old man. Dackins is nuts about animals. Cares about them as much as he does about cricket, and that's saying something. Spent years in the Belgian Congo in his younger days. Palm oil concessions for the soap trade, you know. The creature making that racket must be one he's brought back to England."

"This isn't darkest Africa. We're in Yorkshire. He can't be keeping a lion."

Pennington brayed with laughter. "You couldn't be wider of the mark, old man. And Dackins doesn't stop at a single lion. He has leopards, giraffes, a whole blasted menagerie. Tunnicliffe has the finest private zoo in the county."

Another roar came, louder this time. For all the warmth of the evening, Reggie shivered.

Chapter 16

Jacob had no sooner arrived back in his office than the telephone rang. A messenger had arrived with a special delivery, and insisted on handing the envelope over to Jacob in person.

A solidly built young fellow awaited him in the lobby. If he hadn't worn plain clothes, Jacob would have put money on his being a police constable.

"Mr Flint?"

"Special delivery? It's my lucky day. Who's it from?"

"All I can tell you, Mr Flint, is that I was asked to make sure that it reached your own hands. Nobody else's."

The fellow thrust a small buff envelope into Jacob's hand, and turned to leave.

"Hang on a minute. Who sent you, where do you work?"

He looked over his shoulder. "Sorry, Mr Flint. I wasn't told to answer any questions. Just to pass you the envelope. Good afternoon."

"Well," Maggie said, as the door closed behind the messenger. "Sounds exciting."

"A private message from a secret admirer." He grinned and pointed to her engagement ring. "By the way, I see your dinner and show went swimmingly. I hope you'll both be very happy."

Back in his office, he slit open the envelope. All it contained was an oblong scrap of cardboard, red with black lettering. It bore an address in Gerrard Street, and looked like a membership card, but lacking a name or number. Jacob was willing to bet that if he'd dusted it, he'd have found no fingerprints. There was no covering message. But he had no doubt where the card came from.

Oakes would never admit it, but he'd given Jacob the key to the door of the Clandestine Club.

———

Foibles was a stone's throw from Shaftesbury Avenue, and its walls were devoted to a garish tapestry of theatrical posters. An unctuous head waiter showed Rachel and Louis Morgans to their seats. The booths were panelled in oak, upholstered in red velvet, and had high backs. They were advertised as intimate, a euphemism for cramped.

The only other diners at the rear of the restaurant were a young blonde woman and a silver-haired man in an immaculate pinstripe suit. The place was obviously a haunt of out-of-work actresses and sugar daddies from the City. Perhaps it was the warmth of the evening that had led the woman to wear such a skimpy gown. Rachel's own dress, in peach silk chiffon, left more to the imagination.

"I can recommend the wild Highland red deer, done to a turn," Morgans announced as they studied the menu. "What's your tipple? Take it from me, the 1920 Château Mouton Rothschild is rather fine."

"I'm in your hands."

Morgans ordered, and lit a cigarette. "You really are a remarkable girl. Not a bit like I imagined. I mean, your old man…"

"Let's not talk about the Judge," she said. "I want to know all about you, Louis. And your firm, of course. Leonora Dobell has sung your praises."

"The Dobells have been clients for the past hundred years. I do the muck-and-nettles work, so to speak. Filling in forms, routine correspondence. Deadly boring, if truth be told. Angus doesn't like letting me loose on the clients."

"I'm glad you've made an exception in my case."

"The old boy was pretty put out that you insisted on seeing me." He chortled. "He's afraid you'll decide I'm too louche to be trusted."

"I'm very broad-minded," Rachel said. "As for Mr Mulkerrin, I gather he sympathises with Leonora's need to sell the Dobells' paintings."

"It's no skin off our nose. With taxation so punitive, country house owners are feeling the pinch. The Dobells are better off than many, considering that Felix is a cripple in need of nursing care. Poor blighter. Might have been kinder if the Boche had put him out of his misery."

"I worry what will happen when Felix dies," Rachel sighed. "What with death duties to pay and…"

"The old girl's sitting pretty," Louis said. "Like my old man, God rest his soul, used to say, it's not enough to marry money. You need to marry into a family which is generous with it. Luckily for her, old Oswyn Dobell was the free-and-easy sort. The family settlement gives an heir's widow a life interest in the estate. When Leonora passes away, the Hall may be knocked down or turned into flats or some such. But there's enough in the pot to see her out to a ripe old age. Even though she's probably good for another thirty or forty years. She's not as ancient as she looks."

"So you've met Leonora?"

A wary look entered his eyes. "Briefly, yes. But let's not talk shop. Tell me about yourself, Rachel."

"I've led such a sheltered life," she said. "There's very little to say. I'd much rather listen to you."

"You're very unassuming, Rachel. I like that in a girl. Flappers were never my cup of tea. Brashness simply isn't feminine."

"We should be ogled, not heard?"

"Ha! Very good!" He snorted with laughter.

"I hear you're a writer. A poet, in fact. How marvellous!"

"Well, I can't pretend to be a Robert Graves."

This disclaimer, accompanied by a modest chuckle, prefaced a discourse about English poetry, and the contribution he longed to make to it. This carried them through the hors d'oeuvres, the main course, and two bottles of Château Mouton Rothschild. Rachel confined herself to a single glass of wine, declining each offer of a top-up, as well as a dessert.

"I don't know much about poetry," she said as coffee was served, "but I know what I like. There was someone a few years ago. Gilbert Payne, I think he was called. Do you know him?"

"Payne?" He put down his spoon. "He's dead."

"How awful. You knew him, then?"

"He was a publisher, made his fortune turning out tosh. Ripping yarns." Morgans spoke carefully, as if to avoid slurring his words. "But like the rest of us, he hankered after...well, something a bit different."

"Different?"

He brushed a stray hair out of his eyes; they were no longer quite focusing, but he did his best to subject her to a penetrating gaze. "Why do you ask about old Gilbert? I've not heard his name in ages."

"I was just interested. His name cropped up in connection

with a club... Oh, what was it called?" she pondered. "The Clandestine, that was it."

Morgans struggled to his feet, and glanced around before blundering over to her side of the table, squashing down beside her on the velvet bench. Rachel felt the warmth of his body, and the pressure of his thigh against hers.

"The Clandestine, eh?" He sniggered. "I'm not so sure that you're quite as innocent as you make out. What does a young wench like you know about the Clandestine Club?"

"Why, is there something...not quite proper about it?"

He giggled. "Not quite proper? That's a good one. Who told you about it?"

"I was asking about Gilbert Payne's poetry. I'm sorry to hear he died. What happened?"

He shook his long mane. "You know something, Rachel? I'm beginning to wonder if there's more to you than meets the eye."

"Oh, I hope so, Louis." A coy smile. "Actually, it may have been Reggie Vickers who mentioned the Clandestine. He said Gilbert Payne..."

"You've been out with Reggie too?" He moved his face close to hers. His breath smelled of alcohol, tobacco, and overcooked meat. "For a quiet little thing, you get around. Bet you got no change out of him."

"I'm not sure what you mean," she said. "I just..."

He put a hand on her knee. "Forget Gilbert Payne and Reggie bloody Vickers. You're barking up the wrong tree. I'm not like them."

She lifted his hand. "Louis, please. That woman over there keeps looking at us."

He placed his finger against her lips. "Shhh. I don't care. I've worked out what your game is. It took me a while, but I got there in the end. Not that I object, oh no, not in the least."

"I'm curious, that's all."

"Shhhh," he repeated, replacing his hand on her knee. "You don't have to tell me what you're curious about. You fancy something exotic, don't you? You spent all your life on a godforsaken island in the middle of nowhere. Now you've come down to London and you want a few thrills. Make up for the lost years."

"I just wondered if Gilbert Payne…"

"I hardly knew him," he interrupted. "Come on, high time we left. I've a good mind to take you to the Clandestine. And then, a little of what you fancy."

"Thank you, but no."

"Now don't play hard to get." He pinched her thigh. "It's no use…"

He gave a little yelp of pain as Rachel seized hold of his wrist, and jerked it away.

"Move aside," she whispered, "before you get hurt."

As he tried to get up, she pushed him back down on the bench.

"You're just a rotten tease." His eyes were watering. "A real…"

Bending over the table, she dug her sharp fingernails into his palm and hissed, "Forget this conversation ever took place."

Staring at the trace of blood on his skin, he mumbled, "What are you…?"

"You don't recall a single word," Rachel's glass stood on the edge of the table. Nudging it with an elbow, she tipped the red wine over his lap. "Do you?"

He clutched himself, stifling a sob of self-pity. Spots of colour appeared on each of his pallid cheeks.

"Do you?" she asked again.

He tried to glare at her, but his face had crumpled into a mess of anger and confusion.

"No," he said hoarsely. "We never met."

The young blonde-haired woman in the next booth was watching them with undisguised curiosity. The head waiter came bustling over.

"Monsieur Morgans, is there any difficulty? Can I be of assistance?"

"No difficulty whatsoever." Rachel pointed to Morgans's sodden lap. "This gentleman had a little accident, that's all. By the way, the deer was rather tough, I thought. Good evening."

Once in the street, she looked around, and spotted Trueman. He was in his chauffeur's uniform behind the wheel of the Phantom twenty yards away. He gave her a thumbs up with a gloved hand.

As she climbed in beside him, he said, "Ten minutes later than forecast. Couldn't you tear yourself away?"

She punched him in the ribs. "I wanted to make sure you had enough time. Did you find the Dobell papers?"

"Easy as winking. No bars on the window, no locks. Careless. I suppose that apart from cash in the safe, they think there's nothing worth stealing."

"You took the papers back to the house?"

He nodded. "Between the three of us, we made fair copies of sample letters authorising Leonora to sell the paintings. And the family deed of settlement. Loads of verbiage; lawyers never use one word when twenty will do. I barely had time to break back into Morgans's office and put everything back before getting here."

"Excellent."

"Do you still think Leonora might be defrauding the estate?"

Rachel shook her head. "It looks like a red herring. She's quite open about selling the paintings."

"That doesn't mean she doesn't have a sinister reason for luring you to her Yorkshire lair."

"You're such a comfort."

"What did you pick up?"

"Morgans was acquainted with Payne. And he knows Reggie Vickers."

"Those two are birds of a feather."

"And Morgans invited me to accompany him to the Clandestine."

Trueman gave her a sidelong look. "Don't tell me you weren't tempted."

"Of course I was. But we've agreed that it would be a mistake."

"Where angels fear to tread," he muttered.

She laughed. "Let's see if Jacob Flint rushes in."

Chapter 17

Jacob pulled his hat lower as he turned into Gerrard Street. He cherished his best fedora, and insisted on wearing it at a rakish angle, like Fleet Street's answer to the Prince of Wales. Not that His Royal Highness's hats were made out of rabbit felt and lined with cloth, but the sun had set over Soho, and in the twilight you could get away with...well, murder.

A flight of steps led down to the unmarked entrance of the Clandestine Club. There was no bell, not even a door knocker. At ground level there was a tailor's cutting room, shuttered for the night.

Jacob hesitated. He'd reported on enough nocturnal beatings in this part of London to know he was taking a risk. His mind was made up by the sight of a heavily made-up woman, bare-legged but wearing a fur coat, tottering down the street towards him. He hurried down the steps and knocked on the door.

Nothing happened. He knocked again.

The door opened a couple of inches. A deep voice said, "Yes?"

Jacob held up the membership card, and the man opened the door to admit him. Inside, Jacob found himself confronted by a man who was six feet five, and muscular with it. He wore a dinner suit, but looked as if he'd be more at home in a sergeant major's uniform.

"Evening, sir." He jerked a thumb. "Can I take your hat?"

"Thank you."

Parting with his precious fedora, Jacob followed the man down another short flight of stairs, into a small, cramped room. A handful of smartly dressed men and women lounged around a tiny bar. An elderly pianist was tinkling the ivories and giving a slightly off-key rendition of "Charmaine."

Jacob ordered a gin and tonic from a cockney bartender half the size of the man on the door, and took in his surroundings. The walls were covered in hessian, the decor confined to dried-up palms in chipped pots. The other people in the bar sipped their cocktails with a slightly unfocused look in their eyes. Jacob wasn't sure if they were drug fiends or simply half asleep.

The sense of anticlimax was as overwhelming as the reek of Griselda Farquharson's perfume. If the police had failed to clean up Soho's sinks of iniquity, the economic slump had evidently done their job for them.

The pianist struck up "In a Little Spanish Town," and a bald-headed man in his fifties and his bespectacled young companion made their way to the square space that constituted the dance floor. A senior clerk and his secretary, Jacob guessed. Perhaps a trip to the Clandestine represented a prelude to a night of illicit passion. Judging by their expressions, neither of them was excited by the prospect. He could only assume they were saving themselves for later.

His own prospects of a night of passion were nonexistent. There were just three other couples. No single women on the lookout for adventure. To console himself, he knocked back his gin, and returned to the bar.

"Quiet in here tonight," he said to the barman. Was it worth dropping Gilbert Payne's name into conversation, to see if it provoked a response?

"Might liven up a bit later. Then again, it might not."

Jacob proffered a generous tip and told the barman to have one himself.

"Thanks very much, sir. You're a toff."

"Long time since I was last here," Jacob said, hoping that in such poor light he might look older than his years. "Not quite like the old days, eh? Reminds me of when I came here with a pal of mine…"

"Well, sir," the barman interrupted. "I'd say it's much the same as it ever was. A nod's as good as a wink to a blind horse, if you follow my meaning."

"Absolutely." Jacob raised his glass. He didn't have the faintest idea what the fellow was talking about. "Chin-chin."

"I suppose you'll be wanting to go downstairs, then?" the barman said.

Jacob had thought he was downstairs already. But in for a penny… "Rather."

The barman waved to the sergeant major. "Gent wants to go downstairs."

The big man came over to the bar. "Sorry, sir. Thought you'd just dropped in for a quick one."

Jacob waved away the apology. "A couple of gins as a pick-me-up after a long day never did anyone any harm, eh?"

"You never said a truer word, sir."

Leading Jacob past the dancers, he drew back a velvet curtain. They entered a small vestibule panelled in mahogany. When the man touched the panelling, it slid aside to reveal a wooden door. Fishing a key out of a vast pocket, he unlocked it, and gestured to Jacob to step through.

He found himself at the top of a long, winding flight of steps illuminated by candles occupying niches cut into the brick wall. The key turned in the lock with a decisive click. Jacob felt his chest tighten. But he'd chosen to come here; he had to see it through.

On his way down, he noticed a faint but sickly sweet smell in the air. After counting twenty steps, he reached the bottom, and found himself facing another door, this time made of steel. He turned the handle, but the door would not budge.

If he'd walked into a trap, he told himself, he'd simply have to talk his way out of it. He'd survived worse experiences in the past. Perhaps all this was simply part of an elaborate set of security precautions. No wonder the Clandestine Club managed to dodge police scrutiny.

There was nothing for it but to rap on the door, so he did just that.

The door swung open noiselessly. A dapper little man in a dinner suit stood in front of him, beaming in welcome.

"A very good evening, sir."

"Good evening." Jacob was so relieved not to be confronted by a knife-wielding assassin that he had to restrain himself from throwing his arms around the fellow. "I'm…"

"Please, sir. You have not been here for a long time, perhaps. But you will remember. We don't mention names."

"No, no, of course." Jacob felt his confidence surging back, even though the sickly smell in the air was stronger here. "Absolutely not. I was simply about to say how glad I am to be back."

"Ah, yes, sir. May I see your card?" Jacob took it from his pocket with a flourish. "Splendid. Please go through, and make yourself at home."

The man indicated a beaded curtain patterned with bamboo

leaves. From the other side of the curtain came the sultry sound of a woman crooning "Are You Lonesome Tonight?"

"Thanks very much."

Jacob pushed through the beads. He found himself inside a cavern full of people. The song slid to an end, and there was a burst of applause. A long bar in front of him was doing a roaring trade. The heat was oppressive; there was no hint of damp, despite the depth of the chamber. The lighting was low, the atmosphere so thick with smoke that his eyes stung.

The walls and ceiling were swathed in exotic fabrics. Orange, crimson, yellow, purple. No beige hessian or dying palms here. People lounged on red plush divans or danced cheek to cheek in front of a stage at the far end of the room. Champagne bottles in ice buckets and half-empty glasses occupied half a dozen small tables.

A tall woman in a long evening gown was up on the stage, together with a four-piece band. She started to sing "Ain't She Sweet?"

Jacob peered at the people sprawled over the divans. Several bodies were intertwined. As well as men kissing women, men with rouged faces were caressing each other. Two women in jackets, trousers, and ties were locked in a passionate embrace. Another couple, similarly kitted out, were joining in with the song by way of a satiric serenade. As for the smell in the air, it might be hashish.

He regarded himself as a man of the world. Debauchery denounced by the *Clarion* didn't shock him to the core. Live and let live was his philosophy, though he kept quiet about it in the office. But there were limits. Once, a former colleague had tricked him into visiting a nightclub where men romanced other men; he'd made his excuses and left. Never before, though, had he encountered scenes of such rampant sensuality. He wasn't sure where to look.

His eyes still adjusting to the lack of light, he glanced at the divan nearest to him. A woman in a man's suit and tie was miming the song to amuse a much younger woman whose slender figure was enhanced by a daring evening gown. Her hand rested on the girl's bare shoulder.

The girl's hair was a cloud of blonde curls. Her rosebud lips and round saucer eyes reminded him of Clara Bow, one of his favourite actresses. Looking at her distracted him from her companion. It took him a few seconds to recognise the older woman. In that instant of realisation, his gaze met hers, just as she was mouthing the words *very confidentially*.

He was staring at the woman he thought of as a witch.

Leonora Dobell.

——

Leonora turned her head away the moment she saw Jacob. To hide his embarrassment, he plunged into the crowd at the bar. It took him five minutes to be served, and by the time he'd drunk enough to summon up the courage to look round, the divan was empty. Leonora was nowhere in sight.

"You frightened her away," a voice murmured.

At his side was the woman he'd seen with Leonora. Even in the fug of smoke and dope, he caught a sweet whiff of perfume. At close quarters, perhaps she wasn't quite Clara Bow, but her petite features had a delicate charm.

He cleared his throat. "I'm sorry. I'm not sure…"

"Oh, please don't apologise. I was taken aback, that's all. One minute she was doing her damnedest to amuse me. The next, she caught sight of you. That was enough for her. She jumped up, and said she must go." The girl laughed. "Do you always have this effect on strange women?"

"I'm afraid so. One look at me, and they run a mile."

Her finely pencilled eyebrows lifted. "You don't look utterly terrifying at first glance. Obviously you have hidden depths."

"Yes, they're very well concealed. Can I get you a drink?"

She asked for a Boulevardier, which Jacob had never even heard of, but the barman obliged, and within a couple of minutes he'd joined her on the divan and was sipping his third G and T of the evening.

"I should introduce myself. My name's Jacob."

"We're not supposed to tell each other our real names," she said. "That's the point of this club, isn't it? Clandestine, you see."

"I'm happy to make an exception in your case," he said. "Even if you prefer to remain a Woman of Mystery."

She tried her cocktail, and smiled in approval. "All right, then. I'm Daisy."

"Pleased to make your acquaintance, Daisy."

They exchanged shy smiles, but didn't shake hands. With men and women all around them cavorting in the most licentious way imaginable, such formality would be absurd.

"Actually," she said in a small voice, "there's nothing very mysterious about me. In fact, I'm the definition of ordinary. I've never even been here before."

"Really?" Disappointment needled him. He'd hoped she'd tell him more about Leonora, and the club itself. "But this place is for members only."

"And guests, if you know the right people," Daisy said. "But I'm afraid the person I came with turned out not to be Mr Right."

"You didn't come with Leonora?"

"Is that her real name? She told me to call her Leo. I'd only just met her, five minutes before you arrived and gave her the heebie jeebies."

He leaned towards her. "Who did you come with, if I may ask?"

"You may," she said with mock solemnity. "A colonel, no less."

"I'm impressed," he said.

"I thought my luck was in." She pouted. "I used to be on the chorus line at the Gaiety, but I was sacked a couple of weeks ago, and since then, life has been hand to mouth."

"Sorry to hear that," he said. "There are other chorus lines."

"I'm not so sure. One of the stars misbehaved with me, and took it badly when I complained to the musical director. It was easier to get rid of me than an actor. Even easier to put the word out that I spell trouble. Everyone knows everyone else in theatre land, and it's the old, old story. Give a dog a bad name."

The crooner had moved on to "Stardust." Jacob drank some gin. The lyric was spot on: the melody was haunting his reverie. He was becoming philosophical.

"Life is unfair."

"Too bloody right, if you'll pardon the expression. So when I got talking to a nice respectable gentleman in Hyde Park this afternoon, and he invited me to dinner, I wasn't going to say no, was I? Even if he was old enough to be my father."

"And he brought you here after dinner?"

"Said he'd been a member for years. I'd never even heard of the place, even though I only live round the corner. It all sounded very secret. Exciting, though. After three days of bread and cheese and water, I was ready for some excitement."

She finished her cocktail, and he bought another round of drinks. Oakes was right; the prices were very reasonable. Back on the divan, he settled down close to her. Her perfume was intoxicating as the alcohol.

"Did this colonel tell you his name?"

"Told me to call him Tom." She pouted again. "I bet he wasn't a real colonel. Probably just some married businessman wanting to get away from his missus."

"What happened after you got here?"

"The big chap on the door made a fuss about whether I could be allowed in. Seemed to think I was on the game—sauce! Tom made it all square with him, but the argument upset him. Once we got down here, he bought me a cocktail, but he couldn't settle. I was in my element, watching all this going on!" She waved towards two rouge-lipped men cuddling each other a couple of feet away. "It's the sort of thing you read about in the *News of the World*, isn't it? But worse. Or better. Doesn't seem real somehow. Tom said he needed to do something, and disappeared into the crowd. That was the last I saw of him."

"He abandoned you, just like that?"

"Story of my life, Jacob. My trouble is, men think I'm as common as muck. And cheap too. I'm a flirt, I admit. But I'm not easy. And when they're disappointed, they get cross."

The singer launched into "Blue Skies." As Daisy sipped her cocktail, he felt the pressure of her leg against his. With a head start over dinner, she must have had plenty to drink already.

"You bumped into Leonora by accident?"

"She said I was looking lost and lonely, and what was the matter? When I explained, she said it was shocking that a man could walk out on a pretty girl like me. She bought me a Boulevardier." She took another sip. "I should have said no, I could see what she was after, and I think it's horrid, but I was miserable, so... anyway, nothing came of it. You turned up in the nick of time, and scared her off."

"I hardly know the woman," Jacob said. "We've only met once. Through work. I suppose she was embarrassed to be seen here."

"Dressed like a man, you mean?"

"Yes, I had no idea she was... Well, you know."

He was about to tell her that Leonora was married, but bit

his tongue just in time. What she got up to in her private life was none of his business. Now he understood why she spent so much time in London. In this vast, anonymous city, she could amuse herself in a manner quite impossible on a country estate in Yorkshire.

"What sort of work do you do?"

"I'm a journalist."

Her eyes were like saucers. "Gosh, how marvellous. What newspaper?"

"The *Clarion*."

"Then just remember this." She giggled. "Next time you review a musical, say that the chorus line could have done with legs like Daisy Smith's!"

Had he said too much? He persuaded himself that she'd have forgotten most of their conversation come the morning. There was a touch of bleariness about those lovely big eyes. Before long, she'd be dozing.

"I suppose I'd better be off," he said.

Daisy yawned. "Same here. Nothing to keep me. And I've had more than enough cocktails."

He stood up. It hadn't been a bad evening's work; he'd learned nothing about Gilbert Payne but more than he'd bargained for concerning Leonora.

"Nice to meet you."

"Thanks for driving that woman away, I'd have had a job getting shut of her on my own." She struggled to her feet. "I don't suppose you can do me a favour?"

"You can always ask."

"Would you mind seeing me home, just to my front door? It's only five minutes from here, but at this time of night there are some roughnecks about. If they see a lady on her own, they think they're quids in."

Why not? He didn't mind doing a good deed. And she did look rather like Clara Bow.

"All right, Daisy."

"Thanks, I knew you were a good egg."

The dapper man on the door bade them an effusive goodnight and let them out. They climbed up the stairs, and knocked on the door at the top. The sergeant major greeted them with a brisk nod.

"You'll be wanting your hat, sir. And your coat and bag, madam?"

Jacob collected his fedora, tipped the sergeant major, and stepped out into the night air. Daisy joined him at the top of the stairs outside the building, and they gazed up at the stars together.

"Lovely, isn't it?" she said. "It's not only 'Blue Skies' that make you remember life's probably still worth living."

"Of course it's worth living! No matter what goes wrong, there's always another day, another chance."

"You're lucky. You've got a job. Probably a nice wife or girlfriend. A few bob in the savings bank. It's not like that for everyone." She linked arms with him. "Sorry, don't mean to be maudlin."

As they wove through the maze of streets, he pondered her words. Might he pick up the *Clarion* one day and read a couple of lines about a former chorus girl who had put her head in a gas oven because she couldn't pay the bills? He wished he could help her to find work.

"I haven't got a wife or girlfriend," he said. "Or a boyfriend, in case you're wondering."

She guided him around a barber's shop, and into the narrow entrance of a cramped and insalubrious mews. To left and right were one-storey workshops, most of them derelict. Ahead of them stood a narrow terrace of houses in dingy yellow brick. No lights shone at their windows. In the dull lemon glow cast by a lamp on the street, he saw a rat scampering across the cobblestones.

"Married to your job?" she asked.

"You could say that."

"Watch your footing; some of the cobbles are loose." She halted by a door at the side of the skinny end house. "Here we are. Thanks very much, Jacob. Lucky or not, you're a gentleman, and there's not many I can say that for."

Standing on tiptoe, she pecked him on the cheek. Again he caught her fragrance.

"Goodnight, Daisy."

Clara Bow eyes gazed into his. "I don't suppose you'd fancy a nightcap?"

"I've got work in the morning."

"Don't be frightened. I'll leave your virtue intact. Just one drink, and then I'll shoo you away. Promise."

He felt confused. The gin didn't help. "It's not that I don't think you're very attractive."

"I'm not on the game, if that's what you're scared of." A fierce note entered her voice for the very first time. "A nightcap, and nothing more than a nightcap. What do you say?"

Where was the harm? The truth was, he could do with the company. And if, after the nightcap, they forgot themselves and got carried away, well, they were both adults, with only themselves to blame.

"All right. I mean yes, I'd like that. Thanks."

Taking a key from her bag, she said, "I'm in the garret. Draughty in winter and boiling hot in summer. At least I can afford it for another few weeks."

She led him up two vertiginous flights of uncarpeted stairs before arriving at a miniscule landing. The ceiling was low, and Jacob needed to duck his head.

"Be it ever so humble," she sang softly, "there's no place like home."

He followed Daisy inside, and was assailed by the smell of mildew. She bent over to strike a match. He was right behind her when something hit him hard on the head, and everything dissolved into blackness.

——

When he came round, the back of his head was throbbing. What had happened? Had a burglar broken into the attic? His brain wasn't working as it should. He felt disorientated. Forcing his eyes open, he blinked away tears.

He was lying in bed. A sickening stench of mildew filled his nostrils. The room was pitch black.

And he wasn't wearing a stitch.

Gingerly, he lifted his hand, and brushed the back of his head with his index finger. The matted blood on his scalp was sticky to the touch.

Groaning, he shifted position, only to brush against smooth, chilly flesh. He wasn't alone. The bed was a double, and someone was lying next to him. Also naked.

For heaven's sake, Daisy had taken him to bed with her when he was unconscious.

Wrong, wrong, something was terribly wrong. He was too confused to make sense of things. He touched Daisy's bare back. It was cold. He put his hand on her side, and pulled her to him.

Too weak to scream, he gave a muffled sob of horror.

He was mistaken. Daisy wasn't lying beside him after all.

He was sharing the bed with a corpse.

The lifeless body of a naked man.

Chapter 18

Jacob tumbled out of the bed and onto hard floorboards. They creaked in protest. His bones were aching. As he got to his feet, his sore head almost hit the low ceiling. He felt nauseated, his mind was spinning. Blinking hard, he tried to focus. Moonlight crept through a gap in the curtains. He took a step forward, and his bare foot caught a nail sticking out of the floor. Although he let out a little cry, he was almost beyond pain, beyond caring. Limping to the window, he tore apart the curtains.

A crescent moon illuminated the deserted mews. Through the cobwebs on the window, he could see the way out to the street. In the shadows, he detected movement. The dark shape of a man. The mews was under guard.

At the end of the room was the only door. Someone must have stood behind it as he followed Daisy in. His attacker had been lying in wait. Everything was planned, must have been. The girl was in cahoots with the people at the Clandestine Club. She'd lured him here so that he could be knocked unconscious. And then, while he was out of it, she and his attacker had put him to bed with a dead man.

His gorge rose as he looked at the corpse. The face was

dreadful, the distorted expression a parody of shock and betrayal. The brown hair was long, the cheeks pale, the shoulders narrow. He was thin, not in the least muscular. Only a few years older than Jacob, by the look of him.

A wound gaped in his chest. On the floor by the side of the bed was a steak knife with a wooden handle. The stained blade spoke for itself.

A pound to a penny, Jacob's fingerprints were daubed all over it.

He felt his chest tightening. He must escape, he had no choice. Stay here, and he'd be at the mercy of whoever had done this. They'd allowed him to live. There could only be one reason. They meant to frame him for the murder of this man. Someone he'd never even met.

What on earth could be his motive for such a vile crime? Why would anyone believe he'd killed a perfect stranger?

He forced himself to take a closer look at the body. The smears around the mouth gave him the answer.

The dead man was wearing lipstick.

Jacob's feverish mind worked out the narrative. It made perfect sense. This man had met him at the Clandestine Club, and brought him back here. Once he'd been enticed into bed, a quarrel had started. Perhaps he'd been overcome by shame. Or anger, or both. The knife had been to hand. In a fit of unreasoning rage, Jacob had plunged the blade deep into his new acquaintance's heart.

On a bedside table stood an empty gin bottle and two glasses. A picture of debauchery. Jacob saw in his mind the huge headline on the front page of the *Witness*, as gleeful as it was garish.

House of Horror Slaughter—Clarion *Reporter Arrested*

They'd love it; they'd pump out one special edition after another. An image sprang into his mind of Haydn Williams holding court in the Magpie and Stump, shaking his head and saying that he'd always thought there was something funny about the lad. Couldn't quite put his finger on it, but…

No, no, no. He bit back rising hysteria. If he didn't get out of here, the best he could hope for was ridicule and ruin. The worst was a hood over his head, and a noose around his neck.

He tried the door. Locked, inevitably. The wood was cheap and rotten. It should be easy to charge it down with his shoulder. That still left the door on the ground floor. As he smashed his way through, the racket would bring the guard running.

Next, the window. A forlorn hope, given the height of the attic above ground, but he'd risk anything to escape the dead body. The window was bolted shut and looked as though it hadn't been opened for years. The bolt was covered in rust. After half a minute of trying to shift it, he gave up. Another option gone. Breaking the glass would be far too noisy.

He looked up, but there was no hatch in the ceiling. Even if there had been access to roof space, there would be no way to get outside unless tiles were missing. Not that anything was impossible in this dank hellhole.

Taking a step back, he trod on something. Not a nail this time. Bending down, he picked up a wooden hammer. This must be the weapon someone had used to knock him out when he entered the room. It hurt like hell, but it could have been much worse. If he'd been hit with full force, the blow might have killed him.

Any moment now, a telephone call would be made to Scotland Yard. Daisy, or whatever her real name was, had such a gift for acting. With a tremble in her voice, she'd explain she'd heard terrified cries in this godforsaken mews, and she'd beg the police to take a look at the end terrace house. The police would assume she was a prostitute with public spirit. As soon as a suitable interval had passed to allow Jacob to come round, she'd ring. But not before; it wouldn't do for him still to be unconscious when the police broke into this shabby hovel.

When the police did arrive, his head wound would need explaining. Experienced detectives could work out the sequence of events. They'd conclude that during an argument, the other man had struck him a glancing blow with an old domestic hammer. Just hard enough to enrage Jacob, and provoke him to murder.

What about their clothes? Daisy wouldn't dare to take them away. If the police burst in and found two naked men, but no clothing, they'd draw the obvious conclusion: a third party had been present.

Grubbing around under the bed, he discovered his clothes. His fedora was there too. They'd been dumped there with the corpse's things. Every item stank of gin, even his socks, as if the bottle had been poured all over them. Who cared? Not Jacob. The simple act of getting dressed reminded him that he still belonged to the human race. But time was running out. Daisy was bound to call the police soon. Perhaps she'd already rung them. For all he knew, a car was speeding on its way to the mews at this very moment.

He took another look through the window. No sign of the watchman, no hint of motion among the shadows. That barber's shop on the corner had a canopied entrance, didn't it? The fellow would loiter there, smoking a cigarette to pass the time. In the mews, there was nothing to see.

Dare he risk smashing the glass? Tempted, he weighed the hammer in his hand. A pity his assailant hadn't used a spanner. Then he could have tackled the rusted window bolt. But needs must. He couldn't see that he had any choice but to try to destroy the bolt by brute force, and pray that in the process he didn't shatter the glass.

He struck a lusty blow. Nothing. Another blow. The glass rattled, but the bolt held fast. He felt sick, but kept going. Anything was better than sitting here tamely, waiting for his life to be destroyed. Better to end with a bang than a whimper.

The wooden frame was a wreck of wet rot. He took a breath, and tested it with his index finger. It felt mushy to the touch. Again he lifted the hammer. The sixth blow cracked the bolt. He only needed two more swings to break it apart. His shoulder ached, but he imagined the police car speeding towards Soho, and it gave him the strength to keep battering the window frame. The rotting wood splintered and gave way.

Nearly there. He grasped the wood with both hands, and gave a ferocious wrench. Window and frame came away together. The glass cracked and broke, but the noise was not as loud as he'd feared. He stood at the hole he'd made in the wall. The night air chilled his face. Below in the mews, there was no sign of life.

What next? Beneath the window was an external sill. Narrow as it was, he thought he could just about get a foothold there. He'd have to hope that it didn't crumble under his weight. If it did, he'd be snookered. A drainpipe ran down the side of the property, invitingly within arm's reach. Suppose he clambered down; perhaps he could make it on to the jutting flat roof of the workshop next door. Get that far, and he'd take his chances.

Closing his eyes, he uttered a silent prayer. The risk was enormous, but time was short. Anything was better than being accused of stabbing a man he'd never met after some kind of sordid lovers' tiff. What would happen if he was caught didn't bear thinking about. Better to gamble. If the man guarding the mews challenged him, he'd fight to the death.

Time to summon up his last reserves of courage. He wasn't an athlete or an acrobat, just an awkward young man with too much curiosity for his own good. If he got out of this mess in one piece, he'd... Well, time to think about that if he survived.

Ripping a piece of the dead man's shirt, he wiped the door handle and hammer, as well as the surfaces he remembered touching. This was no time to be squeamish, and he rubbed the handle of the knife as well. He dare not leave the fedora behind, so he put it on. Next he dragged the bed to the window, so that it made a platform for him to climb out. As the bed shifted, the corpse rolled off the far side, and fell on to the floorboards with a thud. When the police did arrive, they'd find a crime scene of chaos.

He began to lever himself out through the window space, and tested the sill with a heel. Bits of stone flaked away, but the sill didn't disintegrate. Clinging onto the uneven wall, he heaved the rest of his body through the opening.

One, two, three. He grabbed at the drainpipe with his right hand, but his foot slipped, and he almost lost his balance and plunged to his death.

No time to think. No time to look down at the yard. Have another go. This time he held on tight to the rusting iron, first with one hand, then with the other, as he swung his body away from the window, and began to descend.

The drainpipe moved under his weight. The bolts fixing it to the wall were coming adrift. Only a madman would linger to see if it would take him crashing down with it. Eyes shut, he twisted his body to his right and jumped down, praying that he'd land with both feet on the workshop roof.

The prayer was answered. His feet hit the roof hard, and the impact sent a brutal shudder through his spine. He fell to his knees rather than to the ground. And the drainpipe didn't break off.

So far, so good. He inched towards another drainpipe, only

to put his foot through a patch of rotting felt. Impossible in the darkness to be sure of the safest way ahead. Better get down before he fell through the roof into the jagged teeth of ancient machinery.

On his haunches at the roof's edge, he measured the drop. It was far less frightening than the prospect of tumbling all the way down from the attic, but it would still be easy to break a leg, or worse. His luck was in. An old signboard protruded from the front of the ramshackle building. It offered him a fingerhold. Taking infinite care, he eased himself over the side, using the signboard to help his descent. Within a few moments, his feet were touching the ground.

Where was his fedora? He'd lost it while clambering out of the window. He looked around frantically and spotted it close to the door which led to the attic. Retrieving it, he thrust it back on his head. A show of defiance.

Someone coughed. Heavy footsteps sounded. The guard was coming to take another look at the mews.

Jacob picked up two loose cobbles. Like any self-respecting Yorkshireman, he'd played his fair share of cricket. His averages had never been anything to write home about, but he was a good cover fieldsman, with a decent throwing arm.

He hurled the smaller cobble across the mews. It struck the wooden door to an old garage in the far corner. The clatter echoed in the confined space. To Jacob, it sounded like a fusillade of bullets. After a second's pause, the guard strode into view. A burly man, with a cosh in one hand and a torch in the other. He moved deliberately, shining a torch in the direction of the noise.

The guard was twenty yards away, less than the length of a cricket pitch, when Jacob threw the larger cobble at him. It hit the man on the temple as he was turning, and knocked him down like a ninepin. Jacob heard a bellow of shock and pain as the hefty body hit the ground. He began to run.

Fleeing the mews, he pounded along the pavement. His foot and head hurt and his whole body ached, but his pace was ferocious. He was running for his life. He spun round the next corner into the adjoining street. There was a passageway between two restaurants. Both were closed, and he wondered what time it was. One o'clock? Two? He'd lost track. Gambling that the alleyway wasn't a dead end, he raced along. Fifty yards later, he reached a main street.

Wonder of wonders, a taxi was approaching. He flagged it down, and to his astonishment, it pulled up at his side. Nervously, he felt inside his jacket pocket. Daisy and her friend hadn't stolen his wallet. He almost wept with relief.

"Where to, governor?"

Jacob said the first thing that came to him. "Gaunt House."

———

"Can you wait for two minutes?" Jacob handed the taxi driver an extravagant tip. The square was silent, and the house in darkness. "I need to see if my friends are still up."

The man peered at him. "You all right, governor?"

"Fine, thanks."

The driver made a sceptical noise. Jacob daren't imagine what he looked like. A bruised parody of a young man-about-town, stinking of gin and with a scalp caked in blood. His body was battered, his brain scrambled. As he rapped on the door, it struck him that he didn't even know why he'd come here.

If no one answered, he daren't go back to Exmouth Market. What if the guard he'd struck with the cobblestone turned up there in search of revenge? What if they knew where he lived?

If…well, the what-ifs were never-ending. He couldn't be sure of anything anymore.

He shifted from one foot to another. The sole which had caught on the nail in the floorboard was stinging. He must get it seen to before it became infected. For the first time, he realised how exhausted he was. He longed for a week of sleep.

If someone was in the house, there was no hint of it. He couldn't hear a sound or see a chink of light. But that was to be expected. Gaunt House was remarkably secure. The ground-floor rooms were soundproofed, and the windows had steel shutters. The swindler who had refurbished the building had his own reasons to ensure he was safe from intruders, and Rachel Savernake had turned the place into a fortress.

A panel in the door slid away to reveal a grille. Trueman's voice said, "What is it?"

"I need to talk to Rachel." Jacob hated sounding so desperate. "I've got myself involved in a murder."

"Wait there."

Jacob gave the taxi driver a nod, and the car moved off into the night. The panel slid back into place, and once again became almost invisible to the naked eye. The door swung open.

Trueman stood before him, in his shirtsleeves. He considered Jacob rather as he might examine a dog which had disgraced itself.

"Go through to the kitchen. Hetty will see you presently."

Jacob did as he was told, and took a seat at the vast pine table in the centre of the kitchen. It was Rachel he wanted to talk to, but he knew better than to argue with Trueman. A clock on the Welsh dresser said half past two. Rachel was probably in bed, although once, in a rare confidence, she'd hinted that she suffered from insomnia.

He slumped back in the chair, and closed his eyes. His

clothes were grubby from lying on the attic floorboards, but he was too exhausted to care. He was drifting off to sleep when a hand tapped his shoulder.

"Your head's cut. Let's have a proper look at it."

Hetty Trueman's stern voice roused him. She was wearing a pinafore, as if about to cook a meal, but she produced a bottle of iodine and bowl of water together with a towel and dressings, and set to work. When she'd dealt with the wound on his scalp, he told her about having cut his foot on the nail, and she attended to that too. She'd have made a good matron of the gruff, no molly-coddling sort. Once or twice the iodine's sting made him yelp, but she took no notice until she'd done.

"There." She surveyed her handiwork. "You'll live."

"Thanks," he said without thinking, "you're an angel."

Hetty made a derisive sound. "And you're a rum one. Not to be trusted out on your own at night, by the look of you. Like something the cat dragged in. Heaven only knows what monkey business you've got up to. You need a good bath, and your suit's ruined. Blood's dripped on the jacket collar, and everything is sodden with gin. Come to that, your breath smells like you spent the night in a distillery."

"Apart from that," he said, "would you agree I'm fairly presentable?"

He detected a glimmer of a smile, but it vanished in a flash. "I've made the best of a bad job. I'd offer you brandy, but I expect you'd be sick. There's nothing more for it. You'll have to do."

He took a breath. "Is Rachel up and about?"

"We don't encourage callers, as well you know." Hetty never made anything easy. "Let alone when decent folk are tucked up in bed."

"But what about Rachel?" Even after all he'd been through, he couldn't quite stop himself.

She scowled. "I'll pretend I didn't hear that, you cheeky young devil."

"Sorry. It's been a difficult night. Let me try again. Might she be kind enough to make an exception? Just this once?"

The kitchen door opened, and Rachel walked in, together with Trueman and Martha. Rachel had a sheaf of papers in her hand. She was wearing a kimono robe in blue silk, decorated with a floral pattern; Martha had on a satin housecoat. Even in his groggy state, he thought they looked ravishing.

"Good evening, Jacob," Rachel said, dropping the papers onto the dresser. "I take it your investigations didn't go to plan?"

———

Rachel held up her hand as Jacob tried to explain. "More haste, less speed. This is such a muddle. Someone has been stabbed to death, and you're mixed it up in it? Fleeing from justice?"

"No!" He was outraged. "I've not done anything wrong. I've committed no crime."

"Now isn't the time to rehearse the case for your defence." Martha had made coffee for them all, and Rachel lifted her china cup. "Never mind the lurid headlines, give us the whole story. Every single thing that's happened in the past twenty-four hours. Tiny points may be crucial. You have an excellent memory; don't leave out a word. Don't exaggerate, either. You're not here to sell newspapers."

He swallowed some coffee. "There's a lot to tell. It'll take ages if I go through every jot and tittle."

She glanced at the clock. "We have the rest of the night. Take your time. The floor is yours."

"If you insist."

Tired and miserable and frustrated as he felt, he must do

Rachel's bidding. Her implacability tormented him, but he needed her on his side. She was his only hope of making sense of what had happened. And of dodging personal disaster.

"I do."

With painstaking attention to detail, and aided by copious quantities of Martha's excellent coffee, he recounted the sequence of events. His long, rambling conversation with Griselda Farquharson, the meeting with Inspector Oakes, the arrival of the membership card, and his visit to the Clandestine Club. Not until he reached the moment when he spotted Leonora Dobell did anyone else utter a word.

"How interesting," Rachel mused. "I did wonder."

"Whether Leonora was a member of the club?"

"Exactly."

"What on earth made you think she might be?"

"It crossed my mind that she'd heard about the place while researching Gilbert Payne. The Clandestine Club is a world away from Mortmain Hall. Curiosity got the better of her."

"She's a married woman."

Rachel groaned. "Oh, Jacob, I've spent most of my life on a tiny island, but there are times when I wonder if you've led a more sheltered existence than me."

"I've certainly not read half as many books as you," he snapped.

She exchanged a smile with Martha, who could scarcely contain her amusement. "It's good to see you've not run out of fighting spirit. Carry on with the story. We're agog."

Jacob scowled but didn't argue. After the drama and excitement of making his escape from the attic, he felt the clammy grip of depression. Now for the tricky part of his story. In the brightly lit kitchen, his sympathy for the pretty girl with the saucer-like eyes didn't seem as selfless as he'd thought at the time.

Rachel listened, expressionless, as he described his conversation with Daisy. When he reached the point where the girl had invited him for a nightcap, Rachel asked a question.

"Describe her dress."

Jacob blinked. "It was revealing, I remember that."

"I'm sure you do. Tell me more."

"Sorry, I'm not very good with women's clothes."

"Don't worry if you don't know your Lanvin from your Florrie Westwood. What colour was it?"

"A sort of bluey-green, I'd say."

Rachel sighed. "Let me help you, then. Was it azure, and made of chiffon? Bare shoulders, and offering a generous glimpse of milky bosom?"

"I suppose it was."

"And did she have blonde hair, bee-stung lips, and nail lacquer the same colour as her gown?" She paused. "Coupled with a faint resemblance to a poor man's Clara Bow?"

He stared. "How did you guess?"

"Put it down to my psychic powers. This colonel, did she tell you anything about him?"

"Only that he was much older." He thought for a moment. "She didn't think he was a real colonel."

"Might calling him a colonel have been a slip of the tongue?"

"I suppose so. Mostly, she called him Tom. Not that it would have been his real name. If he ever existed."

"Oh, he exists, all right," Rachel said. "But I must apologise. You were just about to get to the exciting part of your adventure."

He grimaced, but knew he might as well get it over with. Rachel and the Truemans listened in silence as he rattled through the story, explaining how she'd inveigled him to come up with her, and about recovering consciousness only to find himself stark naked and in bed with the body of a dead man.

"The ruffian who coshed you shouldn't have locked you in," Rachel said.

"I'm glad you think so" Jacob said, with a touch of asperity. "If..."

"I mean, what would the police make of it, if they found you locked up with a corpse? Perhaps he intended to unlock the door before they arrived. But it strikes me as a complication too far."

"I don't..."

"Describe the dead man," Rachel said.

Jacob blushed. "Well, as I say, he wasn't wearing anything apart from lipstick. How much detail do you need?"

"His age, for a start."

"He was in his thirties, probably. Brown hair, on the long side, but starting to thin on top. Grey eyes. Thin, a little less than six feet tall. And apart from the stab wound, there was a nasty scratch on one of his hands."

"I see." Rachel considered. "And you swear that you didn't murder this man? You're not in a state of fugue amnesia?"

His eyes widened in horror and his voice rose as he demanded, "Don't you believe me? Of course I didn't stab the man. I don't know him from Adam. The girl tricked me. I've done my utmost to be totally honest with you. I..."

She smiled. "I just wanted to make sure."

He glowered. "You seem to know a lot about Daisy. The girl, I mean."

"I should do. I saw her in a restaurant this evening, in the company of an older man." She sighed. "I was dining with your bed-mate at the time."

"What?" He gaped. "Not the man who was stabbed?"

"Yes, his name is Louis Morgans. He's a solicitor whose firm acts for the Dobell family." She yawned. "I'm afraid I took a strong dislike to him. His passing will be no great loss to the legal profession."

Chapter 19

Rachel refused to answer any of Jacob's questions until he'd described his escape from the attic. After coming to the end of his tale of woe, he slumped back in his chair while she gave a brief account of her dinner with Morgans. Trueman's burglary wasn't mentioned.

"You look shattered," Martha said. She was the only one to show any sympathy, he thought. "No wonder, after what you've been through."

"Fingerprints, I'm worried about fingerprints," he muttered. "I tried to wipe them off, but I'm sure I missed some."

Martha turned to Rachel. "What will the police make of it?"

"Jacob's right," Rachel said unexpectedly. "The odds are that the woman called the police. By now, they'll have found the body."

"Do you think they'll come knocking at my door?" Jacob asked hoarsely.

"Wipe the sweat off your brow. You escaped, and that makes all the difference. Suppose you did leave fingerprints. How would the police know they are yours? Nobody has given them your name."

"Why not?"

"Think about it. It's all very well to call the police and report mysterious cries from a deserted mews. It's something else to identify one specific journalist. That raises as many questions as answers. With all due respect, you're not a household name. Or a household face. It would have all the hallmarks of what our American cousins call a frame-up."

"Oakes gave me a membership card for the Clan," Jacob said. "He knows I intended to go to Soho. If my name is given to the police, and they want to take my fingerprints, I'm in a cleft stick."

Rachel shook her head. "If you did visit the attic, who is to say it was last night? Nobody saw you with Louis Morgans when he was alive."

"When else might I have gone there? And why else, for that matter?"

"Whoever owns the property," Rachel said, "the police will assume that the attic is used for prostitution. You could have been there on other occasions. Immoral, yes, but not illegal."

"But I've never…"

"Hush," Rachel put a finger to her lips. "Whoever tried to incriminate you has failed. Pinning the murder on you is now more trouble than it's worth."

"After going to such extremes? Bringing me to that mews, killing this fellow Morgans?" He pushed his hand through his hair. "It makes no sense."

"You suppose Morgans was stabbed to death simply so that you could be accused of murder?" Rachel arched her eyebrows. "You flatter yourself. This evening's events have all the hallmarks of improvisation. They had a victim, and you made an obliging scapegoat. Two birds, one stone."

"Improvisation?" He breathed out noisily. "Ridiculous. People don't improvise when it comes to murder."

"Because murder is so solemn and serious?" She shook her head. "Wrong. It's precisely when you're dealing with something out of the ordinary that you need to improvise. There's no instruction manual for murderers."

"The police won't be satisfied." He couldn't let it go. "Morgans was a solicitor, a respected member of the community."

Rachel made a scornful noise. "You think so?"

"They can't ignore his murder. It's not the same as some miserable scoundrel being killed."

"It's exactly the same, in my opinion, but let that pass. What the police will think is this: Morgans was killed in a lover's tiff, or by a prostitute, male or female, following a drink-soaked quarrel. Such crimes aren't unheard of in Soho. There will be a not-very-helpful inquest, and a bland statement to the press. The British public will be assured that such crimes are isolated incidents, that enquiries are being pursued. Nothing for the law-abiding majority to fear. Morgans was playing with fire, and got his fingers burned. If you're not available as a scapegoat, and the investigation runs into a cul-de-sac, people will lose interest. Including Scotland Yard."

His throat dry after talking so long, he said feebly, "What if they do question me?"

"Give them an alibi."

"I don't have an alibi."

"Wrong again." Rachel exchanged a glance with the Truemans.

"What do you mean?"

Martha cleared her throat. "Don't tell me you've forgotten?"

"Forgotten what?"

"Jacob, really! And after I let you stay the night."

"You've been hanging around here lately," Trueman said quietly. "We thought it was Rachel you were interested in. Instead it was my sister."

Jacob's mouth dropped open. He wanted to ask if they were serious, but dreaded sounding ungrateful or causing offence. They were offering him a lifeline. Just like that drainpipe in the dingy mews, he had to grab it.

"Not that we spent the night in bed together," Martha said gently. "I don't trust you that far. We just talked and talked, and then it was too late for you to go back home, so I made up the bed in one of our spare rooms."

"The room you'll sleep in once you've had a hot bath," Hetty said.

Jacob looked at their composed faces. If his brain had been scrambled earlier during this strange and terrible night, it was now well and truly mashed up. He felt more dead than alive. But he had to trust them.

"It's very good of you, Martha." He coughed to hide his embarrassment. "To be prepared to help me...in that way. Thank you."

"You make a lovely couple," Rachel said.

———

"You were right," Hetty told her husband when Jacob had left. "Thank goodness you did return that folder to Morgans's office straight away. The moment the body's identified, the police will go sniffing around."

"I left his room as I found it," Cliff Trueman said. "Not that I expected him to be murdered."

"First Payne, now Morgans," Hetty said. "Where will it end? Was it worth the risk of breaking in?"

"I've read the copies the three of you made," Rachel said. "Martha's handwriting is much better than yours, thank goodness."

"What do you make of the letters?" Trueman asked. "If you managed to decipher my scrawl?"

Rachel sighed. "Leonora has scrupulously obtained permission every time she wanted to sell a picture. There's no hint of fraud."

"And the settlement deed?"

"I wondered if she was lying about being entitled to stay on at Mortmain Hall after her husband died, but Morgans confirmed her understanding. So does the deed. The estate goes to Oswyn Dobell's son or grandson, natural or otherwise. The surviving widow of an incumbent heir is entitled to a life interest, so that the next generation has to wait its turn."

"Oswyn was far more liberal than most testators, then."

"Generous to a fault."

"So even if Felix Dobell had died the very next day after marrying Leonora, she'd have remained as the tenant of Mortmain for the rest of her life?"

"Exactly."

"Quite an incentive for murder."

"Except that her motive would be screamingly obvious. Twelve years since their marriage, Felix is still alive and kicking. Leonora is content to go her own way. While a nurse looks after her husband, she amuses herself at the Old Bailey or the Clandestine Club as the mood takes her. Why risk killing Felix? What would she gain?"

"Unless," Cliff said slowly, "she wanted to kill him for the hell of it. Just for the thrill of seeing if she could commit the perfect murder."

———

"This is your room." Martha indicated an open door on the landing of the second floor. Jacob saw a four-poster bed, with white towels laid on the bedspread.

"Thanks," he said. "And I'm grateful for the alibi."

Her smile showed strong white teeth. "My pleasure. The bathroom is first on the left. The water's hot, you can have a good soak; it'll do you good. Don't fall asleep. It would be a shame if you drowned after surviving so much."

His grin was weary. "You're very kind."

"If you want me to scrub your back, just ring the bell." A cheeky giggle. "Only your back, mind."

With a peal of musical laughter, she skipped off downstairs while he was still blushing.

———

They woke him for a late breakfast in the conservatory at half past nine. He panicked on seeing the time, and stammered incoherently about the *Clarion*, but Rachel put a restraining hand on his arm.

"Martha called your office. She told them you'd be in later."

"She did?" He had visions of colleagues being told he'd spent the night with Rachel's maid. "What did she say?"

"I took the liberty of claiming to be your landlady," Martha said. "They were quite understanding when I told them you were following up a murder that's just been reported."

His eyes widened. "A murder?"

Trueman pointed to the newspapers piled on a chair. "A man's body was found in Soho last night. Cause of death, stabbing. There are veiled hints that the circumstances are unsavoury, and that the deceased was a toff. So far, he hasn't been named."

"It won't take long to identify him." Rachel buttered her toast. "I expect the woman and her associate left his wallet. Just as they left yours, Jacob."

"You think the man who hit me was the man you saw in Foibles? The chap who was squiring Daisy?"

She shook her head. "No, he was too old and too dignified to indulge in violence. Men like that delegate their dirty work to hired hands."

"Who are these people? Why are they doing this?" He gulped some orange juice. "And why did they pick on me?"

"Whoever it is," Rachel said, "is powerful enough to warn you off via a Scotland Yard inspector. Raking over old coals, wasn't that the phrase?"

"You suspect this is connected with Gilbert Payne?"

"Yes."

"And Louis Morgans? Where does he fit in, and why was he murdered?"

"Excellent questions, Jacob." She poured herself a coffee. "If only I had all the answers."

"Is it to do with Leonora Dobell? Is she mixed up in this murky business?"

"At first I doubted it," she said, "The trouble is that wherever we turn, the woman pops up."

"Something odd is going on," Hetty said.

"You have a genius for understatement." Rachel rubbed her chin. "It's almost as if…"

"As if what?" Jacob asked.

She thought for a moment. "As if we're looking at a Cezanne, and noticing brushstrokes by Gauguin."

This was too Delphic for him. "And why has Leonora arranged this house party?"

"There's only place to find the answer, Jacob."

"Namely?"

"We need to go to Mortmain Hall."

———

"Good of you to turn up." Gomersall made a show of checking his watch when he spotted Jacob in the corridor at Clarion House.

"You got my message?" Jacob tried to exude the quiet excitement of a man on a warm trail.

Gomersall frowned. "Those rings under your eyes make you look as though you've been up all night. Burning the candle at both ends, lad?"

"All in the line of duty, sir." Well, it was more or less true. "This murder in Soho."

"Squalid affair." Gomersall snorted. "Is it that really what our readers want to accompany their porridge in the morning? Chap stabbed to death in a dive by some tart or pimp? We're a family newspaper, Jacob, never forget."

"Absolutely."

"Whatever happened to the middle-class murderer?"

An image swam into Jacob's mind. The author of *Respectable Murders*, dressed up as a man, singing "Ain't She Sweet?" to a nubile young woman. Respectability wasn't all it was cracked up to be.

"The professional man at the end of his tether." Gomersall warmed to his theme, sounding almost nostalgic. "Seeing no way out other than a shocking crime. Crippen, Armstrong..."

"Danskin?"

"Defence lawyers are getting smarter," Gomersall muttered. "That's what's wrong with this country."

"Let me run with Soho, sir. I'll file a story as soon as the victim is identified. I've got a first-rate lead, and I'd like to see where it takes me."

Gomersall shrugged. "You're the chief crime correspondent. Ball's in your court."

"Leave it with me," Jacob said, with more confidence than he felt. "By Monday I may have a scoop."

———

"You must see my menagerie." Sir Samuel Dackins's command brooked no argument. "Come on. Plenty of time before the start of play."

The Masqueraders had enjoyed a hearty breakfast around a long table in Tunnicliffe's old cruck barn while their host regaled them with tales of his triumphs in business, jungle exploration, and village cricket. Each field of endeavour, he explained, demanded comparable grit and perseverance.

He led his guests under an ivy-clad loggia at the back of the manor and along a path running beside a colourful herbaceous border. The scent of roses filled the summer air. Shading his eyes from the sun, Dackins opined that it was a perfect day for cricket. Major Whitlow gave a curt nod of agreement.

As they passed a small chapel with an even smaller graveyard, they heard the squawk of birds and screech of monkeys. Reggie exchanged a glance with Pennington, whose ruddy cheeks were almost bursting with suppressed amusement. The din became louder as they reached the front of the stable block. Dackins halted, and raised a hand. The party gathered in a semicircle in front of him, like tourists clustering around a Thomas Cook guide.

"I converted the stables to house the smaller animals as well as my collection of parakeets," he announced. "Listen to them chatter: you can tell how much they love it here."

After inspecting the birds and monkeys and making the requisite murmurs of appreciation, the cricketers entered a stockade containing a pool for penguins as well as the cages of the larger animals. A lion prowled around in front of them, and bared its teeth in greeting.

"Aren't people in the village frightened, having so many

dangerous animals on their doorstep?" asked an earnest little fellow called Turner. He was about thirty, although his thin hair and anxious demeanour made him look ten years older; he worked as a statistician in an office two doors down the corridor from Reggie's.

"One or two malcontents may mumble into their beer," Dackins said. "Ha! You get more sense out of dumb creatures than you do out of the British working man. The blasted farmers moan the most. Mithering that the lions will get out and kill their sheep. Sheer hypocrisy. What happens to their beloved flock, eh? They end up on the dinner table, that's what. Lamb chops and mutton."

Turner was meek but persistent, qualities that suited him admirably for his job, and also for bowling economical spells of off spin. "Doesn't anyone complain that it's cruel to keep wild beasts in captivity?"

Dackins snorted. "There's a ravine over yonder, behind the cricket ground, where my head keeper lets 'em run free. Don't worry, I've had the sides built up so it's impossible for them to escape. Safe as houses. Safer than in the wild, come to that. Perfectly true what they say about nature being red in tooth and claw. Ever seen a lion chewed to death by a pack of hyenas?"

Turner shook his head nervously, and Sir Samuel took them on to the wild cats' cage. A full-grown tigress swished her tail and stalked towards the iron bars. Reggie found himself gazing into yellow eyes with black irises. For all the morning's warmth, he felt a chill.

The menace in her smile reminded him of Rachel Savernake.

———

Major Whitlow won the toss, and elected to bat under a clear blue sky. The Masqueraders amassed one hundred and thirty runs before he declared their innings closed, and the teams adjourned for tea in the thatched pavilion. Reggie set about his egg-and-tomato sandwiches with the zest of a man who had nudged and nurdled fifteen runs before missing a straight ball and hearing the crash of his stumps behind him. He'd made his highest score for two seasons, and worked up an appetite.

Pennington quaffed a tankard of beer. He was basking in the appreciation of his teammates after notching a rapid half-century. Turner, who had vacated the place to Reggie's right a few minutes earlier, sat down beside him again, and poured himself a glass from the jug of ale. Reggie was surprised. Unlike the rest of the Masqueraders, Turner was a modest drinker who usually confined himself to half a pint after the game was over.

"Dutch courage?" Pennington demanded with his customary joviality as Turner took a swig. "Don't worry, your slower ball will bamboozle their batsmen. They won't know whether to slog it for four or for six."

He guffawed at his own wit as Turner frowned. "I went back to change my shirt, and heard the news on the wireless. Chap I was at school with has been murdered. Bad business, by the sound of it."

Pennington patted his stomach. "Don't tell me a maniac has set about ridding the world of old Harrovians."

"You were at Harrow, Turner?" Reggie asked.

The little man nodded. "You weren't, though?"

"No, no, it's just that… I know one or two chaps who were at Harrow."

"Mixing with your betters, eh?" said Pennington, an old Etonian.

Turner's pallor was natural, but there was no mistaking the tremor in his voice. "It's no laughing matter, Pennington. A man, butchered in the middle of London. In some disreputable haunt in Soho. Makes you wonder what the world is coming to."

"What was his name?" Reggie asked.

Turner sighed. "Louis Morgans."

———

"Mortmain?" the taxi driver at Scarborough station repeated. His bushy eyebrows beetled. "Dobell Arms?"

His tone implied that Jacob wished to be conveyed to a distant and inhospitable planet.

"Got it in one," Jacob said cheerfully, climbing into the back.

Following his misadventures of the previous evening, he'd recovered his *sangfroid*. He'd fled from a waking nightmare to find himself safe and sound, with only a few scratches and bruises to show for it. The weather was warm, he was back in his home county, and he'd caught up with some sleep on the journey.

Best of all, he'd just picked up a copy of a late edition of the *Clarion*, hot off the presses. Before dashing to King's Cross for his train, he'd rattled off a dozen crisp paragraphs in record time. Knowing more than the police made his job so much easier. The only concern was to avoid giving too much away. His handiwork filled the front page. It was a good splash.

Soho Murder Victim Identified as Prominent Solicitor

Admittedly *prominent* stretched the truth, but it made for a sharper hook than *odious*. A head-and-shoulders photograph of Louis Morgans smirked from beneath the headline, barely recognisable as the corpse Jacob had seen in that hellhole of an attic. The picture editor had laid his hands on a studio portrait. At first glance, Morgans did bear a passing resemblance to a respectable professional man.

"Not a lot of call for rides to Mortmain, then?" Jacob asked, as they headed out on to the coast road.

The man gave a catarrhal sniff. "It's the back of beyond. Nothing to see, nothing to do. Just a few cliffs and a load of birds making a nuisance of themselves."

"Isn't there a big house? Mortmain Hall?"

"Old mausoleum," the driver said. "Been in the same family for donkey's years, but they've never done owt with it."

"The Dobells, isn't that right? I hear they own a lot of famous paintings."

The driver dismissed the collection of treasures with another sniff. "I don't know owt about art."

"Do you know the Dobell Arms, by any chance? This is my first visit."

The local inn was the one place in the vicinity of Mortmain Hall where you could put up for the night. Martha had telephoned to book him in. She'd amused herself by pretending to be his sister.

"Never set foot in the place." An emphatic sniff. "You're not from these parts, then?"

"Actually, I'm a Yorkshireman myself." Jacob was irked by the implication that he hailed from the soft south. "West Riding, not North. Born and bred in Armley."

"Leeds, is that?"

The driver made it sound as remote as Vladivostok, and as unknowable. He lapsed into silence, and Jacob didn't disturb him again.

———

For Reggie Vickers, the rest of the match passed in a blur. The scoreboard ticked over, but he paid it no heed. He was even oblivious to the occasional roar from the unseen ravine on the far side of the pavilion when the lions felt the need to remind everyone of their presence.

Sir Samuel's team relied on the aggressive batting of a gardener who was built like a blacksmith. He smote the bowling to all four corners of the ground, and although wickets fell regularly at the other end, he was carrying his side to victory. Reggie drifted around the outfield, allowing one fierce shot to pass though his legs to the boundary, to Major Whitlow's displeasure.

Lulu Morgans's death had shaken him to the core. They'd met through the Clan, and their last encounter had ended on bad terms. Lulu was as louche as Doodle was faithless, and they'd quarrelled over the transfer of Doodle's affections to Reggie. Morgans's murder might be a matter of chance. Had he simply been in the wrong place at the wrong time? Soho was full of bad hats, and it was easy to fall foul of them. But Reggie feared there was something more to the crime, something he didn't understand. He only knew enough to make him afraid.

"Catch!"

Turner, whose bowling had taken fearful punishment, had lobbed up an inviting slow ball which the gardener thrashed at with his customary vigour. The ball caught the top edge of his bat and instead of sailing over the boundary, looped up invitingly towards midwicket.

The Masqueraders' fielders had scattered, and Reggie was best placed to take the catch. Pennington's bellow jerked him out of his reverie. He circled beneath the red ball. It took an age to fall from the sky. He cupped his hands in the approved fashion, only for the ball to smack them with such force that he spilled it to the ground. The gasp of dismay from his teammates spoke louder than words. His palm stung as he picked the ball up and hurled it back to the wicketkeeper. The wildness of his throw cost two additional runs.

"Sorry," he called. "Sun in my eyes."

"Bad luck," Turner said stoically. "Catch the next one."

They both knew there wouldn't be another chance. Reggie had not only dropped the catch. He'd let the game slip through his fingers.

He dared not glance at his captain. Major Whitlow was not the forgiving kind.

——

A narrow lane led from the coast road through fields and woodland to Mortmain. The hamlet amounted to a scattering of cottages, a small post office, and a shop. The Dobell Arms was the last building before the lane curved behind a coppice and out of sight, towards the Hall. The inn had a painted signboard battered by the elements and displaying a barely distinguishable coat of arms. Jacob tipped the driver, advised him to take a sightseeing trip to Armley, and strode inside, clutching his suitcase and the *Clarion*.

The inn only had one bar. The ceiling was low, and the floor flagged. There was an inglenook with an unlit log fire. The place was deserted except for a customer who was ringing a bell on the counter. He had a trunk at his feet, a camera case in one hand, and a pair of binoculars hanging from his neck. An Ordnance Survey map peeped out of his coat pocket.

Jacob had decided not to use a false name. He'd tell any casual enquirer that he was taking a short break from the pressures of work. If need be, he'd drop a hint that he suffered from bad nerves, and craved peace and quiet. Given that Mortmain was devoid of tourist attractions, he'd decided to say he was birdwatching. There'd be no shortage of feathered friends in the area. Gulls and suchlike. He'd brought a notebook, pen, and camera to lend credence to his story, but had failed to bargain for bumping into a genuine ornithologist. The sight of the binoculars halted him in his tracks. He'd forgotten to bring any, not that he had a pair of his own.

The man turned and peered suspiciously at him through horn-rimmed spectacles with thick lenses. Jacob's cheeks felt hot. His plumage and colouring were under scrutiny, and had been found wanting. He was too commonplace, he thought glumly. The lesser spotted London journalist.

"Good afternoon," the man said.

His voice was reedy, his accent Scottish. His hair had an indeterminate sandy tint, as did his goatee beard. Jacob would have pigeonholed him as a holidaying schoolmaster but for the fact that it was still term time.

"Afternoon." Jacob joined him at the counter and dropped his suitcase down by his feet. "Waiting long?"

"Four and a half minutes." He rang the bell again.

This prissy and precise fellow looked like one of those pedants who delight in catching other people out. Jacob resolved to claim no expertise whatsoever in the field of ornithology. What else did you look for on the Yorkshire coast? He racked his brains. The landscape was ancient. Jurassic, perhaps? He'd pretend to be interested in fossils.

An elderly man in shirtsleeves emerged from a door at the back of the bar, and scowled at them. "All right, all right. Who's first?"

"Mr Hepton?" the man with the binoculars said.

"Aye."

"Remember me?"

"Happen," the landlord said.

"My name is Siddons, from Inverness. I've stayed here before, as you may recall. Are your sister-in-law and your charming niece well?"

"Happen."

"I've booked the room in the annexe for two nights."

The landlord pushed a dog-eared guestbook across the counter. As Siddons signed his name, Jacob wondered why anyone would want to come back here. Conditions for bird-watching must be more hospitable than those inside the Dobell Arms. Perhaps the real attraction was the charming niece.

He yawned. Fatigue was catching up with him. Placing his copy of the *Clarion* on the bar counter, he sneaked another look at his story on the front page. Did the likes of Renoir feel this satisfaction of a job well done when admiring their latest masterpiece?

The landlord handed a large key to Siddons and said that the door to the inn was locked at a quarter to eleven, sharp. Glancing at the *Clarion* headline, Siddons exclaimed in shock.

"Murder! My goodness." He coughed. "A solicitor, too! What is the world coming to?"

Jacob only just managed to suppress a low groan. He'd committed a cardinal error. The story about Morgans carried his own byline.

As soon as he signed in, it would be obvious that he'd written the story that very day. The landlord's indifference to customers might cause him to ignore it, but Siddons looked like the sort who couldn't mind his own business. So much for the tale about escaping to Mortmain for rest and relaxation.

Muttering vaguely about having left something outside, he fled from the bar, leaving Siddons to stare after him with ill-concealed suspicion. The landlord remained stubbornly indifferent.

Banging the door of the inn behind him, Jacob cursed himself for his carelessness. Last night, overconfidence had come close to costing him his life, but he'd still not learned the lesson. He'd only been here five minutes, and already complacency had caused him to stick out like a sore thumb. A birdwatcher who didn't know the first thing about birds, a man seeking to recuperate but still hard at work.

Thank goodness Rachel Savernake wasn't here to see him squirming with self-abasement. If he were to make sense of what Leonora Dobell was up to, he'd better shape up. He stomped up and down until he was sure that Siddons had departed for his room. The last thing he wanted was to be identified as a crime reporter and trapped in conversation about Louis Morgans's murder by a pernickety nosey parker.

This was the problem with human interest stories, he told himself miserably. They provoked human interest.

When he felt sure the coast must be clear, he went back inside. His suitcase was where he'd left it, but the *Clarion* had vanished, and so had Siddons and Hepton. Jacob rang the bell, but this time more than four and a half minutes passed before mine host deigned to return.

Chapter 20

"What brings you to Mortmain, then?"

Lucy Hepton, the landlord's niece, had lingered after serving Jacob his tea. He was her only customer. Sturdily built, fair-haired, and vivacious, Lucy had a winning smile and a weakness for cheap scent. It was soon clear that she liked a gossip, especially with a young man. The Dobell Arms never got passing trade, she said, because nobody ever passed through it on their way somewhere. The lane came to a dead end at Mortmain Head, and there was only the gloomy old Hall, perched on the clifftops.

"I wanted to relax for a few days. Whitby and Scarborough are too busy. I fancied a bit of peace and quiet."

"You'll get that here, all right. Another birdwatcher, are you?"

"No," he said hastily. "Mr Siddons is the expert."

He was relieved that the ornithologist hadn't put in an appearance. The last thing he wanted was a chat about birdlife.

Lucy sighed. "He's potty about our feathered friends. They're all he really cares about. Goes into raptures if he sees a stonechat perched on a bit of gorse. Their mating call sounds like two pebbles being knocked together, he told me. Takes all sorts, I told him."

She gave him a suggestive wink. Jacob deduced that Siddons hadn't paid her as much attention as she hoped for. He murmured in sympathy.

"He should watch where he's putting his feet, instead of looking up at the sky all the time. He came back an hour ago, limping and moaning like billy-o, and took himself off to bed. He tripped over the cliff edge at Mortmain Head, and sprained his ankle. Mr Dobell's nurse was out, and she bandaged it. He should thank his lucky stars. He could have broken his neck, or drowned, or both. It's a long way down to the sea."

"The cliffs are dangerous?"

"If you don't keep your eye on where you're going. There are paths, but you need to pick your way down like a mountain goat."

"I thought I might look for fossils."

Lucy laughed. "You can start with my old uncle."

———

Beer flowed freely in the cruck barn as Sir Samuel's men celebrated their glorious triumph, and the Masqueraders drowned their sorrows. Reggie drank as if there were no tomorrow. People clapped him on the back, and told him to cheer up. Everyone dropped catches; it was part of the game. None of them realised that the cause of his misery wasn't the mistake that had cost the Masqueraders dear.

Confused and out of his depth, he didn't have a clue what to do next. Two men he knew had been murdered in the space of a week. How could their deaths be a coincidence? He'd known Gilbert Payne's life was in jeopardy; that was why he'd enlisted the aid of the Savernake woman. This second killing, out of the blue, had shredded his nerves. Since Doodle had walked out on him, he had nobody to confide in. He dare not utter a peep to any of his colleagues. Let alone the police. Had he blundered in refusing to talk to Rachel Savernake?

The trouble was that the woman was a mystery. Her name had cropped up at a dinner party. A pal of his godfather, the commissioner of the Metropolitan Police, had gossiped about a judge's daughter with remarkable detective skills. Not that Sir Godfrey approved of outsiders interfering with a police investigation into murder, dear me no. But Rachel Savernake was no shabby inquiry agent, but a judge's daughter with untold wealth and an obsession about murder.

He remembered her name after discovering that Gilbert Payne was still alive but in mortal danger. Consulting the official police was too dangerous—for him, as well as for Gilbert. He'd sought out the Savernake woman and told her as much as he dared. Her coolness as she'd listened to his extraordinary story had impressed and repelled him at one and the same time, but she'd asked enough questions for him to believe she would try to save Gilbert's life.

Knocking back the rest of his pint, he wondered if he'd been too hasty in turning his back on her. Malign and powerful forces were at work. Could Rachel Savernake cast light on the darkness?

And could he trust her?

"Penny for 'em," a voice said.

"Just remembered I've forgotten something."

Pennington chortled. "Contradiction in terms, old man."

"Back in a minute." Reggie got up from his chair. "Call of nature."

"Return fixture is on Saturday, don't forget. Better nip off for some catching practice." Pennington was still braying with laughter as Reggie pushed his way through the crowd.

———

"Funny woman, Mrs Dobell."

"You don't like her?"

After Lucy had cleared the crockery away, she'd come back and pulled up a chair. Jacob had steered the conversation towards Mortmain Hall and its occupants.

"It's not that," Lucy said. "She goes out of her way to make a fuss of me."

Jacob remembered Leonora in the Clandestine Club, singing "Ain't She Sweet?". "Does she really?"

"You'd be surprised." Lucy appeared to be about to share a confidence, before thinking better of it. "And all the time the Hall is going to rack and ruin. Anyhow, she spends a lot of her time down in London."

"What does she get up to there?"

"They say she writes books," Lucy said darkly.

"Goodness," Jacob said. "What about?"

"Murder trials, of all things. Mother says it's nasty. Uncle Bob can't be doing with it, either. Reckons that Mr Dobell ought to put his foot down." She gave a cheeky grin. "Even if he only has one foot."

"Do you see much of him?"

She shook her head. "He was crippled in the war, poor soul. They say he's not really much of a man, if you catch my meaning. He has a nurse to look after him. Not that the nurses last long. There's nothing to keep anyone in Mortmain."

"You've stayed here."

"Twenty-two years," she said dreamily. "A whole lifetime. Not that I could ever leave Mother. So I have to amuse myself as best I can."

She shifted her chair close to his. Acutely conscious of her physical presence, as well as the suffocating perfume, he said, "Do the Dobells...?"

"You don't want to hear me gassing away about the Dobells," she said, placing a hand on his knee. "The gentry aren't like you and me, Jacob."

The door of the inn swung open. Jacob glanced up and saw two old men hobbling towards the bar. He stifled a sigh of relief.

"You've got some customers," he said.

"Two more fossils for your collection," she muttered.

Laughing, he said, "It's been a long day. I can hardly keep my eyes open."

Getting to her feet, she shot him a quizzical look. "Fit young chap like you? It's the fresh air, that's all. A quick nap, and then you'll be ready for anything."

———

Reggie had noticed a telephone in the billiard room where Sir Samuel had entertained his guests the previous evening. He checked his wallet for the piece of paper bearing Rachel's number, but couldn't find it. Irritating, when time was short. He didn't want his absence to arouse comment. He called the operator, and asked to be put through. It took an age, and while he was waiting, Turner popped his head round the door.

"There you are, Vickers! The major is looking for you."

Sweating, Reggie covered the mouthpiece. "What does he want?"

"No need to bite my head off." Turner's tone was injured. "It's not about the cricket."

"Sorry, old man. Still a bit fraught after muffing that catch."

"The major picked up something of yours in the pavilion. At least he thinks it's yours. Asked you to go over there." Turner glanced at his watch. "If you hurry, you'll be back before the soup is served."

"Something of mine?"

"Evidently you dropped it," Turner said with feeling.

Reggie swore under his breath as he put down the telephone receiver. Had the major found the piece of paper on which he'd written Rachel Savernake's address and telephone number? His handwriting, large and childish, was recognisable to anyone familiar with it. Perhaps when he'd changed into his cricket whites, it had fallen out of his pocket. But why did the major want to see him in the pavilion?

There could only be one answer: he wanted a quiet word away from the others, somewhere they wouldn't be disturbed. The major meant to interrogate him about Rachel Savernake.

———

While Lucy was serving the fossils with their beer, Jacob made good his escape. His poky little room was at the top of the stairs. Yawning, he told himself that he hadn't lied to the girl about how weary he felt. It was still light outside, still early, but he was suffering from the effects of his escapade in Soho.

He stripped down to his singlet and shorts, and locked the door, just in case. Lucy appealed to him, and so in theory did the prospect of a frolic with a healthy young woman. But it would take time to recover from his misadventure in Soho. He lay down on the bed and was fast asleep long before a knock came on the bedroom door.

The knocking persisted for fully half a minute, and then the door handle was rattled in vain. None of it woke him up.

———

Reggie slipped out through the French windows at the back of Tunnicliffe. It was a pleasant July evening, the sun's glare no longer ferocious. Hastening towards the cricket ground, he wondered how he might appease the major, and wished he hadn't drunk so much. The brief comfort of alcohol had given way to lethargy and his brain, sluggish at the best of times, was woozy.

In the distance he glimpsed the drive, winding through the trees and towards the main road. Should he make a run for it, take the coward's way out? Wasn't it better to live to fight another day? The snag was, he had nowhere to run to. There was nothing for it but to bluff his way out of trouble. If need be, he'd get down on bended knee and beg for forgiveness. He'd given years of loyal service. Anyone could make a mistake. To err was human.

Better get a move on. The major hated to be kept waiting. Reggie's breath came in ragged spurts as he quickened his pace, and moved beyond the mountainous rhododendrons. The cricket scoreboard came into view, and then the pavilion, its thatched roof pretty under the dipping sun. A tall, upright figure emerged and came down the steps. He stood at the boundary edge, arms folded, and watched as Reggie put on a spurt.

"Sorry if I'm late," he panted.

In his good hand, Major Whitlow held aloft a piece of paper. Sure enough, it was Reggie's note about the Savernake woman's details.

"We need to have a private talk, Vickers."

"Absolutely, sir. I quite understand." What could he do but fawn? "A quiet word. Far from the madding crowd."

The major gave a curt nod. Displeased, Reggie thought, but not spitting feathers. That was something to cling on to; there was hope. He followed the other man along a grass pathway which led away from the pavilion and through a copse of yew trees before descending to a patch of rocky ground. Ahead of them was a knee-high brick wall overlooking a fold in the landscape. The major strode forward and sat down on the wall, facing Reggie. He beckoned Reggie to join him.

"I'm familiar with Miss Savernake's name," he said conversationally, "but I know very little about the woman. Tell me about your relations with her."

"Not much to tell, sir." Reggie struck a casual note; after all, they were two men of the world. "Good family, judge's daughter. Damned attractive, if I may say so. I was given her name by a friend of my godfather's."

"I see."

Reggie wasn't an accomplished liar. It was safest to stick to the truth. The devil of it was, he had no idea how much the major knew, how much he might have guessed. Dangerous to deny having met the woman, if he'd been spotted entering Gaunt House. He was fairly certain he'd not been followed there. But better safe than sorry.

"She invited me to her house once. Rather a home bird. Not a girl for gadding about, parties and suchlike. We took tea, had a natter about this and that…"

"What did you natter about?"

Reggie stroked his jaw. "Between you and me, I found her rather hard work. Not one for small talk. It turned out we didn't have anything in common. She's keen on art, of all things. Her walls are festooned with the most ghastly modern stuff. As for cricket, I doubt she knows an arm ball from a leg bye."

He ventured a man-to-man snigger, but the major's expression didn't flicker. The chap had no sense of humour.

"Was Gilbert Payne mentioned?"

"Payne?" Reggie breathed out. "Lord, no. She's only lived in London a short while. His name would mean nothing to her."

"You didn't discuss him at all?"

"Word of honour, sir." Reggie didn't care to be trapped into the lie direct, but needs must. "Never mix business with pleasure, that's my motto. Not that meeting Rachel Savernake was much fun, between you and me. I've no desire to malign a lady, but she's a cold fish. I decided not to continue the acquaintance."

Major Whitlow's brow furrowed. "I don't believe you."

"I say, sir. That's a bit strong, isn't it?" Reggie began to get to his feet. "Word of a gentleman, and all that?"

"Sit down." Reggie sat. "And Louis Morgans? Were you equally discreet in his company? At the Clandestine Club and elsewhere?"

Reggie felt sick in the pit of his stomach. He'd hoped against hope that the major knew nothing about that side of his life. Damn it all, what a fellow got up to in his private time was nobody else's business. It was simply a matter of letting off steam as far as he was concerned. One of these days, he'd settle down to tedious respectability. He'd marry well, or as well as he could, raise a few nippers, give them the benefit of a proper education. All he needed was to be given a chance. He'd sown his wild oats; he could make a fresh start. It wasn't fair to persecute a chap because he'd made a mistake or two. Anyone could slip off the straight and narrow. It was as easy as dropping a catch.

A glance at Major Whitlow's impassive features told him what he already knew in his heart. Outrage would get him nowhere. Nor would a plea to the major's better nature. He didn't have one.

"I hardly knew Morgans, sir."

"You went as white as a sheet when you heard he was dead."

"Well, of course…"

"Don't bluster, Vickers. It does you no credit." The major tapped Reggie on the knee with his iron claw. A gentle movement, but the sharp fingertips stung. "What did you tell Rachel Savernake?"

He was a jelly of indecision. "I…suppose I may have mentioned Payne, sir."

"An old friend, wasn't he, from the Clandestine Club? When you heard he was still alive, and planning to come back to England, you were concerned for his safety."

"Naturally, sir." Reggie made a brave attempt to muster his dignity. "I hoped…"

"Your work may be mundane, but it is highly confidential." The major's tone hardened. "Have you broken a sacred trust?"

"Sir." Reggie began to flounder. "I mentioned no names, gave nothing away of any substance."

The major's eyes bored into his. Reggie searched in vain for a hint of pity. Mystified, he watched as the other man suddenly bent to pick a pebble from the ground. He lobbed it over his shoulder, over the wall. It made a faint clatter as it fell.

A snarl of anger came from below.

Shifting his position, Reggie saw that the wall separated the grass path from a thick slab of rock overhanging a ravine. He caught a glimpse of a shaggy mane as the creature moved back into the shadows. Its sleep had been disturbed. So this was where the wild animals were allowed to roam free. Thank heaven they couldn't escape.

"You're lying," the major said. "Don't you agree, Pennington?"

Reggie jerked his head again, and saw Pennington's bulky figure emerging from the trees. In his large right hand, he carried a monkey wrench.

"Through his teeth, I'm afraid, sir." Pennington's bonhomie had vanished. His grimness hit Reggie like a blow from the wrench.

In the ravine, the lion snarled again.

"I…I'll tell you everything," Reggie stuttered. "I was fond of

Gilbert, very fond. When I found out that…that he was in danger if he came back to Britain, I was upset. Stupid of me."

"Very," Pennington said.

"I was desperate to save him if I could. I didn't talk to the police, I swear. But I thought the Savernake woman…anyhow, it was a mistake. She did nothing, and Gilbert died."

"Fell out of a train, didn't he?" Pennington asked. "Pure accident."

"If…if you say so."

"Accidents do happen," Pennington said. "And you've had a drop too much to drink, Reggie. You're getting careless. That missed catch this afternoon wasn't the half of it."

Reggie panicked. He jumped down from the wall, and was about to make a dash for it. But the major moved more quickly, and slashed him on the back of the neck with his claw. Reggie fell to the ground, whimpering with shock and pain.

"Not to worry, sir," Pennington said. "The marks won't look much different from those the lions make. Come on, Vickers. Stiff upper lip. Don't make this any more difficult than it needs to be."

He lifted Reggie up as casually as if he were unloading the Bugatti.

"Help!" Reggie screamed.

He struggled to free himself from the muscular arms. But there was no one to hear him or help him. Only the major and Pennington and the animals down in the ravine.

Pennington heaved him over the jutting rock, and let him fall. Reggie screamed as he struck the steep sides of the ravine, before hitting his head on the stony, uneven ground at the bottom.

He lost consciousness as the lion emerged from the shadows.

Chapter 21

"Gorgeous day," Jacob said.

Sun streamed through the windows of the Dobell Arms, but breakfast proved a subdued affair. Siddons, the only other guest, sat by himself. He'd parked his binoculars, map, and walking stick on the chair at opposite side of his little table, to deter anyone from joining him.

He responded to Jacob's pleasantry with a bad-tempered mumble, and drained his coffee cup before struggling to his feet. Wincing as he put weight on his damaged ankle, he limped towards the back door, which led to the tiny outbuilding dignified with the description of an annexe.

On his way out, he passed Mrs Hepton, a dumpy woman with fair hair turning grey. Her cheerful goodbye failed to earn a reply. She presented Jacob with a plate of fat sausages, greasy eggs, and fried bread.

"Sleep well?"

"Like a log, thank you."

He didn't regret his decision not to encourage Lucy's attentions. After his night in Soho, a long uninterrupted and dreamless sleep had done him the world of good.

"Your first time in Mortmain, is it?"

In between mouthfuls, he explained that he'd wanted to get away for a few days. He didn't say what he was getting away from. Mrs Hepton said she gathered he meant to go fossil hunting.

"Ammonites," he said airily, crossing his fingers that Mrs Hepton knew even less about fossils than he did. "Fascinating… um…things."

Mrs Hepton smiled vaguely, and he quizzed her about the Dobells, without learning anything new. When she asked about his plans for the day, he said he'd buy a newspaper in the village, and then stroll around the peninsula.

"Take a gander at our paper if you want," she said obligingly. "The *Witness.*"

"Thanks." He managed not to pour scorn on her taste. "It'll make a change. I usually read the *Clarion.*"

He was glad he hadn't revealed that he was a reporter. The Heptons showed little curiosity about their guests. He suspected none of them had read his story in the copy he'd left on the counter yesterday. In Mortmain, a murder in Soho probably seemed as irrelevant as a hurricane in Hawaii.

A few moments later, she returned to present him with the newspaper. Her pleasant, worn face was sombre.

"Terrible business over at Tunnicliffe. What is the world coming to? Poor man. Fancy being eaten by a lion!"

Jacob's stomach churned as he scanned the front page. His early-morning languor had vanished. Gobbling down the fried breakfast had been a mistake. He felt queasy.

To learn that lions roamed a country estate was startling enough. The news that the animal had feasted on Reggie Vickers sickened him. The *Witness*'s breathless account of the man's fate left as little to the imagination as journalistic decency required. The prurience of the report would have appalled him if he hadn't known that the *Clarion* would be equally gleeful.

So the man who had told Rachel about Gilbert Payne was dead. His grieving friends had told the *Witness* that they'd all been drinking after a cricket match. Reggie had celebrated with more gusto than anyone, even though he'd been on the losing side. It just showed what a sportsman the fellow was. The distressed captain of his team had spoken of Reggie's enthusiasm and loyalty.

The captain was Major Whitlow. The man Jacob had last seen giving evidence at the Old Bailey. Clive Danskin's saviour.

And Danskin was due to arrive in Mortmain later today for a house party with Leonora Dobell and Rachel Savernake.

For all the morning's warmth, Jacob felt a chill.

————

"Vickers died last night," Trueman said.

Rachel and the Truemans had started out early and made excellent progress up the Great North Road even though the fine weather had brought out the traffic. It was a rare outing for them, and their mood was light. Rachel and Martha were both wearing sundresses, daringly short. When Hetty said they might be taken for sisters, Rachel replied that Martha was more than a sister to her. They'd stopped at a roadside tavern near York, and Trueman was returning to their table after going off in search of newspapers.

Rachel put down her knife and fork. "What did they do to him?"

He held up the front page to show the headline: *Cricketer Found Dead in Zoo Tragedy*.

"An appalling accident, if the authorities are to be believed," he said.

"Which they never are," Rachel said. "Go on."

"Happened yesterday evening, after a cricket match at Tunnicliffe. He was playing for the Masqueraders. The team he mentioned to you, captained by Major Whitlow. Not so very far from Mortmain Hall, as it happens."

"The owner of Tunnicliffe bragged about his private zoo in the *Telegraph* a few weeks ago. I suppose the Masqueraders were inspired to combine business with pleasure. Cricket and murder."

Trueman mimed applause. "The police think our friend enjoyed himself too much. Went out to clear his head in the evening air and just happened to fall into a ravine where lions are free to roam."

"Careless."

"The demon drink has a lot to answer for. When his friends realised he was missing, they formed a search party. There wasn't much left to identify by the time they discovered him."

Rachel grimaced. "No doubt tributes have been paid?"

"Poignantly. Vickers was a first-rate public servant, who will be sorely missed."

"In other words, a pawn who outlived his usefulness."

"They have cancelled their return fixture with the Tunnicliffe team as a mark of respect."

"Quite a sacrifice."

"What game are they really playing?" Martha asked.

"We'll soon find out," Rachel said. "At Mortmain Hall."

———

They had arranged to meet Jacob a couple of miles outside Mortmain. He was sitting on the grass verge when the Phantom pulled up. The sun was beating down and he'd just finished an impromptu picnic.

"You heard about Vickers?" Rachel asked.

Jacob nodded. "I thought I might hire a cab and go to Tunnicliffe. Write up the story for the *Clarion*, and…"

"You're forgetting," she said. "Vickers's death was supposedly an accident. You're a crime reporter."

"It would give me a chance to sniff around. See what Major Whitlow and his friends have been getting up to."

"You made enough of a nuisance of yourself in Soho. Don't give them another excuse to use animals as assassins. You might end up being gored by a rhino, or trampled on by elephants. Possibly both."

"Bitten by a boa," Martha said dreamily. "Chewed by a crocodile."

Jacob breathed out. "Perhaps I'll stay in Mortmain."

"Good," Rachel said. "You're learning. Now, have you gleaned anything new about Mortmain Hall and the Dobells?"

"Not a great deal." He gave a brief account of what he'd been up to. "Leonora isn't too popular, and her husband is an object of pity. All rather predictable. I'll keep my eyes and ears open when I go fossil hunting."

"Gastropods or bivalves?"

He blinked. "I'm an amateur, not an expert."

"A rank beginner." She checked her watch. "We'd better get moving. I'm curious to see Mortmain Hall."

"My fossil hunting is sure to take me that way soon," he said breezily.

Rachel shook her head. "Just make sure you don't fall off a cliff."

———

"Mortmain Hall."

Trueman steered the Phantom around the last bend, easing

to a halt as the rutted lane reached a gateway flanked by two old stone pillars topped by crumbling pineapples. The long journey was almost over. They were approaching the tip of the peninsula, Mortmain Head.

The approach to the Hall was an avenue of lime trees bent and twisted by a century of gales. The house loomed up ahead, the angles of roof and chimneys outlined against a brilliant blue sky. A Victorian extravaganza in Gothic, it was an eccentric confection of battlements, pinnacles, and turrets. Ivy crawled over the morose grey stone. Even in the sun, Mortmain Hall looked drab and melancholy.

"Such an eerie place." Hetty Trueman was in the front of the car, next to her husband. "Sends a shiver down my spine."

The Phantom followed a winding drive with views of the sea on either side of the promontory. They glimpsed a domed rotunda lurking beyond a clump of wych elms. There was a disused tennis court, choked with bracken, and a tall dovecote from which grubby paint peeled. As they drew closer to an unkempt gravelled parking area, the Hall cast a large, irregular shadow.

"Journey's end." Rachel's eyes shone as they stopped in front of a gabled porch. Blood-red begonias spilled out of large urns on either side of the entrance.

"Excited, aren't you?" Martha whispered as her brother and his wife clambered out of the car.

"It is what I live for," Rachel murmured.

"The thrill of the chase?"

"The relentless inevitability of the hunt." She hummed a bar or two of "D'ye Ken John Peel?" "From a check to a find, from a find to a view. You know how it ends."

Martha looked at her. "From a view to a death..."

———

"I hope your room is satisfactory," Leonora Dobell said to Rachel in the front hall of the old house.

"The views are magnificent. We're right on top of the sea."

Leonora eyed her curiously. "Does it remind you of the island where you grew up?"

"On Gaunt there are no cliffs," Rachel said. "Only slippery rocks surrounded by the treacherous currents of the sound. Except at low tide, it's cut off from the mainland."

"Do you miss it?"

"After the Judge died," Rachel said, "I was glad to get away."

Leonora took her on a tour of the main rooms. The library was large and well stocked, with rows of ancient leather-bound tomes, although the shelves also revealed Leonora's influence. William Roughead's complete works were present, together with a long run of *Notable British Trials*. Rachel plucked out a book about the Oscar Slater case, and flicked through the pages.

"Murder always fascinated me," Leonora said. "For obvious reasons."

"You didn't write about murder until after the war."

"It took a long time for me to recover from the shock of losing my parents," Leonora said. "I retreated into myself. I'd have loved to go to university, but it was impossible, so I educated myself."

Rachel returned the book to its place. Let the woman talk. The similarities between the two of them were uncanny, but what intrigued her more were their differences.

"I found work as a teacher, but small children are best taken in small doses. I don't have a maternal bone in my body, and I hated every minute." Leonora closed her eyes, remembering. "I suffered from years of poor health, living hand to mouth. What happened to my father led to my fascination with miscarriages of justice, and I adopted the Slaterbeck name. After the war, when I was settled here with time on my hands, I was able to achieve a long-held ambition, and work on a book."

They walked back through the front hall and into a long gallery with a marble fireplace, well-worn chesterfields, and narrow windows of stained glass which let in very little light. The dark-green walls were covered with gilt-framed paintings.

"We still have several of the finest Yorkshire landscapes in private hands," Leonora said. "Despite sending a dozen to auction."

"Your husband must find that heartbreaking," Rachel murmured.

Leonora's mouth tightened. "Felix's grandfather died at the turn of the century, and his father at the end of the war. Two sets of death duties were levied within a generation. This country confiscates landowners' capital with a Communist zeal. Felix has been a home bird ever since he was wounded. He wants to stay at Mortmain for the rest of his life, and so do I. But one must be practical. We economise as much as we can on the servants, as will be evident during your stay. It isn't enough. We have no choice but to realise the family assets."

"And your husband accepts the need to sell?"

"Each time he complains, I remind him that Alaric, his grandfather, was a spendthrift who sold off large parcels of land. Oswyn, his father, was no better. At one time, all the local farmers were tenants of the Dobells. The estate has shrunk to a fraction of its original size. I'm simply carrying on an old family tradition."

Rachel stopped before a painting of Mortmain Hall at twilight. The artist had captured the eeriness of the architecture and the remoteness of the house's clifftop setting. There was no mistaking the combination of masterly detail and vivid hues.

"Holman Hunt."

"He stayed here as a guest of Alaric Dobell, and painted him in return for his hospitality while he explored the Yorkshire coast."

Leonora indicated a portrait of a tall, beaky-nosed man in a frock coat. His bearing was distinguished, but there was an oddly absent look in his brown eyes.

"Alaric's mind gave way in later years. There's a family history of instability. This picture hints at his decline, long before it became apparent to others."

"Diagnosis by artist," Rachel murmured. "Ingenious."

Leonora gave a faint smile. "When Millais came, he painted Felix's father."

Oswyn Dobell's portrait hung opposite the fireplace. Rachel saw a middle-aged man with fair hair and the family eyes and nose, leaning forward in his chair. The artist had captured a sense of suppressed energy. A glint of mischief in his eyes suggested he was about to rebuke Millais for making him sit still for so long.

"You met Felix's father?"

"When I came here, Oswyn was old and plagued by arthritis. But for a Victorian, he was remarkably broad-minded. I felt as if we had something in common."

"Namely Felix?"

"That wasn't what I had in mind," Leonora said drily. "No, Oswyn and I shared a contempt for convention. We judged people on their behaviour, not their birth."

"You sound bitter."

"Who wouldn't be?" Colour rose in Leonora's pallid cheeks. "Many a time, I said to myself that I'd have been no worse off if my father had killed my mother rather than being another victim. Until I changed my name, I felt like an outcast. People talked about me behind my back. Sometimes they gossiped within earshot. I didn't know what to do with my life. And then the war came. I'd never dreamed of nursing, but it gave me a purpose."

"Here at Mortmain Hall," Rachel said.

"With thousands of men wounded in France, the ordinary hospitals were overwhelmed. Country houses like Mortmain were pressed into service. I lived in the North Riding, and joined the local VAD. I was sent here to help out. Felix's wife was matron. She was a martinet; it ran in the family. Oswyn was infirm, and his sons were in France. What we went through was nothing compared to life in the trenches, but things were utterly chaotic. Nobody at Mortmain was a medical expert, apart from one old doctor who was going senile, but I found myself caring for men who were suffering terribly. Even more than I had done. And eventually…"

"Felix became your patient?"

Leonora grunted. "Like Oswyn, I don't care much about what other people think. I'm an outsider, the people in the village have always been suspicious of me. If you believe the local muckrakers, I married Felix for the Dobell fortune, or what was left of it. Why else would a woman marry an older man who was hopelessly crippled?"

She put her hands on her hips and stared defiantly at Rachel. "I've never been a misty-eyed romantic."

Rachel returned her gaze. "I'm sure you're not."

"I can't deny craving comfort and respectability." It was as if she were talking to herself. "When I accepted Felix's proposal, it was because I had to look forward, not back. Do you understand?"

"Yes," Rachel said quietly. "I understand perfectly."

Leonora turned away from her. "In case you're wondering, I haven't forgotten that your father did mine a grievous wrong.

The Judge's summing-up was wicked. But it is clear to me that you are very different from him."

"Yes," Rachel said again. "I am."

———

"And this is my husband, Felix."

The heir to Mortmain Hall was hunched in a bath chair, propped up by pillows, with a plaid rug over his solitary knee, wearing a tartan dressing gown which had seen better days. A nurse in white cap and pinafore stood behind him. He was frail and wrinkled, with straggly grey hair and painfully thin arms poking out of striped pyjama sleeves. His face was a map of lines and his fingernails were bitten to the quick. Little was left of the playboy who had once left Mortmain for the bright lights of London.

As Rachel shook his claw-like hand, she noticed its tremor. How long did the man have left to live? He'd been in his thirties when that German shell changed his life forever. To look at him today, you'd think he was seventy.

"I'm glad to meet you, Mr Dobell."

"Do call me Felix." The feeble hand flapped. Vestiges of charm lingered in the thin, reedy voice. "Daughter of a judge, hey? Got the same bug about murder as my beloved wife?"

"I plead guilty and hope for mercy," Rachel said. "Thank you for putting up with me. The Hall has such a wonderful situation, perched above the sea."

"Ha! We lost a corner of the garden when I was a boy. A stretch of lawn where my brother used to march me up and down, pretending we were soldiers."

His high-pitched laugh turned into a coughing fit. He blew his beaky nose and the nurse patted him on the back.

"There, don't go getting overexcited." She glanced in the direction of his missing leg. "You did enough soldiering in your time. All right now?"

"Yes, yes," the invalid said. "This is my nurse, Bernice Cope. And heaven knows how she manages to cope with me, hey?"

He cackled, a wild, irrational noise. The nurse, unflustered, took no notice.

"How do you do, Miss Savernake."

They shook hands. Bernice Cope was dark-haired, heavily built, in her mid-thirties. Her features were plain, her expression severe, her fingers ringless. So far, she hadn't spared Leonora Dobell a single glance.

"It's a lovely afternoon, Felix," his wife said. "Why don't you go out for a walk?"

Felix's eyelids twitched. The nurse gripped the bath chair, and answered for him. "We had a quarter of an hour on the cliff, didn't we, Felix? But it was too hot. Come on, time for your afternoon nap."

Without more ado, she wheeled him away. Leonora watched her retreating back with undisguised hostility.

"Treats him like a child, and pushes him around to suit herself," she muttered. "Well, this sunshine won't last forever. Thunderstorms are heading this way. Let's take a turn around the grounds."

Without waiting for a reply, she headed through the door, shading her eyes from the sun's harsh glare. Rachel followed her out, fishing out of her bag a pair of tinted glasses with pearl frames and leather blinders.

"You don't care for Nurse Cope?"

Leonora sniffed. "Six months she has been here, and it seems like a lifetime. Felix dotes on her, and she struts around as though she owns the place. No respect. You heard her call my husband by his first name? As for her ideas about nursing, they are ridiculous."

"Is that so?"

"Quite apart from lacking one leg, my husband suffers from an assortment of maladies. The palsy, a weak heart, depression. His health has deteriorated steadily, and his mind is failing, but he's stubborn, won't give up without a fight. I'm sure he's capable of lasting a little longer with the right care."

"Don't you think Bernice Cope cares for him?"

"Oh, she cares for him, all right. After a fashion." She pointed to their left. "This way, Rachel, we'll take a circular tour."

"You suspect Felix of being sweet on her?" Rachel asked.

"My husband always had a roving eye. He adores all his nurses, and this woman is no exception, but it's a long time since he was a debonair man-about-town. He can't do anything more than ogle." Her smile was sardonic. "Felix has married one nurse, and that's plenty, don't you think?"

They followed a path leading to a walled garden. The door to the garden was shut, and the handle rusty. The wall was lichen-stained, the mortar flaking.

"It can't be easy for you," Rachel said.

"I've established a *modus vivendi*. Nowadays, I spend a good deal of my time in London. Of course these surroundings are beautiful. Each evening without fail I take a turn around the grounds before the sun sets. Simply taking in the wild loveliness of the place. Unfortunately, my husband is querulous and increasingly irrational. I don't blame him. The war tore him apart, quite literally. It's a wonder he has kept going so long, but it hasn't been easy. In time, each of his nurses becomes frustrated and bored. With Felix and with Mortmain Hall."

"Bernice Cope doesn't seem bored."

"I'd like to think that she'll be gone soon enough. She

brags to the other servants about her handsome beau, though they've seen neither hide nor hair of him." Leonora's lip curled. "Unfortunately, the way she makes a mystery about her lover convinces me that he is a figment of her overheated imagination."

Beyond the walled garden, on the tip of the promontory, there were no trees. The land narrowed to a point. They could hear and smell the sea before they saw the azure water stretching out on either side below them.

"Breathtaking," Rachel said.

"Gorgeous on a fine day," Leonora said. "When it's foggy and freezing, when the wind lashes the waves against the rocks, Mortmain Head is as welcoming as the North Pole. You see that scar?"

She pointed to a jagged edge of the grounds. "Years ago, during a storm, there was a landslip. A quarter of an acre was lost. The bays on either side of us aren't sandy enough for day trippers, the currents are too dangerous for swimmers. We see an occasional hiker, or birdwatcher or amateur geologist. Apart from that, we're never disturbed. The crowds who flock to Scarborough and Bridlington give us a wide berth. A colony of seals used to come ashore to pup. Now even they have abandoned Mortmain."

"Peace and quiet. How heavenly in these troubled times."

"There are disadvantages to being off the beaten track. Finding capable staff is next to impossible. It's even harder to keep them after they've tasted an east-coast winter. With so many men out of work, you'd expect employers to have the whip hand, but no. I can only pay a pittance. Good servants can do better in the big houses in Scarborough or Whitby. So can good nurses."

"And Nurse Cope?"

Leonora exhaled. "The local quack indulges her, but he's

a fool. So Felix is regularly dosed with heaven knows what. Opium, Indian hemp, henbane."

Rachel raised her eyebrows. "Unorthodox."

"She claims they alleviate the symptoms of Parkinson's disease."

"You don't agree?"

"When I was in the Voluntary Aid Detachment, I worked in a pharmacy for a few months before I was sent to Mortmain. I can assure you, Miss Savernake, I know a thing or two about lethal medicines."

Rachel nodded, knowing that there was more to come.

Leonora took a breath. "If you ask me, she's poisoning him."

Chapter 22

Rachel and Leonora walked to the crest of Mortmain Head in a silence broken only by the screams of the seagulls above them and the splash of waves below. The heat was unrelenting. Even on this most exposed point of the peninsula, Rachel felt only the faintest breath of breeze. She looked over the cliff's ragged edge. The drop to the sea was dizzying.

Turning to face Leonora, she said, "You suspect Nurse Cope of doing your husband harm?"

Leonora sighed. "Her kind of treatment is more dangerous than the disease. Felix should be good for a year or two yet, but that woman might easily kill him off sooner."

Resuming their journey around the headland, they descended the slope in the direction of the Hall, skipping through thick brambles and nettle patches. At one point, they passed a rocky and forbidding trail which followed a precarious route along the vertiginous cliff face before disappearing out of sight.

"This is an ancient landscape," Leonora said. "Folk say you can find dinosaur footprints on ancient blocks of sandstone. The cliffs are riddled with caves, and that path takes you to them. But you need a head for heights."

"Did smugglers hide contraband in caves?"

"Robin Hood's Bay to the north was the smugglers' haven. The village streets are a maze, with endless places to hide from the excise men. Mortmain's caves had more romantic associations, if the folk tales are to be believed."

"Really?"

"To this day, the traditions are kept alive. I heard a malicious rumour that Nurse Cope took a blanket out with her so that she could cavort with her young man in the quiet of a rocky chamber."

"Mortmain is full of stories," Rachel murmured.

Leonora nodded. "But how can one disentangle the truth from make-believe?"

As the grounds broadened out, the main path divided in two, one fork weaving towards the rotunda. Leonora strode out past a small garden of rambling roses. Ahead of them was the stables and the old tennis court.

"Thankfully, I don't care for tennis, so it doesn't matter that the court is going to rack and ruin," Leonora said. "Our head gardener has worked here for fifty years, man and boy. Because he loves the place, he puts up with a rotten wage and the dubious assistance of youths from the village."

A branch of the path led through a clump of trees. The shade was so welcome that they paused close to a small stumpery, a tangle of logs and tree roots with ferns growing through the dead wood.

"I'm curious that you brought three servants with you," Leonora said. "And startled that they comprise the whole of your staff. Forgive my bluntness, but surely you can't be feeling the pinch too? With the upkeep of a large house in London to—"

"Like you," Rachel interrupted, "I'm wary of servants who

can't be trusted. I grew up with the Trueman family. To me, they are like flesh and blood."

"I must apologise. I didn't mean to be rude." Leonora pursed her lips. "Or to sound jealous. You can tell how unaccustomed I am to welcoming guests to Mortmain. How easy it is to forget that I'm a lucky woman. At least I can pursue my interests unhindered. Thank you for indulging me."

"I'm wondering when you'll explain precisely why you invited me to join you and three strangers who were accused of committing murder."

Leonora considered. "I hoped you would be fascinated by the prospect of meeting them."

"And so I am."

"Then that is a good enough answer." Leonora consulted her watch. "Time is moving on. The other guests will arrive soon. Shall we go inside?"

———

"Henry Rolland. Charmed to meet you, Miss Savernake."

Rolland's handshake was brisk, his smile practised, his eyes wary. He resembled a politician attempting to gauge a constituent's allegiance. Rachel thought he'd put on weight since the time of his arrest for the murder of his mistress. In a photograph taken when the Wirral Bungalow Mystery was headline news and reprinted in Leonora's book, Rolland had a lean and hungry look. In retirement, he'd filled out. Immaculate as he was in a double-breasted suit of black Saxony with white pencil stripes, white shirt, and grey tie, not even Savile Row could quite disguise his corpulence, let alone the fleshiness around his jaw.

"Rachel's father was the late Judge Savernake." Leonora was performing introductions in the front hall. "My husband is resting at present, but will join us for dinner. Two more guests are due shortly, and then our party will be complete. Perhaps you'd like to take a turn around the grounds while I have a word with Cook?"

"Admirable suggestion," Rolland said. "We must make the most of this glorious weather before it breaks. A breath of air after the drive over the Pennines will do me a power of good. Care to join me, Miss Savernake? Capital!"

She followed Rolland outside. Squinting into the sun, he said, "This is—ah, a pleasant surprise, Miss Savernake. Mrs Dobell never mentioned that she'd invited you."

Rachel indicated the path they should follow. "I was a last-minute addition to the guest list."

They walked in silence to the furthest point on the headland and looked out at the sea. The heat was more intense than ever. Rachel's skin was burning.

"Have you known Leonora long?" Rolland asked.

"We met for the first time earlier this week."

"So she's a criminologist, eh? Not surprised she hides behind a pen name. Odd sort of a job for a woman."

"You think so?"

"Sordid occupation, delving into old crimes." He thought for a moment. "You're not in the same line?"

"I don't expect I'll ever publish a book," Rachel said. "As you say, a sordid occupation."

He grunted. "She wrote about me, I suppose you know."

"About the case you had the misfortune to be caught up in, yes."

As he fixed a steely gaze on her, Rachel glimpsed a hint of the single-mindedness that had taken him from poverty to riches.

"Read it?" he demanded.

Rachel nodded.

"One minute I was successful, respected. The next, I'd become a pariah. What happened in that bungalow has overshadowed everything else. My life now seems like…marking time. It's a hard thing, to see your world turned inside out like that."

"I'm sure," she said. "And even harder to lose a loved one, or to be murdered."

"Whatever you may think, I cared for the girl," he snapped. "I wasn't simply using her. If anything…"

He broke off, and Rachel finished the sentence for him. "If anything, you cared too much?"

"Yes," he muttered.

Without another word, he marched off in the direction of the house.

———

Outside Mortmain Hall, a man and a woman descended from a taxi. A maid consulted with the Dobells' elderly butler about the destination of their luggage. Clive Danskin was wearing Oxford bags and carrying a straw boater; his gold cufflinks winked in the sun. His demeanour was jaunty, as if he were treating the weekend as a trip to the seaside.

Sylvia Gorrie cut a striking figure, tall and blonde, with high cheekbones and a regal bearing. Her flowing pastel-green summer dress was the epitome of chic. Rachel detected the stylish hallmarks of Elsa Schiaparelli.

Leonora emerged from the house as Henry Rolland approached the newcomers, hand outstretched. Rachel joined the group, and the hostess made the introductions.

"Dinner is at six thirty," Leonora said. "Quite early, I know, but my husband tires easily. He's resting at present, but will join us for a sherry before we dine."

Rolland was sweating. He dabbed his forehead with a handkerchief. "Still damned close to boiling point. Think I'll have a bath, try and cool down."

Leonora smiled. "I'm not surprised your temperature rose, taking a walk with such a beautiful young woman."

Rolland gave a curt nod, and excused himself. Leonora and Sylvia Gorrie followed him inside, leaving Clive Danskin to contemplate Rachel with undisguised interest.

"What brings you to Mortmain Hall, Miss Savernake? Or Rachel, if I may make so bold? We don't want to stand on formality, do we?"

"Leonora made this little party sound irresistible," she said. "I'm no social butterfly, but the guest list is very…select."

"I'll say." Danskin's grin made him look like a schoolboy. His technique with women, Rachel observed, was to be disarmingly frank. "Rolland was accused of murder, you know. And Sylvia—Mrs Gorrie—and I both stood trial at the Old Bailey."

"I'm unsure about the etiquette. Should I offer congratulations on your acquittal, or commiserate because of the injustice of the charge?"

"Very good," Danskin chortled. "You have a pawky sense of humour, Rachel. Admirable. I do appreciate wit in a lady."

"You're not working today, I see."

He stroked his chin. "To tell you the truth, I'm a free agent. The company didn't enjoy the publicity about the trial."

"I'm sorry to hear that."

"Don't be. The change suits me down to the ground." He beamed. "Time to put down a few roots. I want to set up an outfit of my own."

"How brave," Rachel said. "Every newspaper I read tells me that businesses are collapsing across the civilised world. American tycoons queue up to jump from skyscraper windows."

Danskin laughed. "Slump or no slump, ladies will always love silk stockings. Depend upon it. I'm aiming to compete with my old firm. Reckon I can teach them a thing or two about salesmanship. Not that I want to blow my own trumpet."

"Of course not."

The sundress flattered her svelte figure, and he couldn't take his eyes off her. "I'm based in the Smoke. You're there too, aren't you? Perhaps we could get together. I'd be glad to offer you a bite of dinner. I'm sure we'll get on like a house on fire."

"I should have thought you'd had your fill of fires," Rachel said. "After what happened to your car."

Danskin gaped at her for a moment before pulling himself together and bursting into laughter. "A hit, a very palpable hit! My goodness, Rachel, I can see I'm going to have to keep a close watch on you."

"Did the police ever discover the identity of the tramp who died in the blaze?"

"They don't take me into their confidence, sad to say. If their investigations into my alibi are anything to go by, there's no chance they'll discover who he was." He waved airily. "England is full of chaps without jobs, wandering aimlessly around the countryside. Some of the poor beggars are bound to turn to crime. I only wish the police had taken me at my word. A lot of unpleasantness would have been avoided, and taxpayers' money saved. Let me assure you, my dear, the Keystone Cops would have shown more acumen."

"I suppose their excuse is that Major Whitlow was out of the country."

"All I can say is thank the Lord that the blighter turned up in the nick of time." Danskin went through a pantomime of rubbing his neck. "The judge was itching to put on his black cap and send me to the scaffold."

"And now the blighter has turned up in Yorkshire," Rachel said. "Have you seen the news? A man died yesterday evening. A tragic incident at a private zoo a few miles from here. He played cricket for a team captained by the major."

Danskin blinked. "Good Lord. Quite a coincidence."

"Yes," Rachel said. "Isn't it?"

———

"What news from the servants' quarters?" Rachel asked when Martha arrived in her room.

"Hetty's befriended the cook, who is at least a hundred years old, and rather gaga. I'd watch your hors d'oeuvres, if I were you. Cliff's tried talking to the butler, but the man's as deaf as a post. I've had better luck, a long conversation with Leonora's maid. Gladys comes from the village and has worked here since she was fourteen. She's bursting to ask how my face got scarred, but somehow she's restrained herself. Thank goodness she loves to natter. I could hardly get a word in edgeways."

"Perfect." Rachel stood at the window, gazing out over the North Sea. "This is the sort of place where anyone not born and bred within five miles is treated as a suspicious alien."

"Like Leonora Dobell. She only comes from the West Riding, but if you've been stuck in Mortmain all your life, it might as well be Westphalia."

"What do they say about her?"

Martha pondered. "Gladys has a soft spot for her, but even she reckons her mistress has a screw loose."

"Because she sells off her husband's paintings? Or because she's a criminologist?"

"A bit of both. At least she isn't a snob, and doesn't play the lady of the manor. If anything, she goes too far the other way.

She's unconventional. No respect for protocol, or the done thing."

"How dreadful."

"Servants like to know where they stand. They feel more at ease with the gentry than with upstarts who aren't content with their station in life."

"I'll bear that in mind."

Martha stuck out a pink tongue. "Not that any of the gentry ever come near Mortmain. This place has always been stuck out on a limb. Now everyone's forgotten its existence. Folk in the hamlet call it Morgue Hall."

Rachel laughed. "Perfect."

"In case it helps, I've drawn a map of Mortmain and its surroundings, based on what they have told me." Shyly, Martha handed over a sheet of paper. "I'll never get a job with the Ordnance Survey, but you know I love sketching. I'm afraid it's not to scale and..."

"It's marvellous, stop apologising." Rachel dropped a light kiss on Martha's cheek. "Thank you, dear. You'll make an artist yet."

The maid glowed with pleasure. "This is the first house party here since the war. Felix never wanted to see anyone from outside. He's depressed because he's only half a man, and whiles away his time with jigsaw puzzles."

"The Dobells' marriage wasn't a love match on either side, that's as plain as the nose on Leonora's face. But it's hardly unique."

"Leonora hasn't told the servants about her guests."

"That three of them came close to hanging for murder?"

Martha nodded. "Even so, Gladys is worried. She recognised Danskin's photograph from the papers. She doesn't understand why Leonora has suddenly decided to invite all these people here. Including you. Says it's like holding a house party in hell."

"Uncomfortably close to the mark." Rachel rubbed her chin. "When Leonora showed me the Dobells' art collection, I was reminded of a painting I love."

Martha raised her eyes to the heavens. "Surrealism and all that jazz? Give me landscapes any day. I may be a Philistine, but I prefer something I can understand."

"This is an American drawing, *All is Vanity*. You see a woman admiring herself in a mirror. Look again from a distance, and you realise you're gazing at a human skull."

"I might have known that would appeal to you."

"You sound like Hetty." Rachel's smile faded. "The drawing is an optical illusion. Clever artists delight in them. Your eyes are drawn to a picture. But on a second viewing, you realise that you're looking at something else entirely. That's the way I feel about this gathering here at Mortmain Hall. We're seeing one thing, but something very different is going on, without us even realising. Right in front of our eyes."

"That's too deep for me," Martha said.

Rachel sat down on the edge of the four-poster bed. "What does Gladys make of Leonora's passion for criminology?"

"A silly fad which gives her an excuse to dash off to London whenever she's fed up with Felix. What sensible woman would be interested in horrid things like murder? Let alone write books on the subject. It's just not ladylike."

"And does anybody here know what Leonora gets up to in London?"

"There's idle gossip that she might have a lover down there."

"Male or female?"

"Male, of course." Martha smiled. "It's beyond Gladys to imagine a romance between two women. Even though she mutters darkly about Leonora making a favourite of one of Felix's previous nurses. That caused a lot of jealousy. The girl at the

Dobell Arms has also caught Leonora's eye. Some of the lower orders don't know their place."

"How true." Rachel patted her maid's hand.

"People still see her as the nurse who married a crippled soldier when he was still grieving for his first wife. Not that the original Mrs Dobell was popular."

"No?"

"Sounds like a nasty piece of work, a snob and a tyrant. Her father was one of the great and the good in the North Riding. She despised the servants, and even Felix was under her thumb. At least Leonora treats people as human beings."

"With the exception of Felix's nurse?"

"Gladys loathes Bernice Cope. She puts on airs and graces, and brags endlessly about her young man. Not that Gladys believes he exists. Reckons Bernice is too ugly to attract a lover."

Looking at Martha's scarred cheek, Rachel said, "Beauty is in the eye of the beholder."

"So they say." The maid shrugged. "I wonder how many truly believe it?"

Rachel recounted Leonora's remarks about the nurse, and said, "So there is henbane in the house. As well as other poisons."

"Another reason to be careful with your hors d'oeuvres."

Rachel smiled. "Does Gladys think Bernice is a poisoner?"

"On the contrary. She grudgingly admits that Nurse Cope is good at her job. Felix always had a twinkle in his eye, Gladys says. In his younger days, he cut a dashing figure. He's devoted to Bernice, and the twinkle has been spotted again. She helps him with his jigsaw puzzles. All the signs are that she's genuinely fond of him."

"But not of Leonora?"

"She can't bear the woman. And the feeling is mutual. According to Gladys, Leonora would jump at the chance to get rid of her, but Bernice is too canny to give her an excuse." Martha took a tortoiseshell hairbrush from the dressing table. "Come on, you need to be getting ready for dinner."

Rachel pulled off her sundress. Underneath she was wearing a coral step-in chemise of silk crêpe de Chine. Martha sat down beside her on the bed, and began to brush her hair.

"What are the two men like?"

"Henry Rolland spent too long with hundreds of employees at his beck and call. Retirement doesn't suit him. He misses being at the centre of things. Like all businessmen, he's adept at giving the impression that he's robust. My guess is that he's on the brink of a nervous collapse."

"Rolland is in a different position from Danskin and Mrs Gorrie," Martha said. "A court of law found them not guilty. His innocence was never proved."

"Danskin is full of himself after his acquittal. For all the talk at his trial about his financial problems, he doesn't seem short of money now."

"Quite miraculous."

"No doubt he celebrated his good fortune by practising his charm on Sylvia Gorrie on the way here. Now he's invited me to dinner in London."

"Just the two of you? How cosy. First Louis Morgans, now Danskin. Aren't you lucky?"

"I should tell him what happened to Morgans. That would make him think twice."

Martha kept brushing. "Don't be so sure. He'll find your silky hair irresistible. Not to mention everything else about you. What about Mrs Gorrie? If she's as glamorous as people make out, you'll face competition. Have you talked to her yet?"

"No, she fled to her room at the first opportunity. Escaping Danskin, but also Leonora and me."

"Are you still so sure Leonora isn't plotting to kill you?"

"The boot's on the other foot. If I'm not mistaken, she believes that I murdered the Judge."

Martha gave a theatrical groan. "You never hide your hatred of him, that's why."

"The funny thing is, she wouldn't bat an eyelid if I told her I had killed him. It isn't simply murder that interests her. She's obsessed with getting inside the heads of people who commit it."

"Like you, in other words. Promise to be careful." Martha put down the hairbrush. "This is a dangerous pastime."

Rachel shrugged her bare shoulders. "No more so than having a few drinks after a game of cricket, and then blundering around a private zoo full of ravenous lions."

"Vickers's mistake was not to trust you," Martha said. "At least when Jacob gets himself into a mess, he knows where to turn."

"Let's hope he takes more care if he bumps into Major Whitlow than when he went to the Clandestine Club."

"He'll be on his guard with the major. It's the sight of a pretty face that scrambles his brain. Did you notice how coy he was when he talked about the girl at the Dobell Arms?"

"And he thought he was being so discreet." Rachel laughed. "You like him, don't you?"

"So do you," Martha said. "Stop pretending that you don't."

Chapter 23

Sherry was served in the library by two nervous young maids. Felix Dobell insisted on being accompanied by Bernice Cope. Leonora retaliated by refusing to introduce the nurse by name. The lady of the house was wearing an evening dress in navy and purple tulle that might have been fashionable before the war.

Sylvia Gorrie dazzled in a white satin gown which left one shoulder naked. Her skin was tanned a light golden brown. Henry Rolland had buttonholed her, and she contrived to listen with an appearance of interest, while glancing around every now and then, as if in search of sanctuary.

Danskin whispered in Rachel's ear. "Look at that old goat Rolland. He can hardly drag his eyes away from her."

"Can you blame him?" she replied. "Mrs Gorrie is beautiful."

"A good-looking woman, agreed," he said judicially. "Statuesque, to coin a phrase, but she doesn't hold a candle to you, my dear."

Rachel took a sip of Bristol Cream. "You're too generous, Mr Danskin."

"Clive, remember." He patted her hand. "Delightful dress you're wearing, by the way. Just the ticket."

"Thank you. Coco Chanel is the one who deserves congratulation."

He shook his head. "No, you make it look…"

"Your glass is empty, Clive, we can't have that!" Leonora nodded to one of the maids, who promptly spilled Bristol Cream over the floor while attempting to pour. Amid mopping up operations and apologies, the hostess said, "I trust you've recovered from your recent ordeal."

Clive Danskin stared at his hostess for a moment before giving a little laugh. "Oh, at the Bailey? Goodness, it's hard to credit that not much over a week ago I was in the dock. I've quite put it out of my mind. My motto is that one should always look to the future. And how better to celebrate my first full week of freedom than in such a lovely part of the world?"

"You know Yorkshire?" Leonora asked.

"Like the back of my hand," Danskin said. "Not this area, obviously. Not a lot of business to be had in nooks and crannies off the beaten track. But Sheffield, Rotherham, Doncaster, Huddersfield, oh yes. Over the years, I've travelled all over England. Anything to turn an honest penny."

"I'm impressed that you found so many customers in the poorer industrial centres," Rachel said. "In hard economic times, surely people can only afford necessities?"

Danskin frowned. "Ladies love to look nice. Thank goodness for that, I say. Anyway, we mustn't talk shop. Not often I get the chance to look inside an old mansion like this, let alone as an honoured guest. Marvellous library you have here, Leonora."

"You're a fellow book lover, Clive?" Leonora asked.

"Can't say I do a lot of reading. No time, you see. I'm partial to a good thriller, nothing too taxing. Used to enjoy the Mackintosh Trueblood yarns, but I haven't seen them around lately."

Sylvia Gorrie had swept across the room to join them, with Henry Rolland trailing in her wake. "You must choose what you say carefully, Mr Danskin. Our hostess has already told us she attended your trial. I suspect her next project is to write up the blazing car case."

Her white teeth gleamed in a smile, but her words cut like a knife. Danskin's cheeks turned the colour of beetroot. Sylvia turned her back on him and on Leonora, giving her full attention to Rachel.

"Your name is familiar." Her gaze was cold and penetrating. "Are you also an expert in criminology?"

Rachel said calmly, "I can't imagine where you heard that."

"Society tittle-tattle, I expect." Sylvia's expression didn't flicker. "One loses track. But I'm sure I've heard about you in connection with criminal investigation. Don't you have connections with Scotland Yard?"

"Leonora is the specialist. I merely dabble."

"An amateur in detection? How exciting."

"I can't claim any expertise. Think of me just as a nosey parker with a morbid streak."

Sylvia turned to Leonora. "How marvellous that you invited Rachel along. When you first spoke to me, I expected our party to be even smaller."

"It was a pure stroke of luck," Leonora said. "While I was attending Clive's trial, I bumped into a journalist who happens to know Rachel. He kindly passed on my invitation."

"Fortuitous," Sylvia said.

"Absolutely!" Danskin said.

"But you know," Sylvia said thoughtfully, "I almost feel as if I should be on my mettle. Given my unfortunate past, that is. Talking to the country's leading criminologist, and the daughter of an eminent judge. It's rather like being on trial again."

"You need have no fear," Rachel said, so pleasantly that they might be discussing a charity bazaar. "You can't be tried twice. The law forbids it."

Sylvia finished her sherry. "As it happens, I found the court of public opinion more brutal than the Old Bailey. The authorities have installed a barrier protecting the stairs that lead from the dock to the cells. An accused person can't throw herself to her doom. There are no such safeguards in the world outside. No earmuffs to blanket out the mocking whispers. No masks to prevent one noticing an old acquaintance who dodges round a corner so as to avoid a chance encounter."

"You've hit the nail bang on the head," Henry Rolland brayed. "Innocence is no defence. Face a capital charge, and one will be ostracised forever in certain quarters. The members of my club in Liverpool—"

"Dissecting a case in print prolongs the agony," Danskin said. "Leonora, I'll be blunt. I'm hoping that over the course of this weekend I can persuade you that it would serve no useful purpose to write up my trial. All that fuss about nothing, a case of accidental death! Not even a murder."

Nurse Cope had wheeled up Felix Dobell's bath chair. "You see, Leonora," his scratchy voice shrilled. "I warned you this would happen!"

Leonora's face tightened. "A man died in mysterious circumstances. We don't even know his name, far less exactly how he met his end."

"I'll tell you what happened," Danskin snapped. "A victim of crime—yours truly!—was treated like a criminal. Justice? Don't make…"

Felix Dobell took a gulp of sherry only to be convulsed by a fit of coughing. The nurse's customary pat on the back only exacerbated the problem. At first Felix seemed to be choking.

He began to wheeze loudly, but slowly quietened down. His head was bent over. He looked shrunken and sick and very old.

"He's not in a fit state to eat his meal." Nurse Cope spoke with barely suppressed fury. "All this excitement is bad for him."

"You'd better help him upstairs," Leonora retorted. "Make him comfortable, then take the rest of the evening off. I'm sure that's what you want."

The nurse glared. She tucked the rug over Felix's leg and turned the bath chair around without another word.

The shuddering crash of a gong in the front hall shattered the unhappy silence.

"Time for dinner," Leonora said. "Shall we go through?"

———

Yorkshire pudding, drenched in gravy, was served at the start of the meal rather than as part of the main course. In keeping with local tradition, Leonora explained. Making no concession to the heat of the day, the aged cook had produced roast beef, roast potatoes, and steamed vegetables, followed by jam roly-poly. Rachel nibbled modestly, and drank very little of the excellent wine. The room was stuffy, even though the fire was unlit and a mullioned window had been opened.

In the absence of her husband, Leonora sat at the head of the table. Rachel and Henry Rolland were opposite Danskin and Sylvia Gorrie. When Danskin's toes touched hers, Rachel moved her foot away. During the dessert course, Rolland's left hand found its way onto her thigh. She lifted it off as soon as his fingers began to stroke her, but gave no other sign that she'd noticed.

The conversation was stilted and confined to small talk. Rolland described his garden in Great Budworth, and Danskin chipped in to extol the virtues of allotments. Sylvia Gorrie reminisced about a cruise she'd taken around the Mediterranean, and the pleasures of travelling on the *Orient Express*. Rachel contented herself by asking an occasional question and listening to the answers with every appearance of interest. She noticed that Sylvia, like herself, was hardly drinking. Once or twice she asked Sylvia questions about her life since the court case. They were parried with practised ease.

Leonora and the two men made sure that their glasses were refilled at frequent intervals. Rachel calculated that each of them had put away a bottle of wine as well as the sherry. During a lull while the plates were being cleared and coffee served, Leonora leaned back in her chair, and reminisced about coming to Mortmain during the war.

"The library was the nurses' station, the gallery was the main ward. In the front hall, those soldiers who were up and about played cards or listened to the gramophone." She shook her head. "The billiard room became the operating theatre. I remember Felix being brought in on a stretcher. When poor Oswyn offered his home to the Red Cross, he never dreamed his younger son would be one of the casualties we treated."

"War is vile." Sylvia Gorrie's jaw was set. "We need to be vigilant to secure the peace from those who seek to undermine it. We owe it to future generations to make sure the Empire remains so strong that nobody dares to pick a fight with us."

"Take it from me," Danskin said confidentially "There won't be another war. I'm no Conchy, but the simple fact is that the stakes are too high. No government would allow its people to be blown to smithereens."

"We'd all like to think so," Rolland said. "When I ran my business, I saw enough of the armaments trade to understand the havoc that the latest weapons can wreak. Yet who knows what the future will bring? We may have curbed unrest at home, but for how long? Mark my words. As a man of the world, I'm morally certain that dark forces are at work."

"I'm sure you must be right, being a man of the world," Rachel sighed. "We can't have Britain at the mercy of dark forces."

Sylvia Gorrie said, "I understand you spent most of your life on a small island, Rachel? How miserable, being so cut off."

"That's why I'm so gauche in company. Everything I know comes from books."

"Bet you had a big library." Danskin began to hiccup.

Rachel ignored him. "My maid is the same age, we grew up together. She used to test me on what I'd learned. I think of her as a friend and confidante, rather than a servant. That's the trouble, you see, I was never taught how to behave properly in civilised society. I'm not country-house trained."

Rolland forced a laugh. "Not country-house trained! Very good."

Sylvia murmured, "I wonder if we all have more in common than we may realise?"

"I'm absolutely sure we do," Leonora said. "In fact, that's why I invited you all here."

"The length and breadth of England, owners of great houses are entertaining fellow members of the upper classes. But they are a vanishing breed." Sylvia gestured at her dining companions. "Look at the five of us. We're different."

"Tell us more," Rolland said.

"There isn't a trace of blue blood in any of our veins. None of us are 'varsity types, either. You were a nurse, Leonora. Henry, you raised yourself up by your bootstraps. You lived like a recluse, Rachel, despite having a wealthy father. Clive, you worked as a salesman. And I earned a living by tapping away at a typewriter."

"Interesting." Rolland enunciated carefully, as if afraid of slurring his words.

"We've not done so badly for ourselves," Danskin said, fiddling with his bow tie. "School of hard knocks."

Leonora cleared her throat, and lifted her glass of wine. "Through thick and thin, the Dobell family has been renowned for keeping a good cellar. This is a 1911 Burgundy. An excellent year, I'm sure you will agree."

"Ages since I had a spot of '11." Henry Rolland sounded as though he'd been making up for lost time. "Damned fine vintage."

"And now, if you'll indulge an eccentric criminologist, a toast." Leonora took a breath. "To partners in crime!"

The mood in the dining room was becoming febrile. Glasses were raised, but the guests' words were indistinguishable mutterings. Only the voice of Rachel Savernake sounded loud and clear.

"To partners in crime!"

———

The little party adjourned next door in silence. The drawing room had French windows, thrown open to take advantage of the warm weather. The windows gave on to a small paved terrace, and beyond was the main path which wound around the headland.

As the men helped themselves to brandy and cigars, Sylvia Gorrie put a hand on Leonora's arm. "I wonder if you and I could talk privately? It's still so pleasant outside, and I'm feeling rather deprived of oxygen. I'd love to look over the grounds of the Hall. Perhaps you'd accompany me?"

Leonora threw Rachel a glance of triumph. When she

moved, she was slightly unsteady on her feet. "That would be nice. Perhaps in a few minutes? I have something I'd like to say first."

Sylvia's expression gave nothing away. "As you wish."

Leonora clapped her hands, and raised her voice. "I'd like to thank you all for accepting my invitation to come to Mortmain."

Everyone was paying attention now. Rachel thought Jacob had been right to compare Leonora to a witch. She looked as if, at any moment, she would start cackling with malevolent glee.

"I'm sure you are all wondering why I asked you here."

"Glad to be here, interesting part of the country," Rolland said. "Don't mind admitting, I was in two minds at first, given that you'd written about...that rotten business I was dragged into."

"The Wirral Bungalow Murder, yes." Leonora beamed. "I hope you agree that what I wrote was fair."

Rolland pursed his fleshy lips. "Least said, soonest mended. I sympathise with Danskin here. I can see why he wouldn't want you to write up his trial. Damned unfortunate mix-up. Simply because Scotland Yard fell down on the job."

"You've all been caught up in unfortunate events," Leonora said. "Sylvia and Clive were tried for murder, only to be acquitted. Henry would have suffered the same fate if someone else hadn't conveniently killed himself and left a confession. Your circumstances, Rachel, were different. A life spent on a remote island, with only a deranged father and a handful of servants for company. The Judge died a matter of days after your twenty-fifth birthday, didn't he? After which you inherited his fortune, and escaped to London."

"Look here," Rolland said. "I mean, damn it all, what are you implying?"

"I'm sure Rachel can speak for herself," Sylvia Gorrie said coolly.

Everyone's eyes turned to Rachel. "For the Judge," she said softly, "death came as a merciful release."

Danskin stared at her. "Do you mean…?"

Simultaneously, Rolland said, "You're surely not admitting…?"

Sylvia Gorrie held up a slim hand to silence them. "Gentlemen, please. This is most regrettable. Rachel told us a few minutes ago about her unhappy upbringing. To me, it seems admirable that after such experiences, she is so…unflustered. It is neither right nor fair to suggest that she is guilty of some wrongdoing."

"Please," Leonora said loudly.

The drink is talking, Rachel thought. Their hostess, she felt sure, didn't want anyone else to be the centre of attention.

"Please don't think we are enemies. Nothing could be further from the truth. I want you all to understand that I am on your side. My curiosity is boundless. I've spent years studying the criminal mind. The four of you strike me as extraordinary men and women."

"I'm flattered." Rolland seemed to be sobering up. "But let's not beat about the bush. I'm sure Rachel is as innocent as the rest of us. So if you think that we can assist your researches into criminal psychology, you're much mistaken."

"Well said," Sylvia murmured.

"But are you all innocent?" Leonora asked.

"Well, really!" Danskin's voice rose with outrage. "May I remind you that a jury found me not guilty? If you dare to suggest otherwise, you will be hearing from my solicitors."

Leonora indicated their surroundings. The sun was low in the sky. "Though I say it myself, I wrote about the deaths of Phoebe Evison and Walter Gorrie with the utmost discretion. We are grown men and women. This conversation is just between ourselves. The servants are in their rooms. Nobody is listening at a keyhole."

"What are you saying?" Rolland demanded.

"Simply this." Her eyes glittered. "I want to salute your extraordinary achievements, to share in them. That is the truth of it. That is why I begged you all to come to Mortmain Hall."

As they looked at her, again she lifted her glass. "Each of you has committed the perfect murder."

Chapter 24

Clive Danskin took a step forward. For a moment, Rachel thought he would grab Leonora Dobell by the throat, but Rolland seized him by the arm.

"Steady, old chap. We don't want any unpleasantness."

"Unpleasantness?" Danskin's face was crimson with rage. "Did you hear what she said?"

"Yes, I did, and it's very bad form. The four of us have been brought here under false pretences. It's a disgrace. But no sense in losing our tempers. Or our heads."

"Henry is right." Sylvia insinuated herself between the men and Leonora Dobell. "This is no time for speeches, or protestations of innocence. Leonora, you and I should take a walk in the gloaming. We have plenty to chat about."

"Very well," Leonora said. "Let me repeat, I have no wish to cause any offence. Please accept my sincere apologies if I've done so inadvertently."

Danskin snorted. Rolland gave a crisp nod, and lit a cigar. Everyone turned to Rachel. Her face was a mask. She didn't move a muscle or utter a word.

"Come on," Sylvia said, leading their hostess out through the

French windows. As the others watched, the two women joined the main path and kept on walking until they disappeared from sight.

———

"My God." Rolland mopped his brow with a silk handkerchief. "After that performance, I need a snifter. Will you join me?"

He poured himself and Danskin another brandy. Rachel shook her head. The atmosphere was heavy with smoke, heat, and mistrust. For a quarter of an hour, nobody spoke. As an evening's relentless drinking had its inevitable effect, first Rolland excused himself for a few minutes, and then Danskin.

On his return, the silk stocking salesman broke the silence. "Sylvia will knock some sense into the old crone. Got a smart head on her shoulders, that lady."

Rolland loosened his bow tie, eyeing Rachel with naked curiosity. "You've kept very quiet. What do you make of all this tomfoolery?"

"Is it tomfoolery?" Rachel said. "What really happened in that bungalow by the shore? Your mistress was pregnant, no doubt demanding that you leave your wife and children, and make an honest woman of her. Did you kill Phoebe in a fit of rage during a lovers' quarrel? Before panicking, and taking flight?"

Rolland clenched his fists, straining visibly to remain calm in the face of provocation. "That evening was a nightmare. I was in a blue funk, who wouldn't be? Yes, I did make a dash for it. Stupid, but I wasn't thinking straight. I've always stuck to the same story. I found Phoebe's body. Her husband killed her. He confessed and committed suicide to save the hangman a job. Open and shut."

He banged his glass down on the table to emphasise the point. Rachel turned to Danskin.

"Why would I kill a stranger?" the salesman asked. "Utterly ridiculous. And quite intolerable. I'm a victim in this whole brouhaha."

"The prosecution accused you of wanting to start a new life. To flee from the past. And…whatever ties were shackling you."

"Poppycock! My marriage was a dead letter. This week my solicitors wrote to my wife's. Divorce proceedings are under way. As for the other ladies mentioned in court, they were ships passing in the night. It's a lonely life out on the road. You simply wouldn't understand."

"I understand more than you realise," Rachel said. "My life hasn't been entirely sheltered from misfortune. And I have a vivid imagination."

Rolland had regained his composure. "Since we're speaking about your past, I take it you deny murdering your own father?"

"I can swear to that," Rachel said. "As for the Judge, if hating him was a crime, they should lock me up and throw away the key."

"Remarkable." Rolland looked as if he might applaud. "Unusual to find a woman so direct."

"Perhaps that is just as well."

As Danskin tittered, Rolland shifted uneasily. "I don't like to speak about our hostess behind her back, but…ah, Sylvia is coming."

They looked out on to the paved area. The sun was setting. They saw Sylvia striding towards the Hall. She was alone, and her lips were compressed in a tight line. Rachel caught the two men exchanging a worried glance as Sylvia entered the room.

"On your own?" Danskin asked with a show of unconvincing bonhomie. "What on earth have you done with the lady of the manor?"

"She wanted time to reflect on our conversation," Sylvia Gorrie said.

Was this some form of coded message? Rachel had that impression from the men's reaction. A faint nod of assent from Rolland, a ruminative throat-clearing from Danskin. Nothing was said.

"Dashed bad form," Rolland murmured after helping himself to another drink. "Inviting people for a house party, only to accuse them of getting away with murder. And then abandoning them."

"I'll say!" Danskin said. "Never heard of anything like it. I know Leonora Dobell is a criminologist, but really! I hope you gave her a damned good talking-to, Sylvia. Woman to woman."

"I can assure you that I left her in no doubt," Sylvia said.

"What exactly did you say?" Rachel asked.

"Just a moment," Sylvia said. "Let me pour myself a brandy."

"Allow me to do the honours," Rolland said. "Rachel, can I tempt you?"

"Thank you, no."

"Go on," Danskin urged. "A small one won't hurt. It's been a funny old evening. Time to let your hair down."

"Very well."

Rachel's sigh as she allowed Rolland to present her with a drink was heartfelt. Sylvia was giving herself time to make up a story, and the men were helping her to do just that.

Sylvia took a sip. "Ah, that's better. I told Leonora that she'd behaved shabbily. Telling one's guests that they should have been hanged isn't just bad manners. It's an actionable slander."

"Precisely," Rolland growled.

"What she wrote about Henry and me was upsetting but not defamatory. I rather expected that she would make a handsome apology." Sylvia was warming to her theme. "If I'd thought that she intended to accuse me of murdering my husband, I'd never have set foot in this godforsaken old pile."

"Amen to that," Danskin said. "I've a damned good mind to pack my bags and catch the first train back to civilisation."

"I'm inclined to agree," Rolland said. "Feel sorry for the husband. A cripple whose family has owned this place for generations, forced to watch it fall to pieces while his wife squanders his fortune and pretends to be some sort of expert in crime."

"What did Leonora say?" Rachel asked.

"She seemed taken aback by my strength of feeling." Sylvia shook her head. "She told me that whenever she's here at Mortmain, she goes out for an evening stroll. It helps her to clear her mind. She said she'd mull over what I'd said while she walked."

"Not much to think about in my book," Rolland said. "I expect a handsome apology, and won't settle for less."

"Hear, hear," Danskin said.

Sylvia turned to Rachel. "I notice that you like to ask questions, but you give nothing away. Your hostess suspects you of killing your own father. Aren't you outraged? Or do you just play very good poker?"

Rachel shrugged and said nothing. Taking another taste of brandy, Sylvia took a step towards her. "I've heard that since coming to London, you've got mixed up in one or two criminal investigations of your own."

"I can't deny it."

Henry Rolland was losing patience. "You're an enigma."

"I'm afraid," she said, "that there is less to me than meets the eye."

"I don't believe that for a moment," Sylvia said. "I'd love to talk to you, Rachel. Just the two of us women together."

Nodding in the direction of the open French windows, Rachel said, "That's what you said to Leonora."

Sylvia gazed out into the gathering darkness. "She'll be back presently."

"Forgive me." Rachel stretched in an elaborate yawn. "I need to go upstairs and rest for a while."

"I'll be here when you've refreshed yourself," Sylvia said.

"Don't wait up especially for me."

"Oh, I will." Sylvia's tone was cold and insistent. "Of course I will."

———

"Sylvia Gorrie is hand in glove with Rolland and Danskin," Rachel said. "They pretend to be strangers, but I'm sure they're in cahoots."

Cliff, Hetty, and Martha were in her room, in defiance of every social convention. Hetty asked, "What do you think Sylvia has done with Leonora?"

"Nothing, is my guess. Sylvia Gorrie is many things, but she is not lacking in subtlety and she's certainly not stupid."

"But if Leonora doesn't come back to the house?"

"She will." Rachel considered. "Unless Rolland or Danskin have something else in mind."

"There are no wild animals at Mortmain Hall," Martha said.

"Is anything wilder than a human being intent on murder?" Hetty asked. "The cliffs are dangerous. Was it wise to leave the three of them on their own, so they can plot together?"

"There was no alternative." Rachel grimaced. "The three of them are already suspicious. Despite protestations to the contrary, none of them was surprised to find me here. As far as I'm aware, Leonora didn't tell them she'd invited me. Even so, they knew I'd be here at Mortmain Hall."

"Only one way they could have found out," Cliff Trueman said.

Rachel nodded. "Exactly."

Hetty was frowning. "What do you…?"

Someone knocked on the door. A soft, almost timid knock, but persistent. Rachel looked at the Truemans, and they looked at each other. She got up and walked to the door.

"Who is it?"

"Gladys, ma'am." The voice was faint and tremulous. "Mrs Dobell's maid."

Rachel opened the door a fraction. "What's the matter?"

She saw a woman in her fifties, overweight, pasty-faced, and trembling with anxiety.

"It's Mrs Dobell, ma'am."

"What about her?"

"It's pitch black outside; not even she would be out walking this late. But she's nowhere to be found."

———

"We'd better organise a search party," Rolland said. "The lights from the Hall will help us look around nearby, but not if we go through the trees. Do you have torches?"

Gladys nodded. She'd followed Rachel and the Truemans to the morning room, where they found Sylvia and the two men deep in a conversation which came to an abrupt halt as soon as the newcomers arrived. Rachel explained that Leonora wasn't in her room, and there was no sign of her anywhere else in the house.

"I'll run and fetch them," Martha said. "Cliff, Hetty, you come too. Shall we rouse some of the others?"

"Let's not have the whole place in uproar," Rolland said. "I'm sure we'll find her safe and sound, demanding to know what all the fuss is about."

Martha opened the door. "Come on, Gladys, show us where the lights are kept."

As the four servants left the room, Danskin said, "Forceful young woman, that. Shame she's so badly scarred. Otherwise, she'd be quite something."

Rachel glared at him, but held her tongue.

Rolland said, "It may be dark, but it's still warm outside. We'd better show willing, but my guess is that this is a storm in a teacup. Leonora has gone for a longer walk than usual, and she'll be back before long."

"You must have given her plenty to think about," Danskin said to Sylvia.

Sylvia's elegant shoulders moved in a dismissive gesture. "Our hostess has a lot on her mind. Ailing husband, crumbling house."

"What are you suggesting?" Rachel asked.

"When we talked, she seemed abstracted. Even though she'd just accused me of murder. Of course, she'd had plenty to drink, but her behaviour tonight was bizarre. It made me wonder if she was seriously disturbed."

"It would explain a great deal," Rolland said.

"You think she may have harmed herself?" Danskin asked.

"We can't rule anything out," Sylvia said. "With any luck, my fears are misplaced. Ah, here come the servants."

Torches were handed out. Rolland took it upon himself to direct operations, dividing the party into three groups. Hetty and her husband were to check the tip of Mortmain Head. Danskin would lead Martha and Gladys along the south side of the promontory. Rolland, Sylvia, and Rachel would take the north side.

Rachel lingered in the room as the searchers moved outside. She whispered to Martha, "They want to keep an eye on me."

"What do you think has happened?"

"It doesn't look good." She hummed a couple of bars of the old hunting song. "*From a view to a death in the morning.* We weren't meant to know she was missing until tomorrow."

She caught up with her colleagues, and they walked forward together in silence, shining their lamps to make sure they didn't trip over a bramble or stone. When they joined the main path, Sylvia said she and Leonora had parted at that point.

"Which direction did she go in?" Rolland asked.

"That way, I think." Sylvia sounded uncharacteristically hesitant as she pointed towards the clump of trees. "I must admit, I wasn't paying attention. She'd knocked me sideways by suggesting that I had a hand in the death of my husband."

"You and she were out for a while," Rachel said. "You told us about your conversation, but surely more was said?"

"I tried to make her see reason." Sylvia chose her words with care. "She was playing a game with people's lives. I said she'd upset me, but I didn't want to pick a fight. We went round the houses, but that was the gist."

They reached the trees. The wind had sculpted oaks and wych elms into unnatural shapes. Tonight their leaves were hardly disturbed by a breeze. Twigs cracked beneath their feet. An owl hooted. A fox scurried into the undergrowth at their approach. Of the lady of the house, there was no sign.

"Mrs Dobell!" Rolland called. "Are you there? Leonora! Are you all right?"

Nothing.

Beyond the trees stood the rotunda, open to the elements. During the day, one could look out over miles of sea from the stone bench inside. Now it was empty.

Rachel's lamp caught a dark smear on the bench. "Look at that."

"What is it?" Rolland asked.

Rachel bent down and touched the mark. "It's not quite dry."

"It's only a tiny stain." Sylvia sounded unsure of herself. Almost nervous. "Could be anything."

Rachel put her finger to her lips, and sniffed. "Blood, I'd say."

"Come on," Rolland said. "As you say, Sylvia, it's something and nothing. Perhaps Leonora has had a minor accident. Grazed herself."

Leaving the gazebo, they walked to the cliff's edge. Their lights picked out a narrow path which headed downwards. Rachel guessed it connected with the other cliff path she had passed in Leonora's company, the one that led to the caves.

"We shouldn't go down in the dark," Sylvia said. "It's simply not safe. We'll have to get help."

Rachel had moved to the brink. She shone her flashlight over the drop and said, "We won't need to go far."

"What do you mean?" Henry Rolland demanded.

Rachel took a couple of steps along the path. "There's a body down here."

Sylvia looked over the edge and gasped. "Good God. Leonora!"

Rachel inched down, taking care with every step. The crumpled form had come to rest on a narrow ledge of rock jutting out above the sea.

"Watch out, for God's sake!" Rolland made no move to follow her.

"She must have fallen over," Sylvia said in a wondering tone.

"Is she moving?" Rolland asked. "That isn't such a long drop. Even if she's broken a few bones, even if she's unconscious, she may still be alive."

Rachel glanced back at them. She needed to make sure that neither of them was following her. A single push in the small of the back was all it would take, and she'd go tumbling down the side of the cliff to her death.

Her light shone on the faces of Sylvia and Rolland. They were rooted to the clifftop. Their expressions were strained, expectant.

Rachel crouched down and bent over the body. "She's dead."

Rolland swore. Sylvia seemed to choke back a cry of horror.

"Poor woman," she said. "Are you...are you sure?"

"I've checked her pulse," Rachel said. "Nothing."

"How terrible," Sylvia said. "To think we were talking such a short time ago."

"It's not Leonora," Rachel said.

"What?" Rolland and Sylvia spoke in unison, voices cracking with disbelief.

Rachel looked up and saw their faces, peering down in astonishment.

"This is Nurse Cope."

Chapter 25

"Where is Leonora?" Trueman demanded.

The three servants had assembled once again in Rachel's room. Time no longer had meaning. Nobody in Mortmain Hall would sleep tonight. The police were first on the scene, in the burly form of a hapless young constable more familiar with petty larceny than murder. Reinforcements arrived later. An elderly sergeant took statements from the guests and staff while an inspector from Scarborough presided over the examination and removal of the body.

Leonora Dobell had vanished. The servants were speculating excitedly that she'd quarrelled with Bernice Cope and attacked her in a fit of rage, pushing her over the cliff before making a dash for it. The police had roused Felix Dobell from his slumbers, but he'd become tearful and incoherent at the news of his nurse's death. Gladys was trying to care for him. He'd barely asked about his wife.

"Sylvia denies having said anything that would have driven Leonora to murder," Rachel said.

"Surprise, surprise."

"According to Sylvia, Leonora must have bumped into the

woman and quarrelled with her. She killed her, and ran away in a panic. None of the vehicles has been stolen, so she must have escaped on foot."

Trueman groaned. "Madness."

"If that's the case, surely she can't get far," Hetty said. "Not on foot."

"Sylvia pointed out that she had her bag with her," Rachel said. "Perhaps she has money to pay for a taxi and train."

"What if Nurse Cope's death was an accident?" Martha said.

"The bloodstain in the rotunda suggests otherwise."

"We've heard what Mrs Gorrie thinks," Trueman said. "Can you be sure she's not the guilty one?"

"No," Rachel said. "The same old idea keeps whirling round in my brain."

"Namely?"

"Considering murder as a fine art. Imagine a picture painted by two different artists. They belong to different schools, and their brushstrokes have nothing in common. Both are talented, but since their work overlaps, it's impossible to be clear who is doing what." She shook her head. "Or why."

———

Breakfast was provided late and in desultory fashion by servants preoccupied with scandalous theories concerning their absent mistress. Felix Dobell was confined to bed, while the police prowled around as if suspecting that Leonora was lurking somewhere on the premises, in a yet-to-be-discovered secret passage or room. One constable with a poor grasp of architectural history had asked if Mortmain Hall possessed its own priest's hole.

The police had told the guests not to leave the Mortmain estate until further notice. Nobody was under arrest, and they were free to wander around the peninsula, but they should be ready to answer further questions at any time.

Already the sun was beating down. The clamminess of the atmosphere was hard to bear. Flinging open the windows in the dining room made no difference; there wasn't a breath of air. In such sticky and oppressive weather, nerves frayed and so did tempers.

Clive Danskin devoured several rashers of bacon as well as two pork sausages and a mound of scrambled eggs. No one else had much of an appetite. As she picked over a grapefruit, Sylvia Gorrie embellished her theory. Leonora was mentally unbalanced, she said, and excessive drinking had tipped her into an abyss of homicidal fury. Rolland and Danskin agreed. This was a wretched affair. They could only hope that the woman was arrested at the earliest opportunity.

"Why do you think she killed the nurse?" Rachel asked, pouring herself a second cup of coffee. A short doze had been enough to sharpen her up, and she'd already sent Trueman to the Dobell Arms to tell Jacob about the nurse's death.

"Jealousy," Sylvia said. "The poor woman was devoted to Felix; anyone could see that."

"Perhaps the nurse had her eye on becoming the next Mrs Dobell," Danskin suggested.

Rolland addressed Rachel. "Still playing your cards close to your chest, my dear? Surely you realise you're among friends. We're all in the same boat."

"Murder suspects?"

His grunt was dismissive. "The police officers don't strike me as the brightest buttons, but even so. None of us had reason to wish the woman ill."

"Leonora accused each of us of having committed a perfect murder," Rachel said. "Surely that is motive enough?"

"Tommyrot," Rolland said. "Two of us were acquitted. I was never charged. You have never even been suspected of committing a crime."

"Perhaps," Rachel said, "that is because I'm clever rather than innocent."

Sylvia pushed away her plate. "This is getting us nowhere. The last thing we should do is bicker. Rachel, it's time for us to have a serious conversation. I've felt for some time that you and I have a good deal in common."

"Leonora used to say that to me." Rachel paused. "In fact, perhaps that's what she had in mind."

"What?"

"Perhaps she wanted to commit the perfect murder too. The psychology of crime obsessed her. Suppose she wanted to understand the experience. To see what it felt like."

"Absurd." Rolland banged his knife on the table. "For a start, none of us is guilty of anything. Far less murder. Anyway, I can't imagine any crime less perfect than this one. If she wanted to throw the nurse off a cliff, it shouldn't have been so difficult to make sure the body landed in the sea."

"Wait a moment," Danskin said. "Rachel might be on to something. Remember how much the woman drank last night. She may simply have made a terrible hash of things."

They heard a tentative knock, and a ginger-haired constable they hadn't seen before put his head around the door.

"Miss Savernake? Sorry to interrupt, but Inspector Tucker would like to see you."

———

Inspector Tucker was a tall, spare individual with a disconcerting resemblance to Mr Milne's Eeyore. After a night without sleep he looked haggard as well as miserable. In his rural bailiwick, an outbreak of drunkenness and a couple of bicycle thefts constituted a crime wave. The last thing a man trudging towards retirement needed was to be knocked off his stride by murder at a big house.

He began without preamble. "Our local force is hard-pressed at the moment, miss. Barely thirty-six hours ago there was a fatality at a zoo in the area. You may have read about the case. A dreadful accident, but there are still questions to be asked, an inquest to be held. This is a peaceful corner of England. Law-abiding. We're not accustomed to such things."

"I'm sure," Rachel said.

"The chief constable has called in Scotland Yard. Their man is already on his way. Inspector Oakes."

"Ah."

"I understand you are already acquainted with him?"

"That's correct."

"And indeed the commissioner?"

"We have met."

"I've read the statement you gave the sergeant last night. Is there anything you'd care to add?"

Rachel shook her head. "Naturally, I'd assist if I could."

"If I may say so, miss, it is your duty." He gave her a look of undisguised curiosity, and Rachel wondered what Scotland Yard had told his chief constable about her. "Can you really cast no further light on the death of Nurse Cope?"

"It came as a shock. I only met the woman briefly, but she seemed devoted to her patient."

"Not to her patient's wife, however?"

"The antipathy was mutual. I mentioned in my statement Mrs Dobell's disapproval of Nurse Cope's treatment methods, her use of henbane and other poisons. But she didn't seem to suspect Nurse Cope of *deliberately* wanting to harm her patient."

"Indeed." Tucker fiddled with his tie. "Nevertheless, your fellow guests suggest that a few hours later, perhaps influenced by alcohol, she was responsible for Nurse Cope's death."

"At first glance, they are right," Rachel said. "The trouble with first glances is that they never take in the whole picture."

———

"Gentleman to see you, ma'am."

Gladys accosted Rachel as soon as she left the inspector. Overnight, the maid had aged, fresh lines furrowing her brow. Her complexion was the colour of chalk.

"Young fellow with fair hair? Brimming with energy and rather full of himself?"

"That's the one, ma'am. Says he knows you. Sounds almost like a Yorkshireman. Name of Flint."

"Can we talk in the library?"

"Yes, the other guests are in the morning room. That Mrs Gorrie said she wanted to have a word with you as well, when you're free."

"Between you and me, that's a pleasure I'd prefer to postpone. Can you fob her off?"

Gladys had taken a dislike to Sylvia, confiding in Martha that the she found her stand-offish. "Leave it to me, ma'am. I'll show the gentleman straight into the library."

"Thank you."

"Excuse me, ma'am, but what do you think has happened to Mrs Dobell? I'm at my wits' end. I can't help being afraid something terrible has happened. I mean not just to the nurse, God rest her soul."

"I can't offer you much comfort," Rachel said gently. "How is Mr Dobell?"

"Poorly, ma'am. The doctor should be here soon to take a look at him."

The maid was on the verge of tears. Rachel dabbed her cheeks with a handkerchief, and the woman scurried away with muffled words of gratitude.

Rachel took a seat in the library, and when Gladys ushered him in, Jacob sat down beside her. As soon as the door closed behind the maid, he spoke with the glee of a pot finally seizing the chance to call a kettle black.

"Trueman tells me you're a suspect in a murder case. Careless of you, Rachel. I'm disappointed. Was it really wise to allow yourself to be put in such a position?"

His effrontery made Rachel laugh. "Don't be selfish. Surely I'm due a little excitement of my own?"

"Treat me as your father confessor. Miss nothing out. I'm all ears."

"In any case, you're not above suspicion yourself. Perhaps you slipped out of your inn last night to do the foul deed."

"The front door to the inn is locked at a quarter to eleven, and the window of my little room is stuck fast. I almost sweated to death in the heat last night."

"It's not the most watertight of alibis."

"The police have already turned up at the Dobell Arms. A constable was questioning me when Trueman brought your message."

"Did you mention that you've met Leonora?"

Jacob grinned. "It slipped my mind. He told me not to leave Mortmain until further notice. Everyone has to stay put till the cavalry comes, in the shape of Scotland Yard. Their detectives will be questioning us in more detail later."

She exhaled. "The Yard have sent their best man."

"Oakes?" He whistled softly. "Why him, I wonder?"

"My fault, I suppose. The commissioner has heard that I'm a guest here. He's taking no chances. Just in case I've started killing members of the medical profession."

He laughed. "Let's hear what you've been up to. I swear not to write anything down. I've left my pencil and notebook back in my room."

"You're learning."

In her clear, concise fashion she described the previous day's events, culminating in the discovery of the corpse. "I must be slipping. One should always expect the unexpected, but stumbling across Nurse Cope's body knocked the wind out of my sails. I expected to find Leonora."

"Quite a confession," he said. "I thought you anticipate everything."

"Murderers are opportunists, remember. They seize the moment. Nobody can foresee every step they take. And yet…"

"Go on."

"Several people at Mortmain Hall had good reason to murder Leonora. Bernice Cope was one of them. Given her access to poisons, she had the means at her disposal to commit the crime and disguise the death as natural causes. If she had designs on Felix, she had a compelling motive."

"You don't believe this talk about the nurse having a secret lover?"

"Nobody has seen him."

"Even if he does exist," Jacob said, "Bernice may have planned to drop him if she saw the chance to marry money. Perhaps her story was a blind. She set her cap at Felix while pretending that she was already spoken for."

"Certainly, if Felix lost his wife he'd be likely turn to his nurse, just as he did before. The difference is that now he's twelve years older, and in poor health. The old spark hasn't flickered out, but it's dying, and so is he. If Bernice had married him, she'd soon have become a widow. Free to do as she pleased. The mistress of Mortmain Hall."

"You're sure about that, in legal terms?"

"Don't forget, I read the Dobell Family Deed of Settlement. A new wife would be in exactly the same position as Leonora. A tenant for life."

"Legal jargon." Jacob rolled his eyes. "What does it mean?"

"The heir's widow doesn't own the property. She can't pass on the estate under her own will. For as long as she lives, however, for practical purposes she is able to do as she pleases."

"A strong motive, granted," Jacob said. "But Nurse Cope was the one to die."

"Precisely. It's the wrong way round."

"Leonora is a strange woman. Did she kill the nurse out of blind hatred, or because she was afraid that if she didn't, Bernice would dispose of her? Or did Leonora simply shove her over the cliff during an argument which got out of hand?"

Rachel frowned. "Curious that this death coincided with the presence of three individuals who have been suspected of murder. To say nothing of myself. If the crime was premeditated…"

"Perhaps she was simply trying to sow confusion. You said yourself, nobody has a cast-iron alibi. Sylvia could have committed the crime while she was outside. Rolland and Danskin were both out of the room during her absence. You had time on your own after you left them, and before Gladys raised the alarm."

Rachel patted his hand. "On my word of honour, I didn't kill Nurse Cope."

His grin was broad. "You believed me when I denied murdering Louis Morgans. I'm glad to return the compliment. As a bonus, I'll share my theory with you."

"This is why you're my favourite journalist."

"I'm flattered."

"Don't get too cocky. It's just that I despise the rest of Fleet Street. Now tell me what you suspect."

Jacob leaned forward. "The legal process obsesses Leonora, has done since her father's trial. She's not afraid to take risks, her behaviour in the Clandestine Club proves that. What if she's concocted a scheme which makes her appear guilty, but enables her to escape punishment and proclaim herself as the victim of a miscarriage of justice? Exactly like Sylvia Gorrie, Henry Rolland, and Clive Danskin."

"Ingenious."

Jacob relaxed in his chair, beaming broadly. "Thank you."

"Tell me what you've been getting up to since I last saw you," Rachel said. "And then why don't you interview the other three guests, and see if you can trap them in a few damning admissions?"

"You like my theory?"

"I love it." She sighed. "Not that I believe it for a minute."

Chapter 26

Jacob asked the remaining guests if he could speak to them separately, but Sylvia Gorrie insisted that they would talk to him together or not at all.

"Answering questions from a reporter isn't the same as helping the police with their inquiries. You have no right to march into this house demanding a statement from any of us, and I'm surprised the police have allowed it. Does the owner of the house know you're here?"

"Mr Dobell is resting in bed." Jacob was unabashed. "Waiting for a nurse to arrive to take over the dead woman's duties. I'm anxious to talk to him, to see if he can cast any light on this tragedy, but naturally his state of health comes first."

"In other words," Sylvia said, "your answer is no."

"Miss Savernake was happy to talk to me on her own."

"That is a matter for her. I dare say she's unfamiliar with the wiles of Fleet Street. I can't even understand why you're so interested. A member of this household has died in circumstances suggesting that she slipped and fell down the cliff. For all the world, it looks like an accident. As for us, we are merely innocent bystanders."

"But Mrs Dobell is missing, isn't she? And she and the dead woman had a...fractious relationship."

"You're evidently better informed than we are, so I don't see..."

"I'd be happy to interview each of you outside, if that's what you prefer on such a sunny day." Jacob was nothing if not persistent. "Or down at the Dobell Arms, if you prefer."

Sylvia glanced at the other two guests, and said, "I'll give you five minutes. These gentlemen can add or subtract to what I say as they think fit. That is our best offer, Mr Flint, take it or leave it."

Jacob took it. Her version of events contained the bare minimum of detail, and she refused every invitation to speculate on where Leonora Dobell might be. The two men said as little as possible. He detected no obvious lies, but no mention was made of Leonora's allegation that the three of them had actually committed murder. Predictable to a fault.

He'd worked in journalism long enough to know when to abandon an attempt to squeeze blood from a stone, so he wandered out into the grounds of the Hall, venturing as close to the cliff edge as the police allowed. But there was nothing of interest to see.

Rachel was waiting in the rotunda as arranged. She was silent, lost in reflection, and without exchanging a word they set off together towards the Dobell Arms.

Rachel was lithe and fit and her stride was brisk. In the hot and heavy atmosphere, it was all Jacob could do to keep up with her. Why couldn't she be content with a leisurely amble, allowing them to drink in the views? She always seemed to measure herself against a hidden clock, urging herself forward relentlessly. It was almost as if she suffered from some terminal malady, and felt she had little time left to achieve all her goals.

Her sunglasses and hat made an effective mask. It was impossible to gauge her mood. He knew better than to disrupt her train of thought, contenting himself with an occasional surreptitious glance at her figure. The sundress suited her; although the design seemed simple, he supposed it had cost a fortune. Her skin was pale, her dark hair lustrous, her legs long and shapely. He would have loved to slip his hand in hers, just in a companionable way. But he knew he must restrain himself.

Why had she dismissed his reading of Bernice Cope's murder? Admittedly, the theory left questions unanswered. But did any other explanation make better sense of the mystery? What on earth was Leonora up to? His thoughts kept coming back to the Clandestine Club, when their eyes had met for a fleeting instant before she fled and left him to Daisy's tender mercies.

Why had she run? Embarrassment, that must be the answer. She'd supposed that Jacob was there undercover, working on a story that would expose the Clan, and her own proclivities. Unconventional and eccentric she might be, but she was also Felix Dobell's wife and an esteemed criminologist. If her secret way of life in London became common knowledge, it would hurt her reputation. But he didn't believe it was connected with Bernice Cope's death.

"Nearly there," he said as they rounded the last bend in the lane, and the inn came into view.

"Do you think other journalists will be on their way?"

He mopped the sweat off his brow. "Reggie Vickers's death is still the big story in this part of the world. People are arguing about whether private zoos should be allowed, as if what happened was the animals' fault. As for Mortmain Hall, until word gets out that an expert in crime is suspected of murder and has done a flit, the fact that a nurse has tripped over a cliff edge and broken her neck won't cause anyone to hold the presses."

She nodded. "Good. I want to hear what the locals have to say."

———

The sole topics of conversation in the Dobell Arms were the nurse's death and Leonora's disappearance. While Jacob went up to the bar, Rachel found a table in the corner alcove, close enough to eavesdrop.

At the other table in the alcove, a man gnawed at his fingernails as he added a few touches to a sketch of a puffin in his journal. He'd neglected his ham salad and ginger beer. The binoculars at his feet and the walking stick propped against the wall identified him as the ornithologist, Siddons. She tried to engage him in conversation, but every pleasantry was rebuffed with a discouraging grunt. Eventually he squinted at her through his thick glasses with obvious irritation, and didn't even grunt.

Undaunted, Rachel tried again.

"What a wonderful place this must be for spotting seabirds," she said gaily. "Not just puffins, but guillemots…"

"Madam." Her latest interruption provoked him into throwing down his pencil. "With dozens of policeman clumping around, it will be a miracle if there's a single bird left on the peninsula by tomorrow. Now if you'll excuse me."

Picking up his binoculars and stick, he hobbled out of the bar without giving Rachel a backward glance. She turned her attention to the customers at the bar. The pub was an eavesdropper's paradise, given that all the men talked in loud voices and there was no shortage of theories about the mystery of Mortmain Hall.

Opinion was divided between those who regarded Leonora as a deranged killer, and others who blamed passing tramps or disgruntled former servants. One grizzled farm labourer who plainly harboured an ancient grudge insisted that Felix Dobell was a sex maniac whose ill health was feigned. He'd killed his nurse in a fit of homicidal madness. Another fellow was convinced that Nurse Cope was pregnant by Felix, and that she'd committed suicide out of a sense of shame. He reckoned that the story that Felix had been rendered impotent by the blast in which he lost his leg was an ingenious subterfuge to disguise his urge to have his wicked way with every nurse he engaged.

"Then he should have chosen a woman with better looks," a ruddy-faced beer drinker jeered.

"No oil painting, that one," another man agreed. "God rest her soul."

"She used to wheel him out along the cliff," one venerable old codger said. "I often thought she might tip him over the edge, just to put him out of his misery, poor beggar."

The ruddy-faced man nodded sagely. "Who'd have thought he'd outlast her? Makes you think. That's what it does. Makes you think."

The company was united in the belief that the nurse's death was no accident. It wasn't just that it seemed unlikely; it would have been too much of an anticlimax. Especially since two detectives from Scotland Yard were due to arrive at the Dobell Arms that afternoon. An inspector and a sergeant. They'd booked the only remaining rooms.

As the other customers drifted away to share the latest developments in the scandal with everyone else in the hamlet, Lucy served Jacob and Rachel with bread and cheese. He introduced Rachel as a friend, without giving her name. Lucy hid neither her curiosity nor her ample figure; she was coping with the heat by leaving her blouse unbuttoned as far as decency allowed. When she lingered at their table, Rachel seized the chance to interrogate her.

Jacob sat back and admired the skill with which she teased out information. Prior to being elevated to the judiciary, Lionel Savernake QC had been the most formidable cross-examiner at the English Bar, and much as Rachel despised him, she had a similar knack. The difference lay in the subtlety of her probing. Chattering away at nineteen to the dozen, Lucy had no idea how craftily she was being pumped.

"I can't believe Mrs Dobell has run away on purpose," she said. "If you ask me, she's lost her memory."

"Amnesia?"

"That's the word! And it can go on for years, just like shell shock, poor Mr Siddons was telling me only yesterday."

"You don't believe Mrs Dobell is capable of harming anyone?" Rachel suggested.

Lucy hesitated, compelled by honesty to think twice before agreeing. "I suppose anyone is capable of...well, dreadful things. But why would she hurt Nurse Cope? If things were so bad, she could give her a week's notice."

"Mightn't her husband forbid it?"

"Mr Dobell would have hated to lose Bernice Cope, of course." Lucy sighed. "But you have to be practical, don't you? The poor soul is a cripple. Man of the house, yes, but what can he do, apart from his jigsaw puzzles? His wife rules the roost."

"Strong-minded?"

"Oh, yes. My mum says that from the day she came here, Mrs Dobell knew what she wanted, and made sure she got it."

Rachel dabbed her mouth with a handkerchief; the Dobell Arms didn't run to napkins. "Nowadays, she's a respected criminologist."

"Written books, hasn't she?" Lucy shook her head. "Not that I've read any."

"She didn't discuss crime with you?"

"Never. Not a very nice subject, is it? I suppose it's the sort of thing they get up to in places like London. I'm not surprised she's ashamed. You can see why she uses a pen name."

"Does she often call in here?"

"Now and then." Lucy bit her lip. "You probably know, she likes a drink. Sometimes she gets a bit carried away."

"And drinks to excess?"

"Not just that. Her conversation is very personal. I mean, she's always asking after my young man." Lucy blushed. "I tell her I don't have anyone special. I go out with different boys. She keeps saying they aren't good enough for me, and if I tell her I like someone, she gets fidgety and cross. It's not my fault."

"Of course not," Rachel said. "Has she told you about her club in London?"

"The Circe Club?" Lucy nodded. "It's lovely and posh, Leonora says. Mrs Dobell, I mean. She asked me to call her Leonora, even Leo, of all things. But it doesn't seem right. Not with her being a lady."

"I hear the Circe is an excellent club."

"Would you believe it, she even offered to invite me down there, to take a look for myself?" Her tone was wondering. "I've never been to London in my life."

"You must be tempted?"

"I said I'd think it over, and I'd let her know this weekend. But I couldn't see how I might manage it. I can't let Mother down. Or Uncle Bob."

"You'll fly the nest one of these days." Rachel gave a wry smile. "We all do."

"It's different for you, miss. You're a lady, aren't you?"

"Not always," Rachel said.

Lucy giggled, and turned to Jacob. "Then I've got some very good news for you. Mr Siddons is leaving the moment the police give permission. He's not fit enough to go scrambling over the cliffs, and he's annoyed that there's such a to-do about the nurse and Mrs Dobell. Says there's no chance of getting any peace and quiet to watch for rare species."

"Selfish," Jacob said. "If he'd paid attention instead of feeling sorry for himself about his ankle, he might have spotted someone push the nurse to her death through his binoculars. But why is it such good news that he's going?"

"Because it means the annex room will be empty tonight." Giggling, Lucy glanced at Rachel. Her expression was lascivious. "Move in there, if you like. You can come and go as you please, and you won't be disturbed there. If you have company."

———

"Any the wiser?"

Having kept quiet all the way to the Dobell Arms, Jacob found it impossible to repeat the feat on the return journey. While they'd been inside the inn, sombre clouds had gathered. The wind had got up, and the waves were making a more menacing noise. As Mortmain Hall came into view ahead of them, his resolve cracked.

He'd recovered from his embarrassment at the barmaid's suggestion that he might lure Rachel to the annexe room for a night of carnal pleasure. Thank God she hadn't responded to Lucy's offer with mockery or disgust. In fact, she hadn't reacted at all. And now, to his relief, Rachel didn't bite his head off.

"I'm making sense of it all at last." Excitement gave her voice an edge.

"Go on," he said.

"First, I need to find Leonora." She pointed to a narrow dirt path that led from the lane up a grassy knoll and then towards the cliffs. "Let's find the route she used to take for her nocturnal rambling."

He sensed her tension as she lengthened her stride. His forehead dripped with sweat as drops of rain began to fall. Rachel's fitness came from a lifetime of swimming and climbing in the inhospitable environment of the island of Gaunt. Keeping up with her was hard work.

"I've had an idea," he said.

"Congratulations."

"Nurse Cope bragged about having an admirer. Suppose she was telling the truth?"

"You tell me."

"Could it have been Danskin or Rolland? Danskin was a salesman. We know he travelled widely. Nobody kept tabs on his movements. As for Rolland, he's retired, and master of his own destiny. Both men could have spent time here."

"And their motive?"

"They both have a history of philandering. Suppose one or other of them had an affair with the nurse." Jacob was making it up as he went along. "If then she broke the news that she was expecting a child…"

"Come on," Rachel said as they reached the crest of the knoll. A rocky path led down to the cliff.

"You think I might have stumbled on to something?"

"Keep stumbling here and you'll end up in the sea," she said, as he tripped over a rain-dampened stone. "Watch where you're putting your feet."

Panting, he followed as she picked her way forward, and joined her on the brink of the cliff. Far below, waves whipped by a gust of wind were beating against the boulders in a little cove. The seagulls cried, as if in mourning. This spot was exposed and all at once he felt cold.

He was conscious of Rachel stiffening as she scanned the shoreline.

"What is it?"

She pointed down to the water's edge. "Do you see?"

Half hidden by the rocks, something billowed in the breeze. He caught a glimpse of navy and purple and his heart sank.

"It's not...her dress?"

Rachel nodded. "Run back to the Hall and fetch the police. They can call off the search for Leonora."

Chapter 27

Jacob and Rachel left the police officers to their grim work on the shore. Leonora Dobell's body had taken a pounding from the waves and the rocks. As the two of them strode through the rain towards Mortmain Hall, there was a faraway look in Rachel's eyes. Jacob hoped her thoughts were less tangled than his.

"Who's this?" he said. A sleek and shiny red car stood outside the porch, an Alvis Silver Eagle. Jacob hadn't seen it before. Inspector Tucker's rusting Morris was parked at the far end of the building, close to Rachel's Phantom.

"The Romans built a signalling station here, to warn of approaching barbarians." Rachel allowed herself a bleak smile. "An updated version would come in handy."

The front door of the house was flung open, and Gladys blundered out. Her tears were flowing like the rain.

"Oh, miss." Gladys was almost choking with misery. "It's so terrible. First the nurse dies. And now Mrs Dobell…"

Jacob put his arm around Gladys's plump shoulders. Her body shuddered with emotion. And fear too, for what would she do now her mistress was dead? After helping Gladys inside, they found the three Truemans talking to the butler. Hetty took the distraught servants off to the pantry for a restorative cup of tea, while Rachel and the others adjourned to the long gallery.

Trueman consulted his watch. "The inspector is in the library, rewriting his report to incorporate news that Leonora's body has been found. Oakes came up on the *Flying Scotsman*. He should have reached York by now. A police car is bringing him here. He's expected within the hour. Are they treating Leonora's death as murder or suicide?"

"It might even be an accident." Jacob never liked to be left out of a conversation for long.

Trueman's expression was withering. "I suppose she fell from the same stretch of land as Bernice Cope?"

Rachel nodded. "I gather the corpse has a wound to the scalp, but the nurse's head was also gashed. Unless a pathologist says otherwise, there's nothing conclusive. Now, that red car outside. Who does it belong to?"

"Three guesses," Trueman said.

"Major Whitlow?"

Trueman and Martha exchanged glances. "You're so sharp," he said, "one day you'll cut yourself."

"As long as the major doesn't clip my ear with his claw."

"He asked where you were," Martha said. "We didn't give anything away. He said he wanted a private word with you."

"I did wonder if he might."

"What will you do?"

"I need to dry my hair, change out of this dress, and get my story straight," Rachel said. "Then I'll speak to him."

———

Thunder was rumbling as Inspector Oakes marched into Mortmain Hall. He was accompanied by a stockily built sergeant. A few seconds out in the storm was enough to have left their hair wet and their mackintoshes sodden. Trueman strode out of the front gallery, where he'd watched the approach of the police car with Jacob and Martha. He gave the detectives a curt nod.

"Inspector Tucker is on the telephone in the drawing room, speaking to his chief constable. If you want to see Miss Savernake, she's in the morning room. Talking to Major Whitlow."

"Whitlow? The witness from the Danskin trial?"

Before Trueman could answer, the door of the morning room swung open and Rachel strolled out.

"Inspector," she said, "the owner of the house is indisposed, and you will know that his wife has just been found dead. So let me be the one to welcome you to Mortmain Hall."

Oakes's eyes narrowed as he shook her hand. "In the right place at the right time again, Miss Savernake?"

She was amused. "It's a modest talent, but I'm thankful for it. Jacob Flint is here too."

"I should have known."

"Yes, perhaps you should." She pointed to the door which led to the front gallery. "Jacob is in there. Flirting with Martha, I shouldn't wonder, the minute her brother's out of the room."

"I don't want to see him yet," Oakes said. "Sergeant Whealing, can you get an update from Inspector Tucker? In the meantime, perhaps Miss Savernake and I can have a conversation?"

"I'll ring for tea," Rachel said. "You'll need it. Come into the library. We have plenty to discuss."

———

"You realise you are a suspect?" Oakes asked.

Rachel paused in the act of buttering a scone. "Absolutely.

It was as easy for me as for anyone else around here to murder Leonora Dobell. And Nurse Cope, for that matter, if she'd witnessed me committing the crime."

"You think that's the reason why she died? Because of what she saw?"

"Not exactly," Rachel said.

"In other words, no," Oakes muttered. "I'm bound to ask you if you received this note, or something similar."

He flourished a small piece of cheap unwatermarked notepaper bearing a few words in clumsily shaped capitals.

MEET ME AT THE ROTUNDA AT TEN
L

Rachel studied the note as if it were an ancient runic script of fabulous value and scarcity. "I've not seen it before. But it answers one or two questions."

"Such as?"

"Where did you find the note?" When Oakes hesitated, she said briskly, "Come on, no need to make a secret of it."

Oakes sighed. "One of Tucker's men found it upstairs in Leonora Dobell's dressing room."

"And your conclusion?"

"It looks like a note she sent to arrange a meeting. Perhaps a first draft."

"A meeting with whom?"

"Nurse Cope is my bet."

"I'm glad you're not a betting man," Rachel said. "The note didn't come from Leonora and it wasn't sent to the nurse."

———

"Unthinkable," Major Whitlow said. "I refuse to accept your terms."

He'd joined Rachel and Inspector Oakes in the library. Tea and scones had come and gone, and an open bottle of Bristol Cream stood on the table. They might have been debating the choice of guest of honour for a church bazaar.

"I'm afraid I must insist," Rachel said pleasantly. "Blame my taste for the theatrical. But Jacob Flint deserves to hear the story. Without him, we wouldn't know the whole truth."

"How much do you really know?" the major snapped. "I've listened to your outrageous mish-mash of speculation and guesswork. You have no proof."

"Quite," Rachel said. "Think of me as a storyteller with a vivid imagination, not as counsel for the prosecution."

"For my part," Oakes said, "I'm willing to agree to what Miss Savernake proposes, and allow Flint to sit in with us."

"The man is a journalist," the major said. "I don't trust him an inch."

"Just as you didn't trust Reggie Vickers?" Rachel's smile vanished. "I'll speak to Jacob Flint, and I'll answer for him. He won't print a word if he knows what is good for him."

"I don't…"

"If he lets me down, you know what to do. Find a lion hungry for the latest scoop."

"Intolerable!" The major pointed at her with his claw. "You don't understand…"

"Don't patronise me, Major." Her tone cut like a blade. "I've explained my terms. They are perfectly reasonable."

"Miss Savernake!" Major Whitlow banged his claw on the table. "This isn't a game."

"It's certainly not cricket," she said.

"You might as well insist that your servants be allowed to join us."

"I'm sorely tempted." Rachel threw a contemptuous glance at the mark the claw had scored on the varnished table surface. "At least I trust them."

There was a long silence. Rachel turned her back on him and lifted a copy of *Respectable Murders* from the shelf. She leafed through the pages as Oakes addressed Whitlow.

"Major?"

The claw was clenched. "Very well, Miss Savernake. Against my better judgement, I agree."

———

Seven people assembled in the library: Oakes, Major Whitlow, Sylvia Gorrie, Henry Rolland, Clive Danskin, Rachel, and Jacob. Rachel had changed into a dress of orange and yellow brocade. Jacob thought she looked more like a hostess at a pleasant soirée than an expert in murder.

Rolland and Danskin were smoking. The salesman fidgeted incessantly and kept checking his pocket watch. Sylvia had accepted a cigarette. Jacob wondered if she was calming her nerves, but on the surface she remained her usual assured self.

Outside, a storm raged. They heard the crash of a slate tile from the roof as it hit the ground. Oakes had sent his sergeant off to the Dobell Arms, but even such a short drive would be testing in this weather.

"I'd like to tell you a story," Rachel said. "A moral fable, if you like."

Sylvia addressed the inspector. "Is this in order? I know we're in the frozen north, where anything might happen, but Miss Savernake has no official standing here. Or have I overlooked something?"

Oakes glanced at Whitlow. "I have agreed, as has the major, to listen to what Miss Savernake has to say."

As Whitlow inclined his head, Rolland said smoothly, "I don't object. It will kill time until the storm abates, and we can all be on our way."

Danskin was restive. "Let's get on with it, then."

"This all begins with a man called Reginald Vickers," Rachel said. "He was killed by a lion the night before last. Vickers was a fool, but stupidity isn't a capital offence, and he didn't deserve to die. Recently, he contacted me. He was in a blue funk. Said he was desperate, with nowhere else to turn. Certainly not to the police. He'd heard a whisper about my interest in crime, and that whatever my faults, a loose tongue wasn't among them.

"The gist was this. He worked in Whitehall, in an obscure offshoot of the Home Department. The chain of command is unclear to me. I suppose it's an official secret. The major was one of his superiors, and he in turn reports to a colonel whose name I have promised not to mention."

Sylvia Gorrie glanced at Whitlow, who gave a brisk nod of confirmation.

"Reggie was, so to speak, a useful idiot. He was employed because of his stupidity rather than in spite of it. A recruitment policy as daring as it was unwise. However, in the aftermath of the war, those charged with safeguarding this country subordinated everything to a single stark priority. To make sure that Britain did not travel the same path as Russia, with social unrest gathering momentum until the inevitable result was bloody revolution."

"A popular uprising?" Sylvia was derisive. "The term is a misnomer. Ordinary people are duped by demagogues. They always end up worse off. Look at France, look at Russia..."

"Spare us the homily," Rachel said. "The risk was real. After the war came a wave of strikes. Even the police showed signs of insurrection against the establishment. People were angry, making trouble. They believed something must be done to build that land fit for heroes. Equally, the authorities feared the enemy within."

"In the national interest," Sylvia said.

Danskin and Rolland exchanged looks, but said nothing.

"The enemy within," Rachel repeated. "How does one keep an eye on that enemy, and make sure that it fails to thrive? By recruiting ordinary people to help with the task, that's how. Reggie Vickers, an instinctive loyalist, was just a messenger. He was never on the front line. He agreed with the end, but latterly, as he learned more, he began to have qualms about the means."

"Weakness," the major said.

"Human nature," Rachel said. "But you're right. Reggie had weaknesses, plenty of them. It's the main reason he got the job. As for personal matters, his destiny was mapped out from his early days. He was to marry a nice young lady of the same class, and produce nice children to carry on the family name. The trouble was, Reggie yearned for excitement, something different. He was introduced to a club in Soho, and became a member. The Clandestine Club's name spoke for itself. It catered for exotic tastes, forbidden pleasures. And it enjoyed remarkable longevity. Dens of vice usually last only a few months before they are closed down. The Clan escaped a similar fate. Thanks, no doubt, to friends in high places."

The major shook his head. "Wild speculation."

Oakes said, "I told Mr Flint, the Yard could never get the evidence needed to intervene."

Rachel shrugged. "Yes, the Clan is a model of efficiency. Despite not making a profit. Its main *raison d'être* is to make sure that certain individuals are susceptible to blackmail should they behave in a way that the major and his colleagues regard as disobliging. Not that I expect him to admit that."

The major's thin mouth was clamped shut.

"At the Clandestine Club, Reggie met Gilbert Payne. Payne was one of those people who had been recruited to the cause. Reggie was devoted to him, despite realising that Payne was promiscuous and unreliable. He was a publisher, you know. His authors included your husband, Mrs Gorrie, and a poet known for his close ties to the Leninists."

"Rabble rousers," Rolland said.

"Payne's job was to act as a spy. An informer, if you prefer. Passing on any information that might help to defeat the enemy within. But his behaviour became erratic. He talked too much, especially when he was drunk and in the company of a young man. This compromised his usefulness. His masters worried that he risked destroying everything they were trying to do."

"Understandable, surely," Sylvia Gorrie said. "If what you say is correct."

"Four years ago, shortly before this country came close to collapse during a general strike, matters reached a head. Payne was a loose cannon. Although his superiors were ruthless, they preferred to avoid killing their own hirelings if possible. But they feared he would betray himself and the network of informers at a time when Britain was on the brink. It was necessary to stamp out a threat, and send a message to others at one and the same time. *Pour encourager les autres.*"

Lightning flashed. Jacob counted five before the rumble came.

"Payne was given an ultimatum. Leave Britain or face the consequences. He knew enough about his masters to know that defiance was suicidal. He agreed to leave for Tangier, and was given enough money to keep him quiet there. His drowning in the Thames was faked. The body they dredged up belonged, I suppose, to some unfortunate who had got on the wrong side of…well, let's call them the Masqueraders. That's the name of the cricket team they formed to give them an excuse to wander the country unsuspected, when there was dirty work to be done which couldn't be delegated."

Jacob's mouth was dry. He was almost glad he'd sworn never to reveal anything he was told within these four walls. If he was taking notes, he'd already have writer's cramp.

"Reggie wasn't let into the secret, because of his association with Payne. He was only told much later, to make him to understand the importance of absolute discretion. Anybody who failed to toe the line faced dire consequences. Unfortunately, Payne's mother died. He'd cut off all contact with her and she went to her grave thinking her son was dead. In his distress, he vowed that, come what may, he'd pay his last respects at her funeral. He was bored with Tangier, and I suspect he longed to return to Britain and start a new life under a false identity.

"The Masqueraders warned that he'd pay the price if he broke his word, but he defied them. They had to act. There was no telling what he might say or do, once back in England.

"To make matters worse, Leonora Dobell started making a nuisance of herself. Not only had she joined the Clandestine Club, her researches led her to stumble upon the Masqueraders' secrets. Or rather, those involving the three of you."

Rachel gestured towards Sylvia, Rolland, and Danskin. They remained motionless. Listening, watching, waiting.

"Leonora had written about the mystery of Payne's supposed death, and also the cases of Sylvia Gorrie and Henry Rolland. Then out of the blue, she invited Sylvia and Henry to Mortmain Hall. She also sat through Clive Danskin's trial. The Masqueraders didn't know what game she was playing, but she made them nervous. Gilbert Payne's return to Britain was an act of naked provocation. It couldn't pass unpunished.

"Reggie knew enough by this time to believe that Payne would be murdered. He dare not speak to Scotland Yard. The Masqueraders operate in a murky neverland. They have no official status, and few senior politicians are even aware of their existence."

Rachel glanced at Oakes, who was stony-faced. "The Masqueraders are a law unto themselves. They represent the entrepreneurial spirit of a small band of diehard patriots. The government's duty to protect its people from mischief at home has been taken into private hands."

Jacob looked at the major. His expression was impassive. The three other guests were giving nothing away. Rolland blew a smoke ring.

"Calling on my help was an act of desperation. Reggie poured his heart out to me, but soon had second thoughts. Unfortunately, what he'd said about Payne and the guests at the proposed house party at Mortmain Hall piqued my curiosity. I joined Payne on the funeral train, but he refused to admit to his true identity. Or to do anything to save himself from his fate. He finished up on the railway track, sliced into pieces by the Waterloo express.

"Reggie Vickers was appalled and terrified. He'd blabbed too often to be relied upon any longer. The same was true of an acquaintance of his, a solicitor called Louis Morgans. He was another habitué of the Clandestine Club whose tastes ran to both men and women. His nickname there was Lulu. I suspect he'd performed an occasional service for the Masqueraders, but they quickly lost trust in him. They kept a close eye on Reggie, and discovered that he'd spoken to me. When Morgans invited me to dinner, that was enough to convince them that I was a threat, and Morgans a liability."

"Where on earth is this taradiddle taking us?" Sylvia demanded.

"Think of it as a morality tale," Rachel said. "Or rather, a lack-of-morality tale. Reggie Vickers met a ghastly end in a private zoo, and the Masqueraders also dealt with Morgans. They knew of my friendship with Jacob Flint and that he was poking his nose into their business. The possibility of a journalist getting wind of their activities appalled them. So they decided to kill two birds with one stone. Murder Morgans and offer up Jacob as the culprit."

Oakes stared at Jacob; she hadn't mentioned this before. Jacob mustered a sheepish grin.

"Jacob was resourceful enough to dig himself out of the hole he'd tumbled into, but he'd received a savage warning." Rachel gave Jacob a stern glance. "And he'll take heed."

The other heads turned towards him. Jacob toyed with bravado, but thought better of it. He gave a reluctant nod of assent. Everyone looked back at Rachel.

Another flash of lightning, another roar from the heavens.

"I thought I understood why Leonora invited Sylvia, Henry, and Clive to Mortmain Hall. What baffled me was why they agreed to come."

Henry Rolland stubbed out his cigarette in an ashtray. "She'd written about me. I was curious. It seemed—"

Rachel put up a hand to silence him. "Forgive me, but that simply won't do. There had to be a more compelling explanation."

"Such as?" Danskin demanded.

"I believe you were instructed to come to Mortmain Hall."

"Stuff and nonsense. Nobody tells me what to do."

Rachel exhaled. "Leonora was a troubled woman, but she understood the murderous mind. She saw parallels between the killing of Phoebe Evison and the blazing car case."

"Absurd." Rolland guffawed, a burst of noise that seemed strange and contrived in the still of the library. "The strangling of a young woman and the accidental death of a thieving tramp? The cases are chalk and cheese."

"I disagree," Rachel said. "Forget Phoebe's husband for a moment. Forget the alibi conveniently supplied by the major. What are you left with? Two desperate men driven to extremes. Henry and Clive."

"Desperate?" asked Rolland scornfully.

"Bear with my hypothesis. Your lover is pregnant, and argumentative. In the first flush of romance, you promised marriage. Now you're unsure whether she's worth it. You arrive at the bungalow, and you and Phoebe argue. You're under pressure at work, your home life has fallen apart. It all becomes too much to bear. The red mist descends, as Jacob might say, and you strangle her. Your mistress is dead. The respectable businessman has become a killer. Panic-stricken, you run for your life. To London, to find someone who can rescue you from a mess of your own creation."

"A fairy godfather?" Rolland scoffed.

Rachel smiled. "I'm sure the major has been called worse names than that."

"The major?" Rolland paled. "You're…a fantasist, Miss Savernake."

"A fabulist." She took a breath. "You'd worked for the Masqueraders since the end of the war. You were a businessman in Liverpool, a hotbed of unrest. You loathed trade unions, and did your utmost to crush them. That made you invaluable to the major. Evison was a troublemaker who loved fomenting discord. When his wife applied for a job with your firm, the chance to create ructions in Evison's household was too good to miss. Alas for poor Phoebe. You set out to use her, and you succeeded. When she became a nuisance, you killed her.

"My guess is that you'd been promised that if your work for the Masqueraders ever landed you in trouble, they'd bail you out of it. You fled to London, where the major saw a chance to destroy Evison and bind you to him. He seized the moment. Evison was killed, and the death made to look like suicide. A confession was forged. You were off the hook. Never even charged. A perfect outcome, except that Leonora Dobell smelled a rat. But our laws of libel gagged her. She could barely hint at the rat's existence."

Rolland puffed out his cheeks. For a moment, Jacob thought he was about to explode with fury.

Nothing happened. Rachel turned to Danskin.

"You were equally useful to the Masqueraders, moving from town to town, keeping an eye on troublemakers in the poorer quarters under your guise as a lecherous stocking salesman with a taste for low life. Effective, since you were simply playing yourself. But you're easily bored, and you wearied of the game. Because you were so useful to them, you were afraid the Masqueraders wouldn't allow you to resign and lead a normal life. You certainly didn't want to be exiled like Payne. Worse still, you'd racked up debts, and your mistresses were becoming fractious as well as expensive. You yearned for escape, and an idea sprang to mind. Why not pretend to be dead and start all over again?"

"You're forgetting that this case was put before a court of law. I was tried and declared innocent," Danskin snapped.

"Not guilty, rather than innocent. But you're right, this is only a fable in which you pick up a tramp on the road, kill the poor wretch, and then set his body alight in the car. Then you assume a disguise, and catch a train to London. But your plan unravels quickly. You've made too many blunders, and the police get on to your trail. Like Henry, you turn to the Masqueraders for help. They make you suffer, to teach you a lesson. You are forced to go through the ordeal of a trial represented by the Masqueraders' pet lawyer rather than a specialist in criminal advocacy. But they are determined to save you, for fear of what you might say if you were sentenced to death, and had nothing left to lose. Hence the major's last-minute intervention. Your alibi was cast iron, the rescue mission complete.

"It was all too good to be true, and Leonora's instincts told her so. Your complacency in the dock made perfect sense if you knew salvation was at hand. Once again, the rat stank to high heaven. Meanwhile, you were in hock to the Masqueraders. They paid off your debts and looked forward to years of faithful service before you were finally put out to pasture.

"Which brings me to you, Sylvia." She turned to the other woman. "I doubt that Clive has many convictions of any kind. Henry's an old-fashioned capitalist, no more, no less. You strike me as a zealot. Your father was ruined by a labour dispute and you never forgave the agitators whose warped ideals were responsible."

"You seem to forget," Sylvia said, "that I married a distinguished man of the left."

"I haven't forgotten," Rachel said. "It's a mark of your single-mindedness."

Sylvia Gorrie gave a mock bow. Her smile was grim. They could hear the rain pounding the house as if it were a punchbag.

"After moving to London, you worked in a government office, and there I suppose you caught the major's eye. He recruited you and found you a job which brought you into contact with one of the most influential political thinkers of his age. Gorrie's personality was as anaemic as his ideals were red-blooded. He was bad-tempered and excitable, and he was certainly not a man's man. Yet it suited his purpose to have a good-looking young wife."

"If only to disarm his students, the young men he swooned over," Sylvia said.

"Quite. Your husband played a crucial role behind the scenes during the general strike. He did not march or stand on a picket line, but his brains guided the leaders' strategy. The Masqueraders regarded him as one of the most dangerous men in Britain. He certainly wasn't the wisest. He trusted Payne, and he also trusted you. Thanks to your help, the Masqueraders were no longer reliant on Payne. Information you gleaned from Gorrie helped the authorities to crush the strike."

"I had no official role, let me assure you of that."

"That's the drawback of your kind of service," Rachel said. "You are denied public recognition. Gorrie remained a thorn in the establishment's flesh. Like Evison, he represented the enemy within. So the Masqueraders decided he must be dealt with."

"My only observation is this," Sylvia said. "I can see the wisdom of cutting cancerous cells out of a body they are destroying."

"You took a lover, handsome enough to give you some pleasure and stupid enough to do your bidding. You egged him on, hoping that he'd provoke Gorrie into an indiscretion, sexual or otherwise. Gorrie would be ruined, and with any luck he'd kill himself rather than face public shame. Even if he didn't, you'd divorce him amid a blaze of recriminations. His reputation would be destroyed. The scheme was flawed by the Masqueraders' characteristic failing, a tendency to over-elaborate. Your lover was besotted with you. Crazed. The moment Gorrie fell into the lake, you saw a way of ridding society of his idealistic nonsense forever. In a split second, you made up your mind. Your husband died, and you and your lover were tried for his murder."

"The trial was a farce," Sylvia said. "I should never have been charged."

"It wasn't in your script," Rachel agreed. "Your letters to your lover went too far. If only he'd burned them, as you begged, but he broke his promise. All's well that ends well, though. The Masqueraders made sure you were reprieved, and your loyalty duly rewarded. You're now a wealthy woman. The solitary fly in the ointment was Leonora Dobell. She believed the trial process was manipulated to ensure your acquittal, and she was right. A senile judge was given the case. If the worst came to the worst, and you were convicted, the verdict was bound to be overturned on appeal. As things turned out, the jury rebelled against the judge's ravings, and you were set free."

"Rightly so. The proceedings were a farce. An insult to British justice."

"Leonora had her own reasons for questioning the way justice works in our world."

"I was acquitted. No more needs to be said."

"As I said," Rachel murmured, "this is a fable, an exercise in imagination. And the Masqueraders are inventive as well as enterprising. They strive to transform setbacks into fresh opportunities. Leonora Dobell baffled them. They didn't know what to make of her, or of this rather exclusive house party. My presence became another cause of concern. But they came up with a bold solution."

She looked at Sylvia, Rolland, and Danskin. "You were told to accept her invitation and try to recruit Leonora to the ranks of the Masqueraders."

Jacob could contain himself no longer. "Are you serious?"

"Be quiet," she snapped. "The idea was ingenious. Leonora was a dark horse, an eccentric and unpredictable maverick, but that equipped her for unusual, covert activities. As mistress of Mortmain Hall, she had a position in society, and her interest in crime gave her valuable connections."

"Fanciful," Rolland sniffed.

"Your duties didn't end there. You were also told to sound me out to see if I would come on board. That's why Sylvia wanted to talk to me in private, just as she did with Leonora last night."

Rolland breathed out. "This is an extraordinary farrago, Miss Savernake. Not a word of truth in any of it, but I'll say one thing. If this secret body did exist, I can see that you have the qualities to make a mark on it."

"I'm flattered," Rachel said. "Or am I? However, the question doesn't arise, because I've merely beguiled you with a story while the rain teems down."

Sylvia Gorrie could no longer hold back. "And frankly, you are as credible a murder suspect as the rest of us."

"I can't deny it."

Lightning flashed and thunder rumbled, this time almost at the same instant. Sylvia said, "Two women have died here. The nurse and Mrs Dobell. Are you indulging a taste for the fantastic or distracting attention from a crime of your own?"

"A fair question." Rachel glanced through the rain-smeared window. "Did I hear a car pull up outside?"

"Expecting someone else?" Danskin's tone was sardonic. "Surely the party is over?"

"Sergeant Whealing has been busy," Rachel said. "He's brought a number of witnesses up from the village."

"Witnesses?" Rolland glared. "Witnesses to what?"

"Patience," Rachel said. "All will be revealed."

Chapter 28

Sergeant Whealing shepherded the newcomers into the library as soon as their wet coats had been taken away by a maid. He'd brought Lucy Hepton, her mother, old Bob Hepton, and the ornithologist Siddons. All four were pale after their buffeting by the storm. The two men grumbled while Mrs Hepton looked overawed by her surroundings. Lucy, on the other hand, was in her element. She'd put on her best summer frock, and on seeing Jacob, she gave him a delighted wink and shifted her chair so that it was next to his.

Henry Rolland had found the whisky decanter, and he and Danskin had already refilled their tumblers. Siddons, with a disapproving stroke of his goatee, refused a drink and so, with considerable reluctance, did Jacob. Inspector Oakes stared out at the rain through one of the narrow windows. Sylvia Gorrie was whispering in the major's ear.

"Welcome to Yorkshire, Sergeant!" Jacob said. "Foul out there?"

The policeman gave him a sour look. "Never seen anything this bad back home," he said. "Like Armageddon. Pitch-black sky, floods on the lane. The noise of the storm is deafening."

Rachel closed her book and rapped it on the table to gain attention. "Thank you for coming," she said to the new arrivals. "I'm grateful for your help."

"What's this all in aid of?" Mrs Hepton asked. "I've not done owt wrong."

"Perish the thought," Rachel said. "Lucy, I have a question."

Lucy looked around in surprise. "For me?"

Rachel picked up a piece of paper that had lain folded down on the table. It was the message found in Leonora's room. She read it aloud.

"It's a message from someone whose name began with 'L'. Did you send it, by any chance?"

Lucy's face turned scarlet. "I never!"

Mrs Hepton was outraged. "She's a good girl, is Lucy."

"I don't doubt it," Rachel said. "And I never believed you sent the note. But I had to ask."

Danskin said. "Surely 'L' stood for Leonora? So she must have written it."

"That's the obvious conclusion, yes," Rachel said. "And like so many obvious conclusions, it's wrong."

"I don't understand," Rolland said. "What is the significance of this scrap of paper?"

"It's the key to the crime," Rachel said. "The murder of Leonora Dobell, whose body was found a short time ago."

Sylvia Gorrie said, "You're suggesting her death wasn't accidental?"

"Surely," Danskin said, "she murdered the nurse, and then fell into the water while she was trying to get away?"

Rachel shook her head. "That's what we were meant to think."

"What exactly are you saying?" Rolland demanded.

"The murderer knew that Leonora enjoyed the company of

other women, and that she'd taken a shine to Lucy here." The young woman stifled a cry of dismay. "The purpose of the note was to lure Leonora out of the house, so as to kill her. The culprit hit her on the head: there's a bloodstain in the rotunda. And then she was hurled over the side of the cliff, into the sea."

Danskin swore. "Are you saying that the nurse killed her, instead of the other way round?"

"No, Bernice Cope was innocent. Of murder, at least."

"Then how was the nurse killed? Surely it wasn't an accident, a complete coincidence?"

"Not at all. She was integral to the murderer's plan."

"What?" Rolland's eyes almost popped out of his head.

"The murderer asked her to pass the note to Leonora. It must have been in an envelope, and I'm sure there was some elaborate lie about what the note contained, and why it needed to reach Leonora in secret."

"It wasn't Lucy's doing!" Mrs Hepton was appalled. "My daughter had nowt to do with it!"

"No," Rachel said. "Of course she didn't. Nurse Cope had an admirer. She was devoted to him. She'd do anything he said. Including keeping his identity secret."

Jacob shot a glance at Rolland and Danskin. Both men were staring at Rachel.

"With Leonora dead, the nurse had served her purpose. More than that, she was a threat, the one person who might betray him. It wasn't a risk he dared take. So having arranged to meet her on the edge of the cliffs, he killed her too. Two women died, a supposed murderer and her victim."

Sylvia Gorrie said, "Why on earth would anyone go to such lengths?"

"I was puzzled too. It seemed to me that two different minds were at work. Two separate artists in crime. Why would anyone want to commit a murder at precisely the moment when several guests were present at the Hall? People who have previously found themselves mixed up in murder cases?"

Rolland stirred. Shooting a glance at the recent arrivals, he said gruffly, "I trust you're not going to repeat your bizarre... fable, Miss Savernake?"

"No," she replied. "The answer to the conundrum is self-evident. The house party provided the murderer with cover. A chance to confuse the picture. To camouflage a crime that might otherwise have appeared too obvious."

"Too deep for me," Danskin muttered.

"The murderer learned of the forthcoming house party from Reggie Vickers. Poor Reggie has a lot to answer for, including my being here. Louis Morgans was equally indiscreet, and the information he gave was even more important. Not that the murderer was responsible for the recent deaths of either Reggie or Morgans. They were a bonus, although I doubt the murderer had much to worry about from either man. They were Londoners through and through, and he was as sick and tired of them as he was of the city. He wanted to come home."

"Home?" Mrs Hepton asked.

"Yes," Rachel said. "To Mortmain Hall."

She was about to say something else when everyone heard the sound of a terrible crash which made the thunderclaps seem like a throat-clearing. Danskin swore; so did old Bob Hepton. Mrs Hepton shrieked, and Lucy flung her arms around her. Siddons was biting his nails. Everyone turned to the window. Jacob jumped off his chair and took a look outside. Hard as it was to peer through the torrential rain, the sight that greeted him took his breath away.

Rachel was by his side. "Jacob, what is it?"

"It's getting wilder," he said. "The storm has torn the roof right off the stable block."

———

Lucy's mother whimpered and Siddons closed his eyes. Rolland downed the rest of his whisky in a single gulp. Oakes barked at them to keep calm. Sergeant Whealing, closest to the door, stood up.

The door was flung open and Gladys stumbled into the room. Her face was like a ghost's, her voice scratchy and fearful. "Sorry to break in, miss, don't mean to be rude, but the cliff's giving way! The far end of the walled garden is slipping into the sea."

As Mrs Hepton screamed again, Oakes took charge. "Whealing! Take a look outside. Don't go far. See what's going on and report back."

The sergeant raced out of the room as Oakes turned to the others. "Everyone else, stay where you are. I don't want anyone running into danger. We must stick together. Keep you all safe."

"We need to go!" Danskin hissed. "This building was close to the clifftops before they started to crumble. You heard that racket. If the stables are going, it's this place next. It could fall around our necks any moment now. If we don't get away fast, we could be buried alive."

Mrs Hepton wailed loudly and buried her head in her daughter's arms. The major stood up, looking at Danskin with disgust.

"The inspector is right," he barked. "You could be killed by a falling roof tile. Show some discipline. Anyone who leaves may be rushing straight to their death."

"I agree," Rachel said calmly. "Sergeant Whealing will be back in a few moments. Meanwhile, let me resume the story which Mother Nature so rudely interrupted."

Dry-mouthed, Jacob considered her. What had this woman experienced in her life, to harden her nerves so that even the risk of death in a landslide barely caused a flicker of the eyelids?

Oakes nodded. "Very well. But time is short."

Rachel smiled. "Bear with me. I like to build suspense."

"Get on with it, for God's sake!" Danskin yelped.

"What did you mean, the murderer was coming home?" Sylvia demanded.

"He was the heir to Mortmain," Rachel said. "He was Felix Dobell's illegitimate son."

———

For a moment nobody spoke. The crumbling cliffs were forgotten. Everyone in the room, with one exception, stared at Rachel.

"You're wrong," Rolland said. "A bastard can't inherit property. Only a lawful heir."

"A common misconception," Rachel said. "In limited circumstances, it's possible, if the wording of the will or settlement allows it. There is case law on the point. And Oswyn Dobell instructed his solicitor to draft the Dobell Family Settlement in broad and generous terms. When he finally inherited Mortmain, he made sure that in future, the widow of an heir wouldn't be thrown out of her home once her husband died. She'd become a life tenant. Equally, an illegitimate child could inherit, provided he was alive at the time the deed was made. Not that Oswyn expected Felix to inherit the Mortmain Estate, far less his son. But Felix's elder brother never married, and had no offspring. And then he was killed in the war, shortly before Felix was injured."

"Felix's son died," Jacob said. "It says so in *Who's Who*."

"No, you've forgotten what Griselda told you. At seventeen

years old, he suffered shell shock and loss of memory. Frightened to death, he deserted. He risked being shot for cowardice, but he was one of the lucky ones. In view of his age and state of health, he was given a dishonourable discharge. Felix was mortified. Previously, he'd given the boy an allowance, but now he washed his hands of him. In his mind, his son was dead. And that's what he led everyone else to believe. Including *Who's Who*. But the settlement deed prevailed.

"The boy was sick and desperately poor. But time heals some things, and he was able to make a little money, thanks to his remarkable talent."

"Talent?" Rolland demanded.

"He inherited the Dobells' love of art and was skilled at drawing. It took years, but he began to make something of his life."

Rachel moved away from the window, and walked up to Siddons. Without a word, she whipped off his spectacles.

"Recognise him, Jacob?"

Jacob groaned. Of course! How could he not have realised, how had he allowed the glasses and the goatee to mislead him? He was gazing into the eyes of the man who had first drawn his attention to Leonora at the Old Bailey. The courtroom artist.

Siddons the birdwatcher was Felix Dobell's son.

Chapter 29

"This is nonsense." Siddons's Scottish accent had vanished. He sounded frightened. "Despicable."

"I have some sympathy," Rachel said. "You were young and shell-shocked, and your father turned his back on you. To add to your misery, you realised that you were...different from most men. Attracted to your own kind. And because you are handsome, despite your best endeavours to disguise the fact here at Mortmain, you attracted admirers. Eventually you were introduced to the Clandestine Club. At the Club you met Louis Morgans. Lulu, as he was known there. Also Reggie Vickers, who nicknamed you Doodle because of your love of sketching."

Siddons stared in silence, as if Rachel had hypnotised him.

"You'd created a new life under a new name. Calling yourself Siddons after the tragedienne was an act of homage to your actress mother. Valentine Dobell became Valentine Siddons. You knew Morgans's firm acted for the Dobell family, and cultivated his friendship. His father had paid the allowance to you on Felix's behalf, until you were cut off. Did you pretend to have served alongside Valentine Dobell during the war? Perhaps you claimed you were both amused that you shared a Christian name. Whatever the truth, through Morgans you discovered that you were entitled to inherit Mortmain Hall.

"That was a bolt from the blue. The law treat bastards harshly. You'd assumed you'd get nothing. Perhaps you weren't even sure that Morgans understood the law correctly. It didn't matter. Morally, you had a right to the estate when Felix died. He owed it to you. And to your mother, who committed suicide after he deserted you both."

Siddons made a low, keening noise, and buried his head in his hands.

"Still the obstacles were overwhelming. Your father was alive, but might die at any moment. Leonora, on the other hand, was in her early forties and in good health. She might live to eighty or ninety. After Felix died, she'd be tenant for life. Already she was selling off the Dobells' treasures. As an artist, that infuriated you, quite apart from the sadness of losing the family collection. Even if you lived long enough to claim your inheritance, there would be nothing left.

"You deserted Morgans for Vickers. Once he told you what you wanted about the Masqueraders and the plans for this house party, you had no further use for him. Your sole concern was Mortmain Hall. Having inherited your mother's talent for acting, you'd assumed a false identity for your visits to the Mortmain Estate. Hence the tinted hair, thick glasses, and beard. To say nothing of the Scottish accent. This was vital, because one day you'd return in triumph as lord of the manor. Pretending to be a birdwatcher, you roamed as you pleased. Drawing an occasional puffin gave the lie a touch of authenticity.

"You befriended lonely, lovelorn Nurse Cope, and spun her a yarn to persuade her to give nothing away about you. She mentioned Leonora's habit of talking walks before sunset, and you worked out your plan. Leonora's reason for holding a house party didn't matter. The arrangements suited you perfectly. You took the annexe room at the Dobell Arms, so you could slip out quietly, even if the inn itself was locked up. The supposed sprained ankle gave you an alibi. There was never anything wrong with you."

"You cheat!" Lucy shrieked at Siddons. "You lied about your ankle. When you told me about your shell shock and amnesia, I thought you trusted me, like I trusted you. But you lied to me, and that poor woman too!"

She flew at Siddons, scratching at his face with her fingernails. He didn't put up even a token struggle. Oakes moved to intervene.

"Valentine Dobell, you are under…"

Whealing burst into the room. His uniform was wet through and he was panting hard.

"We need to get out!" he bellowed. "The whole house is in danger!"

———

"Follow me!" Oakes shouted.

The roar of the storm was louder than ever. Everyone dashed into the front hall. The Truemans and the Dobells' servants were there, laden down with mackintoshes and surrounded by suitcases.

"Grab your things and run for it!" Trueman threw open the main door. A blast of rain and falling slates greeted them. The noise was deafening. "Mind your heads, keep your eyes on the roof!"

They all ran out into the lashing rain. Jacob's temples pounded. The downpour almost made him blind. A slate crashed to the ground and shattered into pieces. Five yards closer and it would have smashed his head to a pulp.

"My father!" Valentine Dobell screamed. He'd halted just outside the porch. "Where is he?"

Major Whitlow jerked his head towards Mortmain Hall.

"Upstairs," he bellowed. "You'll have to leave him!"

Valentine Dobell turned and headed back into the house.

"Stop!" Oakes yelled.

He and Whealing were about to rush back after Dobell when a menacing rumble came from the back of the building. An ugly crack in the ground spread towards them from the side of the Hall. The land was splitting apart in front of their eyes.

"It's going!" Oakes shouted. "Get down the drive, everyone!"

As Jacob rushed down the drive, he saw Rachel's Phantom parked on the grass. It was out in the open, far enough from the trees to be safe even if they fell. Trueman, like Rachel, thought of everything.

"Oakes!" the major called. "Move, man! It's not safe!"

Trueman yelled at the top of his voice, "Felix Dobell went to hospital. He was taken ill and one of the servants drove him."

Oakes ran towards the major. "Why did you lie?" he cried.

Major Whitlow shrugged. Jacob could barely hear his cool reply.

"I must have panicked."

Another crash made everyone look up. A fissure had appeared in the front wall of the house, just below a gable, and a large chunk of stone fell to the ground.

The major smiled. Jacob could read his mind.

With any luck, the whole place will disintegrate with Valentine Dobell inside, and we'll be spared the fuss and embarrassment of a trial.

Another crash, even louder this time.

Jacob watched, mesmerised by the horror of it all, as the major's wish came true.

Mortmain Hall was falling down.

Chapter 30

"We're lucky to be alive," Jacob said.

"In this life," Rachel said, "we make our own luck."

They were among the crowd of sightseers assembled on the drive up to Mortmain Hall. It was a bright and blustery morning. The violence of the thunderstorm was a memory. Jacob saw men clutching notebooks and pencils approaching people for comments about what had happened. A phrase recurred in the headlines. *The Mortmain Tragedy.*

"You even got your scoop," she said.

"An eyewitness account of a natural disaster." His smile was rueful. "Unusual for a crime correspondent, but better than nothing. If I must keep my mouth shut about everything else."

"Yes, you must."

"The courtroom artist of the *Witness*, guilty of a double murder," he mused. "I'd give my right arm to see that story in print. You don't realise what a sacrifice you've demanded."

"There are animals at Tunnicliffe," Rachel said, "capable of taking off much more than your right arm. Put it down to experience."

The front wall of Mortmain Hall formed a bizarre, broken

folly on the brink of a precipice. Mortmain Head had crumbled into the sea. Just a sliver of land poked out beyond the end of the drive. The wounds in the landscape were savage and deep.

The crowd was subdued. Eventually, vendors would arrive, selling ice cream cornets and souvenirs to tourists with a taste for calamity. For the moment, people hadn't quite forgotten that a man had perished in the landslide.

Jacob spotted the Heptons in the throng. Oakes had ordered them to hold their tongues when questioned by the press. The major had also had a quiet word with them, emphasising one or two points with his claw.

Hoping for silence on the part of Lucy and her mother was futile, but they'd never admit that they'd harboured a killer in their midst, providing a safe haven for him to plot the murder of two women. The shame would be too great. It was so much easier to propagate a fantasy, a story nicer than the truth.

The received wisdom in Mortmain was that Leonora had killed the nurse in a fit of jealous insanity and then committed suicide. Some folk who liked to be contrary reckoned that it was the other way round. Everyone agreed that the precise truth would never be known. So much the better. The uncertainty made fertile territory for guesswork and gossip.

Jacob edged towards the Heptons. Lucy was giving an interview to a stringer from the *Witness*. The man who had died in the landslide had fallen victim to a tragic chance, she said. He was a passionate birdwatcher who yearned to be close to nature. What had happened was awful, but there was some solace for the romantic. Siddons had loved Mortmain; there was nowhere else in the world that he'd rather be. For the record, the reporter asked her uncle if he agreed.

"Happen," the old man said.

The servants and guests from the Hall had been put up

overnight in the Dobell Arms and in villagers' houses. The Truemans were at the inn, preparing for the long drive home. Major Whitlow, Sylvia, Rolland, and Danskin had already departed. Oakes and Sergeant Whealing were closeted with Inspector Tucker and his colleagues at the local police headquarters. There was a lot of work to be done. Loose ends needed to be tied up, paperwork must be put in order before the three inquests reached their preordained conclusions, and everyone was left to get on with their lives.

Jacob rejoined Rachel. The rotunda had survived the catastrophe. They could see it through the trees, a monument to the mistress of Mortmain Hall who had been lured there to her death.

"It's wrong," he said. "It's unjust."

"Life is one injustice after another."

"The major...the Masqueraders...I mean, they can't be allowed to go on like this."

"Like what?" She yawned. "I told everyone a story. I wasn't making out a legal case. It was a moral fable, that's all."

"There was nothing moral about it."

"Think again," she said. "On reflection, don't. It will only make you unhappy. Tell yourself to rejoice that people are working covertly on our behalf, intent on keeping us safe and sound."

"It's disgraceful."

"You've had one brush with death, Jacob. That's enough to be going on with, don't you think?"

"But it isn't right."

"Right and wrong?" She shrugged. "These are dangerous times, Jacob, don't forget that."

He kicked a stray pebble to vent his frustration. "I'm not even sure why Leonora wanted you to come here."

"She fancied herself as a detective, skilled at exploring dark recesses of criminal psychology. Knowing a little of my history, she deduced I'd committed the perfect crime."

He stared at her.

"She was sure I'd murdered my own father."

He said huskily, "And did you?"

She gave him a look. "No, I did not murder my own father."

"But all four guests at Mortmain Hall were people she believed were guilty of murder?"

She clapped her hands.

"Why bring you all together?"

"My theory is that she wanted to find someone to confide in."

"What do you mean?"

"She'd searched for love, but never found it. You must have seen that in her eyes at the Clandestine Club. Perhaps she wasn't quite sane. But then, who is?"

He folded his arms. "I'm not doolally."

"Look where your sanity led you," Rachel said. "To sharing a bed with a naked corpse."

He scowled but said nothing.

"Leonora detected a connection between Sylvia and me, and Rolland, and Danskin. More than that, she regarded herself as one of us. Part of an exclusive band. Men and women capable of committing the perfect crime."

"It makes no sense."

Rachel sighed. "Dear Jacob. You see life in black and white. Really, it's a mess and a muddle of many colours. As if an artist dropped his palette, and the paints splashed everywhere."

Muttering under his breath, Jacob gazed out at Mortmain Hall, its ruined facade outlined against the sky.

"You don't believe me, but you should. Twelve years on, we're still bleeding from a war in which millions died. The lives of men like Felix Dobell were ruined forever. And what provoked the war? Railway timetables for moving troops."

"That's absurd."

"So is life itself. You know why I like those crazy examples of surrealist art? Because there is truth in madness, Jacob. Remember that."

He said mulishly, "Are you telling me you're mad, like Leonora?"

"She reckoned the two of us were peas in a pod. As for her perfect crime, let's hear about it from the man who knows."

He stared. "Who do you mean?"

"Felix Dobell."

Epilogue (Continued)

Felix Dobell tried to sit up in his hospital bed, but the effort was beyond him.

"Elspeth was a wretched woman," he whispered. "I should never have married her."

Rachel gave Jacob a nod. They were in a tiny room with whitewashed walls; the nurse had left her patient to his visitors. The air was pungent with the reek of disinfectant.

"Too respectable for you?"

He gave a feeble nod. "She'd set her cap at my brother, but he was too canny to fall for her. I was the stupid one. Impulsive. Of course I regretted it. When the war came, I was glad to get away. I met Leo when I came back on leave. I liked her. She had…a twinkle in her eye."

Falling back on his pillow, he closed his eye. Talking so much exhausted him. Jacob shot Rachel a glance of warning but she paid no heed.

"So Leo didn't know until then that Elspeth was the chief constable's daughter?"

Felix shook his head.

"She blamed Elspeth's father for persecuting hers," Rachel

said. "He'd demanded Gee's arrest on flimsy evidence. Leonora never forgave, did she?"

"No," Felix mumbled.

"While you were back on the Western Front, the news came that your brother had died. I suppose Elspeth was triumphant. A snob whose husband would inherit Mortmain Hall."

Felix opened his eyes. "Yes," he breathed.

"Leonora poisoned Elspeth, didn't she? My guess is that she used arsenic, and persuaded the old doctor that the cause of death was gastritis. Risky, but nobody suspected. There was a war on, and people were dying all the time. Am I right in supposing that she did it when news came through that you'd been badly injured, that you'd be coming back to Mortmain?"

Felix lifted his head and nodded.

"She'd never had money. Killing Elspeth was an act of revenge which also gave her the security she craved. The fact there couldn't be a physical side to your marriage didn't trouble her. She could do as she pleased; it was a marriage of mutual convenience. You were glad to be rid of Elspeth, and quite content as long as you had company. Especially when a young nurse took a shine to you."

"I thought Bernice…"

"Yes," Rachel said. "She wasn't a beauty, and there was less chance that she'd run off with a suitor. But even she found a lover…"

"All good things…" Felix said faintly.

"They come to an end." Rachel inclined her head.

"I had a son," Felix's tone was wondering. "But he died."

He slumped back on his pillow, and made an odd, guttural sound. His eyes shut. Rachel lifted his thin arms, and folded them across his chest.

"Yes," she said, "he died."

CLUEFINDER

Cluefinders appeared from the late 1920s onward in detective novels by British and American authors as J. J. Connington, Freeman Wills Crofts, Elspeth Huxley, Rupert Penny, John Dickson Carr, C. Daly King, and Edmund Crispin. In a novel which pays homage to the Golden Age of murder, it seemed amusing to revive the tradition. Here are thirty clues in the narrative to the principal strands of the plot.

DOBELL FAMILY RESEMBLANCES

Page 19: *a pale, handsome fellow with straw-coloured hair and a beaky nose*

Page 19: *chewing at his fingernails*

Page 243: *a portrait of a tall, beaky-nosed man*

Page 243: *a middle-aged man with fair hair and the family eyes and nose*

Page 245: *He blew his beaky nose*

Page 245: *his fingernails were bitten to the quick*

THE MURDERER'S INTEREST IN LEONORA

Page 19: *His gaze wandered from Minnie Brown, and came to rest on a woman at the front of the public gallery.*

THE MURDERER'S NAME

Page 47: *It's true. The first time we met, you said I'd always be your Valentine...*

Page 165: *Felix said he'd pay for Valentine's upbringing*

THE MURDERER'S PAST CONNECTION WITH LOUIS MORGANS

Page 47: *There's no going back. Not to you or your posh friend Lulu.*

HOW THE MURDERER LEARNED FROM REGGIE VICKERS

Page 92: *If only he'd never uttered a word. To Doodle... With Doodle, he'd been trying to impress, and failing.*

THE POTENTIAL UNRELIABILITY OF MENTION OF THE MURDERER'S DEMISE IN HIS FATHER'S ENTRY IN *WHO'S WHO*

Page 166: *The boy might as well have died on the front.*

Page 124: Who's Who *relied on the good faith of the great and the good; it wasn't seemly to double-check every piece of information it was given.*

THE MURDERER'S HISTORY OF INSTABILITY

Page 166: *Felix's poor little bastard son suffered shell shock and amnesia.*

Page 300: *"Amnesia?... it can go on for years, just like shell shock, poor Mr Siddons was telling me only yesterday."*

OSWYN'S LIBERAL ATTITUDE

Page 210: *Oswyn was far more liberal than most testators*

Page 243: *for a Victorian, he was remarkably broad-minded.*

THE MURDERER'S PSYCHOLOGICAL MAKE-UP

Page 243: *There's a family history of instability.*

THE MURDERER'S MOTIVE

Page 173: *The family settlement gives an heir's widow a life interest in the estate… there's enough in the pot to see her out to a ripe old age. Even though she's probably good for another thirty or forty years.*

Page 210: *The estate goes to Oswyn Dobell's son or grandson, natural or otherwise.*

WHY THE MURDERER NEEDED TO ACT

Page 210: *The surviving widow of an incumbent heir is entitled to a life interest, so that the next generation has to wait its turn.*

Page 293: *The heir's widow doesn't own the property. She can't pass on the estate under her own will. For as long as she lives, however, for practical purposes she is able to do as she pleases.*

TIMING THE MURDER TO COINCIDE
WITH THE HOUSE PARTY

Page 293: *this death coincided with the presence of three individuals who have been suspected of murder. To say nothing of myself. If the crime was premeditated… trying to sow confusion.*

Page 302: *the annex room will be empty… You can come and go as you please, and you won't be disturbed there.*

LEONORA'S DOUBLE MOTIVE

Page 166: *The only difference was that Felix married the daughter of the chief constable*

Page 260: *Her father was one of the great and the good in the North Riding.*

Page 210: *even if Felix Dobell had died the very next day after* marrying Leonora, she'd have remained as the tenant of Mortmain for the rest of her life

LEONORA'S KNOWLEDGE OF POISONS

Page 249: *I worked in a pharmacy for a few months before I was sent to Mortmain. I know a thing or two about lethal medicines.*

Page 292: *Given her access to poisons, she had the means at her disposal to commit the crime and disguise the death as natural causes.*

HOW LEONORA ESCAPED DETECTION

Page 244: *things were utterly chaotic. Nobody at Mortmain was a medical expert, apart from one old doctor who was going senile*

THE MOTIVATION OF THE MASQUERADERS
AND THEIR ACCOMPLICES

Page 55: *Calling Britain a land fit for heroes might be stretching it somewhat, but at least they were keeping the Bolshies at bay.*

Page 60: *"Lives are at risk. Can't be too careful. Beware the enemy within."*

Page 72: *Sylvia Hardman's father was a Norfolk builder who was bankrupted after a strike by construction workers wrecked his business.*

Page 121: *After that, Evison drifted from job to job; his drinking companions were political agitators, and he was forever arguing for higher wages and better working conditions.*

ACKNOWLEDGMENTS

I've received assistance in the writing of this novel from a wide range of people, and I'd like to mention several of them specifically. John M. Clarke, author of *The Brookwood Necropolis Railway*, gave me a good deal of information about the railway. Tim Benson, a former schoolfriend and nowadays a volunteer guide at the Royal Academy, gave me invaluable help with the chapter set there, as did colleagues of his. Margaret Mackay, librarian of Highgate Literary and Scientific Institution, provided me with information and even photos about the HLSI in the 1930s, and the staff of *Who's Who* and at the National Railway Museum also responded helpfully to my enquiries.

Jonathan Edwards gave me invaluable advice about the legal aspects of inheritance by illegitimate children at the time of the events of the story and also helped with my account of the Old Bailey trial. Helena and Catherine Edwards, James Wills, John M. Clarke, Shawn Reilly Simmons, and Kate Godsmark made very helpful comments on the draft manuscript. The accounts of the fictional criminal cases in the story owe something to real life precedents, but my invented versions are not intended as "explanations" of the actual cases which inspired them, and the characters and events are all products of my imagination. Leonora Dobell's musings on respectability and murder anticipate those articulated by George Orwell in "The Decline of the English Murder." As ever, I'm grateful to my agent, James Wills, and the team at Head of Zeus for their faith in this book.

GALLOWS COURT

Juliet Brentano's Journal

30 JANUARY 1919

My parents died yesterday.

*Henrietta has just broken the news. Tears filled her eyes, and
she put a hand on my arm. I didn't speak, and I didn't cry. The gale
sweeping over the island from the Irish Sea howled for me.*

*Henrietta says Harold Brown sent Judge Savernake a telegram
from London. My parents caught the Spanish flu, he said, like thousands before them. It was all over very quickly, and they passed
away peacefully in each other's arms.*

*It's a fairy story. The emptiness in her voice told me she doesn't
believe a word of it.*

Neither do I. My mother and father were murdered, I'm sure of it.

And Rachel Savernake is responsible.

Chapter 1

'Jacob Flint is watching the house again.' The housekeeper's voice rose. 'Do you think he knows about...?'

'How could he?' Rachel Savernake said. 'Don't worry, I'll deal with him.'

'You can't!' the older woman protested. 'You don't have time.'

Rachel adjusted her cloche hat in front of the looking glass. A demure face returned her gaze. Nobody would guess her nerve-ends were tingling. Was this how the Judge felt, when he put on his black cap?

'There's time enough. The car isn't due for five minutes.'

She slid on her evening gloves. Mrs Trueman handed her the bag, and opened the front door. A voice crooned from the drawing room. Martha was listening to the Dorsey Brothers on the new automatic gramophone. Rachel danced down the short flight of steps in her Pompadour heels, humming Cole Porter's song, 'Let's Do It.'

Fog was slithering over the square, and cold January air nibbled her cheeks. She was glad of her sable coat. The lamp-lights tinged the dirty greyness with an eerie yellow hue. Long years spent on a small island had accustomed her to sea frets. She felt a strange affection for the winter mists drifting in from the water, rippling like gauze curtains, draping the damp landscape. A London particular was a different beast—sooty, sulphurous, and malign, as capable of choking you as a Limehouse ruffian. The greasy air made her eyes smart, and its acrid taste burned her throat. Yet the foul and muddy swirl troubled her no more than pitch darkness frightens a blind man. Tonight she felt invincible.

A figure detached itself from the shadows. Peering through the gloom, she made out a tall, skinny man in coat and trilby. A long woollen scarf, loosely tied, hung from his shoulders. His gait was energetic yet awkward. She guessed he'd been plucking up courage to ring the doorbell.

'Miss Savernake! Sorry to bother you on a Sunday evening!' He sounded young, eager, and utterly unapologetic. 'My name is—'

'I know who you are.'

'But we haven't been introduced.' Unruly strands of fair hair sneaked from under the trilby, and a pompous clearing of the throat couldn't disguise his *gaucherie*. At twenty-four, he had the fresh, scrubbed features of a schoolboy. 'I happen to be—'

'Jacob Flint, a reporter with the *Clarion*. You must know that I never speak to the press.'

'I've done my homework.' He glanced to left and right. 'What I do know is that it's unsafe for a lady to be out while a brutal killer prowls the London streets.'

'Perhaps I'm not really a lady.'

His eyes fastened on the diamond clip in her hat. 'You look every inch—'

'Appearances can be deceptive.'

He leaned towards her. His skin smelled of coal-tar soap. 'If you're not really a lady, all the more reason for you to take care.'

'It is unwise to threaten me, Mr Flint.'

He took a step back. 'I'm desperate to talk to you. You recall the note I left with your housekeeper?'

Of course she did. She'd watched from the window as he'd delivered it. He'd fiddled nervously with his tie while waiting on the step. Surely he wasn't stupid enough to believe she'd answer the door herself?

'My car will arrive presently, and I don't intend to conduct an interview anywhere, let alone on a pavement in the fog.'

'You can trust me, Miss Savernake.'

'Don't be absurd. You're a journalist.'

'Honestly, we have something in common.'

'What, exactly?' She ticked points off on her gloved hand. 'You learned your trade as a reporter in Yorkshire before arriving in London last autumn. You lodge in Amwell Street, and you worry that your landlady's daughter seeks to trade her body for marriage. Ambition drove you to join the muckrakers on the *Clarion* rather than a respectable newspaper. The editor admires your persistence, but frets about your rashness.'

He gulped. 'How…?'

'You have a morbid interest in crime, and regard Thomas Betts's recent accident as both a misfortune and an opportunity. With the *Clarion*'s chief crime reporter on his death bed, you scent a chance to make your name.' She took a breath. 'Be careful what you wish for. If Wall Street can crumble, so can anything. How unfortunate if your promising career were cut short, like his.'

He flinched, as if she'd slapped his face. When he spoke, his voice was hoarse.

'No wonder you solved the Chorus Girl Murder. You're quite a detective; you put the boys in blue to shame.'

'When you sent me a note, did you expect me to do nothing?'

'I'm flattered that you took the trouble to investigate me.' He ventured a grin, showing crooked teeth. 'Or are you brilliant enough to deduce all that from the careless knotting of my scarf, and the fact my shoes need a shine?'

'Find someone else to write about, Mr Flint.'

'My editor would be shocked to hear us described as muck-rakers.' He'd recovered his composure as quickly as he'd lost it. 'The *Clarion* gives the common folk a voice. It's our latest slo-gan. *Our readers need to know.*'

'Not about me.'

'If you leave money out of it, you and I aren't so very different.' He grinned. 'Both new to London, inquisitive, and stubborn as mules. I notice you don't deny solving the Chorus Girl case. So what do you make of the latest sensation, this butchering of poor Mary-Jane Hayes in Covent Garden?'

He paused, but she didn't fill the silence.

'Mary-Jane Hayes's remains were found in a sack, and her head was missing.' He breathed out. 'The details were too foul to print. She was a decent woman—that's what keeps our read-ers awake at night. Not someone who got what she deserved.'

Rachel Savernake's face resembled a porcelain mask. 'Do women ever get what they deserve?'

'This madman won't stop at one. They never do. Before any more women are harmed, he must be brought to justice.'

She considered him. 'So you believe in justice?'

The sleek contours of a Rolls-Royce Phantom loomed through the dirty yellow fog, and the young man skipped out of its path to avoid being crushed. It drew up by Rachel's side.

'Time to go, Mr Flint.'

A broad-shouldered man, six foot four if an inch, climbed out of the car. As he opened the rear door, Rachel handed him her bag. Jacob Flint gave the fellow a wary glance. He looked as if he'd be more at home in a heavyweight boxer's dressing gown than in a chauffeur's livery. His buttons gleamed like warning lights.

Jacob gave a little bow. 'It never does to hide from the press, Miss Savernake. If I don't tell your story, someone less scrupulous will do the job. Let me have a scoop, and you won't regret it.'

Rachel seized hold of the loose ends of his scarf and pulled the knot tight against his neck. Startled, he let out a gasp.

'I never waste time on regrets, Mr Flint,' she whispered.

Releasing the scarf, she took the bag from Trueman and settled herself in the back of the Phantom. As the car glided away into the night, she was conscious of Jacob Flint rubbing his neck as he watched her disappear. Might he prove useful? To give him the story he craved would be risky, but she'd never been afraid to gamble. It was in her blood.

ABOUT THE AUTHOR

Martin Edwards was awarded the highest honor in British crime writing, the Crime Writers' Association (CWA) Diamond Dagger, for his body of work and is president of the Detection Club, consultant to the British Library's Crime Classics, and former chair of the CWA. *Mortmain Hall* is a sequel to *Gallows Court*, which was nominated for both the 2019 eDunnit award for best crime novel and the CWA Historical Dagger.

His contemporary whodunits include *The Coffin Trail*, which was shortlisted for the Theakston's Prize for best crime novel of the year. In addition to his eighteen novels, he has edited forty anthologies and published nine nonfiction books. *The Golden Age of Murder* won the Edgar, Agatha, H. R. F. Keating, and Macavity awards, while *The Story of Classic Crime in 100 Books* also won the Macavity and was shortlisted for four other awards. He has also received the CWA Short Story Dagger, the CWA Margery Allingham Prize, a Red Herring for services to the CWA, and the Poirot Award for his outstanding contribution to the crime genre.